A Victor of Salamis

CW01425686

William Stearns Davis

Alpha Editions

This edition published in 2024

ISBN : 9789362922045

Design and Setting By
Alpha Editions
www.alphaedis.com
Email - info@alphaedis.com

Contents

AUTHOR'S NOTE

The invasion of Greece by Xerxes, with its battles of Thermopylæ, Salamis, and Platæa, forms one of the most dramatic events in history. Had Athens and Sparta succumbed to this attack of Oriental superstition and despotism, the Parthenon, the Attic Theatre, the Dialogues of Plato, would have been almost as impossible as if Phidias, Sophocles, and the philosophers had never lived. Because this contest and its heroes—Leonidas and Themistocles—cast their abiding shadows across our world of to-day, I have attempted this piece of historical fiction.

Many of the scenes were conceived on the fields of action themselves during a recent visit to Greece, and I have tried to give some glimpse of the natural beauty of "The Land of the Hellene,"—a beauty that will remain when Themistocles and his peers fade away still further into the backgrounds of history.

W. S. D.

PROLOGUE
THE ISTHMIAN GAMES NEAR CORINTH

CHAPTER I
GLAUCON THE BEAUTIFUL

The crier paused for the fifth time. The crowd—knotty Spartans, keen Athenians, perfumed Sicilians—pressed his pulpit closer, elbowing for the place of vantage. Amid a lull in their clamour the crier recommenced.

"And now, men of Hellas, another time hearken. The sixth contestant in the pentathlon, most honourable of the games held at the Isthmus, is Glaucon, son of Conon the Athenian; his grandfather—" a jangling shout drowned him.

"The most beautiful man in Hellas!" "But an effeminate puppy!" "Of the noble house of Alcmæon!" "The family's accursed!" "A great god helps him—even Eros." "Ay—the fool married for mere love. He needs help. His father disinherited him."

"Peace, peace," urged the crier; "I'll tell all about him, as I have of the others. Know then, my masters, that he loved, and won in marriage, Hermione, daughter of Hermippus of Eleusis. Now Hermippus is Conon's mortal enemy; therefore in great wrath Conon disinherited his son,—but now, consenting to forgive him if he wins the parsley crown in the pentathlon—"

"A safe promise," interrupted a Spartan in broadest Doric; "the pretty boy has no chance against Lycon, our Laconian giant."

"Boaster!" retorted an Athenian. "Did not Glaucon bend open a horseshoe yesterday?"

"Our Mœrocles did that," called a Mantinean; whereupon the crier, foregoing his long speech on Glaucon's noble ancestry, began to urge the Athenians to show their confidence by their wagers.

"How much is staked that Glaucon can beat Ctesias of Epidaurus?"

"We don't match our lion against mice!" roared the noisiest Athenian.

"Or Amyntas of Thebes?"

"Not Amyntas! Give us Lycon of Sparta."

"Lycon let it be,—how much is staked and by whom, that Glaucon of Athens, contending for the first time in the great games, defeats Lycon of Sparta, twice victor at Nemea, once at Delphi, and once at Olympia?"

The second rush and outcry put the crier nearly at his wits' end to record the wagers that pelted him, and which testified how much confidence the numerous Athenians had in their unproved champion. The brawl of voices drew newcomers from far and near. The chariot race had just ended in the adjoining hippodrome; and the idle crowd, intent on a new excitement, came surging up like waves. In such a whirlpool of tossing arms and shoving elbows, he who was small of stature and short of breath stood a scanty chance of getting close enough to the crier's stand to have his wager recorded. Such, at least, was the fate of a gray but dignified little man, who struggled vainly—even with risk to his long linen chiton—to reach the front.

"Ugh! ugh! Make way, good people,—Zeus confound you, brute of a Spartan, your big sandals crush my toes again! Can I never get near enough to place my two minæ on that Glaucon?"

"Keep back, graybeard," snapped the Spartan; "thank the god if you can hold your money and not lose it, when Glaucon's neck is wrung to-morrow." Whereupon he lifted his own voice with, "Thirty drachmæ to place on Lycon, Master Crier! So you have it—"

"And two minæ on Glaucon," piped the little man, peering up with bright, beady eyes; but the crier would never have heard him, save for a sudden ally.

"Who wants to stake on Glaucon?" burst in a hearty young Athenian who had wagered already. "You, worthy sir? Then by Athena's owls they shall hear you! Lend us your elbow, Democrates."

The latter request was to a second young Athenian close by. With his stalwart helpers thrusting at either side, the little man was soon close to the crier.

"Two minæ?" quoth the latter, leaning, "two that Glaucon beats Lycon, and at even odds? But your name, sir—"

The little man straightened proudly.

"Simonides of Ceos."

The crowd drew back by magic. The most bristling Spartan grew respectful. The crier bowed as his ready stylus made the entry.

"Simonides of Ceos, Simonides the most noted poet in Hellas!" cried the first of his two rescuers; "it's a great honour to have served so famous a man. Pray let me take your hand."

"With all the joy in the world." The little poet coloured with delight at the flattery. "You have saved me, I avow, from the forge and anvil of Hephæstus. What a vulgar mob! Do stand apart; then I can try to thank you."

Aided again by his two protectors, Simonides was soon clear of the whirlpool. Under one of the graceful pines, which girded the long stadium, he recovered breath and looked at leisure upon his new acquaintances. Both were striking men, but in sharp contrast: the taller and darker showed an aquiline visage betraying a strain of non-Grecian blood. His black eyes and large mouth were very merry. He wore his green chiton with a rakishness that proved him anything but a dandy. His companion, addressed as Democrates, slighter, blonder, showed Simonides a handsome and truly Greek profile, set off by a neatly trimmed reddish beard. His purple-edged cloak fell in statuesque folds of the latest mode, his beryl signet-ring, scarlet fillet, and jewelled girdle bespoke wealth and taste. His face, too, might have seemed frank and affable, had not Simonides suddenly recalled an old proverb about mistrusting a man with eyes too close together.

"And now," said the little poet, quite as ready to pay compliments as to take them, "let me thank my noble deliverers, for I am sure two such valorous young men as you must come of the best blood of Attica."

"I am not ashamed of my father, sir," spoke the taller Athenian; "Hellas has not yet forgotten Miltiades, the victor of Marathon."

"Then I clasp the hand of Cimon, the son of the saviour of Hellas." The little poet's eyes danced. "Oh! the pity I was in Thessaly so long, and let you grow up in my absence. A noble son of a noble father! And your friend—did you name him Democrates?"

"I did so."

"Fortunate old rascal I am! For I meet Cimon the son of Miltiades, and Democrates, that young lieutenant of Themistocles who all the world knows is gaining fame already as Nestor and Odysseus, both in one, among the orators of Athens."

"Your compliments exceed all truth," exclaimed the second Athenian, not at all angered by the praise. But Simonides, whose tongue was brisk, ran on with a torrent of flattery and of polite insinuation, until Cimon halted him, with a query.

"Yet why, dear Cean, since, as you say, you only arrived this afternoon at the Isthmus, were you so anxious to stake that money on Glaucon?"

"Why? Because I, like all Greece outside of Sparta, seem to be turning Glaucon-mad. All the way from Thessaly—in Bœotia, in Attica, in Megara— men talked of him, his beauty, his prowess, his quarrel with his father, his marriage with Hermione, the divinest maiden in Athens, and how he has gone to the games to win both the crown and crusty Conon's forgiveness. I tell you, every mule-driver along the way seemed to have staked his obol on him. They praise him as 'fair as Delian Apollo,' 'graceful as young Hermes,' and—here I wonder most,—'modest as an unwedded girl.' " Simonides drew breath, then faced the others earnestly, "You are Athenians; do you know him?"

"Know him?" Cimon laughed heartily; "have we not left him at the wrestling ground? Was not Democrates his schoolfellow once, his second self to-day? And touching his beauty, his valour, his modesty," the young man's eyes shone with loyal enthusiasm, "do not say 'over-praised' till you have seen him."

Simonides swelled with delight.

"Oh, lucky genius that cast me with you! Take me to him this moment."

"He is so beset with admirers, his trainers are angry already; besides, he is still at the wrestling ground."

"But soon returns to his tents," added Democrates, instantly; "and Simonides—is Simonides. If Themistocles and Leonidas can see Glaucon, so must the first poet of Hellas."

"O dearest orator," cried the little man, with an arm around his neck, "I begin to love you already. Away this moment, that I may worship your new divinity."

"Come, then," commanded Cimon, leading off with strides so long the bard could hardly follow; "his tent is not distant: you shall see him, though the trainers change to Gorgons."

The "Precinct of Poseidon," the great walled enclosure where were the temples, porticos, and the stadium of the Isthmus, was quickly behind them. They walked eastward along the sea-shore. The scene about was brisk enough, had they heeded. A dozen chariots passed. Under every tall pine along the way stood merchants' booths, each with a goodly crowd. Now a herd of brown goats came, the offering of a pious Phocian; now a band of Aphrodite's priestesses from Corinth whirled by in no overdecorous dance, to a deafening noise of citharas and castanets. A soft breeze was sending the brown-sailed fisher boats across the heaving bay. Straight before the three spread the white stuccoed houses of Cenchræa, the eastern haven of Corinth; far ahead in smooth semicircle rose the green crests of the Argive mountains, while to their right upreared the steep lonely pyramid of brown rock, Acro-Corinthus, the commanding citadel of the thriving city. But above, beyond these, fairer than them all, spread the clear, sun-shot azure of Hellas, the like whereof is not over any other land, save as that land is girt by the crisp foam of the blue Ægean Sea.

So much for the picture, but Simonides, having seen it often, saw it not at all, but plied the others with questions.

"So this Hermione of his is beautiful?"

"Like Aphrodite rising from the sea foam." The answer came from Democrates, who seemed to look away, avoiding the poet's keen glance.

"And yet her father gave her to the son of his bitter enemy?"

"Hermippus of Eleusis is sensible. It is a fine thing to have the handsomest man in Hellas for son-in-law."

"And now to the great marvel—did Glaucon truly seek her not for dowry, nor rank, but for sheer love?"

"Marriages for love are in fashion to-day," said Democrates, with a side glance at Cimon, whose sister Elpinice had just made a love match with Callias the Rich, to the scandal of all the prudes in Athens.

"Then I meet marvels even in my old age. Another Odysseus and his Penelope! And he is handsome, valiant, high-minded, with a wife his peer? You raise my hopes too high. They will be dashed."

"They will not," protested Democrates, with every sign of loyalty; "turn here: this lane in the pines leads to his tent. If we have praised too much, doom us to the labours of Tantalus."

But here their progress was stopped. A great knot of people were swarming about a statue under a pine tree, and shrill, angry voices proclaimed not trafficking, but a brawl.

CHAPTER II
THE ATHLETE

There was ceaseless coming and going outside the Precinct of Poseidon. Following much the same path just taken by Simonides and his new friends, two other men were walking, so deep in talk that they hardly heeded how many made respectful way for them, or how many greeted them. The taller and younger man, to be sure, returned every salute with a graceful flourish of his hands, but in a mechanical way, and with eye fixed on his companion.

The pair were markedly contrasted. The younger was in his early prime, strong, well developed, and daintily dressed. His gestures were quick and eloquent. His brown beard and hair were trimmed short to reveal a clear olive face—hardly regular, but expressive and tinged with an extreme subtilty. When he laughed, in a strange, silent way, it was to reveal fine teeth, while his musical tongue ran on, never waiting for answer.

His comrade, however, answered little. He barely rose to the other's shoulder, but he had the chest and sinews of an ox. Graces there were none. His face was a scarred ravine, half covered by scanty stubble. The forehead was low. The eyes, gray and wise, twinkled from tufted eyebrows. The long gray hair was tied about his forehead in a braid and held by a golden circlet. The "chlamys" around his hips was purple but dirty. To his companion's glib Attic he returned only Doric monosyllables.

"Thus I have explained: if my plans prosper; if Corcyra and Syracuse send aid; if Xerxes has trouble in provisioning his army, not merely can we resist Persia, but conquer with ease. Am I too sanguine, Leonidas?"

"We shall see."

"No doubt Xerxes will find his fleet untrustworthy. The Egyptian sailors hate the Phœnicians. Therefore we can risk a sea fight."

"No rashness, Themistocles."

"Yes—it is dicing against the Fates, and the stake is the freedom of Hellas. Still a battle must be risked. If we quit ourselves bravely, our names shall be remembered as long as Agamemnon's."

"Or Priam's?—his Troy was sacked."

"And you, my dear king of Sparta, will of course move heaven and earth to have your Ephors and Council somewhat more forward than of late in preparing for war? We all count on you."

"I will try."

"Who can ask more? But now make an end to statecraft. We were speaking about the pentathlon and the chances of—"

Here the same brawling voices that had arrested Simonides broke upon Themistocles and Leonidas also. The cry "A fight!" was producing its inevitable result. Scores of men, and those not the most aristocratic, were running pell-mell whither so many had thronged already. In the confusion scant reverence was paid the king of Sparta and the first statesman of Athens, who were thrust unceremoniously aside and were barely witnesses of what followed.

The outcry was begun, after-report had it, by a Sicyonian bronze-dealer finding a small but valuable lamp missing from the table whereon he showed his wares. Among the dozen odd persons pressing about the booth his eye singled out a slight, handsome boy in Oriental dress; and since Syrian serving-lads were proverbially light-fingered, the Sicyonian jumped quickly at his conclusion.

"Seize the Barbarian thief!" had been his shout as he leaped and snatched the alleged culprit's mantle. The boy escaped easily by the frailness of his dress, which tore in the merchant's hands; but a score of bystanders seized the fugitive and dragged him back to the Sicyonian, whose order to "search!" would have been promptly obeyed; but at this instant he stumbled over the missing lamp on the ground before the table, whence probably it had fallen. The bronze-dealer was now mollified, and would willingly have released the lad, but a Spartan bystander was more zealous.

"Here's a Barbarian thief and spy!" he began bellowing; "he dropped the lamp when he was detected! Have him to the temple and to the wardens of the games!"

The magic word "spy" let loose the tongues and passions of every man within hearing. The unfortunate lad was seized again and jostled rudely, while questions rattled over him like hailstones.

"Whose slave are you? Why here? Where's your master? Where did you get that outlandish dress and gold-laced turban? Confess, confess,—or it'll be whipped out of you! What villany are you up to?"

If the prisoner had understood Greek,—which was doubtful,—he could scarce have comprehended this babel. He struggled vainly; tears started to his eyes. Then he committed a blunder. Not attempting a protest, he thrust a small hand into his crimson belt and drew forth a handful of gold as bribe for release.

"A slave with ten darics!" bawled the officious Spartan, never relaxing his grip. "Hark you, friends, it's plain as day. Dexippus of Corinth has a Syrian lad like this. The young scoundrel's robbed his master and is running away."

"That's it! A runaway! To the temple with him!" chimed a dozen. The prisoner's outcries were drowned. He would have been swept off in ungentle custody had not a strong hand intervened in his favor.

"A moment, good citizens," called a voice in clear Attic. "Release this lad. I know Dexippus's slave; he's no such fellow."

The others, low-browed Spartans mostly, turned, ill-pleased at the interruption of an Athenian, but shrank a step as a name went among them.

"Castor and Pollux—it's Glaucon the Beautiful!"

With two thrusts of impetuous elbows, the young man was at the assailed lad's side. The newcomer was indeed a sight for gods. Beauty and power seemed wholly met in a figure of perfect symmetry and strength. A face of fine regularity, a chiselled profile, smooth cheeks, deep blue eyes, a crown of closely cropped auburn hair, a chin neither weak nor stern, a skin burnt brown by the sun of the wrestling schools—these were parts of the picture, and the whole was how much fairer than any part! Aroused now, he stood with head cast back and a scarlet cloak shaking gracefully from his shoulders.

"Unhand the lad!" he repeated.

For a moment, compelled by his beauty, the Spartans yielded. The Oriental pressed against his protector; but the affair was not to end so easily.

"Hark you, Sir Athenian," rejoined the Spartan leader, "don't presume on your good looks. Our Lycon will mar them all to-morrow. Here's Dexippus's slave or else a Barbarian spy: in either case to the temple with him, and don't you hinder."

He plucked at the boy's girdle; but the athlete extended one slim hand, seized the Spartan's arm, and with lightning dexterity laid the busybody flat on Mother Earth. He staggered upward, raging and calling on his fellows.

"Sparta insulted by Athens! Vengeance, men of Lacedæmon! Fists! Fists!"

The fate of the Oriental was forgotten in the storm of patriotic fury that followed. Fortunately no one had a weapon. Half a dozen burly Laconians precipitated themselves without concert or order upon the athlete. He was hidden a moment in the rush of flapping gowns and tossing arms. Then like a rock out of the angry sea shone his golden head, as he shook off the attack. Two men were on their backs, howling. The others stood at respectful distance, cursing and meditating another rush. An Athenian pottery merchant from a neighbouring booth began trumpeting through his hands.

"Men of Athens, this way!"

His numerous countrymen came scampering from far and wide. Men snatched up stones and commenced snapping off pine boughs for clubs. The athlete, centre of all this din, stood smiling, with his glorious head held high, his eyes alight with the mere joy of battle. He held out his arms. Both pose and face spoke as clearly as words,—"Prove me!"

"Sparta is insulted. Away with the braggart!" the Laconians were clamouring. The Athenians answered in kind. Already a dark sailor was drawing a dirk. Everything promised broken heads, and perhaps blood, when Leonidas and his friend,—by laying about them with their staves,—won their way to the front. The king dashed his staff upon the shoulder of a strapping Laconian who was just hurling himself on Glaucon.

"Fools! Hold!" roared Leonidas, and the moment the throng saw what newcomers they faced, Athenian and Spartan let their arms drop and stood sheepish and silent. Themistocles instantly stepped forward and held up his hand. His voice, trumpet-clear, rang out among the pines. In three sentences he dissolved the tumult.

"Fellow-Hellenes, do not let Dame Discord make sport of you. I saw all that befell. It is only an unlucky misunderstanding. You are quite satisfied, I am sure, Master Bronze-Dealer?"

The Sicyonian, who saw in a riot the ruin of his evening's trade, nodded gladly.

"He says there was no thieving, and he is entirely satisfied. He thanks you for your friendly zeal. The Oriental was not Dexippus's slave, and Xerxes does not need such boys for spies. I am certain Glaucon would not insult Sparta. So let us part without bad blood, and await the judgment of the god in the contest to-morrow."

Not a voice answered him. The crash of music from the sacrificial embassy of Syracuse diverted everybody's attention; most of the company streamed away to follow the flower-decked chariots and cattle back to the temple. Themistocles and Leonidas were left almost alone to approach the athlete.

"You are ever Glaucon the Fortunate," laughed Themistocles; "had we not chanced this way, what would not have befallen?"

"Ah, it was delightful," rejoined the athlete, his eyes still kindled; "the shock, the striving, the putting one's own strength and will against many and feeling 'I am the stronger.' "

"Delightful, no doubt" replied the statesman, "though Zeus spare me fighting one against ten! But what god possessed you to meddle in this brawl, and imperil all chances for to-morrow?"

"I was returning from practice at the palæstra. I saw the lad beset and knew he was not Dexippus's slave. I ran to help him. I thought no more about it."

"And risked everything for a sly-eyed Oriental. Where is the rascal?"

But the lad—author of the commotion—had disappeared completely.

"Behold his fair gratitude to his rescuer," cried Themistocles, sourly, and then he turned to Leonidas. "Well, very noble king of Sparta, you were asking to see Glaucon and judge his chances in the pentathlon. Your Laconians have just proved him; are you satisfied?"

But the king, without a word of greeting, ran his eyes over the athlete from head to heel, then blurted out his verdict:

"Too pretty."

Glaucon blushed like a maid. Themistocles threw up his hands in deprecation.

"But were not Achilles and many another hero beautiful as brave? Does not Homer call them so many times 'godlike'?"

"Poetry doesn't win the pentathlon," retorted the king; then suddenly he seized the athlete's right arm near the shoulder. The muscles cracked. Glaucon did not wince. The king dropped the arm with a *"Euge!"* then extended his own hand, the fingers half closed, and ordered, "Open."

One long minute, just as Simonides and his companions approached, Athenian and Spartan stood face to face, hand locked in hand, while Glaucon's forehead grew redder, not with blushing. Then blood rushed to the king's brow also. His fingers were crimson. They had been forced open.

"Euge!" cried the king, again; then, to Themistocles, "He will do."

Whereupon, as if satisfied in his object and averse to further dalliance, he gave Cimon and his companions the stiffest of nods and deliberately turned on his heel. Speech was too precious coin for him to be wasted on mere adieus. Only over his shoulder he cast at Glaucon a curt mandate.

"I hate Lycon. Grind his bones."

Themistocles, however, lingered a moment to greet Simonides. The little poet was delighted, despite overweening hopes, at the manly beauty yet modesty of the athlete, and being a man who kept his thoughts always near his tongue, made Glaucon blush more manfully than ever.

"Master Simonides is overkind," had ventured the athlete; "but I am sure his praise is only polite compliment."

"What misunderstanding!" ran on the poet. "How you pain me! I truly desired to ask a question. Is it not a great delight to know that so many people are gladdened just by looking on you?"

"How dare I answer? If 'no,' I contradict you—very rude. If 'yes,' I praise myself—far ruder."

"Cleverly turned. The face of Paris, the strength of Achilles, the wit of Periander, all met in one body;" but seeing the athlete's confusion more profound than ever, the Cean cut short. "Heracles! if my tongue wounds you, lo! it's clapped back in its sheath; I'll be revenged in an ode of fifty iambs on your victory. For that you will conquer, neither I nor any sane man in Hellas has the least doubt. Are you not confident, dear Athenian?"

"I am confident in the justice of the gods, noble Simonides," said the athlete, half childishly, half in deep seriousness.

"Well you may be. The gods are usually 'just' to such as you. It's we graybeards that Tyche, 'Lady Fortune,' grows tired of helping."

"Perhaps!" Glaucon passed his hand across his eyes with a dreamy gesture. "Yet sometimes I almost say, 'Welcome a misfortune, if not too terrible,' just to ward off the god's jealousy of too great prosperity. In all things, save my father's anger, I have prospered. To-morrow I can appease that, too. Yet you know Solon's saying, 'Call no man fortunate till he is dead.' "

Simonides was charmed at this frank confession on first acquaintance. "Yes, but even one of the Seven Sages can err."

"I do not know. I only hope—"

"Hush, Glaucon," admonished Democrates. "There's no worse dinner before a contest than one of flighty thoughts. When safe in Athens—"

"In Eleusis you mean," corrected the athlete.

"Pest take you," cried Cimon; "you say Eleusis because there is Hermione. But make this day-dreaming end ere you come to grips with Lycon."

"He will awaken," smiled Themistocles. Then, with another gracious nod to Simonides, the statesman hastened after Leonidas, leaving the three young men and the poet to go to Glaucon's tent in the pine grove.

"And why should Leonidas wish Glaucon to grind the bones of the champion of Sparta?" asked Cimon, curiously.

"Quickly answered," replied Simonides, who knew half the persons of the nobility in Hellas; "first, Lycon is of the rival kingly house at Sparta; second, he's suspected of 'Medizing,' of favouring Persia."

"I've heard that story of 'Medizing,'" interrupted Democrates, promptly; "I can assure you it is not true."

"Enough if he's suspected," cried the uncompromising son of Miltiades; "honest Hellenes should not even be blown upon in times like this. Another reason then for hating him—"

"Peace!" ordered Glaucon, as if starting from a long revery, and with a sweep of his wonderful hands; "let the Medes, the Persians, and their war wait. For me the only war is the pentathlon,—and then by Zeus's favour the victory, the glory, the return to Eleusis! Ah—wish me joy!"

"Verily, the man is mad," reflected the poet; "he lives in his own bright world, sufficient to himself. May Zeus never send storms to darken it! For to bear disaster his soul seems never made."

* * * * * *

At the tent Manes, the athlete's body-servant, came running to his master, with a small box firmly bound.

"A strange dark man brought this only a moment since. It is for Master Glaucon."

On opening there was revealed a bracelet of Egyptian turquoise; the price thereof Simonides wisely set at two minæ. Nothing betrayed the identity of the giver save a slip of papyrus written in Greek, but in very uncertain hand. *"To the Beautiful Champion of Athens: from one he has greatly served."*

Cimon held the bracelet on high, admiring its perfect lustre.

"Themistocles was wrong," he remarked; "the Oriental was not ungrateful. But what 'slave' or 'lad' was this that Glaucon succoured?"

"Perhaps," insinuated Simonides, "Themistocles was wrong yet again. Who knows if a stranger giving such gifts be not sent forth by Xerxes?"

"Don't chatter foolishness," commanded Democrates, almost peevishly; but Glaucon replaced the bracelet in the casket.

"Since the god sends this, I will rejoice in it," he declared lightly. "A fair omen for to-morrow, and it will shine rarely on Hermione's arm." The mention of that lady called forth new protests from Cimon, but he in turn was interrupted, for a half-grown boy had entered the tent and stood beckoning to Democrates.

CHAPTER III
THE HAND OF PERSIA

The lad who sidled up to Democrates was all but a hunchback. His bare arms were grotesquely tattooed, clear sign that he was a Thracian. His eyes twinkled keenly, uneasily, as in token of an almost sinister intelligence. What he whispered to Democrates escaped the rest, but the latter began girding up his cloak.

"You leave us, *philotate*?" cried Glaucon. "Would I not have all my friends with me to-night, to fill me with fair thoughts for the morrow? Bid your ugly Bias keep away!"

"A greater friend than even Glaucon the Alcmæonid commands me hence," said the orator, smiling.

"Declare his name."

"Declare *her* name," cried Simonides, viciously.

"Noble Cean, then I say I serve a most beautiful, high-born dame. Her name is Athens."

"Curses on your public business," lamented Glaucon. "But off with you, since your love is the love of us all."

Democrates kissed the athlete on both cheeks. "I leave you to faithful guardians. Last night I dreamed of a garland of lilies, sure presage of a victory. So take courage."

"*Chaire! chaire!*"[1] called the rest; and Democrates left the tent to follow the slave-boy.

Evening was falling: the sea, rocks, fields, pine groves, were touched by the red glow dying behind Acro-Corinthus. Torches gleamed amid the trees where the multitudes were buying, selling, wagering, making merry. All Greece seemed to have sent its wares to be disposed of at the Isthmia. Democrates idled along, now glancing at the huckster who displayed his painted clay dolls and urged the sightseers to remember the little ones at home. A wine-seller thrust a sample cup of a choice vintage under the Athenian's nose, and vainly adjured him to buy. Thessalian easy-chairs, pottery, slaves kidnapped from the Black Sea, occupied one booth after another. On a pulpit before a bellowing crowd a pair of marionettes were rolling their eyes and gesticulating, as a woman pulled the strings.

But there were more exalted entertainments. A rhapsodist stood on a pine stump chanting in excellent voice Alcæus's hymn to Apollo. And more willingly the orator stopped on the edge of a throng of the better sort, which listened to a man of noble aspect reading in clear voice from his scroll.

"Æschylus of Athens," whispered a bystander. "He reads choruses of certain tragedies he says he will perfect and produce much later."

Democrates knew the great dramatist well, but what he read was new—a "Song of the Furies" calling a terrific curse upon the betrayer of friendship. "Some of his happiest lines," meditated Democrates, walking away, to be held a moment by the crowd around Lamprus the master-harpist. But now, feeling that he had dallied long enough, the orator turned his back on the two female acrobats who were swinging on a trapeze and struck down a long, straight road which led toward the distant cone of Acro-Corinthus. First, however, he turned on Bias, who all the time had been accompanying, dog-fashion.

"You say he is waiting at Hegias's inn?"

"Yes, master. It's by the temple of Bellerophon, just as you begin to enter the city."

"Good! I don't want to ask the way. Now catch this obol and be off."

The boy snatched the flying coin and glided into the crowd.

Democrates walked briskly out of the glare of the torches, then halted to slip the hood of his cloak up about his face.

"The road is dark, but the wise man shuns accidents," was his reflection, as he strode in the direction pointed by Bias.

The way was dark. No moon; and even the brilliant starlight of summer in Hellas is an uncertain guide. Democrates knew he was traversing a long avenue lined by spreading cypresses, with a shimmer of white from some tall, sepulchral monument. Then through the dimness loomed the high columns of a temple, and close beside it pale light spread out upon the road as from an inn.

"Hegias's inn," grumbled the Athenian. "Zeus grant it have no more fleas than most inns of Corinth!"

At sound of his footsteps the door opened promptly, without knocking. A squalid scene revealed itself,—a white-washed room, an earthen floor, two clay lamps on a low table, a few stools,—but a tall, lean man in Oriental dress greeted the Athenian with a salaam which showed his own gold earrings, swarthy skin, and black mustache.

"Fair greetings, Hiram," spoke the orator, no wise amazed, "and where is your master?"

"At service," came a deep voice from a corner, so dark that Democrates had not seen the couch where lolled an ungainly figure that now rose clumsily.

"Hail, Democrates."

"Hail, Lycon."

Hand joined in hand; then Lycon ordered the Oriental to "fetch the noble Athenian some good Thasian wine."

"You will join me?" urged the orator.

"Alas! no. I am still in training. Nothing but cheese and porridge till after the victory to-morrow; but then, by Castor, I'll enjoy 'the gentleman's disease'— a jolly drunkenness."

"Then you are sure of victory to-morrow?"

"Good Democrates, what god has tricked you into believing your fine Athenian has a chance?"

"I have seven minæ staked on Glaucon."

"Seven staked in the presence of your friends; how many in their absence?"

Democrates reddened. He was glad the room was dark. "I am not here to quarrel about the pentathlon," he said emphatically.

"Oh, very well. Leave your dear sparrow to my gentle hands." The Spartan's huge paws closed significantly: "Here's the wine. Sit and drink. And you, Hiram, get to your corner."

The Oriental silently squatted in the gloom, the gleam of his beady eyes just visible. Lycon sat on a stool beside his guest, his Cyclops-like limbs sprawling down upon the floor. Scarred and brutish, indeed, was his face, one ear missing, the other beaten flat by boxing gloves; but Democrates had a distinct feeling that under his battered visage and wiry black hair lurked greater penetration of human motive and more ability to play therewith than the chance observer might allow. The Athenian deliberately waited his host's first move.

"The wine is good, Democrates?" began Lycon.

"Excellent."

"I presume you have arranged your wagers to-morrow with your usual prudence."

"How do you know about them?"

"Oh, my invaluable Hiram, who arranged this interview for us through Bias, has made himself a brother to all the betting masters. I understand you have arranged it so that whether Glaucon wins or loses you will be none the poorer."

The Athenian set down his cup.

"Because I would not let my dear friend's sanguine expectations blind all my judgment is no reason why you should seek this interview, Lycon," he rejoined tartly. "If this is the object of your summons, I'm better back in my own tent."

Lycon tilted back against the table. His speech was nothing curt or "Laconic"; it was even drawling. "On the contrary, dear Democrates, I was only commending your excellent foresight, something that I see characterizes all you do. You are the friend of Glaucon. Since Aristeides has been banished, only Themistocles exceeds you in influence over the Athenians. Therefore, as a loyal Athenian you must support your champion. Likewise, as a man of judgment you must see that I—though this pentathlon is only a by-play, not my business—will probably break your Glaucon's back to-morrow. It is precisely this good judgment on your part which makes me sure I do well to ask an interview—for something else."

"Then quickly to business."

"A few questions. I presume Themistocles to-day conferred with Leonidas?"

"I wasn't present with them."

"But in due time Themistocles will tell you everything?"

Democrates chewed his beard, not answering.

"*Pheu!* you don't pretend Themistocles distrusts you?" cried the Spartan.

"I don't like your questions, Lycon."

"I am very sorry. I'll cease them. I only wished to-night to call to your mind the advantage of two such men as you and I becoming friends. I may be king of Lacedæmon before long."

"I knew that before, but where's your chariot driving?"

"Dear Athenian, the Persian chariot is now driving toward Hellas. We cannot halt it. Then let us be so wise that it does not pass over us."

"Hush!" Democrates spilled the cup as he started. "No 'Medizing' talk before me. Am I not Themistocles's friend?"

"Themistocles and Leonidas will seem valiant fools after Xerxes comes. Men of foresight—"

"Are never traitors."

"Beloved Democrates," sneered the Spartan, "in one year the most patriotic Hellene will be he who has made the Persian yoke the most endurable. Don't blink at destiny."

"Don't be overcertain."

"Don't grow deaf and blind. Xerxes has been collecting troops these four years. Every wind across the Ægean tells how the Great King assembles millions of soldiers, thousands of ships: Median cavalry, Assyrian archers, Egyptian battle-axemen—the best troops in the world. All the East will be marching on our poor Hellas. And when has Persia failed to conquer?"

"At Marathon."

"A drop of rain before the tempest! If Datis, the Persian general, had only been more prudent!"

"Clearly, noblest Lycon," said Democrates, with a satirical smile, "for a taciturn Laconian to become thus eloquent for tyranny must have taken a bribe of ten thousand gold darics."

"But answer my arguments."

"Well—the old oracle is proved: 'Base love of gain and naught else shall bear sore destruction to Sparta.' "

"That doesn't halt Xerxes's advance."

"An end to your croakings,"—Democrates was becoming angry,—"I know the Persian's power well enough. Now why have you summoned me?"

Lycon looked on his visitor long and hard. He reminded the Athenian disagreeably of a huge cat just considering whether a mouse were near enough to risk a spring.

"I sent for you because I wished you to give a pledge."

"I'm in no mood to give it."

"You need not refuse. Giving or withholding the fate of Hellas will not be altered, save as you wish to make it so."

"What must I promise?"

"That you will not reveal the presence in Greece of a man I intend to set before you." Another silence. Democrates knew even then, if vaguely, that he was making a decision on which might hinge half his future. In the after days he looked back on this instant with unspeakable regret. But the Laconian sat before him, smiling, sneering, commanding by his more dominant will. The Athenian answered, it seemed, despite himself:—

"If it is not to betray Hellas."

"It is not."

"Then I promise."

"Swear it then by your native Athena."

And Democrates—perhaps the wine was strong—lifted his right hand and swore by Athena Polias of Athens he would betray no secret.

Lycon arose with what was part bellow, part laugh. Even then the orator was moved to call back the pledge, but the Spartan acted too swiftly. The short moments which followed stamped themselves on Democrates's memory. The flickering lamps, the squalid room, the long, dense shadows, the ungainly movements of the Spartan, who was opening a door,—all this passed after the manner of a vision. And as in a vision Democrates saw a stranger stepping through the inner portal, as at Lycon's summons—a man of no huge stature, but masterful in eye and mien. Another Oriental, but not as the obsequious Hiram. Here was a lord to command and be obeyed. Gems flashed from the scarlet turban, the green jacket was embroidered with pearls—and was not half the wealth of Corinth in the jewels studding the sword hilt? Tight trousers and high shoes of tanned leather set off a form supple and powerful as a panther's. Unlike most Orientals the stranger was fair. A blond beard swept his breast. His eyes were sharp, steel-blue. Never a word spoke he; but Democrates looked on him with wide eyes, then turned almost in awe to the Spartan.

"This is a prince—" he began.

"His Highness Prince Abairah of Cyprus," completed Lycon, rapidly, "now come to visit the Isthmian Games, and later your Athens. It is for this I have brought you face to face—that he may be welcome in your city."

The Athenian cast at the stranger a glance of keenest scrutiny. He knew by every instinct in his being that Lycon was telling a barefaced lie. Why he did not cry out as much that instant he hardly himself knew. But the gaze of the "Cyprian" pierced through him, fascinating, magnetizing, and Lycon's great hand was on his victim's shoulder. The "Cyprian's" own hand went out seeking Democrates's.

"I shall be very glad to see the noble Athenian in his own city. His fame for eloquence and prudence is already in Tyre and Babylon," spoke the stranger, never taking his steel-blue eyes from the orator's face. The accent was Oriental, but the Greek was fluent. The prince—for prince he was, whatever his nation—pressed his hand closer. Almost involuntarily Democrates's hand responded. They clasped tightly; then, as if Lycon feared a word too much, the unknown released his hold, bowed with inimitable though silent courtesy, and was gone behind the door whence he had come.

It had taken less time than men use to count a hundred. The latch clicked. Democrates gazed blankly on the door, then turned on Lycon with a start.

"Your wine was strong. You have bewitched me. What have I done? By Zeus of Olympus—I have given my hand in pledge to a Persian spy."

" 'A prince of Cyprus'—did you not hear me?"

"Cerberus eat me if that man has seen Cyprus. No Cyprian is so blond. The man is Xerxes's brother."

"We shall see, friend; we shall see: 'Day by day we grow old, and day by day we grow wiser.' So your own Solon puts it, I think."

Democrates drew himself up angrily. "I know my duty; I'll denounce you to Leonidas."

"You gave a pledge and oath."

"It were a greater crime to keep than to break it."

Lycon shrugged his huge shoulders. "*Eu!* I hardly trusted to that. But I do trust to Hiram's pretty story about your bets, and still more to a tale that's told about where and how you've borrowed money."

Democrates's voice shook either with rage or with fear when he made shift to answer.

"I see I've come to be incriminated and insulted. So be it. If I keep my pledge, at least suffer me to wish you and your 'Cyprian' a very good night."

Lycon good-humouredly lighted him to the door. "Why so hot? I'll do you a service to-morrow. If Glaucon wrestles with me, I shall kill him."

"Shall I thank the murderer of my friend?"

"Even when that friend has wronged you?"

"Silence! What do you mean?"

Even in the flickering lamplight Democrates could see the Spartan's evil smile.

"Of course—Hermione."

"Silence, by the infernal gods! Who are you, Cyclops, for *her* name to cross your teeth?"

"I'm not angry. Yet you will thank me to-morrow. The pentathlon will be merely a pleasant flute-playing before the great war-drama. You will see more of the 'Cyprian' at Athens—"

Democrates heard no more. Forth from that wine-house he ran into the sheltering night, till safe under the shadow of the black cypresses. His head glowed. His heart throbbed. He had been partner in foulest treason. Duty to friend, duty to country,—oath or no oath,—should have sent him to Leonidas. What evil god had tricked him into that interview? Yet he did not denounce the traitor. Not his oath held him back, but benumbing fear,—and what sting lay back of Lycon's hints and threats the orator knew best. And how if Lycon made good his boast and killed Glaucon on the morrow?

CHAPTER IV
THE PENTATHLON

In a tent at the lower end of the long stadium stood Glaucon awaiting the final summons to his ordeal. His friends had just cried farewell for the last time: Cimon had kissed him; Themistocles had gripped his hand; Democrates had called "Zeus prosper you!" Simonides had vowed that he was already hunting for the metres of a triumphal ode. The roar from without told how the stadium was filled with its chattering thousands. The athlete's trainers were bestowing their last officious advice.

"The Spartan will surely win the quoit-throw. Do not be troubled. In everything else you can crush him."

"Beware of Mœrocles of Mantinea. He's a knavish fellow; his backers are recalling their bets. But he hopes to win on a trick; beware, lest he trip you in the foot-race."

"Aim low when you hurl the javelin. Your dart always rises."

Glaucon received this and much more admonition with his customary smile. There was no flush on the forehead, no flutter of the heart. A few hours later he would be crowned with all the glory which victory in the great games could throw about a Hellene, or be buried in the disgrace to which his ungenerous people consigned the vanquished. But, in the words of his day, "he knew himself" and his own powers. From the day he quitted boyhood he had never met the giant he could not master; the Hermes he could not outrun. He anticipated victory as a matter of course, even victory wrested from Lycon, and his thoughts seemed wandering far from the tawny track where he must face his foes.

"Athens,—my father,—my wife! I will win glory for them all!" was the drift of his revery.

The younger rubber grunted under breath at his athlete's vacant eye, but Pytheas, the older of the pair, whispered confidently that "when he had known Master Glaucon longer, he would know that victories came his way, just by reaching out his hands."

"Athena grant it," muttered the other. "I've got my half mina staked on him, too." Then from the tents at either side began the ominous call of the heralds:—

"Amyntas of Thebes, come you forth."

"Ctesias of Epidaurus, come you forth."

"Lycon of Sparta, come you forth."

Glaucon held out his hands. Each trainer seized one.

"Wish me joy and honour, good friends!" cried the athlete.

"Poseidon and Athena aid you!" And Pytheas's honest voice was husky. This was the greatest ordeal of his favourite pupil, and the trainer's soul would go with him into the combat.

"Glaucon of Athens, come you forth."

The curtains of the tent swept aside. An intense sunlight sprang to meet the Athenian. He passed into the arena clad only in his coat of glistering oil. Scolus of Thasos and Mœrocles of Mantinea joined the other four athletes; then, escorted each by a herald swinging his myrtle wand, the six went down the stadium to the stand of the judges.

Before the fierce light of a morning in Hellas beating down on him, Glaucon the Alcmæonid was for an instant blinded, and walked on passively, following his guide. Then, as from a dissolving mist, the huge stadium began to reveal itself: line above line, thousand above thousand of bright-robed spectators, a sea of faces, tossing arms, waving garments. A thunderous shout rose as the athletes came to view,—jangling, incoherent; each city cheered its champion and tried to cry down all the rest: applause, advice, derision. Glaucon heard the derisive hootings, "pretty girl," "pretty pullet," from the serried host of the Laconians along the left side of the stadium; but an answering salvo, "Dog of Cerberus!" bawled by the Athenian crowds opposite, and winged at Lycon, returned the taunts with usury. As the champions approached the judges' stand a procession of full twenty pipers, attended by as many fair boys in flowing white, marched from the farther end of the stadium to meet them. The boys bore cymbals and tambours; the pipers struck up a brisk marching note in the rugged Dorian mode. The boys' lithe bodies swayed in enchanting rhythm. The roaring multitude quieted, admiring their grace. The champions and the pipers thus came to the pulpit in the midst of the long arena. The president of the judges, a handsome Corinthian in purple and a golden fillet, swept his ivory wand from right to left. The marching note ceased. The whole company leaped as one man to its feet. The pipes, the cymbals were drowned, whilst twenty thousand voices—Doric, Bœotian, Attic—chorused together the hymn which all Greece knew: the hymn to Poseidon of the Isthmus, august guardian of the games.

Louder it grew; the multitude found one voice, as if it would cry, "We are Hellenes all; though of many a city, the same fatherland, the same gods, the same hope against the Barbarian."

"Praise we Poseidon the mighty, the monarch,

Shaker of earth and the harvestless sea;

King of wide Ægæ and Helicon gladsome

Twain are the honours high Zeus sheds on thee!

Thine to be lord of the mettlesome chargers,

Thine to be lord of swift ships as they wing!

Guard thou and guide us, dread prince of the billows,

Safe to their homeland, thy suppliants bring;

Faring by land or by clamorous waters

Be thou their way-god to shield, to defend,

Then shall the smoke of a thousand glad altars,

To thee in reverent gladness ascend!"

Thus in part. And in the hush thereafter the president poured a libation from a golden cup, praying, as the wine fell on the brazier beside him, to the "Earth Shaker," seeking his blessing upon the contestants, the multitude, and upon broad Hellas. Next the master-herald announced that now, on the third day of the games, came the final and most honoured contest: the pentathlon, the fivefold struggle, with the crown to him who conquered thrice. He proclaimed the names of the six rivals, their cities, their ancestry, and how they had complied with the required training. The president took up his tale, and turning to the champions, urged them to strive their best, for the eyes of all Hellas were on them. But he warned any man with blood-guiltiness upon his soul not to anger the gods by continuing in the games.

"But since," the brief speech concluded, "these men have chosen to contend, and have made oath that they are purified or innocent, let them join, and Poseidon shed fair glory upon the best!"

More shouting; the pipers paraded the arena, blowing shriller than ever. Some of the athletes shifted uneasily. Scolus the Thasian—youngest of the six—was pale, and cast nervous glances at the towering bulk of Lycon. The Spartan gave him no heed, but threw a loud whisper at Glaucon, who stood silently beside him:—

"By Castor, son of Conon, you are extremely handsome. If fine looks won the battle, I might grow afraid."

The Athenian, whose roving eye had just caught Cimon and Democrates in the audience, seemed never to hear him.

"And you are passing stalwart. Still, be advised. I wouldn't harm you, so drop out early."

Still no answer from Glaucon, whose clear eye seemed now to be wandering over the bare hills of Megara beyond.

"No answer?" persisted the giant. "*Eu!* don't complain that you've lacked warning, when you sit to-night in Charon's ferry-boat."

The least shadow of a smile flitted across the Athenian's face; there was a slight deepening of the light in his eye. He turned his head a bit toward Lycon:—

"The games are not ended, dear Spartan," he observed quietly.

The giant scowled. "I don't like you silent, smiling men! You're warned. I'll do my worst—"

"Let the leaping begin!" rang the voice of the president,—a call that changed all the uproar to a silence in which one might hear the wind moving in the firs outside, while every athlete felt his muscles tighten.

The heralds ran down the soft sands to a narrow mound of hardened earth, and beckoned to the athletes to follow. In the hands of each contestant were set a pair of bronze dumb-bells. The six were arrayed upon the mound with a clear reach of sand before. The master-herald proclaimed the order of the leaping: that each contestant should spring twice, and he whose leaps were the poorest should drop from the other contests.

Glaucon stood, his golden head thrown back, his eyes wandering idly toward his friends in the stadium. He could see Cimon restless on his seat, and Simonides holding his cloak and doubtless muttering wise counsel. The champion was as calm as his friends were nervous. The stadium had grown oppressively still; then broke into along "ah!" Twenty thousand sprang up together as Scolus the Thasian leaped. His partisans cheered, while he rose from a sand-cloud; but ceased quickly. His leap had been poor. A herald with a pick marked a line where he had landed. The pipers began a rollicking catch to which the athletes involuntarily kept time with their dumb-bells.

Glaucon leaped second. Even the hostile Laconians shouted with pleasure at sight of his beautiful body poised, then flung out upon the sands far beyond the Thasian. He rose, shook off the dust, and returned to the mound, with a graceful gesture to the cheer that greeted him; but wise heads knew the contest was just beginning.

Ctesias and Amyntas leaped beyond the Thasian's mark, short of the Athenian's. Lycon was fifth. His admirers' hopes were high. He did not blast them. Huge was his bulk, yet his strength matched it. A cloud of dust hid him from view. When it settled, every Laconian was roaring with delight. He had passed beyond Glaucon. Mœrocles of Mantinea sprang last and badly. The second round was almost as the first; although Glaucon slightly surpassed his former effort. Lycon did as well as before. The others hardly bettered their early trial. It was long before the Laconians grew quiet enough to listen to the call of the herald.

"Lycon of Sparta wins the leaping. Glaucon of Athens is second. Scolus of Thasos leaps the shortest and drops from the pentathlon."

Again cheers and clamour. The inexperienced Thasian marched disconsolately to his tent, pursued by ungenerous jeers.

"The quoit-hurling follows," once more the herald; "each contestant throws three quoits. He who throws poorest drops from the games."

Cimon had risen now. In a momentary lull he trumpeted through his hands across the arena.

"Wake, Glaucon; quit your golden thoughts of Eleusis; Lycon is filching the crown."

Themistocles, seated near Cimon's side, was staring hard, elbows on knees and head on hands. Democrates, next him, was gazing at Glaucon, as if the athlete were made of gold; but the object of their fears and hopes gave back neither word nor sign.

The attendants were arraying the five remaining champions at the foot of a little rise in the sand, near the judges' pulpit. To each was brought a bronze quoit, the discus. The pipers resumed their medley. The second contest was begun.

First, Amyntas of Thebes. He took his stand, measured the distance with his eye, then with a run flew up the rising, and at its summit his body bent double, while the heavy quoit flew away. A noble cast! and twice excelled. For a moment every Theban in the stadium was transported. Strangers sitting together fell on one another's necks in sheer joy. But the rapture ended quickly. Lycon flung second. His vast strength could now tell to the uttermost. He was proud to display it. Thrice he hurled. Thrice his discus sped out as far as ever man had seen a quoit fly in Hellas. Not even Glaucon's best wishers were disappointed when he failed to come within three cubits of the Spartan. Ctesias and Mœrocles realized their task was hopeless, and strove half heartedly. The friends of the huge Laconian were almost beside themselves with joy; while the herald called desperately that:—

"Lycon of Sparta wins with the discus. Glaucon of Athens is second. Ctesias of Epidaurus throws poorest and drops from the games."

"Wake, Glaucon!" trumpeted Cimon, again his white face shining out amid the thousands of gazers now. "Wake, or Lycon wins again and all is lost!"

Glaucon was almost beyond earshot; to the frantic entreaty he answered by no sign. As he and the Spartan stood once more together, the giant leered on him civilly:—

"You grow wise, Athenian. It's honour enough and to spare to be second, with Lycon first. *Eu!*—and here's the last contest."

"I say again, good friend,"—there was a slight closing of the Athenian's lips, and deepening in his eyes,—"the pentathlon is not ended."

"The harpies eat you, then, if you get too bold! The herald is calling for the javelin-casting. Come,—it's time to make an end."

But in the deep hush that spread again over the thousands Glaucon turned toward the only faces that he saw out of the innumerable host: Themistocles, Democrates, Simonides, Cimon. They beheld him raise his arm and lift his glorious head yet higher. Glaucon in turn saw Cimon sink into his seat. "He wakes!" was the appeased mutter passing from the son of Miltiades and running along every tier of Athenians. And silence deeper than ever held the stadium; for now, with Lycon victor twice, the literal turning of a finger in the next event might win or lose the parsley crown.

The Spartan came first. The heralds had set a small scarlet shield at the lower end of the course. Lycon poised his light javelin thrice, and thrice the slim dart sped through the leathern thong on his fingers. But not for glory. Perchance this combat was too delicate an art for his ungainly hands. Twice the missile lodged in the rim of the shield; once it sprang beyond upon the sand. Mœrocles, who followed, surpassed him. Amyntas was hardly worse. Glaucon came last, and won his victory with a dexterous grace that made all but the hottest Laconian swell the "*Io! paian!*" of applause. His second cast had been into the centre of the target. His third had splintered his second javelin as it hung quivering.

"Glaucon of Athens wins the javelin-casting. Mœrocles of Mantinea is second. Amyntas of Thebes is poorest and drops from the games." But who heard the herald now?

By this time all save the few Mantineans who vainly clung to their champion, and the Laconians themselves, had begun to pin their hopes on the beautiful son of Conon. There was a steely glint in the Spartan athlete's eye that made the president of the games beckon to the master-herald.

"Lycon is dangerous. See that he does not do Glaucon a mischief, or transgress the rules."

"I can, till they come to the wrestling."

"In that the god must aid the Athenian. But now let us have the foot-race."

In the little respite following the trainers entered and rubbed down the three remaining contestants with oil until their bodies shone again like tinted ivory. Then the heralds conducted the trio to the southern end farthest from the tents. The two junior presidents left their pulpit and took post at either end of a line marked on the sand. Each held the end of a taut rope. The contestants drew lots from an urn for the place nearest the lower turning goal,—no trifling advantage. A favouring god gave Mœrocles the first; Lycon was second; Glaucon only third. As the three crouched before the rope with hands dug into the sand, waiting the fateful signal, Glaucon was conscious that a strange blond man of noble mien and Oriental dress was sitting close by the starting line and watching him intently.

It was one of those moments of strain, when even trifles can turn the overwrought attention. Glaucon knew that the stranger was looking from him to Lycon, from Lycon back to himself, measuring each with shrewd eye. Then the gaze settled on the Athenian. The Oriental called to him:—

"Swift, godlike runner, swift;"—they were so close they could catch the Eastern accent—"the Most High give you His wings!"

Glaucon saw Lycon turn on the shouter with a scowl that was answered by a composed smile. To the highly strung imagination of the Athenian the wish became an omen of good. For some unknown cause the incident of the Oriental lad he rescued and the mysterious gift of the bracelet flashed back to him. Why should a stranger of the East cast him fair wishes? Would the riddle ever be revealed?

A trumpet blast. The Oriental, his wish, all else save the tawny track, flashed from Glaucon's mind. The rope fell. The three shot away as one.

Over the sand they flew, moving by quick leaps, their shining arms flashing to and fro in fair rhythm. Twice around the stadium led the race, so no one strained at first. For a while the three clung together, until near the lower goal the Mantinean heedlessly risked a dash. His foot slipped on the sands. He recovered; but like arrows his rivals passed him. At the goal the inevitable happened. Lycon, with the shorter turn, swung quickest. He went up the homeward track ahead, the Athenian an elbow's length behind. The stadium seemed dissolving in a tumult. Men rose; threw garments in the air; stretched out their arms; besought the gods; screamed to the runners.

"Speed, son of Conon, speed!"

"Glory to Castor; Sparta is prevailing!"

"Strive, Mantinean,—still a chance!"

"Win the turn, dear Athenian, the turn, and leave that Cyclops behind!"

But at the upper turn Lycon still held advantage, and down the other track went the twain, even as Odysseus ran behind Ajax, "who trod in Ajax' footsteps ere ever the dust had settled, while on his head fell the breath of him behind." Again at the lower goal the Mantinean was panting wearily in the rear. Again Lycon led, again rose the tempest of voices. Six hundred feet away the presidents were stretching the line, where victory and the plaudits of Hellas waited Lycon of Lacedæmon.

Then men ceased shouting, and prayed under breath. They saw Glaucon's shoulders bend lower and his neck strain back, while the sunlight sprang all over his red-gold hair. The stadium leaped to their feet, as the Athenian landed by a bound at his rival's side. Quick as the bound the great arm of the Spartan flew out with its knotted fist. A deadly stroke, and shunned by a hair's-breadth; but it was shunned. The senior president called angrily to the herald; but none heard his words in the rending din. The twain shot up the track elbow to elbow, and into the rope. It fell amid a blinding cloud of dust. All the heralds and presidents ran together into it. Then was a long, agonizing moment, while the stadium roared, shook, and raged, before the dust settled and the master-herald stood forth beckoning for silence.

"Glaucon of Athens wins the foot-race. Lycon of Sparta is second. Mœrocles of Mantinea drops from the contest. Glaucon and Lycon, each winning twice, shall wrestle for the final victory."

And now the stadium grew exceeding still. Men lifted their hands to their favourite gods, and made reckless, if silent, vows,—geese, pigs, tripods, even oxen,—if only the deity would strengthen their favourite's arm. For the first time attention was centred on the tall "time pointer," by the judges' stand, and how the short shadow cast by the staff told of the end of the morning. The last wagers were recorded on the tablets by nervous styluses. The readiest tongues ceased to chatter. Thousands of wistful eyes turned from the elegant form of the Athenian to the burly form of the Spartan. Every outward chance, so many an anxious heart told itself, favoured the oft-victorious giant; but then,—and here came reason for a true Hellene,—"the gods could not suffer so fair a man to meet defeat." The noonday sun beat down fiercely. The tense stillness was now and then broken by the bawling of a swarthy hawker thrusting himself amid the spectators with cups and a jar of sour wine. There was a long rest. The trainers came forward again and dusted the two remaining champions with sand that they might grip fairly. Pytheas looked keenly in his pupil's face.

" 'Well begun is half done,' my lad; but the hottest battle is still before," said he, trying to cover his own consuming dread.

"Faint heart never won a city," smiled Glaucon, as if never more at ease; and Pytheas drew back happier, seeing the calm light in the athlete's eyes.

"Ay," he muttered to his fellow-trainer, "all is well. The boy has wakened."

But now the heralds marched the champions again to the judges. The president proclaimed the rules of the wrestling,—two casts out of three gave victory. In lower tone he addressed the scowling Spartan:—

"Lycon, I warn you: earn the crown only fairly, if you would earn it. Had that blow in the foot-race struck home, I would have refused you victory, though you finished all alone."

A surly nod was the sole answer.

The heralds led the twain a little way from the judges' stand, and set them ten paces asunder and in sight of all the thousands. The heralds stood, crossing their myrtle wands between. The president rose on his pulpit, and called through the absolute hush:—

"Prepared, Spartan?"

"Yes."

"Prepared, Athenian?"

"Yes."

"Then Poseidon shed glory on the best!"

His uplifted wand fell. A clear shrill trumpet pealed. The heralds bounded back in a twinkling. In that twinkling the combatants leaped into each other's arms. A short grapple; again a sand cloud; and both were rising from the ground. They had fallen together. Heated by conflict, they were locked again ere the heralds could proclaim a tie. Cimon saw the great arms of the Spartan twine around the Athenian's chest in fair grapple, but even as Lycon strove with all his bull-like might to lift and throw, Glaucon's slim hand glided down beneath his opponent's thigh. Twice the Spartan put forth all his powers. Those nearest watched the veins of the athletes swell and heard their hard muscles crack. The stadium was in succession hushed and tumultuous. Then, at the third trial, even as Lycon seemed to have won his end, the Athenian smote out with one foot. The sands were slippery. The huge Laconian lunged forward, and as he lunged, his opponent by a masterly effort tore himself loose. The Spartan fell heavily,—vanquished by a trick, though fairly used.

The stadium thundered its applause. More vows, prayers, exhortations. Glaucon stood and received all the homage in silence. A little flush was on his forehead. His arms and shoulders were very red. Lycon rose slowly. All could hear his rage and curses. The heralds ordered him to contain himself.

"Now, fox of Athens," rang his shout, "I will kill you!"

Pytheas, beholding his fury, tore out a handful of hair in his mingled hope and dread. No man knew better than the trainer that no trick would conquer Lycon this second time; and Glaucon the Fair might be nearer the fields of Asphodel than the pleasant hills by Athens. More than one man had died in the last ordeal of the pentathlon.

The silence was perfect. Even the breeze had hushed while Glaucon and Lycon faced again. The twenty thousand sat still as in their sepulchres, each saying in his heart one word—"Now!" If in the first wrestling the attack had been impetuous, it was now painfully deliberate. When the heralds' wands fell, the two crept like mighty cats across the narrow sands, frames bent, hands outstretched, watching from the corners of their eyes a fair chance to rush in and grapple. Then Lycon, whose raging spirit had the least control, charged. Another dust cloud. When it cleared, the two were locked together as by iron.

For an instant they swayed, whilst the Spartan tried again his brute power. It failed him. Glaucon drew strength from the earth like Antæus. The hushed stadium could hear the pants of the athletes as they locked closer, closer. Strength failing, the Spartan snatched at his enemy's throat; but the Athenian had his wrist gripped fast before the clasp could tighten, and in the melée Glaucon's other hand passed beneath Lycon's thigh. The two seemed deadlocked. For a moment they grinned face to face, almost close enough to bite each other's lips. But breath was too precious for curses. The Spartan flung his ponderous weight downward. A slip in the gliding sand would have ruined the Athenian instantly; but Poseidon or Apollo was with him. His feet dug deep, and found footing. Lycon drew back baffled, though the clutches of their hands were tightening like vices of steel. Then again face to face, swaying to and fro, panting, muttering, while the veins in the bare backs swelled still more.

"He cannot endure it. He cannot! Ah! Athena Polias, pity him! Lycon is wearing him down," moaned Pytheas, beside himself with fear, almost running to Glaucon's aid.

The stadium resumed its roaring. A thousand conflicting prayers, hopes, counsels, went forth to the combatants. The gods of Olympus and Hades; all demigods, heroes, satyrs, were invoked for them. They were besought to conquer in the name of parents, friends, and native land. Athenians and Laconians, sitting side by side, took up the combat, grappling fiercely. And all this time the two strove face to face.

How long had it lasted? Who knew? Least of all that pair who wrestled perchance for life and for death. Twice again the Spartan strove with his weight to crush his opponent down. Twice vainly. He could not close his grip around the Athenian's throat. He had looked to see Glaucon sink exhausted; but his foe still looked on him with steadfast, unweakening eyes. The president was just bidding the heralds, "Pluck them asunder and declare a tie!" when the stadium gave a shrill long shout. Lycon had turned to his final resource. Reckless of his own hurt, he dashed his iron forehead against the Athenian's, as bull charges bull. Twice and three times, and the blood leaped out over Glaucon's fair skin. Again—the rush of blood was almost blinding. Again—Pytheas screamed with agony—the Athenian's clutch seemed weakening. Again—flesh and blood could not stand such battering long. If Lycon could endure this, there was only one end to the pentathlon.

"Help thou me, Athena of the Gray Eyes! For the glory of Athens, my father, my wife!"

The cry of Glaucon—half prayer, half battle-shout—pealed above the bellowing stadium. Even as he cried it, all saw his form draw upward as might Prometheus's unchained. They saw the fingers of the Spartan unclasp. They saw his bloody face upturned and torn with helpless agony. They saw his great form totter, topple, fall. The last dust cloud, and into it the multitude seemed rushing together....

... They caught Glaucon just as he fell himself. Themistocles was the first to kiss him. Little Simonides wept. Cimon, trying to embrace the victor, hugged in the confusion a dirty Platæan. Democrates seemed lost in the whirlpool, and came with greetings later. Perhaps he had stopped to watch that Oriental who had given Glaucon good wishes in the foot-race. The fairest praise, however, was from a burly man, who merely held out his hand and muttered, "Good!" But this was from Leonidas.

* * * * * * *

Very late a runner crowned with pink oleanders panted up to the Athenian watch by Mount Icarus at the custom-house on the Megarian frontier.

"*Nika!*—He conquers."

The man fell breathless; but in a moment a clear beacon blazed upon the height. From a peak in Salamis another answered. In Eleusis, Hermippus the Noble was running to his daughter. In Peiræus, the harbour-town, the sailor folk were dancing about the market-place. In Athens, archons, generals, and elders were accompanying Conon to the Acropolis to give thanks to Athena. Conon had forgotten how he had disowned his son. Another beacon glittered from the Acropolis. Another flashed from the lordly crest of Pentelicus, telling the news to all Attica. There was singing in the fishers' boats far out upon the bay. In the goat-herds' huts on dark Hymethus the pan-pipes blew right merrily. Athens spent the night in almost drunken joy. One name was everywhere:—

"Glaucon the Beautiful who honours us all! Glaucon the Fortunate whom the High Gods love!"

BOOK I
THE SHADOW OF THE PERSIAN

CHAPTER V
HERMIONE OF ELEUSIS

A cluster of white stuccoed houses with a craggy hill behind, and before them a blue bay girt in by the rocky isle of Salamis—that is Eleusis-by-the-Sea. Eastward and westward spreads the teeming Thrasian plain, richest in Attica. Behind the plain the encircling mountain wall fades away into a purple haze. One can look southward toward Salamis; then to the left rises the rounded slope of brown Pœcilon sundering Eleusis from its greater neighbour, Athens. Look behind: there is a glimpse of the long violet crests of Cithæron and Parnes, the barrier mountains against Bœotia. Look to right: beyond the summits of Megara lifts a noble cone. It is an old friend, Acro-Corinthus. The plain within the hills is sprinkled with thriving farmsteads, green vineyards, darker olive groves. The stony hill-slopes are painted red by countless poppies. One hears the tinkling of the bells of roving goats. Thus the more distant view; while at the very foot of the hill of vision rises a temple with proud columns and pediments,—the fane of Demeter the "Earth Mother" and the seat of her Mysteries, renowned through Hellas.

The house of Hermippus the Eumolpid, first citizen of Eleusis, stood to the east of the temple. On three sides gnarled trunks and sombre leaves of the sacred olives almost hid the white low walls of the rambling buildings. On the fourth side, facing the sea, the dusty road wound east toward Megara. Here, by the gate, were gathered a rustic company: brown-faced village lads and lasses, toothless graybeards, cackling old wives. Above the barred gate swung a festoon of ivy, whilst from within the court came the squeaking of pipes, the tuning of citharas, and shouted orders—signs of a mighty bustling. Then even while the company grew, a half-stripped courier flew up the road and into the gate.

"They come," ran the wiseacre's comment; but their buzzing ceased, as again the gate swung back to suffer two ladies to peer forth. Ladies, in the truth, for the twain had little in common with the ogling village maids, and whispers were soon busy with them.

"Look—his wife and her mother! How would you, Praxinœ, like to marry an Isthmionices?"

"Excellently well, but your Hermas won't so honour you."

"*Eu!* see, she lifts her pretty blue veil; I'm glad she's handsome. Some beautiful men wed regular hags."

The two ladies were clearly mother and daughter, of the same noble height, and dressed alike in white. Both faces were framed in a flutter of Amorgos gauze: the mother's was saffron, crowned with a wreath of golden wheatears; the daughter's blue with a circlet of violets. And now as they stood with arms entwined the younger brushed aside her veil. The gossips were right. The robe and the crown hid all but the face and tress of the lustrous brown hair,—but that face! Had not King Hephæstos wrought every line of clear Phœnician glass, then touched them with snow and rose, and shot through all the ichor of life? Perhaps there was a fitful fire in the dark eyes that awaited the husband's coming, or a slight twitching of the impatient lips. But nothing disturbed the high-born repose of face and figure. Hermione was indeed the worthy daughter of a noble house, and happy the man who was faring homeward to Eleusis!

Another messenger. Louder bustle in the court, and the voice of Hermippus arraying his musicians. Now a sharp-faced man, who hid his bald pate under a crown of lilies, joined the ladies,—Conon, father of the victor. He had ended his life-feud with Hermippus the night the message flashed from Corinth. Then a third runner; this time in his hand a triumphant palm branch, and his one word—"Here!" A crash of music answered from the court, while Hermippus, a stately nobleman, his fine head just sprinkled with gray, led out his unmartial army.

Single pipes and double pipes, tinkling lyres and many-stringed citharas, not to forget herdsmen's reed flutes, cymbals, and tambours, all made melody and noise together. An imposing procession that must have crammed the courtyard wound out into the Corinth road.

Here was the demarch[2] of Eleusis, a pompous worthy, who could hardly hold his head erect, thanks to an exceeding heavy myrtle wreath. After him, two by two, the snowy-robed, long-bearded priests of Demeter; behind these the noisy corps of musicians, and then a host of young men and women,—bright of eye, graceful of movement,—twirling long chains of ivy, laurel, and myrtle in time to the music. Palm branches were everywhere. The procession moved down the road; but even as it left the court a crash of cymbals through the olive groves answered its uproar. Deep now and sonorous sounded manly voices as in some triumphal chant. Hermione, as she stood by the gate, drew closer to her mother. Inflexible Attic custom seemed to hold her fast. No noblewoman might thrust herself boldly under the public eye—save at a sacred festival—no, not when the centre of the gladness was her husband.

"He comes!" So she cried to her mother; so cried every one. Around the turn in the olive groves swung a car in which Cimon stood proudly erect, and at his side another. Marching before the chariot were Themistocles, Democrates, Simonides; behind followed every Athenian who had visited the Isthmia. The necks of the four horses were wreathed with flowers; flowers hid the reins and bridles, the chariot, and even its wheels. The victor stood aloft, his scarlet cloak flung back, displaying his godlike form. An unhealed scar marred his forehead—Lycon's handiwork; but who thought of that, when above the scar pressed the wreath of wild parsley? As the two processions met, a cheer went up that shook the red rock of Eleusis. The champion answered with his frankest smile; only his eyes seemed questioning, seeking some one who was not there.

"Io! Glaucon!" The Eleusinian youths broke from their ranks and fell upon the chariot. The horses were loosed in a twinkling. Fifty arms dragged the car onward. The pipers swelled their cheeks, each trying to outblow his fellow. Then after them sped the maidens. They ringed the chariot round with a maze of flowers chains. As the car moved, they accompanied it with a dance of unspeakable ease, modesty, grace. A local poet—not Simonides, not Pindar, but some humbler bard—had invoked his muse for the grand occasion. Youths and maidens burst forth into singing.

"Io! Io, pæan! the parsley-wreathed victor hail!

Io! Io, pæan! sing it out on each breeze, each gale!

He has triumphed, our own, our beloved,

Before all the myriad's ken.

He has met the swift, has proved swifter!

The strong, has proved stronger again!

Now glory to him, to his kinfolk,

To Athens, and all Athens' men!

Meet, run to meet him,

The nimblest are not too fleet.

Greet him, with raptures greet him,

With songs and with twinkling feet.

He approaches,—throw flowers before him.

Throw poppy and lily and rose;

Blow faster, gay pipers, faster,

Till your mad music throbs and flows,

For his glory and ours flies through Hellas,

Wherever the Sun-King goes.

Io! Io, pæan! crown with laurel and myrtle and pine,

Io, pæan! haste to crown him with olive, Athena's dark vine.

He is with us, he shines in his beauty;

Oh, joy of his face the first sight;

He has shed on us all his bright honour,

Let High Zeus shed on him his light,

And thou, Pallas, our gray-eyed protectress,

Keep his name and his fame ever bright!"

Matching action to the song, they threw over the victor crowns and chains beyond number, till the parsley wreath was hidden from sight. Near the gate of Hermippus the jubilant company halted. The demarch bawled long for silence, won it at last, and approached the chariot. He, good man, had been a long day meditating on his speech of formal congratulation and enjoyed his opportunity. Glaucon's eyes still roved and questioned, yet the demarch rolled out his windy sentences. But there was something unexpected. Even as the magistrate took breath after reciting the victor's noble ancestry, there was a cry, a parting of the crowd, and Glaucon the Alcmæonid leaped from the chariot as never on the sands at Corinth. The veil and the violet wreath fell from the head of Hermione when her face went up to her husband's. The blossoms that had covered the athlete shook over her like a cloud as his face met hers. Then even the honest demarch cut short his eloquence to swell the salvo.

"The beautiful to the beautiful! The gods reward well. Here is the fairest crown!"

For all Eleusis loved Hermione, and would have forgiven far greater things from her than this.

* * * * * *

Hermippus feasted the whole company,—the crowd at long tables in the court, the chosen guests in a more private chamber. "Nothing to excess" was the truly Hellenic maxim of the refined Eleusinian; and he obeyed it. His banquet was elegant without gluttony. The Syracusan cook had prepared a lordly turbot. The wine was choice old Chian but well diluted. There was no vulgar gorging with meat, after the Bœotian manner; but the great Copaic eel, "such as Poseidon might have sent up to Olympus," made every gourmand clap his hands. The aromatic honey was the choicest from Mt. Hymettus.

Since the smaller company was well selected, convention was waived, and ladies were present. Hermione sat on a wide chair beside Lysistra, her comely mother; her younger brothers on stools at either hand. Directly across the narrow table Glaucon and Democrates reclined on the same couch. The eyes of husband and wife seldom left each other; their tongues flew fast; they never saw how Democrates hardly took his gaze from the face of Hermione. Simonides, who reclined beside Themistocles,—having struck a firm friendship with that statesman on very brief acquaintance,—was overrunning with humour and anecdote. The great man beside him was hardly his second in the fence of wit and wisdom. After the fish had given way to the wine, Simonides regaled the company with a gravely related story of how the Dioscuri had personally appeared to him during his last stay in Thessaly and saved him from certain death in a falling building.

"You swear this is a true tale, Simonides?" began Themistocles, with one eye in his head.

"It's impiety to doubt. As penalty, rise at once and sing a song in honour of Glaucon's victory."

"I am no singer or harpist," returned the statesman, with a self-complacency he never concealed. "I only know how to make Athens powerful."

"Ah! you son of Miltiades," urged the poet, "at least you will not refuse so churlishly."

Cimon, with due excuses, arose, called for a harp, and began tuning it; but not all the company were destined to hear him. A slave-boy touched Themistocles on the shoulder, and the latter started to go.

"The Dioscuri will save you?" demanded Simonides, laughing.

"Quite other gods," rejoined the statesman; "your pardon, Cimon, I return in a moment. An agent of mine is back from Asia, surely with news of weight, if he must seek me at once in Eleusis."

But Themistocles lingered outside; an instant more brought a summons to Democrates, who found Themistocles in an antechamber, deep in talk with Sicinnus,—nominally the tutor of his sons, actually a trusted spy. The first glance at the Asiatic's keen face and eyes was disturbing. An inward omen— not from the entrails of birds, nor a sign in the heavens—told Democrates the fellow brought no happy tidings.

With incisive questions Themistocles had been bringing out everything.

"So it is absolutely certain that Xerxes begins his invasion next spring?"

"As certain as that Helios will rise to-morrow."

"Forewarned is forearmed. Now where have you been since I sent you off in the winter to visit Asia?"

The man, who knew his master loved to do the lion's share of the talking, answered instantly:—

"Sardis, Emesa, Babylon, Susa, Persepolis, Ecbatana."

"*Eu!* Your commission is well executed. Are all the rumours we hear from the East well founded? Is Xerxes assembling an innumerable host?"

"Rumour does not tell half the truth. Not one tribe in Asia but is required to send its fighting men. Two bridges of boats are being built across the Hellespont. The king will have twelve hundred war triremes, besides countless transports. The cavalry are being numbered by hundreds of thousands, the infantry by millions. Such an army was never assembled since Zeus conquered the Giants."

"A merry array!" Themistocles whistled an instant through his teeth; but, never confounded, urged on his questions. "So be it. But is Xerxes the man to command this host? He is no master of war like Darius his father."

"He is a creature for eunuchs and women; nevertheless his army will not suffer."

"And wherefore?"

"Because Prince Mardonius, son of Gobryas, and brother-in-law of the king, has the wisdom and valour of Cyrus and Darius together. Name him, and you name the arch-foe of Hellas. He, not Xerxes, will be the true leader of the host."

"You saw him, of course?"

"I did not. A Magian in Ecbatana told me a strange story. 'The Prince,' said he, 'hates the details of camps; leaving the preparation to others, he has gone to Greece to spy out the land he is to conquer.' "

"Impossible, you are dreaming!" The exclamation came not from Themistocles but Democrates.

"I am not dreaming, worthy sir," returned Sicinnus, tartly; "the Magian may have lied, but I sought the Prince in every city I visited; they always told me, 'He is in another.' He was not at the king's court. He may have gone to Egypt, to India, or to Arabia;—he *may* likewise have gone to Greece."

"These are serious tidings, Democrates," remarked Themistocles, with an anxiety his voice seldom betrayed. "Sicinnus is right; the presence of such a man as Mardonius in Hellas explains many things."

"I do not understand."

"Why, the lukewarmness of so many friends we had counted on, the bickerings which arose among the Confederates when we met just now at the Isthmus, the slackness of all Spartans save Leonidas in preparing for war, the hesitancy of Corcyra in joining us. Thebes is Medizing, Crete is Medizing, so is Argos. Thessaly is wavering. I can almost name the princes and great nobles over Hellas who are clutching at Persian money. O Father Zeus," wound up the Athenian, "if there is not some master-spirit directing all this villany, there is no wisdom in Themistocles, son of Neocles."

"But the coming of Mardonius to Greece?" questioned the younger man; "the peril he runs? the risk of discovery—"

"Is all but nothing, except as he comes to Athens, for Medizers will shelter him everywhere. Yet there is one spot—blessed be Athena—" Themistocles's hands went up in easy piety—"where, let him come if come he dare!" Then with a swift change, as was his wont, the statesman looked straight on Democrates.

"Hark you, son of Myscelus; those Persian lords are reckless. He may even test the fates and set foot in Attica. I am cumbered with as many cares as Zeus, but this commission I give to you. You are my most trusted lieutenant; I can risk no other. Keep watch, hire spies, scatter bribe-money. Rest not day nor night to find if Mardonius the Persian enters Athens. Once in our clutches—and you have done Hellas as fair a turn as Miltiades at Marathon. You promise it? Give me your hand."

"A great task," spoke Democrates, none too readily.

"And one you are worthy to accomplish. Are we not co-workers for Athens and for Hellas?"

Themistocles's hawklike eyes were unescapable. The younger Athenian thought they were reading his soul. He held out his hand....

When Democrates returned to the hall, Cimon had ended his song. The guests were applauding furiously. Wine was still going round, but Glaucon and Hermione were not joining. Across the table they were conversing in low sentences that Democrates could not catch. But he knew well enough the meaning as each face flashed back the beauty of the other. And his mind wandered back darkly to the day when Glaucon had come to him, more radiant than even his wont, and cried, "Give me joy, dear comrade, joy! Hermippus has promised me the fairest maiden in Athens." Some evil god had made Democrates blind to all his boon-companion's wooing. How many hopes of the orator that day had been shattered! Yet he had even professed to rejoice with the son of Conon.... He sat in sombre silence, until the piping voice of Simonides awakened him.

"Friend, if you are a fool, you do a wise thing in keeping still; if a wise man, a very foolish thing."

"Wine, boy," ordered Democrates; "and less water in it. I feel wretchedly stupid to-day."

He spent the rest of the feast drinking deeply, and with much forced laughter. The dinner ended toward evening. The whole company escorted the victor toward Athens. At Daphni, the pass over the hills, the archons and strategi— highest officials of the state—met them with cavalry and torches and half of the city trailing at their heels. Twenty cubits of the city wall were pulled down to make a gate for the triumphal entry. There was another great feast at the government house. The purse of an hundred drachmæ, due by law to Isthmian victors, was presented. A street was named for Glaucon in the new port-town of Peiræus. Simonides recited a triumphal ode. All Athens, in short, made merry for days. Only one man found it hard to join the mirth whole-heartedly. And this was the victor's bosom friend,—Democrates.

CHAPTER VI
ATHENS

In Athens! Shall one mount the Acropolis or enter the market place? Worship in the temple of the Virgin Athena, or descend to the Agora and the roar of its getters and spenders? For Athens has two faces—toward the ideal, toward the commonplace. Who can regard both at once? Let the Acropolis, its sculptures, its landscape, wait. It has waited for men three thousand years. And so to the Agora.

"Full market time." The Agora was a beehive. From the round Tholus at the south to the long portico at the north all was babel and traffic. Donkeys raised their wheezing protest against too heavy loads of farm produce. Megarian swine squealed and tugged at their leg-cords. An Asiatic sailor clamoured at the money-changer's stall for another obol in change for a Persian daric. "Buy my oil!" bawled the huckster from his wicker booth beside the line of Hermes-busts in the midst of the square. "Buy my charcoal!" roared back a companion, whilst past both was haled a grinning negro with a crier who bade every gentleman to "mark his chance" for a fashionable servant. Phocian the quack was hawking his toothache salve from the steps of the Temple of Apollo. Deira, the comely flower girl, held out crowns of rose, violet, and narcissus to the dozen young dandies who pressed about her. Around the Hermes-busts idle crowds were reading the legal notices plastered on the base of each statue. A file of mules and wagons was ploughing through the multitude with marble for some new building. Every instant the noise grew. Pandora's box had opened, and every clamour had flitted out.

At the northern end, where the porticos and the long Dromos street ran off toward the Dipylon gate, stood the shop of Clearchus the potter. A low counter was covered with the owner's wares,—tall amphoræ for wine, flat beakers, water-pots, and basins. Behind, two apprentices whirled the wheel, another glazed on the black varnish and painted the jars with little red loves and dancing girls. Clearchus sat on the counter with three friends,—come not to trade but to barter the latest gossip from the barber-shops: Agis the sharp, knavish cockpit and gaming-house keeper, Crito the fat mine-contractor, and finally Polus, gray and pursy, who "devoted his talents to the public weal," in other words was a perpetual juryman and likewise busybody.

The latest rumour about Xerxes having been duly chewed, conversation began to lag.

"An idle day for you, my Polus," threw out Clearchus.

"Idle indeed! No jury sits to-day in the King Archon's Porch or the 'Red Court'; I can't vote to condemn that Heraclius who's exported wheat contrary to the law."

"Condemn?" cried Agis; "wasn't the evidence very weak?"

"Ay," snorted Polus, "very weak, and the wretch pleaded piteously, setting his wife and four little ones weeping on the stand. But we are resolved. 'You are boiling a stone—your plea's no profit,' thought we. Our hearts vote 'guilty,' if our heads say 'innocent.' One mustn't discourage honest informers. What's a patriot on a jury for if only to acquit? Holy Father Zeus, but there's a pleasure in dropping into the voting-urn the black bean which condemns!"

"Athena keep us, then, from litigation," murmured Clearchus; while Crito opened his fat lips to ask, "And what adjourns the courts?"

"A meeting of the assembly, to be sure. The embassy's come back from Delphi with the oracle we sought about the prospects of the war."

"Then Themistocles will speak," observed the potter; "a very important meeting."

"Very important," choked the juror, fishing a long piece of garlic from his wallet and cramming it into his mouth with both hands. "What a noble statesman Themistocles is! Only young Democrates will ever be like him."

"Democrates?" squeaked out Crito.

"Why, yes. Almost as eloquent as Themistocles. What zeal for democracy! What courage against Persia! A Nestor, I say, in wisdom—"

Agis gave a whistle.

"A Nestor, perhaps. Yet if you knew, as I do, how some of his nights pass,—dice, Rhodian fighting-cocks, dancing-girls, and worse things,—"

"I'll scarce believe it," grunted the juror; yet then confessed somewhat ruefully, "however, he is unfortunate in his bosom friend."

"What do you mean?" demanded the potter.

"Glaucon the Alcmæonid, to be sure. I cried 'Io, pæan!' as loud as the others when he came back; still I weary of having a man always so fortunate."

"Even as you voted to banish Aristeides, Themistocles's rival, because you were tired of hearing him called 'the Just.' "

"There's much in that. Besides, he's an Alcmæonid, and since their old murder of Cylon the house has been under a blood curse. He has married the daughter of Hermippus, who is too highly born to be faithful to the democracy. He carries a Laconian cane,—sure sign of Spartanizing tendencies. He may conspire any day to become tyrant."

"Hush," warned Clearchus, "there he passes now, arm in arm with Democrates as always, and on his way to the assembly."

"The men are much alike in build," spoke Crito, slowly, "only Glaucon is infinitely handsomer."

"And infinitely less honest. I distrust your too beautiful and too lucky men," snapped Polus.

"Envious dog," commented Agis; and bitter personalities might have followed had not a bell jangled from an adjacent portico.

"Phormio, my brother-in-law, with fresh fish from Phaleron," announced Polus, drawing a coin from his wonted purse,—his cheek; "quick, friends, we must buy our dinners."

Between the columns of the portico stood Phormio the fishmonger, behind a table heaped with his scaly wares. He was a thick, florid man with blue eyes lit by a humourous twinkle. His arms were crusted with brine. To his waist he was naked. As the friends edged nearer he held up a turbot, calling for a bid. A clamour answered him. The throng pressed up the steps, elbowing and scrambling. The competition was keen but good-natured. Phormio's broad jests and witticisms—he called all his customers by name—aided in forcing up the price. The turbot was knocked down to a rich gentleman's cook marketing for his master. The pile of fish decreased, the bidding sharpened. The "Market Wardens" seemed needed to check the jostling. But as the last eel was held up, came a cry—

"Look out for the rope!"

Phormio's customers scattered. Scythian constables were stretching cords dusted with red chalk across all exits from the Agora, save that to the south. Soon the band began contracting its nets and driving a swarm of citizens toward the remaining exit, for a red chalk-mark on a mantle meant a fine. Traffic ceased instantly. Thousands crowded the lane betwixt the temples and porches, seeking the assembly place,—through a narrow, ill-built way, but the great area of the Pnyx opened before them like the slopes of some noble theatre.

No seats; rich and poor sat down upon the rocky ground. Under the open azure, at the focus of the semicircle, with clear view before of the city, and to right of the red cliffs of the Acropolis, rose a low platform hewn in the rock,—the "Bema," the orator's pulpit. A few chairs for the magistrates and a small altar were its sole furnishings. The multitude entered the Pnyx through two narrow entrances pierced in the massy engirdling wall and took seats at pleasure; all were equals—the Alcmæonid, the charcoal-seller from Acharnæ. Amid silence the chairman of the Council arose and put on the myrtle crown,—sign that the sitting was opened. A herald besought blessings on the Athenians and the Platæans their allies. A wrinkled seer carefully slaughtered a goose, proclaimed that its entrails gave good omen, and cast the carcass on the altar. The herald assured the people there was no rain, thunder, or other unlucky sign from heaven. The pious accordingly breathed easier, and awaited the order of the day.

The decree of the Council convening the assembly was read; then the herald's formal proclamation:—

"Who wishes to speak?"

The answer was a groan from nigh every soul present. Three men ascended the Bema. They bore the olive branches and laurel garlands, suppliants at Delphi; but their cloaks were black. "The oracle is unfavourable! The gods deliver us to Xerxes!" The thrill of horror went around the Pnyx.

The three stood an instant in gloomy silence. Then Callias the Rich, solemn and impressive, their spokesman, told their eventful story.

"Athenians, by your orders we have been to Delphi to inquire of the surest oracle in Greece your destinies in the coming war. Hardly had we completed the accustomed sacrifices in the Temple of Apollo, when the Pythoness Aristonice, sitting above the sacred cleft whence comes the inspiring vapour, thus prophesied." And Callias repeated the hexameters which warned the Athenians that resistance to Xerxes would be worse than futile; that Athens was doomed; concluding with the fearful line, "Get from this temple afar, and brood on the ills that await ye."

In the pause, as Callias's voice fell, the agony of the people became nigh indescribable. Sturdy veterans who had met the Persian spears at Marathon blinked fast. Many groaned, some cursed. Here and there a bold spirit dared to open his heart to doubt, and to mutter, "Persian gold, the Pythoness was corrupted," but quickly hushed even such whispers as rank impiety. Then a voice close to the Bema rang out loudly:—

"And is this all the message, Callias?"

"The voice of Glaucon the Fortunate," cried many, finding relief in words. "He is a friend to the ambassador. There is a further prophecy."

The envoy, who had made his theatrical pause too long, continued:—

"Such, men of Athens, was the answer; and we went forth in dire tribulation. Then a certain noble Delphian, Timon by name, bade us take the olive branches and return to the Pythoness, saying, 'O King Apollo, reverence these boughs of supplication, and deliver a more comfortable answer concerning our dear country. Else we will not leave thy sanctuary, but stay here until we die.' Whereat the priestess gave us a second answer, gloomy and riddling, yet not so evil as the first."

Again Callias recited his lines of doom, "that Athena had vainly prayed to Zeus in behalf of her city, and that it was fated the foe should overrun all Attica, yet

" 'Safe shall the wooden wall continue for thee and thy children;

Wait not the tramp of the horse, nor the footmen mightily moving

Over the land, but turn your back to the foe, and retire ye.

Yet a day shall arrive when ye shall meet him in battle.

Oh, holy Salamis, thou shalt destroy the offspring of women

When men scatter the seed, or when they gather the harvest.' "

"And that is all?" demanded fifty voices.

"That is all," and Callias quitted the Bema. Whereupon if agony had held the Pnyx before, perplexity held it now. "The wooden wall?" "Holy Salamis?" "A great battle, but who is to conquer?" The feverish anxiety of the people at length found its vent in a general shout.

"The seers! Call the seers! Explain the oracle!"

The demand had clearly been anticipated by the president of the Council.

"Xenagoras the Cerycid is present. He is the oldest seer. Let us hearken to his opinion."

The head of the greatest priestly family in Athens arose. He was a venerable man, wearing his ribbon-decked robes of office. The president passed him the myrtle crown, as token that he had the Bema. In a tense hush his voice sounded clearly.

"I was informed of the oracles before the assembly met. The meaning is plain. By the 'wooden wall' is meant our ships. But if we risk a battle, we are told slaughter and defeat will follow. The god commands, therefore, that without resistance we quit Attica, gathering our wives, our children, and our goods, and sail away to some far country."

Xenagoras paused with the smile of him who performs a sad but necessary duty, removed the wreath, and descended the Bema.

"Quit Attica without a blow! Our fathers' fathers' sepulchres, the shrines of our gods, the pleasant farmsteads, the land where our Attic race have dwelt from dimmest time!"

The thought shot chill through the thousands. Men sat in helpless silence, while many a soul, as the gaze wandered up to the temple-crowned Acropolis, asked once, yes twice, "Is not the yoke of Persia preferable to that?" Then after the silence broke the clamour of voices.

"The other seers! Do all agree with Xenagoras? Stand forth! stand forth!"

Hegias, the "King Archon," chief of the state religion, took the Bema. His speech was brief and to the point.

"All the priests and seers of Attica have consulted. Xenagoras speaks for them all save Hermippus of the house of Eumolpus, who denies the others' interpretation."

Confusion followed. Men rose, swung their arms, harangued madly from where they stood. The chairman in vain ordered "Silence!" and was fain to bid the Scythian constables restore order. An elderly farmer thrust himself forward, took the wreath, and poured out his rustic wisdom from the Bema. His advice was simple. The oracle said "the wooden wall" would be a bulwark, and by the wooden wall was surely meant the Acropolis which had once been protected by a palisade. Let all Attica shut itself in the citadel and endure a siege.

So far he had proceeded garrulously, but the high-strung multitude could endure no more. "*Kataba! Kataba!*" "Go down! go down!" pealed the yell, emphasized by a shower of pebbles. The elder tore the wreath from his head and fled the Bema. Then out of the confusion came a general cry.

"Cimon, son of Miltiades, speak to us!"

But that young nobleman preserved a discreet silence, and the multitude turned to another favourite.

"Democrates, son of Myscelus, speak to us!"

The popular orator only wrapped his cloak about him, as he sat near the chairman's stand, never answering the call he rejoiced of wont to hear.

There were cries for Hermippus, cries even for Glaucon, as if prowess in the pentathlon gave ability to unravel oracles. The athlete sitting beside Democrates merely blushed and drew closer to his friend. Then at last the despairing people turned to their last resource.

"Themistocles, son of Neocles, speak to us!"

Thrice the call in vain; but at the fourth time a wave of silence swept across the Pnyx. A figure well beloved was taking the wreath and mounting the Bema.

The words of Themistocles that day were to ring in his hearer's ears till life's end. The careless, almost sybaritic, man of the Isthmus and Eleusis seemed transfigured. For one moment he stood silent, lofty, awe-inspiring. He had a mighty task: to calm the superstitious fears of thirty thousand, to silence the prophets of evil, to infuse those myriads with his own high courage. He began with a voice so low it would have seemed a whisper if not audible to all the Pnyx. Quickly he warmed. His gestures became dramatic. His voice rose to a trumpet-call. He swept his hearers with him as dry leaves before the blast. "When he began to weave his words, one might have deemed him churlish, nay a fool, but when from his chest came his deep voice, and words like unto flakes of winter snow, then who could with him contend?" Thus Homer of Odysseus the Guileful, thus as truly of Themistocles saviour of Hellas.

First he told the old, but never wearisome story of the past of Athens. How, from the days of Codrus long ago, Athens had never bowed the knee to an invader, how she had wrested Salamis from greedy Megara, how she had hounded out the tyrannizing sons of Peisistratus, how she had braved all the wrath of Persian Darius and dashed his huge armament back at Marathon. With such a past, only a madman as well as traitor would dream of submitting to Xerxes now. But as for the admonition of Xenagoras to quit Attica and never strike a blow, Themistocles would have none of it. With a clearness that appealed to every home-loving Hellene he pictured the fate of wanderers as only one step better than that of slaves. What, then, was left? The orator had a decisive answer. Was not the "wooden wall" which should endure for the Athenians the great fleet they were just completing? And as for the fate of the battle the speaker had an unexpected solution. "Holy Salamis," spoke the Pythoness. And would she have said "holy," if the issue had been only woe to the sons of Athens? "Luckless Salamis" were then more reasonably the word; yet the prophetess so far from predicting defeat had assured them victory.

Thus ran the substance of the speech on which many a soul knew hung the mending or ending of Hellas, but lit all through with gleams of wit, shades of pathos, outbursts of eloquence which burned into the hearers' hearts as though the speaker were a god. Then at the end, Themistocles, knowing his audience was with him, delivered his peroration:—

"Let him who trusts in oracles trust then in this, and in the old prophecy of Epimenides that when the Persian comes it is to his hurt. But I will say with Hector of Troy, 'One oracle is best—to fight for one's native country.' Others may vote as they will. My vote is that if the foe by land be too great, we retire before him to our ships, ay, forsake even well-loved Attica, but only that we may trust to the 'wooden wall,' and fight the Great King by sea at Salamis. We contend not with gods but with men. Let others fear. I will trust to Athena Polias,—the goddess terrible in battle. Hearken then to Solon the Wise (the orator pointed toward the temple upon the soaring Acropolis):—

" 'Our Athens need fear no hurt

Though gods may conspire her ill.

The hand that hath borne us up,

It guides us and guards us still.

Athena, the child of Zeus,

She watches and knows no fear.

The city rests safe from harm

Beneath her protecting spear.'

Thus trusting in Athena, we will meet the foe at Salamis and will destroy him.''

"Who wishes to speak?" called the herald. The Pnyx answered together. The vote to retire from Attica if needs be, to strengthen the fleet, to risk all in a great battle, was carried with a shout. Men ran to Themistocles, calling him, "Peitho,—Queen Persuasion." He made light of their praises, and walked with his handsome head tossed back toward the general's office by the Agora, to attend to some routine business. Glaucon, Cimon, and Democrates went westward to calm their exhilaration with a ball-game at the gymnasium of Cynosarges. On the way Glaucon called attention to a foreigner that passed them.

"Look, Democrates, that fellow is wonderfully like the honest barbarian who applauded me at the Isthmus."

Democrates glanced twice.

"Dear Glaucon," said he, "that fellow had a long blond beard, while this man's is black as a crow." And he spoke the truth; yet despite the disguise he clearly recognized the "Cyprian."

CHAPTER VII
DEMOCRATES AND THE TEMPTER

In the northern quarter of Athens the suburb of Alopece thrust itself under the slopes of Mt. Lycabettus, that pyramid of tawny rock which formed the rear bulwark, as it were, of every landscape of Athens. The dwellings in the suburb were poor, though few even in the richer quarters were at all handsome; the streets barely sixteen feet wide, ill-paved, filthy, dingy. A line of dirty gray stucco house-fronts was broken only by the small doors and the smaller windows in the second story. Occasionally a two-faced bust of Hermes stood before a portal, or a marble lion's head spouted into a corner water trough. All Athenian streets resembled these. The citizen had his Pnyx, his Jury-Court, his gossiping Agora for his day. These dingy streets sufficed for the dogs, the slaves, and the women, whom wise Zeus ordered to remain at home.

Phormio the fishmonger had returned from his traffic, and sat in his house-door meditating over a pot of sour wine and watching the last light flickering on the great bulk of the mountain. He had his sorrows,—good man,—for Lampaxo his worthy wife, long of tongue, short of temper, thrifty and very watchful, was reminding him for the seventh time that he had sold a carp half an obol too cheap. His patience indeed that evening was so near to exhaustion that after cursing inwardly the "match-maker" who had saddled this Amazon upon him, he actually found courage for an outbreak. He threw up his arms after the manner of a tragic actor:—

"True, true is the word of Hesiod!"

"True is what?" flew back none too gently.

" 'The fool first suffers and is after wise.' Woman, I am resolved."

"On what?" Lampaxo's voice was soft as broken glass.

"Years increase. I shan't live long. We are childless. I will provide for you in my will by giving you in marriage to Hyperphon."[2]

"Hyperphon!" screamed the virago, "Hyperphon the beggarly hunchback, the laughing-stock of Athens! O Mother Hera!—but I see the villain's aim. You are weary of me. Then divorce me like an honourable man. Send me back to Polus my dear brother. Ah, you sheep, you are silent! You think of the two-minæ dowry you must then refund. Woe is me! I'll go to the King Archon. I'll charge you with gross abuse. The jury will condemn you. There'll be fines, fetters, stocks, prison—"

"Peace," groaned Phormio, terrified at the Gorgon, "I only thought—"

"How dared you think? What permitted—"

"Good evening, sweet sister and Phormio!" The salutation came from Polus, who with Clearchus had approached unheralded. Lampaxo smoothed her ruffled feathers. Phormio stifled his sorrows. Dromo, the half-starved slave-boy, brought a pot of thin wine to his betters. The short southern twilight was swiftly passing into night. Groups of young men wandered past, bound homeward from the Cynosarges, the Academy, or some other well-loved gymnasium. In an hour the streets would be dark and still, except for a belated guest going to his banquet, a Scythian constable, or perhaps a cloak thief. For your Athenian, when he had no supper invitation, went to bed early and rose early, loving the sunlight far better than the flicker of his uncertain lamps.

"And did the jury vote 'guilty'?" was Phormio's first question of his brother-in-law.

"We were patriotically united. There were barely any white beans for acquittal in the urn. The scoundrelly grain-dealer is stripped of all he possesses and sent away to beg in exile. A noble service to Athens!"

"Despite the evidence," murmured Clearchus; but Lampaxo's shrill voice answered her brother:—

"It's my opinion you jurors should look into a case directly opposite this house. Spies, I say, Persian spies."

"Spies!" cried Polus, leaping up as from a coal; "why, Phormio, haven't you denounced them? It's compounding with treason even to fail to report—"

"Peace, brother," chuckled the fishmonger, "your sister smells for treason as a dog for salt fish. There is a barbarian carpet merchant—a Babylonian, I presume—who has taken the empty chambers above Demas's shield factory opposite. He seems a quiet, inoffensive man; there are a hundred other foreign merchants in the city. One can't cry 'Traitor!' just because the poor wight was not born to speak Greek."

"I do not like Babylonish merchants," propounded Polus, dogmatically; "to the jury with him, I say!"

"At least he has a visitor," asserted Clearchus, who had long been silent. "See, a gentleman wrapped in a long himation is going up to the door and standing up his walking stick."

"And if I have eyes," vowed the juror, squinting through his hands in the half light, "that closely wrapped man is Glaucon the Alcmæonid."

"Or Democrates," remarked Clearchus; "they look much alike from behind. It's getting dark."

"Well," decided Phormio, "we can easily tell. He has left his stick below by the door. Steal across, Polus, and fetch it. It must be carved with the owner's name."

The juror readily obeyed; but to read the few characters on the crooked handle was beyond the learning of any save Clearchus, whose art demanded the mystery of writing.

"I was wrong," he confessed, after long scrutiny, " 'Glaucon, son of Conon.' It is very plain. Put the cane back, Polus."

The cane was returned, but the juror pulled a very long face.

"Dear friends, here is a man I've already suspected of undemocratic sentiments conferring with a Barbarian. Good patriots cannot be too vigilant. A plot, I assert. Treason to Athens and Hellas! Freedom's in danger. Henceforth I shall look on Glaucon the Alcmæonid as an enemy of liberty."

"*Phui!*" almost shouted Phormio, whose sense of humour was keen, "a noble conspiracy! Glaucon the Fortunate calls on a Babylonish merchant by night. You say to plot against Athens. I say to buy his pretty wife a carpet."

"The gods will some day explain," said Clearchus, winding up the argument,—and so for a little while the four forgot all about Glaucon.

* * * * * *

Despite the cane, Clearchus was right. The visitor was Democrates. The orator mounted the dark stair above the shield-factory and knocked against a door, calling, "*Pai! Pai!*" "Boy! boy!" a summons answered by none other than the ever smiling Hiram. The Athenian, however, was little prepared for the luxury, nay splendour, which greeted him, once the Phœnician had opened the door. The bare chamber had been transformed. The foot sank into the glowing carpets of Kerman and Bactria. The gold-embroidered wall tapestries were of Sidonian purple. The divans were covered with wondrous stuff which Democrates could not name,—another age would call it silk. A tripod smoked with fragrant Arabian frankincense. Silver lamps, swinging from silver chains, gave brilliant light. The Athenian stood wonderbound, until a voice, not Hiram's, greeted him.

"Welcome, Athenian," spoke the Cyprian, in his quaint, eastern accent. It was the strange guest in the tavern by Corinth. The Prince—prince surely, whatever his other title—was in the same rich dress as at the Isthmus, only his flowing beard had been dyed raven black. Yet Democrates's eyes were diverted instantly to the peculiarly handsome slave-boy on the divan beside his master. The boy's dress, of a rare blue stuff, enveloped him loosely. His hair was as golden as the gold thread on the round cap. In the shadows the face almost escaped the orator,—he thought he saw clear blue eyes and a marvellously brilliant, almost girlish, bloom and freshness. The presence of this slave caused the Athenian to hesitate, but the Cyprian bade him be seated, with one commanding wave of the hand.

"This is Smerdis, my constant companion. He is a mute. Yet if otherwise, I would trust him as myself."

Democrates, putting by surprise, began to look on his host fixedly.

"My dear Barbarian, for that you are a Hellene you will not pretend, you realize, I trust, you incur considerable danger in visiting Athens."

"I am not anxious," observed the Prince, composedly. "Hiram is watchful and skilful. You see I have dyed my hair and beard black and pass for a Babylonish merchant."

"With all except me, *philotate*,—'dearest friend,' as we say in Athens." Democrates's smile was not wholly agreeable.

"With all except you," assented the Prince, fingering the scarlet tassel of the cushion whereon he sat. "I reckoned confidently that you would come to visit me when I sent Hiram to you. Yes—I have heard the story that is on your tongue: one of Themistocles's busybodies has brought a rumour that a certain great man of the Persian court is missing from the side of his master, and you have been requested to greet that nobleman heartily if he should come to Athens."

"You know a great deal!" cried the orator, feeling his forehead grow hot.

"It is pleasant to know a great deal," smiled back the Prince, carelessly, while Hiram entered with a tray and silver goblets brimming with violet-flavoured sherbet; "I have innumerable 'Eyes-and-ears.' You have heard the name? One of the chief officers of his Majesty is 'The Royal Eye.' You Athenians are a valiant and in many things a wise people, yet you could grow in wisdom by looking well to the East."

"I am confident," exclaimed Democrates, thrusting back the goblet, "if your Excellency requires a noble game of wits, you can have one. I need only step to the window, and cry 'Spies!'—after which your Excellency can exercise your wisdom and eloquence defending your life before one of our Attic juries."

"Which is a polite and patriotic manner of saying, dearest Athenian, you are not prepared to push matters to such unfortunate extremity. I omit what his Majesty might do in the way of taking vengeance; sufficient that if aught unfortunate befalls me, or Hiram, or this my slave Smerdis, while we are in Athens, a letter comes to your noble chief Themistocles from the banker Pittacus of Argos."

Democrates, who had risen to his feet, had been flushed before. He became pale now. The hand that clutched the purple tapestry was trembling. The words rose to his lips, the lips refused to utter them. The Prince, who had delivered his threat most quietly, went on, "In short, good Democrates, I was aware before I came to Athens of our necessities, and I came because I was certain I could relieve them."

"Never!" The orator shot the word out desperately.

"You are a Hellene."

"Am I ashamed of it?"

"Do not, however, affect to be more virtuous than your race. Persians make their boast of truth-telling and fidelity. You Hellenes, I hear, have even a god—Hermes Dolios,—who teaches you lying and thieving. The customs of nations differ. Mazda the Almighty alone knoweth which is best. Follow then the customs of Hellenes."

"You speak in riddles."

"Plainer, then. You know the master I serve. You guess who I am, though you shall not name me. For what sum will you serve Xerxes the Great King?"

The orator's breath came deep. His hands clasped and unclasped, then were pressed behind his head.

"I told Lycon, and I tell you, I am no traitor to Hellas."

"Which means, of course, you demand a fair price. I am not angry. You will find a Persian pays like the lord he is, and that his darics always ring true metal."

"I'll hear no more. I was a fool to meet Lycon at Corinth, doubly a fool to meet you to-night. Farewell."

Democrates seized the latch. The door was locked. He turned furiously on the Barbarian. "Do you keep me by force? Have a care. I can be terrible if driven to bay. The window is open. One shout—"

The Cyprian had risen, and quietly, but with a grip like iron on Democrates's wrist, led the orator back to the divan.

"You can go free in a twinkling, but hear you shall. Before you boast of your power, you shall know all of mine. I will recite your condition. Contradict if I say anything amiss. Your father Myscelus was of the noble house of Codrus, a great name in Athens, but he left you no large estate. You were ambitious to shine as an orator and leader of the Athenians. To win popularity you have given great feasts. At the last festival of the Theseia you fed the poor of Athens on sixty oxen washed down with good Rhodian wine. All that made havoc in your patrimony."

"By Zeus, you speak as if you lived all your life in Athens!"

"I have said 'I have many eyes.' But to continue. You gave the price of the tackling for six of the triremes with which Themistocles pretends to believe he can beat back my master. Worse still, you have squandered many minæ on flute girls, dice, cock-fights, and other gentle pleasures. In short your patrimony is not merely exhausted but overspent. That, however, is not the most wonderful part of my recital."

"How dare you pry into my secrets?"

"Be appeased, dear Athenian; it is much more interesting to know you deny nothing of all I say. It is now five months since you were appointed by your sagacious Athenian assembly as commissioner to administer the silver taken from the mines at Laurium and devoted to your navy. You fulfilled the people's confidence by diverting much of this money to the payment of your own great debts to the banker Pittacus of Argos. At present you are 'watching the moon,' as you say here in Athens,—I mean, that at the end of this month you must account to the people for all the money you have handled, and at this hour are at your wits' ends to know whence the repayment will come."

"That is all you know of me?"

"All."

Democrates sighed with relief. "Then you have yet to complete the story, my dear Barbarian. I have adventured on half the cargo of a large merchantman bringing timber and tin from Massalia; I look every day for a messenger from Corinth with news of her safe arrival. Upon her coming I can make good all I owe and still be a passing rich man."

If the Cyprian was discomposed at this announcement, he did not betray it.

"The sea is frightfully uncertain, good Democrates. Upon it, as many fortunes are lost as are made."

"I have offered due prayers to Poseidon, and vowed a gold tripod on the ship's arrival."

"So even your gods in Hellas have their price," was the retort, with an ill-concealed sneer. "Do not trust them. Take ten talents from me and to-night sleep sweetly."

"Your price?" the words slipped forth involuntarily.

"Themistocles's private memoranda for the battle-order of your new fleet."

"Avert it, gods! The ship will reach Corinth, I warn you—" Democrates's gestures became menacing, as again he rose, "I will set you in Themistocles's hand as soon—"

"But not to-night." The Prince rose, smiled, held out his hand. "Unbar the door for his Excellency, Hiram. And you, noble sir, think well of all I said at Corinth on the certain victory of my master; think also—" the voice fell— "how Democrates the Codrid could be sovereign of Athens under the protection of Persia."

"I tyrant of Athens?" the orator clapped his hand behind his back; "you say enough. Good evening."

He was on the threshold, when the slave-boy touched his master's hand in silent signal.

"And if there be any fair woman you desire,"—how gliding the Cyprian's voice!—"shall not the power of Xerxes the great give her unto you?"

Why did Democrates feel his forehead turn to flame? Why—almost against will—did he stretch forth his hand to the Cyprian? He went down the stair scarce feeling the steps beneath him. At the bottom voices greeted him from across the darkened street.

"A fair evening, Master Glaucon."

"A fair evening," his mechanical answer; then to himself; as he walked away, "Wherefore call me Glaucon? I have somewhat his height, though not his shoulder. Ah,—I know it, I have chanced to borrow his carved walking-stick. Impudent creatures to read the name!"

He had not far to go. Athens was compactly built, all quarters close together. Yet before he reached home and bed, he was fighting back an ill-defined but terrible thought. "Glaucon! They think I am Glaucon. If I chose to betray the Cyprian—" Further than that he would not suffer the thought to go. He lay sleepless, fighting against it. The dark was full of the harpies of uncanny suggestion. He arose unrefreshed, to proffer every god the same prayer: "Deliver me from evil imaginings. Speed the ship to Corinth."

CHAPTER VIII
ON THE ACROPOLIS

The Acropolis of Athens rises as does no other citadel in the world. Had no workers in marble or bronze, no weavers of eloquence or song, dwelt beneath its shadow, it would stand the centre and cynosure of a remarkable landscape. It is *"The Rock,"* no other like unto it. Is it enough to say its ruddy limestone rises as a huge boulder one hundred and fifty feet above the plain, that its breadth is five hundred, its length one thousand? Numbers and measures can never disclose a soul,—and the Rock of Athens has all but a soul: a soul seems to glow through its adamant when the fire-footed morning steals over the long crest of Hymettus, and touches the citadel's red bulk with unearthly brightness; a soul when the day falls to sleep in the arms of night as Helios sinks over the western hill by Daphni. Then the Rock seems to throb and burn with life again.

It is so bare that the hungry goats can hardly crop one spear of grass along its jagged slopes. It is so steep it scarce needs defence against an army. It is so commanding that he who stands on the westmost pinnacle can look across the windy hill of the Pnyx, across the brown plain-land and down to the sparkling blue sea with the busy havens of Peiræus and Phalerum, the scattered gray isles of the Ægean, and far away to the domelike crest of Acro-Corinthus. Let him turn to the right: below him nestles the gnarled hill of Areopagus, home of the Furies, the buzzing plaza of the Agora, the closely clustered city. Behind, there spread mountain, valley, plain,—here green, here brown, here golden,—with Pentelicus the Mighty rearing behind all, his summits fretted white, not with winter snows, but with lustrous marble. Look to the left: across the view passes the shaggy ridge of Hymettus, arid and scarred, as if wrought by the Titans, home only of goats and bees, of nymphs and satyrs.

That was almost the self-same vision in the dim past when the first savage clambered this "Citadel of Cecrops" and spoke, "Here is my dwelling-place." This will be the vision until earth and ocean are no more. The human habitation changes, the temples rise and crumble; the red and gray rock, the crystalline air, the sapphire sea, come from the god, and these remain.

Glaucon and Hermione were come together to offer thanks to Athena for the glory of the Isthmus. The athlete had already mounted the citadel heading a myrtle-crowned procession to bear a formal thanksgiving, but his wife had not then been with him. Now they would go together, without pomp. They walked side by side. Nimble Chloë tripped behind with her mistress's parasol. Old Manes bore the bloodless sacrifice, but Hermione said in her heart there came two too many.

Many a friendly eye, many a friendly word, followed as they crossed the Agora, where traffic was in its morning bustle. Glaucon answered every greeting with his winsome smile.

"All Athens seems our friend!" he said, as close by the Tyrannicides' statues at the upper end of the plaza a grave councilman bowed and an old bread woman left her stall to bob a courtesy.

"Is *your* friend," corrected Hermione, thinking only of her husband, "for I have won no pentathlon."

"Ah, *makaira*, dearest and best," he answered, looking not on the glorious citadel but on her face, "could I have won the parsley wreath had there been no better wreath awaiting me at Eleusis? And to-day I am gladdest of the glad. For the gods have sent me blessings beyond desert, I no longer fear their envy as once. I enjoy honour with all good men. I have no enemy in the world. I have the dearest of friends, Cimon, Themistocles—beyond all, Democrates. I am blessed in love beyond Peleus espoused to Thetis, or Anchises beloved of Aphrodite, for my golden Aphrodite lives not on Olympus, nor Paphos, nor comes on her doves from Cythera, but dwells—"

"Peace." The hand laid on his mouth was small but firm. "Do not anger the goddess by likening me unto her. It is joy enough for me if I can look up at the sun and say, 'I keep the love of Glaucon the Fortunate and the Good.'"

Walking thus in their golden dream, the two crossed the Agora, turned to the left from the Pnyx, and by crooked lanes went past the craggy rock of Areopagus, till before them rose a wooden palisade and a gate. Through this a steep path led upward to the citadel. Not to the Acropolis of fame. The buildings then upon the Rock in one short year would lie in heaps of fire-scarred ruin. Yet in that hour before Glaucon and Hermione a not unworthy temple rose, the old "House of Athena," prototype of the later Parthenon. In the morning light it stood in beauty—a hundred Doric columns, a sculptured pediment, flashing with white marble and with tints of scarlet, blue, and gold. Below it, over the irregular plateau of the Rock, spread avenues of votive statues of gods and heroes in stone, bronze, or painted wood. Here and there were numerous shrines and small temples, and a giant altar for burning a hundred oxen. So hand in hand the twain went to the bronze portal of the Temple. The kindly old priest on guard smiled as he sprinkled them with the purifying salt water out of the brazen laver. The door closed behind them. For a moment they seemed to stand in the high temple in utter darkness. Then far above through the marble roof a softened light came creeping toward them. As from unfolding mist, the great calm face of the ancient goddess looked down with its unchanging smile. A red coal glowed on the tripod at her feet. Glaucon shook incense over the brazier. While it smoked, Hermione laid the crown of lilies between the knees of the half-seen image, then her husband lifted his hands and prayed aloud.

"Athena, Virgin, Queen, Deviser of Wisdom,—whatever be the name thou lovest best,—accept this offering and hear. Bless now us both. Give us to strive for the noblest, to speak the wise word, to love one another. Give us prosperity, but not unto pride. Bless all our friends; but if we have enemies, be thou their enemy also. And so shall we praise thee forever."

This was all the prayer and worship. A little more meditation, then husband and wife went forth from the sacred cella. The panorama—rocks, plain, sea, and bending heavens—opened before them in glory. The light faded upon the purple breasts of the western mountains. Behind the Acropolis, Lycabettus's pyramid glowed like a furnace. The marble on distant Pentelicus shone dazzlingly.

Glaucon stood on the easternmost pinnacle of the Rock, watching the landscape.

"Joy, *makaira*, joy," he cried, "we possess one another. We dwell in 'violet-crowned Athens'; for what else dare we to pray?"

But Hermione pointed less pleased toward the crest of Pentelicus.

"Behold it! How swiftly yonder gray cloud comes on a rushing wind! It will cover the brightness. The omen is bad."

"Why bad, *makaira*?"

"The cloud is the Persian. He hangs to-day as a thunder-cloud above Athens and Hellas. Xerxes will come. And you—"

She pressed closer to her husband.

"Why speak of me?" he asked lightly.

"Xerxes brings war. War brings sorrow to women. It is not the hateful and old that the spears and the arrows love best."

Half compelled by the omen, half by a sudden burst of unoccasioned fear, her eyes shone with tears; but her husband's laugh rang clearly.

"*Euge!* dry your eyes, and look before you. King Æolus scatters the cloud upon his briskest winds. It breaks into a thousand bits. So shall Themistocles scatter the hordes of Xerxes. The Persian shadow shall come, shall go, and again we shall be happy in beautiful Athens."

"Athena grant it!" prayed Hermione.

"We can trust the goddess," returned Glaucon, not to be shaken from his happy mood. "And now that we have paid our vows to her, let us descend. Our friends are already waiting for us by the Pnyx before they go down to the harbours."

As they went down the steep, Cimon and Democrates came running to join them, and in the brisk chatter that arose the omen of the cloud and fears of the Persian faded from Hermione's mind.

* * * * * *

It was a merry party such as often went down to the havens of Athens in the springtime and summer: a dozen gentlemen, old and young, for the most part married, and followed demurely by their wives with the latter's maids, and many a stout Thracian slave tugging hampers of meat and drink. Laughter there was, admixed with wiser talk; friends walking by twos and threes, with Themistocles, as always, seeming to mingle with all and to surpass every one both in jests and in wisdom. So they fared down across the broad plain-land to the harbours, till the hill Munychia rose steep before them. A scramble over a rocky, ill-marked way led to the top; then before them broke a second view comparable almost to that from the Rock of Athena: at their feet lay the four blue havens of Athens, to the right Phaleron, closer at hand the land-locked bay of Munychia, beyond that Zea, beyond that still a broader sheet—Peiræus, the new war-harbour of Athens. They could look down on the brown roofs of the port-town, the forest of masts, the merchantman unloading lumber from the Euxine, the merchantman loading dried figs for Syria; but most of all on the numbers of long black hulls, some motionless on the placid harbour, some propped harmlessly on the shore. Hermione clouded as she saw them, and glanced away.

"I do not love your new fleet, Themistocles," she said, frowning at the handsome statesman; "I do not love anything that tells so clearly of war. It mars the beauty."

"Rather you should rejoice we have so fair a wooden wall against the Barbarian, dear lady," answered he, quite at ease. "What can we do to hearten her, Democrates?"

"Were I only Zeus," rejoined the orator, who never was far from his best friend's wife, "I would cast two thunderbolts, one to destroy Xerxes, the second to blast Themistocles's armada,—so would the Lady Hermione be satisfied."

"I am sorry, then, you are not the Olympian," said the woman, half smiling at the pleasantry. Cimon interrupted them. Some of the party had caught a sun-burned shepherd in among the rocks, a veritable Pan in his shaggy goat-skin. The bribe of two obols brought him out with his pipe. Four of the slave-boys fell to dancing. The party sat down upon the burnt grass,—eating, drinking, wreathing poppy-crowns, and watching the nimble slaves and the ships that crawled like ants in the haven and bay below. Thus passed the noon, and as the sun dropped toward craggy Salamis across the strait, the men of the party wandered down to the ports and found boats to take them out upon the bay.

The wind was a zephyr. The water spread blue and glassy. The sun was sinking as a ball of infinite light. Themistocles, Democrates, and Glaucon were in one skiff, the athlete at the oars. They glided past the scores of black triremes swinging lazily at anchor. Twice they pulled around the proudest of the fleet,—the *Nausicaä*, the gift of Hermippus to the state, a princely gift even in days when every Athenian put his all at the public service. She would be Themistocles's flag-ship. The young men noted her fine lines, her heavy side timbers, the covered decks, an innovation in Athenian men-of-war, and Themistocles put a loving hand on the keen bronze beak as they swung around the prow.

"Here's a tooth for the Persian king!" he was laughing, when a second skiff, rounding the trireme in an opposite direction, collided abruptly. A lurch, a few splinters was all the hurt, but as the boats parted Themistocles rose from his seat in the stern, staring curiously.

"Barbarians, by Athena's owls, the knave at the oars is a sleek Syrian, and his master and the boy from the East too. What business around our war-fleet? Row after them, Glaucon; we'll question—"

"Glaucon does no such folly," spoke Democrates, instantly, from the bow; "if the harbour-watch doesn't interfere with honest traders, what's it to us?"

"As you like it." Themistocles resumed his seat. "Yet it would do no harm. Now they row to another trireme. With what falcon eyes the master of the trio examines it! Something uncanny, I repeat."

"To examine everything strange," proclaimed Democrates, sententiously, "needs the life of a crow, who, they say, lives a thousand years, but I don't see any black wings budding on Themistocles's shoulders. Pull onward, Glaucon."

"Whither?" demanded the rower.

"To Salamis," ordered Themistocles. "Let us see the battle-place foretold by the oracle."

"To Salamis or clear to Crete," rejoined Glaucon, setting his strength upon the oars and making the skiff bound, "if we can find water deep enough to drown those gloomy looks that have sat on Democrates's brows of late."

"Not gloomy but serious," said the young orator, with an attempt at lightness; "I have been preparing my oration against the contractor I've indicted for embezzling the public naval stores."

"Destroy the man!" cried the rower.

"And yet I really pity him; he was under great temptation."

"No excuses; the man who robs the city in days like these is worse than he who betrays fortresses in most wars."

"I see you are a savage patriot, Glaucon," said Themistocles, "despite your Adonis face. We are fairly upon the bay; our nearest eavesdroppers, yon fishermen, are a good five furlongs. Would you see something?" Glaucon rested on the oars, while the statesman fumbled in his breast. He drew out a papyrus sheet, which he passed to the rower, he in turn to Democrates.

"Look well, then, for I think no Persian spies are here. A month long have I wrought on this bit of papyrus. All my wisdom flowed out of my pen when I spread the ink. In short here is the ordering of the ships of the allied Greeks when we meet Xerxes in battle. Leonidas and our other chiefs gave me the task when we met at Corinth. To-day it is complete. Read it, for it is precious. Xerxes would give twenty talents for this one leaf from Egypt."

The young men peered at the sheet curiously. The details and diagrams were few and easy to remember, the Athenian ships here, the Æginetan next, the Corinthian next, and so with the other allies. A few comments on the use of the light pentaconters behind the heavy triremes. A few more comments on Xerxes's probable naval tactics. Only the knowledge that Themistocles never committed himself in speech or writing without exhausting every expedient told the young men of the supreme importance of the paper. After due inspection the statesman replaced it in his breast.

"You two have seen this," he announced, seemingly proud of his handiwork; "Leonidas shall see this, then Xerxes, and after that—" he laughed, but not in jest—"men will remember Themistocles, son of Neocles!"

The three lapsed into silence for a moment. The skiff was well out upon the sea. The shadows of the hills of Salamis and of Ægelaos, the opposing mountain of Attica, were spreading over them. Around the islet of Psyttaleia in the strait the brown fisher-boats were gliding. Beyond the strait opened the blue hill-girdled bay of Eleusis, now turning to fire in the evening sun. Everything was peaceful, silent, beautiful. Again Glaucon rested on his oars and let his eyes wander.

"How true is the word of Thales the Sage," he spoke; " 'the world is the fairest of all fair things, because it is the work of God.' It cannot be that, here, between these purple hills and the glistening sea, there will come that battle beside which the strife of Achilles and Hector before Troy shall pass as nothing!"

Themistocles shook his head.

"We do not know; we are dice in the high gods' dice-boxes.

" 'Man all vainly shall scan the mind of the Prince of Olympus.'

"We can say nothing wiser than that. We can but use our Attic mother wit, and trust the rest to destiny. Let us be satisfied if we hope that destiny is not blind."

They drifted many moments in silence.

"The sun sinks lower," spoke Democrates, at length; "so back again to the havens."

On the return Themistocles once more vowed he caught a glimpse of the skiff of the unknown foreigners, but Democrates called it mere phantasy. Hermione met them at the Peiræus, and the party wandered back through the gathering dusk to the city, where each little group went its way. Themistocles went to his own house, where he said he expected Sicinnus; Cimon and Democrates sought a tavern for an evening cup; Glaucon and Hermione hastened to their house in the Colonus suburb near the trickling Cephissus, where in the starlit night the tettix[4] in the black old olives by the stream made its monotonous music, where great fireflies gleamed, where Philomela the nightingale called, and the tall plane trees whispered softly to the pines. When Hermione fell asleep, she had forgotten about the coming of the Persian, and dreamed that Glaucon was Eros, she was Psyche, and that Zeus was giving her the wings of a butterfly and a crown of stars.

Democrates went home later. After the heady Pramnian at the tavern, he roved away with Cimon and others to serenade beneath the lattice of a lady—none too prudish—in the Ceramicus quarter. But the fair one was cruel that night, and her slaves repelled the minstrels with pails of hot water from an upper window. Democrates thereupon quitted the party. His head was very befogged, but he could not expel one idea from it—that Themistocles had revealed that day a priceless secret, that the statesman and Glaucon and he himself were the only men who shared it, and that it was believed that Glaucon had visited the Babylonish carpet-seller. Joined to this was an overpowering consciousness that Helen of Troy was not so lovely as Hermione of Eleusis. When he came to his lodgings, however, his wits cleared in a twinkling after he had read two letters. The first was short.

"Themistocles to Democrates:—This evening I begin to discover something. Sicinnus, who has been searching in Athens, is certain there is a Persian agent in the city. Seize him.—*Chaire.*"

The second was shorter. It came from Corinth.

"Socias the merchant to Democrates:—Tyrrhenian pirates have taken the ship. Lading and crew are utterly lost.—*Chaire.*"

The orator never closed his eyes that night.

- 73 -

CHAPTER IX
THE CYPRIAN TRIUMPHS

Democrates fronted ruin. What profit later details from Socias of the capture of the merchantman? Unless three days before the coming festival of the Panathenæa the orator could find a large sum, he was forever undone. His sequestering of the ship-money would become public property. He would be tried for his life. Themistocles would turn against him. The jury would hardly wait for the evidence. He would drink the poisonous hemlock and his corpse be picked by the crows in the Barathrum,—an open pit, sole burial place for Athenian criminals.

One thing was possible: to go to Glaucon, confess all, and beg the money. Glaucon was rich. He could have the amount from Conon and Hermippus for the asking. But Democrates knew Glaucon well enough to perceive that while the athlete might find the money, he would be horrified at the foul disclosure. He would save his old comrade from death, but their friendship would be ended. He would feel in duty bound to tell Themistocles enough to ruin Democrates's political prospects for all time. An appeal to Glaucon was therefore dismissed, and the politician looked for more desperate remedies.

Democrates enjoyed apartments on the street of the Tripods east of the Acropolis, a fashionable promenade of Athens. He was regarded as a confirmed bachelor. If, therefore, two or three dark-eyed flute girls in Phaleron had helped him to part with a good many minæ, no one scolded too loudly; the thing had been done genteelly and without scandal. Democrates affected to be a collector of fine arms and armour. The ceiling of his living room was hung with white-plumed helmets, on the walls glittered brass greaves, handsomely embossed shields, inlaid Chalcidian scimitars, and bows tipped with gold. Under foot were expensive rugs. The orator's artistic tastes were excellent. Even as he sat in the deeply pillowed arm-chair his eye lighted on a Nike,—a statuette of the precious Corinthian bronze, a treasure for which the dealer's unpaid account lay still, alas! in the orator's coffer.

But Democrates was not thinking so much of the unpaid bronze-smith as of divers weightier debts. On the evening in question he had ordered Bias, the sly Thracian, out of the room; with his own hands had barred the door and closed the lattice; then with stealthy step thrust back the scarlet wall tapestry to disclose a small door let into the plaster. A key made the door open into a cupboard, out of which Democrates drew a brass-bound box of no great size, which he carried gingerly to a table and opened with a complex key.

The contents of the box were curious, to a stranger enigmatic. Not money, nor jewels, but rolls of closely written papyri, and things which the orator studied more intently,—a number of hard bits of clay bearing the impressions of seals. As Democrates fingered these, his face might have betrayed a mingling of keen fear and keener satisfaction.

"There is no such collection in all Hellas,—no, not in the world," ran his commentary; "here is the signet of the Tagos of Thessaly, here of the Bœotarch of Thebes, here of the King of Argos. I was able to secure the seal of Leonidas while in Corinth. This, of course, is Themistocles's,—how easily I took it! And this—of less value perhaps to a man of the world—is of my beloved Glaucon. And here are twenty more. Then the papyri,"—he unrolled them lovingly, one after another,—"precious specimens, are they not? Ah, by Zeus, I must be a very merciful and pious man, or I'd have used that dreadful power heaven has given me and never have drifted into these straits."

What that "power" was with which Democrates felt himself endued he did not even whisper to himself. His mood changed suddenly. He closed the box with a snap and locked it hurriedly.

"Cursed casket!—I think I would be happier if Phorcys, the old man of the deep, could drown it all! I would be better for it and kept from foul thoughts."

He thrust the box back in the cupboard, drew forth a second like it, unlocked it, and took out more writings. Selecting two, he spread ink and papyrus before him, and copied with feverish haste. Once he hesitated, and almost flung back the writings into the casket. Once he glanced at the notes he had prepared for his speech against the defrauding contractor. He grimaced bitterly. Then the hesitation ended. He finished the copying, replaced the second box, and barred and concealed the cupboard. He hid his new copies in his breast and called in Bias.

"I am going out, but I shall not be late."

"Shall not Hylas and I go with lanterns?" asked the fellow. "Last night there were foot-pads."

"I don't need you," rejoined his master, brusquely.

He went down into the dimly lighted street and wound through the maze of back alleys wherein Athens abounded, but Democrates never missed his way. Once he caught the glint of a lantern—a slave lighting home his master from dinner. The orator drew into a doorway; the others glided by, seeing nothing. Only when he came opposite the house of the Cyprian he saw light spreading from the opposite doorway and knew he must pass under curious eyes.

Phormio was entertaining friends very late. But Democrates took boldness for safety, strode across the illumined ring, and up to the Cyprian's stairway. The buzz of conversation stopped a moment. "Again Glaucon," he caught, but was not troubled.

"After all," he reflected, "if seen at all, there is no harm in such a mistake."

The room was again glittering in its Oriental magnificence. The Cyprian advanced to meet his visitor, smiling blandly.

"Welcome, dear Athenian. We have awaited you. We are ready to heal your calamity."

Democrates turned away his face.

"You know it already! O Zeus, I am the most miserable man in all Hellas!"

"And wherefore miserable, good friend?" The Cyprian half led, half compelled the visitor to a seat on the divan. "Is it such to be enrolled from this day among the benefactors of my most gracious lord and king?"

"Don't goad me!" Democrates wrung his hands. "I am desperate. Take these papyri, read, pay, then let me never see your face again." He flung the two rolls in the Prince's lap and sat in abject misery.

The other unrolled the writings deliberately, read slowly, motioned to Hiram, who also read them with catlike scrutiny. During all this not a word was spoken. Democrates observed the beautiful mute emerge from an inner chamber and silently take station at his master's side, following the papers also with wonderful, eager eyes. Only after a long interval the Prince spoke.

"Well—you bring what purports to be private memoranda of Themistocles on the equipment and arraying of the Athenian fleet. Yet these are only copies."

"Copies; the originals cannot stay in my possession. It were ruin to give them up."

The Prince turned to Hiram.

"And do you say, from what you know of these things, these memoranda are genuine?"

"Genuine. That is the scanty wisdom of the least of your Highness's slaves."

The Oriental bowed himself, then stood erect in a manner that reminded Democrates of some serpent that had just coiled and uncoiled.

"Good," continued the emissary; "yet I must ask our good Athenian to confirm them with an oath."

The orator groaned. He had not expected this last humiliation; but being forced to drink the cup, he drained it to the lees. He swore by Zeus Orchios, Watcher of Oaths, and Dike, the Eternal Justice, that he brought true copies, and that if he was perjured, he called a curse upon himself and all his line. The Cyprian received his oath with calm satisfaction, then held out the half of a silver shekel broken in the middle.

"Show this to Mydon, the Sicyonian banker at Phaleron. He holds its counterpart. He will pay the man who completes the coin ten talents."

Democrates received the token, but felt that he must stand upon his dignity.

"I have given an oath, stranger, but give the like to me. What proof have I of this Mydon?"

The question seemed to rouse the unseen lion in the Cyprian. His eye kindled. His voice swelled.

"We leave oaths, Hellene, to men of trade and barter, to men of trickery and guile. The Aryan noble is taught three things: to fear the king, to bend the bow, to speak the truth. And he learns all well. I have spoken,—my word is my oath."

The Athenian shrank at the storm he had roused. But the Prince almost instantly curbed himself. His voice sank again to its easy tone of conciliation.

"So much for my word, good friend; yet better than an oath, look here. Can the man who bears this ring afford to tell a lie?"

He extended his right hand. On the second finger was a huge beryl signet. Democrates bent over it.

"Two seated Sphynxes and a winged cherub flying above,—the seal of the royal Achæmenians of Persia! You are sent by Xerxes himself. You are—"

The Prince raised a warning finger. "Hush, Athenian. Think what you will, but do not name me, though soon my name shall fly through all the world."

"So be it," rejoined Democrates, his hands clutching the broken coin as at a last reprieve from death. "But be warned, even though I bear you no good-will. Themistocles is suspicious. Sicinnus his agent, a sly cat, is searching for you. The other day Themistocles, in the boat at Peiræus, was fain to have you questioned. If detected, I cannot save you."

The Prince shrugged his shoulders.

"Good Democrates, I come of a race that trusts in the omnipotence of God and does the right. Duty requires me in Athens. What Ahura-Mazda and Mithra his glorious vicegerent will, that shall befall me, be I in Hellas or in safe Ecbatana. The decree of the Most High, written among the stars, is good. I do not shun it."

The words were spoken candidly, reverently. Democrates drew toward the door, and the others did not strive to detain him.

"As you will," spoke the Athenian; "I have warned you. Trust then your God. I have sold myself this once, but do not call me friend. Necessity is a sharp goad. May our paths never cross again!"

"Until you again have need," said the Prince, not seeking to wring from the other any promise.

Democrates muttered a sullen farewell and went down the dark stairs. The light in Phormio's house was out. No one seemed to be watching. On the way homeward Democrates comforted himself with the reflection that although the memoranda he sold were genuine, Themistocles often changed his plans, and he could see to it this scheme for arraying the war fleet was speedily altered. No real harm then would come to Hellas. And in his hand was the broken shekel,—the talisman to save him from destruction. Only when Democrates thought of Glaucon and Hermione he was fain to grit his teeth, while many times it returned to him, "They think it was *Glaucon* who has been twice now to visit the Babylonish carpet-seller."

* * * * * * *

As the door had closed behind the orator, the Prince had strode across the rugs to the window—and spat forth furiously as in extreme disgust.

"Fool, knave, villain! I foul my lips by speaking to his accursed ears!"

The tongue in which he uttered this was the purest "Royal Persian," such as one might hear in the king's court. The beautiful "mute," mute no longer, glided across the chamber and laid both hands upon his shoulder with a gracious caress.

"And yet you bear with these treacherous creatures, you speak them fair?" was the remark in the same musical tongue.

"Yes, because there is sore need. Because, with all their faithlessness, covetousness, and guile, these Hellenes are the keenest, subtlest race beneath

Mithra's glorious light. And we Persians must play with them, master them, and use them to make us lords of all the world."

Hiram had disappeared behind a curtain. The Prince lifted her silver embroidered red cap. Over the graceful shoulders fell a mass of clear gold hair, so golden one might have hidden shining darics within it. The shining head pressed against the Persian's breast. In this attitude, with the loose dress parting to show the tender lines, there could be no doubt of the other's sex. The Prince laid his hand upon her neck and drew her bright face nearer.

"This is a mad adventure on which we two have come," he spoke; "how nearly you were betrayed at the Isthmus, when the Athenian saved you! A blunder by Hiram, an ill-turn of Fate, will ruin us yet. It is far, Rose of Eran, from Athens to the pleasant groves of Susa and the sparkling Choaspes."

"But the adventure is ending," answered she, with smiling confidence; "Mazda has guarded us. As you have said—we are in his hand, alike here and in my brother's palace. And we have seen Greece and Athens—the country and city which you will conquer, which you will rule."

"Yes," he said, letting his eyes pass from her face to the vista of the Acropolis, which lay in fair view under the moonlight. "How noble a city this! Xerxes has promised that I shall be satrap of Hellas, Athens shall be my capital, and you, O best beloved, you shall be mistress of Athens."

"I shall be mistress of Athens," echoed she, "but you, husband and lord, would that men might give you a higher name than satrap, chief of the Great King's slaves!"

"Xerxes is king," he answered her.

"My brother wears the purple cap. He sits on the throne of Cyrus the Great and Darius the Dauntless. I would be a loyal Aryan, the king is indeed in Susa or Babylon. But for me the true king of Media and Persia—is here." And she lifted proud eyes to her husband.

"You are bold, Rose of Eran," he smiled, not angry at her implication; "more cautious words than these have brought many in peril of the bow-string. But, by Mithra the Fiend-Smiter, why were you not made a man? Then truly would your mother Atossa have given Darius an heir right worthy the twenty kingdoms!"

She gave a gentle laugh.

"The Most High ordains the best. Have I not the noblest kingdom? Am I not your wife?"

His laugh answered her.

"Then I am greater than Xerxes. I love my empire the best!"

He leaned again from the lattice, "O, fairest of cities, and we shall win it! See how the tawny rock turns to silver beneath the moonbeams! How clearly burn the stars over the plain and the mountain! And these Greeks, clever, wise, beautiful, when we have mastered them, have taught them our Aryan obedience and love of truth, what servants will they not become! For we are ordained to conquer. Mazda has given us empire without limit, from the Indus to the Great Ocean of the West,—all shall be ours; for we are Persians, the race to rule forever."

"We will conquer," she said dreamily, as enchanted as was he by the beauties of the night.

"From the day Cyrus your grandfather flung down Cambyses the Mede, the High God has been with us. Egypt, Assyria, Babylon—have all bowed under our yoke. The Lydian at golden Sardis, the Tartar on the arid steppes, the Hindoo by his sacred river, all send tribute to our king, and Hellas—" he held out his arms confidently—"shall be the brightest star in the Persian tiara. When Darius your father lay dying, I swore to him, 'Master, fear not; I will avenge you on Athens and on all the Greeks.' And in one brief year, O *fravashi*, soul of the great departed, I may make good the vow. I will make these untamed Hellenes bow their proud necks to a king."

Her own eyes brightened, looking on him, as he spoke in pride and power.

"And yet," she could not keep back the question, "as we have moved through this Hellas, and seen its people, living without princes, or with princes of little power, sometimes a strange thought comes. These perverse, unobedient folk, false as they are, and ununited, have yet a strength to do great things, a strength which even we Aryans lack."

He shook his head.

"It cannot be. Mazda ordained a king to rule, the rest to obey. And all the wits of Hellas have no strength until they learn that lesson well. But I will teach it them."

"For some day you will be their king?" spoke the woman. He did not reprove, but stood beside her, gazing forth upon the night. In the moonlight the columns and sculptures of the great temple on the Acropolis stood out in minute tracery They could see all the caverns and jagged ledges on the massy Rock. The flat roofs of the sleeping city lay like a dark and peaceful ocean. The mountains spread around in shadow-wrapped hush. Far away the dark stretch of the sea sent back a silver shimmering in answer to the moon. A landscape only possible at Athens! The two sensitive Orientals' souls were deeply touched. For long they were silent, then the husband spoke.

"Twenty days more; we are safe in Sardis, the adventure ended. The war only remains, and the glory, the conquest,—and thou. O Ahura-Mazda," he spoke upward to the stars, "give to thy Persians this land. For when Thou hast given this, Thou wilt keep back nothing of all the world."

CHAPTER X
DEMOCRATES RESOLVES

Democrates surpassed himself when arraigning the knavish contractor. "Nestor and Odysseus both speak to us," shouted Polus in glee, flinging his black bean in the urn. "What eloquence, what righteous fury when he painted the man's infamy to pillage the city in a crisis like this!"

So the criminal was sent to death and Democrates was showered with congratulations. Only one person seemed hardly satisfied with all the young orator did,—Themistocles. The latter told his lieutenant candidly he feared all was not being done to apprehend the Persian emissary. Themistocles even took it upon himself to send Sicinnus to run down several suspects, and just on the morning of the day preceding the Panathenæa—the great summer festival—Democrates received a hint which sent him home very thoughtful. He had met his chief in the Agora as he was leaving the Government-House, and Themistocles had again asked if he had smelt aught of the Persian agent. He had not.

"Then you would well devote more time to finding his scent, and less to convicting a pitiful embezzler. You know the Alopece suburb?"

"Certainly."

"And the house of Phormio the fishmonger?" to which Democrates nodded.

"Well, Sicinnus has been watching the quarter. A Babylonish carpet-seller has rooms opposite Phormio. The man is suspicious, does no trading, and Phormio's wife told Sicinnus an odd tale."

"What tale?" Democrates glanced at a passing chariot, avoiding Themistocles's gaze.

"Why, twice the Barbarian, she swears, has had an evening visitor—and he our dear Glaucon."

"Impossible."

"Of course. The good woman is mistaken. Still, question her. Pry into this Babylonian's doings. He may be selling more things than carpets. If he has corrupted any here in Athens,—by Pluto the Implacable, I will make them tell out the price!"

"I'll inquire at once."

"Do so. The matter grows serious."

Themistocles caught sight of one of the archons and hastened across the Agora to have a word with him. Democrates passed his hand across his forehead, beaded with sudden sweat-drops. He knew—though Themistocles had said not a word—that his superior was beginning to distrust his efforts, and that Sicinnus was working independently. Democrates had great respect for the acuteness of that Asiatic. He was coming perilously near the truth already. If the Cyprian and Hiram were arrested, the latter at least would surely try to save his life by betraying their nocturnal visitor. To get the spy safely out of Athens would be the first step,—but not all. Sicinnus once upon the scent would not readily drop it until he had discovered the emissary's confederate. And of the fate of that confederate Themistocles had just given a grim hint. There was one other solution possible. If Democrates could discover the confederate *himself*, Sicinnus would regard the matter as cleared up and drop all interest therein. All these possibilities raced through the orator's head, as does the past through one drowning. A sudden greeting startled him.

"A fair morning, Democrates." It was Glaucon. He walked arm-in-arm with Cimon.

"A fair morning, indeed. Where are you going?"

"To the Peiræus to inspect the new tackling of the *Nausicaä*. You will join us?"

"Unfortunately I argue a case before the King Archon."

"Be as eloquent as in your last speech. Do you know, Cimon declares I am disloyal too, and that you will soon be prosecuting me?"

"Avert it, gods! What do you mean?"

"Why, he is sending a letter to Argos," asserted Cimon. "Now I say Argos has Medized, therefore no good Hellene should correspond with a traitorous Argive."

"Be jury on my treachery," commanded Glaucon. "Ageladas the master-sculptor sends me a bronze Perseus in honour of my victory. Shall I churlishly send him no thanks because he lives in Argos?"

" 'Not guilty' votes the jury; the white beans prevail. So the letter goes to-day?"

"To-morrow afternoon. You know Seuthes of Corinth—the bow-legged fellow with a big belly. He goes home to-morrow afternoon after seeing the procession and the sacrifice."

"He goes by sea?" asked Democrates, casually.

"By land; no ship went to his liking. He will lie overnight at Eleusis."

The friends went their ways. Democrates hardly saw or heard anything until he was in his own chambers. Three things were graven on his mind: Sicinnus was watching, the Babylonian was suspected, Glaucon was implicated and was sending a letter to Argos.

* * * * * *

Bias the Thracian was discovered that afternoon by his master lurking in a corner of the chamber. Democrates seized a heavy dog-whip, lashed the boy unmercifully, then cast him out, threatening that eavesdropping would be rewarded by "cutting into shoe soles." Then the master resumed his feverish pacings and the nervous twisting of his fingers. Unfortunately, Bias felt certain the threat would never have been uttered unless the weightiest of matters had been on foot. As in all Greek dwellings, Democrates's rooms were divided not by doors but by hanging curtains, and Bias, letting curiosity master fear, ensconced himself again behind one of these and saw all his master's doings. What Democrates said and did, however, puzzled his good servant quite sufficiently.

Democrates had opened the privy cupboard, taken out one of the caskets and scattered its contents upon the table, then selected a papyrus, and seemed copying the writing thereon with extreme care. Next one of the clay seals came into play. Democrates was testing it upon wax. Then the orator rose, dashed the wax upon the floor, put his sandal thereon, tore the papyrus on which he wrote to bits. Again he paced restlessly, his hands clutching his hair, his forehead frowns and blackness, while Bias thought he heard him muttering as he walked:—

"O Zeus! O Apollo! O Athena! I cannot do this thing! Deliver me! Deliver!"

Then back to the table again, once more to pick up the mysterious clay, again to copy, to stamp on the wax, to fling down, mutilate, and destroy. The pantomime was gone through three times. Bias could make nothing of it. Since the day his parents—following the barbarous Thracian custom—had sold him into slavery and he had passed into Democrates's service, the lad had never seen his master acting thus.

"Clearly the *kyrios* is mad," was his own explanation, and growing frightened at following the strange movements of his lord, he crept from his retreat and tried to banish uncanny fears at a safe distance, by tying a thread to the leg of a gold-chafer[5] and watching its vain efforts at flight. Yet had he continued his eavesdropping he might have found—if not the key to all Democrates's doings—at least a partial explanation. For the fourth time the papyrus had been written, for the fourth time the orator had torn it up. Then his eyes went down to the lump of clay before him on the table.

"Curses upon the miserable stuff!" he swore almost loudly; "it is this which has set the evil thoughts to racing. Destroy *that*, and the deed is beyond my power."

He held up the clay and eyed it as a miser might his gold.

"What a little lump! Not very hard. I can dash it on the floor and it dissolves in dust. And yet, and yet—all Elysium, all Tartarus, are pent up for me in just this bit of clay."

He picked at it with his finger and broke a small piece from the edge.

"A little more, the stamp is ruined. I could not use it. Better if it were ruined. And yet,—and yet,—"

He laid the clay upon the table and sat watching it wistfully.

"O Father Zeus!" he broke out after silence, "if I were not compelled by fear! Sicinnus is so sharp, Themistocles so unmerciful! It would be a terrible death to die,—and every man is justified in shunning death."

He looked at the inanimate lump as if he expected it to answer him.

"Ah, I am all alone. No one to counsel me. In every other trouble when has it been as this? Glaucon? Cimon? Themistocles?—What would they advise?"—he ended with a laugh more bitter than a sob. "And I must save myself, but at such a price!"

He pressed his hands over his eyes.

"Curses on the hour I met Lycon! Curses on the Cyprian and his gold! It would have been better to have told Glaucon and let him save me now and hate me forever after. But I have sold myself to the Cyprian. The deed cannot be taken back."

But as he said it, he arose, took the charmed bit of clay, replaced in the box, and locked the coffer. His hand trembled as he did it.

"I cannot do this thing. I have been foolish, wicked,—but I must not be driven mad by fear. The Cyprian must quit Athens to-morrow. I can throw Sicinnus off the scent. I shall never be the worse."

He walked with the box toward the cupboard, but stopped halfway.

"It is a dreadful death to die;"—his thoughts raced and were half uttered,—"hemlock!—men grow cold limb by limb and keep all their faculties to the end. And the crows in the Barathrum, and the infamy upon my father's name!

When was a son of the house of Codrus branded 'A Traitor to Athens'? Is it wickedness to save one's own life?"

Instead of going to the cupboard he approached the window. The sun beat hotly, but as he leaned forth into the street he shivered as on a winter's morn. In blank wretchedness he watched the throng beneath the window, pannier-laden asses, venders of hot sausage with their charcoal stoves and trays, youths going to and from the gymnasium, slaves returning from market. How long he stood thus, wretched, helpless, he did not know. At last he stirred himself.

"I cannot stand gaping like a fool forever. An omen, by every god an omen! Ah! what am I to do?" He glanced toward the sky in vain hope of a lucky raven or eagle winging out of the east, but saw only blue and brightness. Then his eye went down the street, and at the glance the warm blood tingled from his forehead to his heels.

She was passing,—Hermione, child of Hermippus. She walked before, two comely maids went after with her stool and parasol; but they were the peonies beside the rose. She had thrown her blue veil back. The sun played over the sheen of her hair. As she moved, her floating saffron dress of the rare muslin of Amorgos now revealed her delicate form, now clothed her in an enchanting cloud. She held her head high, as if proud of her own grace and of the beauty and fair name of her husband. She never looked upward, nor beheld how Democrates's eyes grew like bright coals as he gazed on her. He saw her clear high forehead, he heard—or thought he heard despite the jar of the street—the rustle of the muslin robe. Hermione passed, nor ever knew how, by taking this way from the house of a friend, she coloured the skein of life for three mortals—for herself, her husband, and Democrates.

Democrates followed her with his eyes until she vanished around the fountain at the street corner; then sprang back from the window. The workings of his face were terrible. It was an instant when men grasp the godlike or sink to the demon, when they do deeds never to be recalled.

"The omen!" he almost cried, "the omen! Not Zeus but Hermes the Guileful sent it. He will be with me. She is Glaucon's wife. But if not his, whose then but mine? I will do the deed to the uttermost. The god is with me."

He flung the casket upon the table and spread its fateful contents again before him. His hand flew over the papyrus with marvellous speed and skill. He knew that all his faculties were at his full command and unwontedly acute.

Bias was surprised at his sport by a sudden clapping of his master's hands.

"What is it, *kyrie?*"

"Go to Agis. He keeps the gaming-house in the Ceramicus. You know where. Tell him to come hither instantly. He shall not lack reward. Make your feet fly. Here is something to speed them."

He flung at the boy a coin. Bias opened eyes and mouth in wonder. It was not silver, but a golden daric.

"Don't blink at it, sheep, but run. Bring Agis," ordered the master,—and Bias's legs never went faster than on that afternoon.

Agis came. Democrates knew his man and had no difficulty in finding his price. They remained talking together till it was dark, yet in so guarded a tone that Bias, though he listened closely, was unable to make out anything. When Agis went away, he carried two letters. One of these he guarded as if holding the crown jewels of the Great King; the second he despatched by a discreet myrmidon to the rooms of the Cyprian in Alopece. Its contents were pertinent and ran thus:—

"Democrates to the stranger calling himself a prince of Cyprus, greeting:— Know that Themistocles is aware of your presence in Athens, and grows suspicious of your identity. Leave Athens to-morrow or all is lost. The confusion accompanying the festival will then make escape easy. The man to whom I entrust this letter will devise with Hiram the means for your flight by ship from the havens. May our paths never cross again!—*Chaire.*"

After Agis was gone the old trembling came again to Democrates. He had Bias light all the lamps. The room seemed full of lurking goblins,—harpies, gorgons, the Hydra, the Minotaur, every other foul and noxious shape was waiting to spring forth. And, most maddening of all, the chorus of Æschylus, that Song of the Furies Democrates had heard recited at the Isthmus, rang in the miserable man's ears:—

"With scourge and with ban

We prostrate the man,

Who with smooth-woven wile,

And a fair-facèd smile

Hath planted a snare for his friend.

Though fleet, we shall find him;

Though strong, we shall bind him,

Who planted a snare for his friend."

Democrates approached the bust of Hermes standing in one corner. The brazen face seemed to wear a smile of malignant gladness at the fulfilment of his will.

"Hermes," prayed the orator, "Hermes Dolios, god of craft and lies, thieves' god, helper of evil,—be with me now. To Zeus, to Athena the pure, I dare not pray. Prosper me in the deed to which I set my hand,"—he hesitated, he dared not bribe the shrewd god with too mean a gift, "and I vow to set in thy temple at Tanagra three tall tripods of pure gold. So be with me on the morrow, and I will not forget thy favour."

The brazen face still smiled on; the room was very still. Yet Democrates took comfort. Hermes was a great god and would help him. When the song of the Furies grew too loud, Democrates silenced it by summoning back Hermione's face and asking one triumphant question:—

"She is Glaucon's wife. But if not his, whose then but mine?"

CHAPTER XI
THE PANATHENÆA

Flowers on every head, flowers festooned about each pillar, and flowers under foot when one crossed the Agora. Beneath the sheltering porticos lurked bright-faced girls who pelted each passer with violets, narcissus, and hyacinths. For this was the morn of the final crowning day of the Panathenæa, greatest, gladdest of Athenian festivals.

Athletic contests had preceded it and stately Pyrrhic dances of men in full armour. There had been feasting and merry-making despite the darkening shadow of the Persian. Athens seemed awakened only to rejoice. To-day was the procession to the Acropolis, the bearing of the sacred robe to Athena, the public sacrifice for all the people. Not even the peril of Xerxes could hinder a gladsome holiday.

The sun had just risen above Hymettus, the Agora shops were closed, but the plaza itself and the lesches—the numerous little club houses about it—overran with gossipers. On the stone bench before one of these buzzed the select coterie that of wont assembled in Clearchus's booth; only Polus the juror now and then nodded and snored. He had sat up all night hearing the priestesses chant their ceaseless litanies on the Acropolis.

"Guilty—I vote guilty," the others heard him muttering, as his head sank lower.

"Wake up, friend," ordered Clearchus; "you're not condemning any poor scoundrel now."

"*Ai!* ah!" Polus rubbed his eyes, "I only thought I was dropping the black bean—"

"Against whom?" quoth Crito, the fat contractor.

"Whom? Why that aristocrat Glaucon, surely,—to-night—" Polus suddenly checked himself and began to roll his eyes.

"You've a dreadful grievance against him," remarked Clearchus; "the gods know why."

"The wise patriot can see many things," observed Polus, complacently, "only I repeat—wait till to-night—and then—"

"What then?" demanded all the others.

"Then you shall see," announced the juror, with an oratorical flourish of his dirty himation, "and not you only but all of Athens."

Clearchus grinned.

"Our dear Polus has a vast sense of his own importance. And who has been making you partner of the state secrets—Themistocles?"

"A man almost his peer, the noble patriot Democrates. Ask Phormio's wife, Lampaxo; ask—" Once more he broke off to lay a finger on his lips. "This will be a notable day for Athens!"

"Our good friend surely thinks so!" rejoined the potter, dryly; "but since he won't trust us with his precious secret, I think it much more interesting to watch the people crossing the square. The procession must be gathering outside the Dipylon Gate. Yonder rides Themistocles now to take command."

The statesman cantered past on a shining white Thessalian. At his heels were prancing Cimon, Democrates, Glaucon, and many another youth of the noble houses of Athens. At sight of the son of Conon, Polus had wagged his head in a manner utterly perplexing to his associates, and they were again perplexed when they saw Democrates wheel back from the side of his chief and run up for a hurried word with a man in the crowd they recognized as Agis.

"Agis is a strange fish to have dealings with a 'steward' of the procession to-day," wondered Crito.

"You'll be enlightened to-morrow," said Polus, exasperatingly. Then as the band of horsemen cantered down the broad Dromos street, "Ah, me,—I wish I could afford to serve in the cavalry. It's far safer than tugging a spear on foot. But there's one young man out yonder on whose horse I'd not gladly be sitting."

"*Phui*," complained Clearchus, "you are anxious to eat Glaucon skin and bones! There goes his wife now, all in white flowers and ribbons, to take her place in the march with the other young matrons. Zeus! But she is as handsome as her husband."

"She needn't 'draw up her eyebrows,' "⁶ growled the juror, viciously; "they're marks of disloyalty even in her. Can't you see she wears shoes of the Theban model, laced open so as to display her bare feet, though everybody knows Thebes is Medizing? She's no better than Glaucon."

"Hush," ordered Clearchus, rising, "you have spoken folly enough. Those trumpets tell us we must hasten if we hope to join in the march ourselves."

* * * * * *

Who can tell the great procession? Not the maker of books,—what words call down light on the glancing eyes, on the moving lines of colour? Not the artist,—his pencil may not limn ten thousand human beings, beautiful and glad, sweeping in bright array across the welcoming city. Nor can the sculptor's marble shape the marching forms, the rippling draperies, the warm and buoyant life. The life of Athens was the crown of Greece. The festival of the Panathenæa was the crown of Athens.

Never had Helios looked down on fairer landscape or city. The doors of the patrician houses were opened; for a day unguarded, unconstrained, the daughters, wives, and mothers of the nobility of Athens walked forth in their queenly beauty. One could see that the sculptor's master works were but rigid counterparts of lovelier flesh and blood. One could see veterans, stalwart almost as on the day of the old-time battles, but crowned with the snow of years. One could see youths, and need no longer marvel the young Apollo was accounted fair. Flowers, fluttering mantles, purple, gold, the bravery of armour, rousing music—what was missing? All conjoined to make a perfect spectacle.

The sun had chased the last vapours from the sky. The little ravines on distant Hymettus stood forth sharply as though near at hand. The sun grew hot, but men and women walked with bared heads, and few were the untanned cheeks and shoulders. Children of the South, and lovers of the Sun-King, the Athenians sought no shelter, their own bright humour rejoicing in the light.

On the broad parade ground outside the Dipylon, the towering northwestern gate, the procession gathered. Themistocles the Handsome, never more gallant than now upon the white Thessalian, was ordering the array, the ten young men, "stewards of the Panathenæa," assisting. He sent his last glance down the long files, his ivory wand signed to the musicians in the van.

"Play! march!"

Fifty pipers blew, fifty citharas tinkled. The host swept into the city.

Themistocles led. Under the massy double gate caracoled the charger. The robe of his rider blew out behind him like purple wings. There was the cry and clang of cymbals and drums. From the gray battlement yellow daisies rained down like gold. Cantering, halting, advancing, beckoning, the chief went forward, and behind swept the "knights," the mounted chivalry of Athens,—three hundred of the noblest youths of Attica, on beasts sleek and spirited, and in burnished armour, but about every helm a wreath. Behind the "knights" rode the magistracy, men white-headed and grave, some riding, some in flower-decked cars. After these the victors in the games and contests of the preceding day. Next the elders of Athens—men of blameless life, beautiful in hale and honoured age. Next the *ephebi*,—the youths close to manhood, whose fair limbs glistened under their sweeping chitons. Behind them, their sisters, unveiled, the maidens of Athens, walking in rhythmic beauty, and with them their attendants, daughters of resident foreigners. Following upon these was the long line of bleating victims, black bulls with gilded horns and ribbon-decked rams without blemish. And next—but here the people leaned from parapet, house-roof, portico, and shouted louder than ever:

"The car and the robe of Athena! Hail, *Io, pæan!* hail!"

Up the street on a car shaped like a galley moved the peplus, the great robe of the sovran goddess. From afar one could see the wide folds spread on a shipyard and rippling in the breeze. But what a sail! One year long had the noblest women of Attica wrought on it, and all the love and art that might breathe through a needle did not fail. It was a sheen of glowing colour. The strife of Athena with the brutish giants, her contest with Arachne, the deeds of the heroes of Athens—Erechtheus, Theseus, Codrus: these were some of the pictures. The car moved noiselessly on wheels turned by concealed mechanism. Under the shadow of the sail walked the fairest of its makers, eight women, maids and young matrons, clothed in white mantles and wreaths, going with stately tread, unmoved by the shouting as though themselves divine. Seven walked together. But one, their leader, went before,—Hermione, child of Hermippus.

Many an onlooker remembered this sight of her, the deep spiritual eyes, the symmetry of form and fold, the perfect carriage. Fair wishes flew out to her like doves.

"May she be blessed forever! May King Helios forever bring her joy!"

Some cried thus. More thought thus. All seemed more glad for beholding her.

Behind the peplus in less careful array went thousands of citizens of every age and station, all in festival dress, all crowned with flowers. They followed the car up the Dromos Street, across the cheering Agora, and around the southern side of the Acropolis, making a full circuit of the citadel. Those who watched saw Glaucon with Democrates and Cimon give their horses to slaves, and mount the bare knoll of Areopagus, looking down upon the western face of the Acropolis. As the procession swung about to mount the steep, Hermione lifted her glance to Areopagus, saw her husband gazing down on her, raised her hands in delighted gesture, and he answered her. It was done in the sight of thousands, and the thousands smiled with the twain.

"Justice! The beautiful salutes the beautiful." And who thought the less of Hermione for betraying the woman beneath the mien of the goddess?

But now the march drew to an end. The procession halted, reformed, commenced the rugged way upward. Suddenly from the bastion of the Acropolis above wafted new music. Low, melancholy at first, as the pipers and harpers played in the dreamy Lydian mode, till, strengthening into the bolder Æolic, the strains floated down, inviting, "Come up hither," then stronger still it pealed in the imperious crash of the Doric as the procession mounted steadily. Now could be seen great Lamprus, Orpheus's peer, the master musician, standing on the balcony above the gate, beating time for the loud choral.

A chorus amongst the marchers and a second chorus in the citadel joined together, till the red crags shook,—singing the old hymn of the Homeridæ to Athena, homely, rude, yet dear with the memory of ages:—

"Pallas Athena, gray-eyed queen of wisdom,

Thy praise I sing!

Steadfast, all holy, sure ward of our city,

Triton-born rule whom High Zeus doth bring

Forth from his forehead.

Thou springest forth valiant;

The clangour swells far as thy direful arms ring.

"All the Immortals in awed hush are bending,

Beautiful, terrible, thy light thou'rt sending

Flashed from thine eyes and thy pitiless spear.

Under thy presence Olympus is groaning,

Earth heaves in terrors, the blue deeps are moaning;

   'Wisdom, the All-Seeing Goddess is here!'

"Now the sea motionless freezes before thee;

Helios, th' Sun-Lord, draws rein to adore thee;

   Whilst thou, O Queen, puttest on divine might.

Zeus, the deep-councillor, gladly greets thee!

Hail, Holy Virgin—our loud pæan meets thee,

   Pallas, Chaste Wisdom, Dispeller of Night!'"

Up the face of the Rock, up the long, statue-lined way, till through the gate the vision burst,—the innumerable fanes and altars, the assembly of singers and priests, the great temple in its pride of glittering marble. Clearer, stronger sounded the choral, shot up through the limpid azure; swaying, burning, throbbing, sobs and shouting, tears and transports, so mounted new strains of the mighty chorus, lit through with the flames of Homeric verse. Then stronger yet was the mingling of voices, earth, sky, deep, beasts' cry and gods' cry, all voiced, as chorus answered to chorus. Now the peplus was wafted on a wave of song toward the temple's dawn-facing portal, when from beneath the columns, as the tall valves turned and the sun leaped into the cella, hidden voices returned the former strains—mournful at first. Out of the adytum echoed a cry of anguish, the lament of the Mother of Wisdom at her children's deathly ignorance, which plucks them down from the Mount of the Beautiful Vision. But as the thousands neared, as its pæans became a prayer, as yearning answered to yearning, lo! the hidden song swelled and soared,—for the goddess looked for her own, and her own were come to her. And thus in beneath the massy pediment, in through the wide-flung doors, floated the peplus, while under its guardian shadow walked Hermione.

So they brought the robe to Athena.

＊ ＊ ＊ ＊ ＊ ＊

Glaucon and his companions had watched the procession ascend, then followed to see the sacrifice upon the giant altar. The King Archon cut the throat of the first ox and made public prayer for the people. Wood soaked in perfumed oil blazed upon the huge stone platform of the sacrifice. Girls flung frankincense upon the roaring flames. The music crashed louder. All Athens seemed mounting the citadel. The chief priestess came from the holy house, and in a brief hush proclaimed that the goddess had received the robe with all favour. After her came the makers of the peplus, and Hermione rejoined her husband.

"Let us not stay to the public feast," was her wish; "let these hucksters and charcoal-burners who live on beans and porridge scramble for a bit of burned meat, but we return to Colonus."

"Good then," answered Glaucon, "and these friends of course go with us."

Cimon assented readily. Democrates hesitated, and while hesitating was seized by the cloak by none other than Agis, who gave a hasty whisper and vanished in the swirling multitude before Democrates could do more than nod.

"He's an uncanny fox," remarked Cimon, mystified; "I suppose you know his reputation?"

"The servant of Athens must sometimes himself employ strange servants," evaded the orator.

"Yet you might suffer your friends to understand—"

"Dear son of Miltiades," Democrates's voice shook in the slightest, "the meaning of my dealings with Agis I pray Athena you may never have cause to know."

"Which means you will not tell us. Then by Zeus I swear the secret no doubt is not worth the knowing." Cimon stopped suddenly, as he saw a look of horror on Hermione's face. "Ah, lady! what's the matter?"

"Glaucon," she groaned, "frightful omen! I am terrified!"

Glaucon's hands dropped at her cry. He himself paled slightly. In one of his moods of abstraction he had taken the small knife from his belt and begun to pare his nails,—to do which after a sacrifice was reputed an infallible means of provoking heaven's anger. The friends were grave and silent. The athlete gave a forced laugh.

"The goddess will be merciful to-day. To-morrow I will propitiate her with a goat."

"Now, now, not to-morrow," urged Hermione, with white lips, but her husband refused.

"The goddess is surfeited with sacrifices this morning. She would forget mine."

Then he led the rest, elbowing the way through the increasing swarms of young and old, and down into the half-deserted city. Democrates left them in the Agora, professing great stress of duties.

"Strange man," observed Cimon, as he walked away; "what has he this past month upon his mind? That Persian spy, I warrant. But the morning wanes. It's a long way to Colonus. 'Let us drink, for the sun is in the zenith.' So says Alcæus—and I love the poet, for he like myself is always thirsty."

The three went on to the knoll of Colonus where Glaucon dwelt. Cimon was overrunning with puns and jests, but the others not very merry. The omen of Glaucon's thoughtlessness, or something else, made husband and wife silent, yet it was a day when man or maid should have felt their spirits rise. The sky had never been brighter, not in Athens. Never had the mountains and sea spread more gloriously. From the warm olive-groves sounded the blithesome note of the Attic grasshopper. The wind sweeping over the dark cypresses by the house set their dark leaves to talking. The afternoon passed in pleasure, friends going and coming; there was laughter, music, and good stories. Hermione at least recovered part of her brightness, but her husband, contrary to all custom, remained taciturn, even melancholy. At last as the gentle tints of evening began to cover hill and plain and the red-tiled roofs of the ample city, all the friends were gone, saving only Cimon, and he— reckless fellow—was well able to dispense with companionship, being, in the words of Theognis, "not absolutely drunk, nor sober quite." Thus husband and wife found themselves alone together on the marble bench beneath the old cypress.

"Oh, *makaire*! dearest and best," asked Hermione, her hands touching his face, "is it the omen that makes you grow so sad? For the sun of your life is so seldom under clouds that when it is clouded at all, it seems as deep darkness."

He answered by pressing back her hair, "No, not the omen. I am not a slave to chance like that. Yet to-day,—the wise God knows wherefore,—there comes a sense of brooding fear. I have been too happy—too blessed with friendship, triumph, love. It cannot last. Clotho the Spinner will weary of making my thread of gold and twine in a darker stuff. Everything lovely must pass. What said Glaucus to Diomedes? 'Even as the race of leaves, so likewise are those of men; the leaves that now are, the wind scattereth, and the forest buddeth forth more again; thus also with the race of men, one putteth forth, another ceaseth.' So even my joy must pass—"

"Glaucon,—take back the words. You frighten me."

He felt her in his arms trembling, and cursed himself for what he had uttered.

"A blight upon my tongue! I have frightened you, and without cause. Surely the day is bright enough, surely Athena having been thus far good we can trust her goodness still. Who knows but that it be many a year before our sun comes to his setting!"

He kissed her many times. She grew comforted, but they had not been together long when they were surprised by the approach of Themistocles and Hermippus. Hermione ran to her father.

"Themistocles and I were summoned hither," explained Hermippus, "by a message from Democrates bidding us come to Colonus at once, on an urgent matter touching the public weal."

"He is not here. I cannot understand," marvelled Glaucon; but while he spoke, he was interrupted by the clatter of hoofs from a party of horsemen spurring furiously and heading from the pass of Daphni.

CHAPTER XII
A TRAITOR TO HELLAS

Before the house six riders were reining,—five Scythian "bowmen" of the constabulary of Athens, tow-headed Barbarians, grinning but mute; the sixth was Democrates. He dismounted with a bound, and as he did so the friends saw that his face was red as with pent-up excitement. Themistocles advanced hastily.

"What's this? Your hands seem a-quiver. Whom has that constable tied up behind him?"

"Seuthes!" cried Glaucon, bounding back, "Seuthes, by every god, and pinioned like a felon."

"Ay!" groaned the prisoner, lashed to a horse, "what have I done to be seized and tried like a bandit? Why should I be set upon by these gentlemen while I was enjoying a quiet pot of wine in the tavern at Daphni, and be haled away as if to crucifixion? *Mu! Mu!* make them untie me, dear Master Glaucon."

"Put down your prisoner," ordered Democrates, "and all you constables stay without the house. I ask Themistocles, Hermippus, and Glaucon to come to an inner room. I must examine this man. The matter is serious."

"Serious?" echoed the bewildered athlete, "I can vouch for Seuthes—an excellent Corinthian, come to Athens to sell some bales of wool—"

"Answer, Glaucon," Democrates's voice was stern. "Has he no letters from you for Argos?"

"Certainly."

"You admit it?"

"By the dog of Egypt, do you doubt my word?"

"Friends," called Democrates, dramatically, "mark you that Glaucon admits he has employed this Seuthes as his courier."

"Whither leads this mummery?" cried the athlete, growing at last angry.

"If to nothing, I, Democrates, rejoice the most. Now I must bid you to follow me."

Seizing the snivelling Seuthes, the orator led into the house and to a private chamber. The rest followed, in blank wonderment. Cimon had recovered enough to follow—none too steadily. But when Hermione approached, Democrates motioned her back.

"Do not come. A painful scene may be impending."

"What my husband can hear, that can I," was her retort. "Ah! but why do you look thus dreadfully on Glaucon?"

"I have warned you, lady. Do not blame me if you hear the worst," rejoined Democrates, barring the door. A single swinging lamp shed a fitful light on the scene—the whimpering prisoner, the others all amazed, the orator's face, tense and white. Democrates's voice seemed metallic as he continued:—

"Now, Seuthes, we must search you. Produce first the letter from Glaucon."

The fat florid little Corinthian was dressed as a traveller, a gray chalmys to his hips, a brimmed brown hat, and high black boots. His hands were now untied. He tugged from his belt a bit of papyrus which Democrates handed to Themistocles, enjoining "Open."

Glaucon flushed.

"Are you mad, Democrates, to violate my private correspondence thus?"

"The weal of Athens outweighs even the pleasure of Glaucon," returned the orator, harshly, "and you, Themistocles, note that Glaucon does not deny that the seal here is his own."

"I do not deny," cried the angry athlete. "Open, Themistocles, and let this stupid comedy end."

"And may it never change to tragedy!" proclaimed Democrates. "What do you read, Themistocles?"

"A courteous letter of thanks to Ageladas." The senior statesman was frowning. "Glaucon is right. Either you are turned mad, or are victim of some prank,—is it yours, Cimon?"

"I am as innocent as a babe. I'd swear it by the Styx," responded that young man, scratching his muddled head.

"I fear we are not at the end of the examination," observed Democrates, with ominous slowness. "Now, Seuthes, recollect your plight. Have you no other letter about you?"

"None!" groaned the unheroic Corinthian. "Ah! pity, kind sirs; what have I done? Suffer me to go."

"It is possible," remarked his prosecutor, "you are an innocent victim, or at least do not realize the intent of what you bear. I must examine the lining of your chalmys. Nothing. Your girdle. Nothing. Your hat, remove it. Quite empty. Blessed be Athena if my fears prove groundless. But my first duty is to Athens and Hellas. Ah! Your high boots. Remove the right one." The orator felt within, and shook the boot violently. "Nothing again. The left one, empty it seems. *Ei!* what is this?"

In a tense silence he shook from the boot a papyrus, rolled and sealed. It fell on the floor at the feet of Themistocles, who, watching all his lieutenant did, bent and seized it instantly; then it dropped from his hands as a live coal.

"The seal! The seal! May Zeus smite me blind if I see aright!"

Hermippus, who had been following all the scene in silence, bent, lifted the fateful paper, and he too gave a cry of grief.

"It is the seal of Glaucon. How came it here?"

"Glaucon,"—hard as Democrates's voice had been that night, it rang like cold iron now,—"as the friend of your boyhood, and one who would still do for you all he may, I urge you as you love me to look upon this seal."

"I am looking," but as he spoke paleness followed the angry flush on the athlete's forehead. He needed no omen to tell him something fearful was about to ensue.

"The seal is yours?"

"The very same, two dancing mænads and over them a winged Eros. But how came this letter here? I did not—"

"As you love life or death, as you preserve any regard for our friendship, I adjure you,—not to brave it longer, but to confess—"

"Confess what? My head is reeling."

"The treason in which you have dipped your hands, your dealings with the Persian spy, your secret interviews, and last of all this letter,—I fear a gross betrayal of all trust,—to some agent of Xerxes. I shudder when I think of what may be its contents."

"And—this—from—you! Oh,—Democrates,—"

The accused man's hands snatched at the air. He sank upon a chest.

"He does not deny it," threw out the orator, but Glaucon's voice rang shrilly:—

"Ever! Ever will I deny! Though the Twelve Gods all cried out 'guilty!' The charge is monstrous."

"It is time, Democrates," said Themistocles, who had preserved a grim silence, "that you showed us clearly whither your path is leading. This is a fearful accusation you launch against your best-loved friend."

"Themistocles is right," assented the orator, moving away from the luckless Seuthes as from a pawn no longer important in the game of life and death. "The whole of the wretched story I fear I must tell on the Bema to all Athens. I must be brief, but believe me, I can make good all I say. Since my return from the Isthmia, I have been observed to be sad. Rightly—for knowing Glaucon as I did, I grew suspicious, and I loved him. You have thought me not diligent in hunting down the Persian spy. You were wrong. But how could I ruin my friend without full proof? I made use of Agis,—no genteel confederate, to be sure, but honest, patriotic, indefatigable. I soon had my eyes on the suspected Babylonish carpet-seller. I observed Glaucon's movements closely, they gave just ground for suspicion. The Babylonian, I came to feel, was none other than an agent of Xerxes himself. I discovered that Glaucon had been making this emissary nocturnal visits."

"A lie!" groaned the accused, in agony.

"I would to Athena I believed you," was the unflinching answer; "I have direct evidence from eye-witnesses that you went to him. In a moment I can produce it. Yet still I hesitated. Who would blast a friend without damning proof? Then yesterday with your own lips you told me you sent a messenger to disloyal Argos. I suspected two messages, not one, were entrusted to Seuthes, and that you proclaimed the more innocent matter thus boldly simply to blind my eyes. Before Seuthes started forth this morning Agis informed me he had met him in a wine-shop—"

"True," whimpered the unhappy prisoner.

"And this fellow as much as admitted he carried a second and secret message—"

"Liar!" roared Seuthes.

"Men hint strange things in wine-shops," observed Democrates, sarcastically. "Enough that a second papyrus with Glaucon's seal has been found hidden upon you."

"Open it then, and know the worst," interjected Themistocles, his face like a thunder-cloud; but Democrates forbade him.

"A moment. Let me complete my story. This afternoon I received warning that the Babylonish carpet-vender had taken sudden flight, presumably toward Thebes. I have sent mounted constables after him. I trust they can seize him at the pass of Phyle. In the meantime, I may assure you I have irrefutable evidence—needless to present here—that the man was a Persian agent, and to more purpose hear this affidavit, sworn to by very worthy patriots.

"Polus, son of Phodrus of the Commune of Diomea, and Lampaxo his sister take oath by Zeus, Dike, and Athena, thus: We swear we saw and recognized Glaucon, son of Conon, twice visiting by night in the past month of Scirophorion a certain Babylonish carpet-seller, name unknown, who had lodgings above Demas's shield factory in Alopece."

"Details lack," spoke Themistocles, keenly.

"To be supplied in full measure at the trial," rejoined the orator. "And now to the second letter itself."

"Ay, the letter, whatever the foul Cyclops that wrought it!" groaned Glaucon through his teeth.

Themistocles took the document from Hermippus's trembling hands. His own trembled whilst he broke the seal.

"The handwriting of Glaucon. There is no doubt," was his despairing comment. His frown darkened. Then he attempted to read.

"Glaucon of Athens to Cleophas of Argos wishes health:—

"Cleophas leads the Medizers of Argos, the greatest friend of Xerxes in Greece. O Zeus, what is this next—

"Our dear friend, whom I dare not name, to-day departs for Thebes, and in a month will be safe in Sardis. His visit to Athens has been most fruitful. Since you at present have better opportunity than we for forwarding packets to Susa, do not fail to despatch this at once. A happy chance led Themistocles to explain to me his secret memorandum for the arraying of the Greek fleet. You can apprize its worth, for the only others to whom it is entrusted are Democrates and later Leonidas—"

Themistocles flung the papyrus down. His voice was broken. Tears stood in his eyes.

"O Glaucon, Glaucon,—whom I have trusted? Was ever trust so betrayed! May Apollo smite me blind, if so I could forget what I read here! It is all written—the secret ordering of the fleet—"

For a terrible moment there was silence in the little room, a silence broken by a wild, shrill cry,—Hermione's, as she cast her arms about her husband.

"A lie! A snare! A wicked plot! Some jealous god has devised this guile, seeing we were too happy!"

She shook with sobs, and Glaucon, roused to manhood by her grief, uprose and faced the stern face of Democrates, the blenching faces of the rest.

"I am the victim of a conspiracy of all the fiends in Tartarus,"—he strove hard to speak steadily; "I did not write that second letter. It is a forgery."

"But who, then," groaned Themistocles, hopelessly, "*can* claim this handiwork? Democrates or I?—for no other has seen the memorandum,— that I swear. It has not yet gone to Leonidas. It has been guarded as the apple of my eye. We three alone knew thereof. And it is in this narrow room the betrayer of Hellas must stand."

"I cannot explain." Glaucon staggered back to his seat. His wife's head sank upon his lap. The two sat in misery.

"Confess, by the remnants of our friendship I implore, confess," ordered Democrates, "and then Themistocles and I will strive to lighten if possible your inevitable doom."

The accused man sat dumb, but Hermione struck back as some wild creature driven to bay. She lifted her head.

"Has Glaucon here no friend but me, his wife?" She sent beseeching eyes about the room. "Do you all cry 'guilty, guilty'? Then is your friendship false, for when is friendship proved, save in the hour of need?"

The appeal brought an answer from her father, who had been standing silent; and in infinite distress kindly, cautious, charitable Hermippus began:—

"Dear Glaucon, Hermione is wrong; we were never more your friends. We are willing to believe the best and not the worst. Therefore tell all frankly. You have been a victim of great temptation. The Isthmian victory has turned your head. The Persian was subtle, plausible. He promised I know not what. You did not realize all you were doing. You had confederates here in Athens who are more guilty. We can make allowances. Tell only the truth, and the purse and influence of Hermippus of Eleusis shall never be held back to save his son-in-law."

"Nor mine, nor mine," cried Themistocles, snatching at every straw; "only confess, the temptation was great, others were more guilty, everything then may be done—"

Glaucon drew himself together and looked up almost proudly. Slowly he was recovering strength and wit.

"I have nothing to confess," he spoke, "nothing. I know nothing of this Persian spy. Can I swear the god's own oath—by Earth, by Sky, by the Styx—"

Themistocles shook his head wearily.

"How can we say you are innocent? You never visited the Babylonian?"

"Never. Never!"

"Polus and Lampaxo swear otherwise. The letter?"

"A forgery."

"Impossible. Is the forger Democrates or I?"

"Some god has done this thing in malice, jealous of my great joy."

"I fear Hermes no longer strides so frequently about Athens. The hand and seal are yours,—and still you do not confess?"

"If I must die," Glaucon was terribly pale, but his voice was steady, "it is not as a perjurer!"

Themistocles turned his back with a groan.

"I can do nothing for you. This is the saddest hour in my life." He was silent, but Democrates sprang to the athlete's side.

"Have I not prayed each god to spare me this task?" he spoke. "Can I forget our friendship? Do not brave it to the end. Pity at least your friends, your wife—"

He threw back his cloak, pointing to a sword.

"*Ai,*" cried the accused, shrinking. "What would you have me do?"

"Save the public disgrace, the hooting jury, the hemlock, the corpse flung into the Barathrum. Strike this into your breast and end the shame."

No further. Glaucon smote him so that he reeled. The athlete's tone was terrible.

"Villain! You shall not tempt me." Then he turned to the rest, and stood in his white agony, yet beautiful as ever, holding out his arms.

"O friends, do you all believe the worst? Do you, Themistocles, turn silently against me?" No answer. "And you, Hermippus?" No answer again. "And you, Cimon, who praised me as the fairest friend in all the world?" The son of Miltiades simply tore his hair. Then the athlete turned to Democrates.

"And you I deemed more than comrade, for we were boys at school together, were flogged with the same rod, and drank from the same cup, had like friends, foes, loves, hates; and have lived since as more than brothers,—do you too turn utterly away?"

"I would it were otherwise," came the sullen answer. Again Democrates pointed to the sword, but Glaucon stood up proudly.

"No. I am neither traitor, nor perjurer, nor coward. If I must perish, it shall be as becomes an Alcmæonid. If you have resolved to undo me, I know your power over Athenian juries. I must die. But I shall die with unspotted heart, calling the curse of the innocent upon the god or man who plotted to destroy me."

"We have enough of this direful comedy," declared Democrates, pale himself. "Only one thing is left. Call in the Scythians with their gyves, and hale the traitor to prison."

He approached the door; the others stood as icy statues, but not Hermione. She had her back against the door before the orator could open.

"Hold," she commanded, "for you are doing murder!"

Democrates halted at the menacing light in her eyes. All the fear had gone out of them. Athena Promachos, "Mistress of Battles," must have stood in that awful beauty when aroused. Did the goddess teach her in that dread moment of her power over the will of the orator? Glaucon was still standing motionless, helpless, his last appeal having ended in mute resignation to inevitable fate. She motioned to him desperately.

"Glaucon! Glaucon!" she adjured, "do not throw your life away. They shall not murder you. Up! Rouse yourself! There is yet time. Fly, or all is lost."

"Fly!" spoke the athlete, almost vacantly. "No, I will brave them to the end."

"For my sake, fly," she ordered, and conjured by that potent talisman, Glaucon moved toward her.

"How? Whither?"

"To the ends of the earth, Scythia, Atlantis, India, and remain till all Athens knows you are innocent."

As men move who know not what they do, he approached the door. Held by the magic of her eyes the others stood rigid. They saw Hermione raise the latch. Her husband's face met hers in one kiss. The door opened, closed. Glaucon was gone, and as the latch clicked Democrates shook off the charm and leaped forward.

"After the traitor! Not too late!—"

For an instant he wrestled with Hermione hand to hand, but she was strong through fear and love. He could not master her. Then a heavy grasp fell on his shoulder—Cimon's.

"You are beside yourself, Democrates. My memory is longer than yours. To me Glaucon is still a friend. I'll not see him dragged to death before my eyes. When we follow even a fox or a wolf, we give fair start and fair play. You shall not pursue him yet."

"Blessing on you!" cried the wife, falling on her knees and seizing Cimon's cloak. "Oh, make Themistocles and my father merciful!"

Hermippus—tender-hearted man—was in tears. Themistocles was pacing the little chamber, his hand tugging his beard, clearly in grievous doubt.

"The Scythians! The constables!" Democrates clamoured frantically; "every instant gives the traitor better start."

But Cimon held him fast, and Themistocles was not to be interrupted. Only after a long time he spoke, and then with authority which brooked no contradiction.

"There is no hole in the net of Democrates's evidence that Glaucon is guilty of foul disloyalty, disloyalty worthy of shameful death. Were he any other there would be only one way with him and that a short one. But Glaucon I know, if I know any man. The charges even if proved are nigh incredible. For of all the thousands in Hellas his soul seemed the purest, noblest, most ingenuous. Therefore I will not hasten on his death. I will give the gods a chance to save him. Let Democrates arraign me for 'misprision of treason' if he will, and of failing in duty to Athens. There shall be no pursuit of Glaucon until morning. Then let the Eleven[1] issue their hue and cry. If they take him, let the law deal with him. Till then give respite."

Democrates attempted remonstrance. Themistocles bade him be silent sharply, and the other bowed his head in cowed acquiescence. Hermione staggered from the door, her father unbarred, and the whole wretched company went forth. In the passage hung a burnished steel mirror; Hermione gave a cry as she passed it. The light borne by Hermippus showed her in her festival dress, the rippling white drapery, the crown of white violets.

"My father!" she cried, falling into his arms, "is it still the day of the Panathenæa, when I marched in the great procession, when all Athens called me happy? It was a thousand years ago! I can never be glad again—"

He lifted her tenderly as she fainted. Old Cleopis, the Spartan nurse who had kissed her almost before her mother, ran to her. They carried her to bed, and Athena in mercy hid her from consciousness that night and all the following day.

CHAPTER XIII
THE DISLOYALTY OF PHORMIO

On the evening of the Panathenæa, Bias, servant of Democrates, had supped with Phormio,—for in democratic Athens a humble citizen would not disdain to entertain even a slave. The Thracian had a merry wit and a story-teller's gift that more than paid for the supper of barley-porridge and salt mackerel, and after the viands had disappeared was ready even to tell tales against his master.

"I've turned my brain inside out, and shaken it like a meal sack. No wisdom comes. The *kyrios* has something on his mind. He prays to Hermes Dolios as often as if he were a cut-purse. Then yesterday he sent me for Agis—"

"Agis?" Phormio pricked up his ears. "The gambling-house keeper? What does Democrates with *him*?"

"Answer yourself. My master has been to Agis's pretty place before to see his cocks. However, this is different. To-day I met Theon."

"Who's he?"

"Agis's slave, the merriest scoundrel in Athens. Agis, he says, has been prancing like an ass stuffed with barley. He gave Theon a letter from Democrates to take to your Babylonian opposite; Theon must hunt up Seuthes, a Corinthian, and worm out of him when and how he was leaving Athens. Agis promised Theon a gold stater if all was right."

Phormio whistled. "You mean the carpet-dealer here? By Athena's owls, there is no light in his window to-night!"

"None, indeed," crackled Lampaxo; "didn't I see that cursed Babylonian with his servants gliding out just as Bias entered? Zeus knows whither! I hope ere dawn Democrates has them by the heels."

"Democrates does something to-night," asserted Bias, extending his cup for wine. "At noon Agis flew up to him, chattered something in his ear, whereupon Democrates bade me be off and not approach him till to-morrow, otherwise a cane gets broken on my shoulders."

"It's not painful to have a holiday," laughed Phormio.

"It's most painful to be curious yet unsatisfied."

"But why did not you take the letter to the Babylonian?" observed Phormio, shrewdly.

"I'm perplexed, indeed. Only one thing is possible."

"And that is—"

"Theon is not known in this street. I am. Perhaps the *kyrios* didn't care to have it rumoured he had dealings with that Babylonian."

"Silence, undutiful scoundrel," ordered Lampaxo, from her corner; "what has so noble a patriot as Democrates to conceal? Ugh! Be off with you! Phormio, don't dare to fill up the tipsy fox's beaker again. I want to pull on my nightcap and go to bed."

Bias did not take the hint. Phormio was considering whether it was best to join combat with his redoubtable spouse, or save his courage for a more important battle, when a slight noise from the street made all listen.

"Pest light on those bands of young roisterers!" fumed Lampaxo. "They go around all night, beating on doors and vexing honest folk. Why don't the constables trot them all to jail?"

"This isn't a drunken band, good wife," remarked Phormio, rising; "some one is sitting on the stones by the Hermes, near the door, groaning as if in pain."

"A drunkard? Let him lie then," commanded Lampaxo; "let the coat-thieves come and filch his chiton."

"He's hardly drunken," observed her husband, peering through the lattice in the door, "but sick rather. Don't detain me, *philotata*,"—Lampaxo's skinny hand had tried to restrain. "I'll not let even a dog suffer."

"You'll be ruined by too much charity," bewailed the woman, but Bias followed the fishmonger into the night. The moon shone down the narrow street, falling over the stranger who half lay, half squatted by the Hermes. When the two approached him, he tried to stagger to his feet, then reeled, and Phormio's strong arms seized him. The man resisted feebly, and seemed never to hear the fishmonger's friendly questions.

"I am innocent. Do not arrest me. Help me to the temple of Hephæstos, where there's asylum for fugitives. Ah! Hermione, that I should bring you this!"

Bias leaped back as the moonlight glanced over the face of the stranger.

"Master Glaucon, half naked and mad! *Ai!* woe!"

"Glaucon the Alcmæonid," echoed Phormio, in amazement, and the other still struggled to escape.

"Do you not hear? I am innocent. I never visited the Persian spy. I never betrayed the fleet. By what god can I swear it, that you may believe?"

Phormio was a man to recover from surprise quickly, and act swiftly and to the purpose. He made haste to lead his unfortunate visitor inside and lay him on his one hard couch. Scarcely was this done, however, when Lampaxo ran up to Glaucon in mingled rage and exultation.

"Phormio doesn't know what Polus and I told Democrates, or what he told us! So you thought to escape, you white-skinned traitor? But we've watched you. We know how you went to the Babylonian. We know your guilt. And now the good gods have stricken you mad and delivered you to justice." She waved her bony fists in the prostrate man's face. "Run, Phormio! don't stand gaping like a magpie. Run, I say—"

"Whither? For a physician?"

"To Areopagus, fool! There's where the constables have their camp. Bring ten men with fetters. He's strong and desperate. Bias and I will wait and guard him. If you stir, traitor,—" she was holding a heavy meat-knife at the fugitive's throat,—"I'll slit your weasand like a chicken."

But for once in his life Phormio defied his tyrant effectively. With one hand he tore the weapon from her clutch, the other closed her screaming mouth.

"Are you mad yourself? Will you rouse the neighbourhood? I don't know what you and Polus tattled about to Democrates. I don't greatly care. As for going for constables to seize Glaucon the Fortunate—"

"Fortunate!" echoed the miserable youth, rising on one elbow, "say it never again. The gods have blasted me with one great blow. And you—you are Phormio, husband and brother-in-law of those who have sworn against me,—you are the slave of Democrates my destroyer,—and you, woman,— Zeus soften you!—already clamour for my worthless life, as all Athens does to-morrow!"

Lampaxo suddenly subsided. Resistance from her spouse was so unexpected she lost at once arguments and breath. Phormio continued to act promptly; taking a treasured bottle from a cupboard he filled a mug and pressed it to the newcomer's lips. The fiery liquor sent the colour back into Glaucon's face. He raised himself higher—strength and mind in a measure returned. Bias had whispered to Phormio rapidly. Perhaps he had guessed more of his master's doings than he had dared to hint before.

"Hark you, Master Glaucon," began Phormio, not unkindly. "You are with friends, and never heed my wife. She's not so steely hearted as she seems."

"Seize the traitor," interjected Lampaxo, with a gasp.

"Tell your story. I'm a plain and simple man, who won't believe a gentleman with your fair looks, fame, and fortune has pawned them all in a night. Bias has sense. First tell how you came to wander down this way."

Glaucon sat upright, his hands pressing against his forehead.

"How can I tell? I have run to and fro, seeing yet not seeing whither I went. I know I passed the Acharnican gate, and the watch stared at me. Doubtless I ran hither because here they said the Babylonian lived, and he has been ever in my head. I shudder to go over the scene at Colonus. I wish I were dead. Then I could forget it!"

"Constables—fetters!" howled Lampaxo, as a direful interlude, to be silenced by an angry gesture from her helpmeet.

"Nevertheless, try to tell what you can," spoke Phormio, mildly, and Glaucon, with what power he had, complied. Broken, faltering, scarce coherent often, his story came at last. He sat silent while Phormio clutched his own head. Then Glaucon darted around wild and hopeless eyes.

"*Ai!* you believe me guilty. I almost believe so myself. All my best friends have cast me off. Democrates, my friend from youth, has wrought my ruin. My wife I shall never see again. I am resolved—" He rose. A desperate purpose made his feet steady.

"What will you do?" demanded Phormio, perplexed.

"One thing is left. I am sure to be arrested at dawn if not before. I will go to the 'City-House,' the public prison, and give myself up. The ignominy will soon end. Then welcome the Styx, Hades, the never ending night—better than this shame!"

He started forth, but Phormio's hand restrained him. "Not so fast, lad! Thank Olympus, I'm not Lampaxo. You're too young a turbot for Charon's fish-net. Let me think a moment."

The fishmonger stood scratching his thin hairs. Another howl from Lampaxo decided him.

"Are you a traitor, too? Away with the wretch to prison!"

"I'm resolved," cried Phormio, striking his thigh. "Only an honest man could get such hatred from my wife. If they've not tracked you yet, they're not likely to find you before morning. My cousin Brasidas is master of the *Solon*, and owes a good turn—"

Quick strides took him to a chest. He dragged forth a sleeveless sailor's cloak of hair-cloth. To fling this over Glaucon's rent chiton took an instant, another instant to clap on the fugitive's head a brimless red cap.

"*Euge!*—you grow transformed. But that white face of yours is dangerous. See!" he rubbed over the Alcmæonid's face two handfuls of black ashes snatched from the hearth and sprang back with a great laugh, "you're a sailor unlading charcoal now. Zeus himself would believe it. All is ready—"

"For prison?" asked Glaucon, clearly understanding little.

"For the sea, my lad. For Athens is no place for you to-morrow, and Brasidas sails at dawn. Some more wine? It's a long, brisk walk."

"To the havens? You trust me? You doubt the accusation which every friend save Hermione believes? O pure Athena—and this is possible!" Again Glaucon's head whirled. It took more of the fiery wine to stay him up.

"Ay, boy," comforted Phormio, very gruff, "you shall walk again around Athens with a bold, brave face, though not to-morrow, I fear. Polus trusts his heart and not his head in voting 'guilty,' so I trust it voting 'innocent.'"

"I warn you," Glaucon spoke rapidly, "I've no claim on your friendship. If your part in this is discovered, you know our juries."

"That I know," laughed Phormio, grimly, "for I know dear Polus. So now my own cloak and we are off."

But Lampaxo, who had watched everything with accumulating anger, now burst loose. She bounded to the door.

"Constables! Help! Athens is betrayed!"

She bawled that much through the lattice before her husband and Bias dragged her back. Fortunately the street was empty.

"That I should see this! My own husband betraying the city! Aiding a traitor!" Then she began whimpering through her nose. "*Mu! mu!* leave the villain to his fate. Think of me if not of your own safety. Woe! when was a woman more misused?"

But here her lament ended, for Phormio, with the firmness of a man thoroughly determined, thrust a rag into her mouth and with Bias's help bound her down upon the couch by means of a convenient fish-cord.

"I am grieved to stop your singing, blessed dear," spoke the fishmonger, indulging in a rare outburst of sarcasm against his formidable helpmeet, "but we play a game with Fate to-night a little too even to allow unfair chances.

Bias will watch you until I return, and then I can discover, *philotata*, whether your love for Athens is so great you must go to the Archon to denounce your husband."

The Thracian promised to do his part. His affection for Democrates was clearly not the warmest. Lampaxo's farewell, as Phormio guided his half-dazed companion into the street, was a futile struggle and a choking. The ways were empty and silent. Glaucon allowed himself to be led by the hand and did not speak. He hardly knew how or whither Phormio was taking him. Their road lay along the southern side of the Acropolis, past the tall columns of the unfinished Temple of Zeus, which reared to giant height in the white moonlight. This, as well as the overshadowing Rock itself, they left behind without incident. Phormio chose devious alleys, and they met neither Scythian constables nor bands of roisterers. Only once the two passed a house bright with lamps. Jovial guests celebrated a late wedding feast. Clearly the two heard the marriage hymn of Sappho.

"The bridegroom comes tall as Ares,

Ho, Hymenæus!

Taller than a mighty man,

Ho, Hymenæus!"

Glaucon stopped like one struck with an arrow.

"They sang that song the night I wedded Hermione. Oh, if I could drink the Lethe water and forget!"

"Come," commanded Phormio, pulling upon his arm. "The sun will shine again to-morrow."

Thus the twain went forward, Glaucon saying not a word. He hardly knew how they passed the Itonian Gate and crossed the long stretch of open country betwixt the city and its havens. No pursuit as yet—Glaucon was too perplexed to reason why. At last he knew they entered Phaleron. He heard the slapping waves, the creaking tackle, the shouting sailors. Torches gleamed ruddily. A merchantman was loading her cargo of pottery crates and oil jars,—to sail with the morning breeze. Swarthy shipmen ran up and down the planks betwixt quay and ship, balancing their heavy jars on their heads as women bear water-pots. From the tavern by the mooring came harping and the clatter of cups, while two women—the worse for wine—ran out to drag the newcomers in to their revel. Phormio slapped the slatterns aside with his staff. In the same fearful waking dream Glaucon saw Phormio demanding the shipmaster. He saw Brasidas—a short man with the face of a hound and arms to hug like a bear—in converse with the fishmonger, saw the master at first refusing, then gradually giving reluctant assent to some demand. Next Phormio was half leading, half carrying the fugitive aboard the ship, guiding him through a labyrinth of bales, jars, and cordage, and pointing to a hatchway ladder, illumined by a swinging lantern.

"Keep below till the ship sails; don't wipe the charcoal from your face till clear of Attica. Officers will board the vessel before she puts off; yet have no alarm, they'll only come to see she doesn't violate the law against exporting grain." Phormio delivered his admonitions rapidly, at the same time fumbling in his belt. "Here—here are ten drachmæ, all I've about me, but something for bread and figs till you make new friends,—in which there'll be no trouble, I warrant. Have a brave heart. Remember that Helios can shine lustily even if you are not in Athens, and pray the gods to give a fair return."

Glaucon felt the money pressed within his palm. He saw Phormio turning away. He caught the fishmonger's hard hand and kissed it twice.

"I can never reward you. Not though I live ten thousand years and have all the gold of Gyges."

"*Phui!*" answered Phormio, with a shrug; "don't detain me, it's time I was home and was unlashing my loving wife."

And with that he was gone. Glaucon descended the ladder. The cabin was low, dark, unfurnished save with rude pallets of straw, but Glaucon heeded none of these things. Deeper than the accusation by Democrates, than the belief therein by Themistocles and the others, the friendship of the fishmonger touched him. A man base-born, ignorant, uncivil, had believed him, had risked his own life to save him, had given him money out of his poverty, had spoken words of fair counsel and cheer. On the deck above the sailors were tumbling the cargo, and singing at their toil, but Glaucon never heard them. Flinging himself on a straw pallet, for the first time came the comfort of hot tears.

* * * * * *

Very early the *Solon's* square mainsail caught the breeze from the warm southwest. The hill of Munychia and the ports receded. The panorama of

Athens—plain, city, citadel, gray Hymettus, white Pentelicus—spread in a vista of surpassing beauty—so at least to the eyes of the outlaw when he clambered to the poop. As the ship ran down the low coast, land and sea seemed clothed with a robe of rainbow-woven light. Far, near,—islands, mountains, and deep were burning with saffron, violet, and rose, as the Sun-God's car climbed higher above the burning path it marked across the sea. Glaucon saw all in clear relief,—the Acropolis temple where he had prayed, the Pnyx and Areopagus, the green band of the olive groves, even the knoll of Colonus,—where he had left his all. Never had he loved Athens more than now. Never had she seemed fairer to his eyes than now. He was a Greek, and to a Greek death was only by one stage a greater ill than exile.

"O Athena Polias," he cried, stretching his hands to the fading beauty, "goddess who determineth all aright,—bless thou this land, though it wakes to call me traitor. Teach it to know I am innocent. Comfort Hermione, my wife. And restore me to Athens, after doing deeds which wipe out all my unearned shame!"

The *Solon* rounded the cape. The headland concealed the city. The Saronian bay opened into the deeper blue of the Ægean and its sprinkling of brown islands. Glaucon looked eastward and strove to forget Attica.

* * * * * *

Two hours later all Athens seemed reading this placard in the Agora:—

NOTICE

For the arrest of GLAUCON, SON OF CONON, charged with high treason, I will pay one talent.

DEXILEUS, Chairman of the Eleven.

Other such placards were posted in Peiræus, in Eleusis, in Marathon, in every Attic village. Men could talk of nothing else.

CHAPTER XIV
MARDONIUS THE PERSIAN

Off Andros the northern gale smote them. The ship had driven helplessly.

Off Tenos only the skill of Brasidas kept the *Solon* clear of the rocky shores.

As they raced past holy Delos the frightened passengers had vowed twelve oxen to Apollo if he saved them.

Near Naxos, Brasidas, after vainly trying to make a friendly haven, bade his sailors undergird the ship with heavy cables, for the timbers seemed starting. Finally he suffered his craft to drive,—hoping at least to find some islet with a sandy shore where he could beach her with safety.

The *Solon*, however, was near her doom. She was built on the Samian model, broad, flat, high in poop, low in prow,—excellent for cargo, but none too seaworthy. The foresail blew in tatters. The closely brailed mainsail shook the weakened mast. The sailors had dropped their quaint oaths, and began to pray—sure proof of danger. The dozen passengers seemed almost too panic-stricken to aid in flinging the cargo overboard. Several were raving.

"Hearken, Poseidon of Calauria," howled a Peiræus merchant against the screeching blasts, "save from this peril and I vow thee and thy temple two mixing bowls of purest gold!"

"A great vow," suggested a calmer comrade. "All your fortune can hardly pay it."

"Hush," spoke the other, in undertone, "don't let the god overhear me; let me get safe to Mother Earth and Poseidon has not one obol. His power is only over the sea."

A creaking from the mainmast told that it might fall at any moment. Passengers and crew redoubled their shouts to Poseidon and to Zeus of Ægina. A fat passenger staggered from his cabin, a huge money-bag bound to his belt,—as if gold were the safest spar to cling to in that boiling deep. Others, less frantic, gave commissions one to another, in case one perished and another escaped.

"You alone have no messages, pray no prayers, show no fear!" spoke a grave, elderly man to Glaucon, as both clutched the swaying bulwark.

"And wherefore?" came the bitter answer; "what is left me to fear? I desire no life hereafter. There can be no consciousness without sad memory."

"You are very young to speak thus."

"But not too young to have suffered."

A wave dashed one of the steering rudders out of the grip of the sailor guiding it. The rush of water swept him overboard. The *Solon* lurched. The wind smote the straining mainsail, and the shivered mainmast tore from its stays and socket. Above the bawling of wind and water sounded the crash. The ship, with only a small sail upon the poop, blew about into the trough of the sea. A mountain of green water thundered over the prow, bearing away men and wreckage. The "governor," Brasidas's mate, flung away the last steering tiller.

"The *Solon* is dying, men," he trumpeted through his hands. "To the boat! Save who can!"

The pinnace set in the waist was cleared away by frantic hands and axes. Ominous rumblings from the hold told how the undergirding could not keep back the water. The pinnace was dragged to the ship's lee and launched in the comparative calm of the *Solon's* broadside. Pitifully small was the boat for five and twenty. The sailors, desperate and selfish, leaped in first, and watched with jealous eyes the struggles of the passengers to follow. The noisy merchant slipped in the leap, and they heard him scream once as the wave swallowed him. Brasidas stood in the bow of the pinnace, clutching a sword to cut the last rope. The boat filled to the gunwales. The spray dashed into her. The sailors bailed with their caps. Another passenger leaped across, whereat the men yelled and drew their dirks.

"Three are left. Room for one more. The rest must swim!"

Glaucon stood on the poop. Was life still such a precious thing to some that they must clutch for it so desperately? He had even a painful amusement in watching the others. Of himself he thought little save to hope that under the boiling sea was rest and no return of memory. Then Brasidas called him.

"Quick! The others are Barbarians and you a Hellene. Your chance—leap!"

He did not stir. The "others"—two strangers in Oriental dress—were striving to enter the pinnace. The seamen thrust their dirks out to force them back.

"Full enough!" bawled the "governor." "That fellow on the poop is mad. Cut the rope, or we are caught in the swirl."

The elder Barbarian lifted his companion as if to fling him into the boat, but Brasidas's sword cut the one cable. The wave flung the *Solon* and the pinnace asunder. With stolid resignation the Orientals retreated to the poop. The people in the pinnace rowed desperately to keep her out of the deadly trough of the billows, but Glaucon stood erect on the drifting wreck and his voice rang through the tumult of the sea.

"Tell them in Athens, and tell Hermione my wife, that Glaucon the Alcmæonid went down into the deep declaring his innocence and denouncing the vengeance of Athena on whosoever foully destroyed him!—"

Brasidas waved his sword in last farewell. Glaucon turned back to the wreck. The *Solon* had settled lower. Every wave washed across the waist. Nothing seemed to meet his gaze save the leaden sky, the leaden green water, the foam of the bounding storm-crests. He told himself the gods were good. Drowning was more merciful death than hemlock. Pelagos, the untainted sea, was a softer grave than the Barathrum. The memory of the fearful hour at Colonus, the vision of the face of Hermione, of all things else that he would fain forget—all these would pass. For what came after he cared nothing.

So for some moments he stood, clinging upon the poop, awaiting the end. But the end came slowly. The *Solon* was a stoutly timbered ship. Much of her lading had been cast overboard, but more remained and gave buoyancy to the wreckage. And as the Athenian awaited, almost impatiently, the final disaster, something called his eye away from the heaving sky-line. Human life was still about him. Wedged in a refuge, betwixt two capstans, the Orientals were sitting, awaiting doom like himself. But wonder of wonders,—he had not relaxed his hold on life too much to marvel,—the younger Barbarian was beyond all doubt a woman. She sat in her companion's lap, lifting her white face to his, and Glaucon knew she was of wondrous beauty. They were talking together in some Eastern speech. Their arms were closely twined. It was plain they were passing the last love messages before entering the great mystery together. Of Glaucon they took no heed. And he at first was almost angered that strangers should intrude upon this last hour of life. But as he looked, as he saw the beauty of the woman, the sheen of her golden hair, the interchange of love by touch and word,—there came across his own spirit a most unlooked-for change. Suddenly the white-capped billows seemed pitiless and chill. The warm joy of life returned. Again memory surged back, but without its former pang. He saw again the vision of Athens, of Colonus, of Eleusis-by-the-Sea. He saw Hermione running through the throng to meet him the day he returned from the Isthmia. He heard the sweet wind singing over the old olives beside the cool Cephissus. Must these all pass forever? forever? Were life, friends, love, the light of the sun, eternally lost, and nothing left save the endless sleep in the unsunned caves of Oceanus? With one surge the desire to live, to bear hard things, to conquer them, returned. He dashed the water from his eyes. What he did next was more by instinct than by reason. He staggered across the reeling deck, approached the Barbarians, and seized the man by the arm.

"Would you live and not die? Up, then,—there is still a chance."

The man gazed up blankly.

"We are in Mazda's hands," he answered in foreign accent. "It is manifestly his will that we should pass now the Chinvat bridge. We are helpless. Where is the pinnace?"

Glaucon dragged him roughly to his feet.

"I do not know your gods. Do not speak of their will to destroy us till the destruction falls. Do you love this woman?"

"Save her, let me twice perish."

"Rouse yourself, then. One hope is left!"

"What hope?"

"A raft. We can cast a spar overboard. It will float us. You look strong,—aid me."

The man rose and, thoroughly aroused, seconded the Athenian intelligently and promptly. The lurches of the merchantman told how close she was to her end. One of the seamen's axes lay on the poop. Glaucon seized it. The foremast was gone and the mainmast, but the small boat-mast still stood, though its sail had blown to a thousand flapping streamers. Glaucon laid his axe at the foot of the spar. Two fierce strokes weakened so that the next lurch sent it crashing overboard. It swung in the mælstrom by its stays and the halyards of the sail. Tossing to and fro like a bubble, it was a fearful hope, but a louder rumbling from the hold warned how other hope had fled. The Barbarian recoiled as he looked on it.

"It can never float through this storm," Glaucon heard him crying between the blasts, but the Athenian beckoned him onward.

"Leap!" commanded Glaucon; "spring as the mast rises on the next wave."

"I cannot forsake her," called back the man, pointing to the woman, who lay with flying hair between the capstans, helpless and piteous now that her lover was no longer near.

"I will provide for her. Leap!"

Glaucon lifted the woman in his arms. He took a manner of pride in showing the Barbarian his skill. The man looked at him once, saw he could be trusted, and took the leap. He landed in the water, but caught the sail-cloth drifting from the mast, climbed beside it, and sat astride. The Athenian sprang at the next favoring wave. His burden made the task hard, but his stadium training never stood in better stead. The cold water closed around him. The wave dragged down in its black abyss, but he struck boldly upward, was beside the friendly spar, and the Barbarian aided him to mount beside him, then cut the lashings to the *Solon* with the dagger that still dangled at his belt. The billows swept them away just as the wreck reared wildly, and bow foremost plunged into the deep. They bound the woman—she was hardly conscious now—into the little shelter formed by the junction of the broken sail-yard and the mast. The two men sat beside her, shielding her with their bodies from the beat of the spray. Speech was all but impossible. They were fain to close their eyes and pray to be delivered from the unceasing screaming of the wind, the howling of the waters. And so for hours....

Glaucon never knew how long they thus drifted. The *Solon* had been smitten very early in the morning. She had foundered perhaps at noon. It may have been shortly before sunset—though Helios never pierced the clouds that storm-racked day—when Glaucon knew that the Barbarian was speaking to him.

"Look!" The wind had lulled a little; the man could make himself heard. "What is it?"

Through the masses of gray spray and driving mist Glaucon gazed when the next long wave tossed them. A glimpse,—but the joys of Olympus seemed given with that sight; wind-swept, wave-beaten, rock-bound, that half-seen ridge of brown was land,—and land meant life, the life he had longed to fling away in the morning, the life he longed to keep that night. He shouted the discovery to his companion, who bowed his head, manifestly in prayer.

The wind bore them rapidly. Glaucon, who knew the isles of the Ægean as became a Hellene, was certain they drove on Astypalæa, an isle subject to Persia, though one of the outermost Cyclades. The woman was in no state to realize their crisis. Only a hand laid on her bosom told that her heart still fluttered. She could not endure the surge and the suffocating spray much longer. The two men sat in silence, but their eyes went out hungrily toward the stretch of brown as it lifted above the wave crests. The last moments of the desperate voyage crept by like the pangs of Tantalus. Slowly they saw unfolding the fog-clothed mountains, a forest, scattered bits of white they knew were stuccoed houses; but while their eyes brought joy, their ears brought sadness. The booming of the surf upon an outlying ledge grew ever clearer. Almost ere they knew it the drifting mast was stayed with a shock. They saw two rocks swathed in dripping weed that crusted with knife-like barnacles, thrust their black heads out of the boiling water. And beyond— fifty paces away—the breakers raced up the sandy shore where waited refuge.

The spar wedged fast in the rocks. The waves beat over it pitilessly. He who stayed by it long had better have sunk with the *Solon*,—his would have been an easier death. Glaucon laid his mouth to the man's ear.

"Swim through the surf. I will bear the woman safely."

"Save her, and be you blessed forever. I die happy. I cannot swim."

The moment was too terrible for Glaucon to feel amazed at this confession. To a Hellene swimming was second nature. He thought and spoke quickly.

"Climb on the higher rock. The wave does not cover it entirely. Dig your toes in the crevices. Cling to the seaweed. I will return for you."

He never heard what the other cried back to him. He tore the woman clear of her lashings, threw his left arm about her, and fought his way through the surf. He could swim like a Delian, the best swimmers in Hellas; but the task was mighty even for the athlete. Twice the deadly undertow almost dragged him downward. Then the soft sand was oozing round his feet. He knew a knot of fisher folk were running to the beach, a dozen hands took his fainting burden from him. One instant he stood with the water rushing about his ankles, gasped and drew long breaths, then turned his face toward the sea.

"Are you crazed?" he heard voices clamouring—they seemed a great way off,—"a miracle that you lived through the surf once! Leave the other to fate. Phorcys has doomed him already."

But Glaucon was past acting by reason now. His head seemed a ball of fire. Only his hands and feet responded mechanically to the dim impulse of his bewildered brain. Once more the battling through the surf, this time against it and threefold harder. Only the man whose strength had borne the giant Spartan down could have breasted the billows that came leaping to destroy him. He felt his powers were strained to the last notch. A little more and he knew he might roll helpless, but even so he struggled onward. Once again the two black rocks were springing out of the swollen water. He saw the Barbarian clinging desperately to the higher. Why was he risking his life for a man who was not a Hellene, who might be even a servant of the dreaded Xerxes? A strange moment for such questionings, and no time to answer! He clung to the seaweed beside the Barbarian for an instant, then through the gale cried to the other to place his hands upon his shoulders. The Oriental complied intelligently. For a third time Glaucon struggled across the raging flood. The passage seemed endless, and every receding breaker dragging down to the graves of Oceanus. The Athenian knew his power was failing, and doled it out as a miser, counting his strokes, taking deep gulps of air between each wave. Then, even while consciousness and strength seemed passing together, again beneath his feet were the shifting sands, again the voices encouraging, the hands outstretched, strange forms running down into the surf, strange faces all around him. They were bearing him and the Barbarian high upon the beach. They laid him on the hard, wet sand—never a bed more welcome. He was naked. His feet and hands bled from the tearing of stones and barnacles. His head was in fever glow. Dimly he knew the Barbarian was approaching him.

"Hellene, you have saved us. What is your name?"

The other barely raised his head. "In Athens, Glaucon the Alcmæonid, but now I am without name, without country."

The Oriental answered by kneeling on the sands and touching his head upon them close to Glaucon's feet.

"Henceforth, O Deliverer, you shall be neither nameless nor outcast. For you have saved me and her I love more than self. You have saved Artazostra, sister of Xerxes, and Mardonius, son of Gobryas, who is not the least of the Princes of Persia and Eran."

"Mardonius—arch foe of Hellas!" Glaucon spoke the words in horror. Then reaction from all he had undergone robbed him of sense. They carried him to the fisher-village. That night he burned with fever and raved wildly. It was many days before he knew anything again.

* * * * * *

Six days later a Byzantine corn-ship brought from Amorgos to Peiræus two survivors of the *Solon*,—the only ones to escape the swamping of the pinnace. Their story cleared up the mystery of the fate of "Glaucon the Traitor." "The gods," said every Agora wiseacre, "had rewarded the villain with their own hands." The Babylonish carpet-seller and Hiram had vanished, despite all search, but everybody praised Democrates for saving the state from a fearful peril. As for Hermione, her father took her to Eleusis that she might be free from the hoots of the people. Themistocles went about his business very sorrowful. Cimon lost half his gayety. Democrates, too, appeared terribly worn. "How he loved his friend!" said every admirer. Beyond doubt for long Democrates was exceeding thoughtful. Perhaps a reason for this was that about a month after the going of Glaucon he learned from Sicinnus that Prince Mardonius was at length in Sardis,—and possibly Democrates knew on what vessel the carpet-seller had taken flight.

BOOK II
THE COMING OF THE PERSIAN

CHAPTER XV
THE LOTUS-EATING AT SARDIS

When Glaucon awoke to consciousness, it was with a sense of absolute weakness, at the same moment with a sense of absolute rest. He knew that he was lying on pillows "softer than sleep," that the air he breathed was laden with perfume, that the golden light which came through his half-closed eyelids was deliciously tempered, that his ears caught a musical murmur, as of a plashing fountain. So he lay for long, too impotent, too contented to ask where he lay, or whence he had departed. Athens, Hermione, all the thousand and one things of his old life, flitted through his brain, but only as vague, far shapes. He was too weak even to long for them. Still the fountain plashed on, and mingling with the tinkling he thought he heard low flutes breathing. Perhaps it was only a phantasy of his flagging brain. Then his eyes opened wider. He lifted his hand. It was a task even to do that little thing,—he was so weak. He looked at the hand! Surely his own, yet how white it was, how thin; the bones were there, the blue veins, but all the strength gone out of them. Was this the hand that had flung great Lycon down? It would be mere sport for a child to master him now. He touched his face. It was covered with a thick beard, as of a long month's growth. The discovery startled him. He strove to rise on one elbow. Too weak! He sank back upon the cushions and let his eyes rove inquiringly. Never had he seen tapestries the like of those that canopied his bed. Scarlet and purple and embroidered in gold thread with elaborate hunting scenes,—the dogs, the chariots, the slaying of the deer, the bearing home of the game. He knew the choicest looms of Sidon must have wrought them. And the linen, so cool, so grateful, underneath his head—was it not the almost priceless fabric of Borsippa? He stirred a little, his eyes rested on the floor. It was covered with a rug worth an Athenian patrician's ransom,—a lustrous, variegated sheen, showing a new tint at each change of the light. So much he saw from the bed, and curiosity was wakened. Again he put forth his hand, and touched the hanging curtains. The movement set a score of little silver bells that dangled over the canopy to jingling. As at a signal the flutes grew louder, mingling with them was the clearer note of lyres. Now the strains swelled sweetly, now faded away into dreamy sighing, as if bidding the listener to sink again into the arms of sleep. Another vain effort to rise on his elbow. Again he was helpless. Giving way to the charm of the music, he closed his eyes.

"Either I am awaking in Elysium, or the gods send to me pleasant dreams before I die."

He was feebly wondering which was the alternative when a new sound roused him, the sweep and rustle of the dresses of two women as they approached the bed. He gazed forth listlessly, when lo! above his couch stood two strangers,—strangers, but either as fair as Aphrodite arising from the sea. Both were tall, and full of queenly grace, both were dressed in gauzy white, but the hair of the one was of such gold that Glaucon hardly saw the circlet which pressed over it. Her eyes were blue, the lustre of her face was like a white rose. The other's hair shone like the wing of a raven. A wreath of red poppies covered it, but over the softly tinted forehead there peered forth a golden snake with emerald eyes—the Egyptian uræus, the crown of a princess from the Nile. Her eyes were as black as the other's were blue, her lips as red as the dye of Tyre, her hands—But before Glaucon looked and wondered more, the first, she of the golden head, laid her hand upon his face,—a warm, comforting hand that seemed to speed back strength and gladness with the touch. Then she spoke. Her Greek was very broken, yet he understood her.

"Are you quite awakened, dear Glaucon?"

He looked up marvelling, not knowing how to answer; but the golden goddess seemed to expect none from him.

"It is now a month since we brought you from Astypalæa. You have wandered close to the Portals of the Dead. We feared you were beloved by Mazda too well, that you would never wake that we might bless you. Night and day have my husband and I prayed to Mithra the Merciful and Hauratât the Health-Giver in your behalf; each sunrise, at our command, the Magians have poured out for you the Haôma, the sacred juice dear to the Beautiful Immortals, and Amenhat, wisest of the physicians of Memphis, has stood by your bedside without rest. Now at last our prayers and his skill have conquered; you awake to life and gladness."

Glaucon lay wondering, not knowing how to reply, and only understanding in half, when the dark-haired goddess spoke, in purer Greek than her companion.

"And I, O Glaucon of Athens, would have you suffer me to kiss your feet. For you have given my brother and my sister back to life." Then drawing near she took his hand in hers, while the two smiling looked down on him.

Then at last he found tongue to speak. "O gracious Queens, for such you are, forgive my roving wits. You speak of great service done. But wise Zeus knoweth we are strangers—"

The golden goddess tossed her shining head and smiled,—still stroking with her hand.

"Dear Glaucon, do you remember the Eastern lad you saved from the Spartans at the Isthmus? Behold him! Recall the bracelet of turquoise,—my first gratitude. Then again you saved me with my husband. For I am the woman you bore through the surf at the island. I am Artazostra, wife of Mardonius, and this is Roxana, his half-sister, whose mother was a princess in Egypt."

Glaucon passed his fingers before his face, beckoning back the past.

"It is all far away and strange: the flight, the storm, the wreck, the tossing spar, the battling through the surges. My head is weak. I cannot picture it all."

"Do not try. Lie still. Grow strong and glad, and suffer us to teach you," commanded Artazostra.

"Where do I lie? We are not upon the rocky islet still?"

The ladies laughed, not mockingly but so sweetly he wished that they would never cease.

"This is Sardis," spoke Roxana, bending over him; "you lie in the palace of the satrap."

"And Athens—" he said, wandering.

"Is far away," said Artazostra, "with all its griefs and false friends and foul remembrances. The friends about you here will never fail. Therefore lie still and have peace."

"You know my story," cried he, now truly in amaze.

"Mardonius knows all that passes in Athens, in Sparta, in every city of Hellas. Do not try to tell more. We weary you already. See—Amenhat comes to bid us begone."

The curtains parted again. A dark man in a pure white robe, his face and head smooth-shaven, approached the bed. He held out a broad gold cup, the rim whereof glinted with agate and sardonyx. He had no Greek, but Roxana took the cup from him and held it to Glaucon's lips.

"Drink," she commanded, and he was fain to obey. The Athenian felt the heavily spiced liquor laying hold of him. His eyes closed, despite his wish to gaze longer on the two beautiful women. He felt their hands caressing his cheeks. The music grew ever softer. He thought he was sinking into a kind of euthanasy, that his life was drifting out amid delightful dreams. But not cold Thanatos, but health-bearing Hypnos was the god who visited him now. When next he woke, it was with a clearer vision, a sounder mind.

* * * * * *

Sardis the Golden, once capital of the Lydian kings and now of the Persian satraps, had recovered from the devastation by the Ionians in their ill-starred revolt seventeen years preceding. The city spread in the fertile Sardiene, one of the garden plains of Asia Minor. To the south the cloud-crowned heights of Tmolus ever were visible. To the north flowed the noble stream of Hebrus, whilst high above the wealthy town, the busy agora, the giant temple of Lydian Cybele, rose the citadel of Meles, the palace fortress of the kings and the satraps. A frowning castle it was without, within not the golden-tiled palaces of Ecbatana and Susa boasted greater magnificence and luxury than this one-time dwelling of Crœsus. The ceilings of the wide banqueting halls rose on pillars of emerald Egyptian malachite. The walls were cased with onyx. Winged bulls that might have graced Nineveh guarded the portals. The lions upbearing the throne in the hall of audience were of gold. The mirrors in the "House of the Women" were not steel but silver. The gorgeous carpets were sprinkled with rose water. An army of dark Syrian eunuchs and yellow-faced Tartar girls ran at the beck of the palace guests. Only the stealthy entrance of Sickness and Death told the dwellers here they were not yet gods.

Artaphernes, satrap of Lydia, had his divan, his viziers, and his audiences,— a court worthy of a king,—but the real lord of Western Asia was the prince who was nominally his guest. Mardonius had his own retinue and wing of the palace. On him fell the enormous task of organizing the masses of troops already pouring into Sardis, and he discharged his duty unwearyingly. The completion of the bridges of boats across the Hellespont, the assembling of the fleet, the collecting of provisions, fell to his province. Daily a courier pricked into Sardis with despatches from the Great King to his trusted general. Mardonius left the great levees and public spectacles to Artaphernes, but his hand was everywhere. His decisions were prompt. He was in constant communication with the Medizing party in Hellas. He had no time for the long dicing and drinking bouts the Persians loved, but he never failed to find each day an hour to spend with Artazostra his wife, with Roxana his half-sister, and with Glaucon his preserver.

Slowly through the winter health had returned to the Athenian. For days he had lain dreaming away the hours to the tune of the flutes and the fountains. When the warm spring came, the eunuchs carried him in a sedan-chair through the palace garden, whence he could look forth on the plain, the city, the snow-clad hills, and think he was on Zeus's Olympian throne, surveying all the earth. Then it was he learned the Persian speech, and easily, for were not his teachers Artazostra and Roxana? He found it no difficult tongue, simple and much akin to Greek, and unlike most of the uncouth tongues the

Oriental traders chattered in Sardis. The two women were constantly with him. Few men were admitted to a Persian harem, but Mardonius never grudged the Greek the company of these twain.

"Noble Athenian," said the Prince, the first time he visited Glaucon's bed, "you are my brother. My house is yours. My friends are yours. Command us all."

* * * * * * *

Every day Glaucon was stronger. He tested himself with dumb-bells. Always he could lift a heavier weight. When the summer was at hand, he could ride out with Mardonius to the "Paradise," the satrap's hunting park, and be in at the death of the deer. Yet he was no more the "Fortunate Youth" of Athens. Only imperfectly he himself knew how complete was the severance from his old life. The terrible hour at Colonus had made a mark on his spirit which not all Zeus's power could take away. No doubt all the one-time friends believed him dead. Had Hermione's confidence in him remained true? Would she not say "guilty" at last with all the rest? Mardonius might have answered, he had constant letters from Greece, but the Prince was dumb when Glaucon strove to ask of things beyond the Ægean.

Day by day the subtle influence of the Orient—the lotus-eating,—"tasting the honey-sweet fruit which makes men choose to abide forever, forgetful of the homeward way"—spread its unseen power over the Alcmæonid. Athens, the old pain, even the face of Hermione, would rise before him only dimly. He fought against this enchantment. But it was easier to renew his vow to return to Athens, after wiping out his shame, than to break these bands daily tightening.

He heard little Greek, now that he was learning Persian. Even he himself was changed. His hair and beard grew long, after the Persian manner. He wore the loose Median cloak, the tall felt cap of a Persian noble. The elaborate genuflexions of the Asiatics no longer astonished him. He learned to admire the valiant, magnanimous lords of the Persians. And Xerxes, the distant king, the wielder of all this power, was he not truly a god on earth, vicegerent of Lord Zeus himself?

"Forget you are a Hellene. We will talk of the Nile, not of the Cephissus," Artazostra said, whenever he spoke of home. Then she would tell of Babylon and Persepolis, and Mardonius of forays beside the wide Caspian, and Roxana of her girlhood, while Gobryas was satrap of Egypt, spent beside the magic river, of the Pharaohs, the great pyramid, of Isis and Osiris and the world beyond the dead. Before the Athenian was opened the golden East, its glitter, its wonderment, its fascination. He even was silent when his hosts talked boldly of the coming war, how soon the Persian power would rule from the Pillars of Heracles to Ind.

Yet once he stood at bay, showing that he was a Hellene still. They were in the garden. Mardonius had come to them where under the pomegranate tree the women spread their green tapestry which their nimble needles covered with a battle scene in scarlet. The Prince told of the capture and crucifixion of the chiefs of a futile revolt in Armenia. Then Artazostra clapped her hands to cry.

"Fools! Fools whom Angra-Mainyu the Evil smites blind that he may destroy them!"

Glaucon, sitting at her feet, looked up quickly. "Valiant fools, lady; every man must strike for his own country."

Artazostra shook her shining head.

"Mazda gives victory to the king of Eran alone. Resisting Xerxes is not rebellion against man, it is rebellion against Heaven."

"Are you sure?" asked the Athenian, his eye lighting ominously. "Are yours the greatest gods?"

But Roxana in turn cast down the tapestry and opened her arms with a charming gesture.

"Be not angry, Glaucon, for will you not become one with us? I dare to prophesy like a seer from old Chaldea. Assur of Nineveh, Marduk of Babylon, Baal of Tyre, Ammon of Memphis—all have bent the knee to Mazda the Glorious, to Mithra the Fiend-Smiting, and shall the weak *dævas*, the puny gods of Greece, save their land, when greater than they bow down in sore defeat?"

Yet Glaucon still looked on her boldly.

"You have your mighty gods, but we have ours. Pray to your Mazda and Mithra, but we will still trust Zeus of the Thunders and Athena of the Gray Eyes, the bulwarks of our fathers. And Fate must answer which can help the best."

The Persians shook their heads. It was time to return to the palace. All that Glaucon had seen of the Barbarian's might, since awakening in Sardis, told him Xerxes was indeed destined to go forth conquering and to conquer. Then the vision of the Acropolis, the temples, the Guardian Goddess, returned. He banished all disloyal thoughts for the instant. The Prince walked with his wife, Glaucon with Roxana. He had always thought her beautiful; she had never seemed so beautiful as now. Did he imagine whither Mardonius perhaps was leading him?

CHAPTER XVI
THE COMING OF XERXES THE GOD-KING

At last the lotus-eating ended. Repeated messengers told how Xerxes was quitting Babylon, was holding a muster in Cappadocia, and now was crossing Asia Minor toward Sardis. Mardonius and his companions had returned to that capital. Daily the soldiery poured into Sardis by tens of thousands. Glaucon knew now it was not a vain boast that for ten years the East had been arming against Hellas, that the whole power of the twenty satrapies would be flung as one thunderbolt upon devoted Greece.

In the plain about Sardis a second city was rising, of wicker booths and gay pavilions. The host grew hourly. Now a band of ebony archers in leopard skins entered from far Ethiopia, now Bactrian battle-axemen, now yellow-faced Tartars from the northeast, now bright-turbaned Arabs upon their swaying camels,—Syrians, Cilicians, black-bearded Assyrians and Babylonians, thick-lipped Egyptians, came, and many a strange race more.

But the core of the army were the serried files of Aryan horse and foot,—blond-headed, blue-eyed men, Persians and Medes, veterans of twenty victories. Their muscles were tempered steel. Their unwearying feet had tramped many a long parasang. Some were light infantry with wicker shields and powerful bows, but as many more horsemen in gold-scaled armour and with desert steeds that flew like Pegasus.

"The finest cavalry in the world!" Mardonius vaunted, and his guest durst not answer nay.

Satrap after satrap came. When at last a foaming Arab galloping to the castle proclaimed, "Next morn the Lord of the World will enter Sardis," Glaucon could scarce have looked for a greater, though he had expected Cronian Zeus himself.

Mardonius, as "bow-bearer to the king," a semi-regal office, rode forth a stage to meet the sovran. The streets of Sardis were festooned with flowers. Thousands of spearmen held back the crowds. The Athenian stood beside Roxana and Artazostra at the upper window of a Lydian merchant prince, and his eyes missed nothing.

Never had the two women seemed lovelier than when their hearts ran out to their approaching king. He felt now the power of personal sovranty, how these children of the East awaited not Xerxes the Master, but Xerxes the Omnipotent, God-Manifest, whose decrees were as the decrees of Heaven. And their awe could not fail to awe the Athenian.

At noon the multitude caught the first token of the king. Down the road, through the gate, walked a man, bare-headed, bare-footed, alone,—Artaphernes, despot of all Lydia, going to pay his abject homage. Presently the eunuch priests of Cybele, perched above the gate, clashed their cymbals and raised their hymn of welcome. To the boom of drums the thousand chosen cavalry and as many picked footmen of the Life Guard entered, tall, magnificent soldiers,—caps and spear butts shining with gold. After these a gilded car drawn by the eight sacred horses, each milk-white, and on the car an altar bearing the eternal fire of Mazda. Then, each in his flashing chariot, moved the "Six Princes," the heads of the great clans of the Achæmenians, then two hundred led desert horses, in splendid trappings, and then—after a long interval, that the host might cast no dust upon its lord, rode a single horseman on a jet-black steed, Artabanus—the king's uncle and vizier. He beckoned to the people.

"Have fear, Lydians, the giver of breath to all the world comes now beneath your gates!"

The lines of soldiers flung down their spears and dropped upon their knees. The multitude imitated. A chariot came running behind four of the sacred steeds of Nisæa,—their coats were like new snow, their manes braided with gold thread, bridle, bits, pole, baseboard, shone with gems and the royal metal. The wheel was like the sun. A girl-like youth guided the crimson reins, a second held the tall green parasol. Its shadow did not hide the commanding figure upon the car. Glaucon looked hard. No mistaking—Xerxes was here, the being who could say to millions "Die!" and they perished like worms; in verity "God-Manifest."

For in looks Xerxes, son of Darius, was surely the Great King. A figure of august height was set off nobly by the flowing purple caftan and the purple cap which crowned the curling black hair. The riches of satrapies were in the rubies and topazes on sword sheath and baldric. The head was raised. The face was not regular, but of a proud, aquiline beauty. The skin was olive, the eyes dark, a little pensive. If there were weak lines about the mouth, the curling beard covered them. The king looked straight on, unmoved by the kneeling thousands, but as he came abreast of the balcony, chance made him look upward. Perhaps the sight of the beautiful Greek caused Xerxes to smile winsomely. The smile of a god can intoxicate. Caught away from himself, Glaucon the Alcmæonid joined in the great salvo of cheering.

"Victory to Xerxes! Let the king of kings reign forever!"

The chariot was gone almost instantly, a vast retinue—cooks, eunuchs, grooms, hunters, and many closed litters bearing the royal concubines—followed, but all these passed before Glaucon shook off the spell the sight of royalty cast on him.

* * * * * * *

That night in the palace Xerxes gave a feast in honour of the new campaign. The splendours of a royal banquet in the East need no retelling. Silver lamps, carpets of Kerman rugs or of the petals of fresh roses, a thousand lutes and dulcimers, precious Helbon wine flowing like water, cups of Phœnician crystal, tables groaning with wild boars roasted whole, dancing women none too modest,—these were but the incidentals of a gorgeous confusion. To Glaucon, with the chaste loveliness of the Panathenæa before his mind, the scene was one of vast wonderment but scarcely of pleasure. The Persian did nothing by halves. In battle a hero, at his cups he became a satyr. Many of the scenes before the guests emptied the last of the tall silver tankards were indescribable.

* * * * * * *

On the high dais above the roaring hall sat Xerxes the king,—adored, envied, pitiable.

When Spitames, the seneschal, brought him the cup, the bearer bowed his face, not daring to look on his dread lord's eyes.

When Artabanus, the vizier, approached with a message, he first kissed the carpet below the dais.

When Hydarnes, commander of the Life Guard, drew near to receive the watchword for the night, he held his mantle before his mouth, lest his breath pollute the world monarch.

Yet of all forms of seeming prosperity wherewith Fate can curse a man, the worst was the curse of Xerxes. To be called "god" when one is finite and mortal; to have no friends, but only a hundred million slaves; to be denied the joys of honest wish and desire because there were none left unsatisfied; to have one's hastiest word proclaimed as an edict of deity; never to be suffered to confess a mistake, cost what the blunder might, that the "king of kings" might seem lifted above all human error; in short, to be the bondsman of one's own deification,—this was the hard captivity of the lord of the twenty satrapies.

For Xerxes the king was a man,—of average instincts, capacities, goodness, wickedness. A god or a genius could have risen above his fearful isolation. Xerxes was neither. The iron ceremonial of the Persian court left him of genuine pleasures almost none. Something novel, a rare sensation, an opportunity to vary the dreary monotony of splendour by an astounding act of generosity or an act of frightful cruelty,—it mattered little which,—was snatched at by the king with childlike eagerness. And this night Xerxes was in an unwontedly gracious mood. At his elbow, as he sat on the throne cased with lapis lazuli and onyx, waited the one man who came nearest to being a friend and not a slave,—Mardonius, son of Gobryas, the bow-bearer,—and therefore more entitled than any other prince of the Persians to stand on terms of intimacy with his lord.

While Spitames passed the wine, the king hearkened with condescending and approving nod to the report of the Prince as to his mad adventure in Hellas. Xerxes even reproved his brother-in-law mildly for hazarding his own life and that of his wife among those stiff-necked tribesmen who were so soon to taste the Aryan might.

"It was in your service, Omnipotence," the Prince was rejoining blandly; "what if not I alone, but a thousand others of the noblest of the Persians and the Medes may perish, if only the glory of their king is advanced?"

"Nobly said; you are a faithful slave, Mardonius. I will remember you when I have burned Athens."

He even reached forth and stroked the bow-bearer's hand, a condescension which made the footstool-bearer, parasol-bearer, quiver-bearer, and a dozen great lords more gnaw their lips with envy. Hydarnes, the commander who had waited an auspicious moment, now thought it safe to kneel on the lowest step of the throne.

"Omnipotence, I am constrained to tell you that certain miserable Hellenes have been seized in the camp to-night—spies sent to pry out your power. Do you deign to have them impaled, crucified, or cast into the adders' cage?"

The king smiled magnanimously.

"They shall not die. Show them the host, and all my power. Then send them home to their fellow-rebels to tell the madness of dreaming to withstand my might."

The smile of Xerxes had spread, like the ripple from a pebble splashing in a pool, over the face of every nobleman in hearing. Now their praises came as a chant.

"O Ocean of Clemency and Wisdom! Happy Eran in thy sagacious yet merciful king!"

Xerxes, not heeding, turned to Mardonius.

"Ah! yes,—you were telling how you corrupted one of the chief Athenians, then had to flee. On the voyage you were shipwrecked?"

"So I wrote to Babylon, to your Eternity."

"And a certain Athenian fugitive saved your lives? And you brought him to Sardis?"

"I did so, Omnipotence."

"Of course he is at the banquet."

"The king speaks by the promptings of Mazda. I placed him with certain friends and bade them see he did not lack good cheer."

"Send,—I would talk with him."

"Suffer me to warn your Majesty," ventured Mardonius, "he is an Athenian and glories in being of a stubborn, Persian-hating stock. I fear he will not perform due obeisance to the Great King."

"I can endure his rudeness," spoke Xerxes, for once in excellent humour; "let the 'supreme usher' bring him with full speed."

The functionary thus commanded bowed himself to the ground and hastened on his errand.

But well that Mardonius had deprecated the wrath of the monarch. Glaucon came with his head high, his manner almost arrogant. The mere fact that his boldness might cost him his life made him less bending than ever. He trod firmly upon the particular square of golden carpet at the foot of the dais which none, saving the king, the vizier, and the "Six Princes," could lawfully tread. He held his hands at his sides, firmly refusing to conceal them in his cloak, as court etiquette demanded. As he stood on the steps of the throne, he gave the glittering monarch the same familiar bow he might have awarded a friend he met in the Agora. Mardonius was troubled. The supreme usher was horrified. The master-of-punishments, ever near his chief, gazed eagerly to see if Xerxes would not touch the audacious Hellene's girdle—a sign for prompt decapitation. Only the good nature of the king prevented a catastrophe, and Xerxes was moved by two motives, pleasure at meeting a fellow-mortal who could look him in the eye without servility or fear, delight at the beautiful features and figure of the Athenian. For an instant monarch and fugitive looked face to face, then Xerxes stretched out, not his hand, but the gold tip of his ivory baton. Glaucon had wisdom enough to touch it,—a token that he was admitted to audience with the king.

"You are from Athens, beautiful Hellene," spoke Xerxes, still admiring the stranger. "I will question you. Let Mardonius interpret."

"I have learned Persian, great sir," interposed Glaucon, never waiting for the bow-bearer.

"You have done well," rejoined the smiling monarch; "yet better had you learned our Aryan manners of courtliness. No matter—you will learn them likewise in good time. Now tell me your name and parentage."

"I am Glaucon, son of Conon, of the house of the Alcmæonidæ."

"Great nobles, Omnipotence," interposed Mardonius, "so far as nobility can be reckoned among the Greeks."

"I have yet to learn their genealogies," remarked Xerxes, dryly; then he turned back to Glaucon. "And do your parents yet live, and have you any brethren?" The question was a natural one for an Oriental. Glaucon's answer came with increased pride.

"I am a child of my parent's old age. My mother is dead. My father is feeble. I have no brethren. Two older brothers I had. One fell here at Sardis, when we Athenians sacked the city. One fell victorious at Marathon, while he burned a Persian ship. Therefore I am not ashamed of their fates."

"Your tongue is bold, Hellene," said the good-natured king; "you are but a lame courtier. No matter. Tell me, nevertheless, why you churlishly refuse to do me reverence. Do you set yourself above all these princes of the Persians who bow before me?"

"Not so, great sir. But I was born at Athens, not at Susa. We Hellenes pray standing even to Zeus, stretching forth our hands and looking upward. Can I honour the lord of all the satrapies above the highest god?"

"A nimble tongue you have, Athenian, though an unbending neck." Xerxes sat and stroked his beard, pleased at the frank reply. "Mardonius has told how you saved his and my sister's lives, and that you are an outlaw from Athens."

"The last is all too true, great sir."

"Which means you will not pray your gods too hard for my defeat? ha?"

Glaucon blushed, then looked up boldly.

"A Persian king, I know, loves truth-telling. I still love and pray for Athens, even if unknown enemies conspired against me."

"Humph! You can learn our other virtues later. Are you blind to my power? If so, I pity more than I blame you."

"The king is kind," returned Glaucon, putting by a part of his hauteur. "I would not anger him. I only know he would rather have men say, 'Xerxes conquered a proud nation, hard to subdue,' than, 'He conquered a feeble race of whining slaves.'"

"Excellent! In all save your vain confidence of victory, you seem wise beyond your youth. You are handsome. You are noble—"

"Very noble," interposed Mardonius.

"And you saved the lives of Mardonius and Artazostra. Did you know their nobility when you rescued them?"

"Not so. I would not let them drown like sheep."

"The better, then. You acted without low motive of reward. Yet let the day never come when Xerxes is called 'ungrateful' for benefits done his servants. You shall come to love me by beholding my magnanimity. I will make you a Persian, despite your will. Have you seen battle?"

"I was too young to bear a spear at Marathon," was the unflinching answer.

"Learn then to wield it in another army. Where is the archsecretary?"

That functionary was present instantly. Mardonius, taking the whispers of the king, dictated an order which the scribe stamped on his tablet of wet clay with a rapid stylus.

"Now the chief proclaimer," was the king's order, which brought a tall man in a bright scarlet caftan salaaming to the dais.

He took the tablet from the secretary and gave a resounding blow upon the brass gong dangling from his elbow. The clatter of wine cups ceased. The drinkers were silent on pain of death. The herald sent his proclamation in stentorian voice down the hall:—

"In the name of Xerxes the Achæmenian, king of kings, king of Persia, Media, Babylon, and Lydia; smiter of the Scythians, dominator of the Indians, terror of the Hellenes; to all peoples of the world his slaves,—hear ye!

"Says Xerxes the king, whose word changes not. Forasmuch as Glaucon the Athenian did save from death my servant and my sister, Mardonius and Artazostra, I do enroll him among the 'Benefactors of the King,' a sharer of my bounty forever. Let his name henceforth be not Glaucon, but Prexaspes. Let my purple cap be touched upon his head. Let him be given the robe of honour and the girdle of honour. Let the treasurer pay him a talent of gold. Let my servants honour him. Let those who mock at him be impaled. And this I proclaim as my decree."

What followed Glaucon was too bewildered to recall clearly. He knew that the archchamberlain lifted the great jewel-crusted hat from the king's head and set it on his own for an instant, that they brought him a flowing purple robe, and clasped about his waist a golden belt, every link set with a stone of price. The hall arose *en masse* to drink to the man whom the sovran delighted to honour.

"Hail! Thrice hail to the Lord Prexaspes! Justly rewarded by our gracious king!"

No man refused his plaudit, and Glaucon never knew how many envious courtiers cheered with their lips and in their hearts muttered dark things against "the manner in which his Majesty loved to play the god and promote this unknown Hellene above the heads of so many faithful subjects."

Glaucon had made shift to speak some words of deprecation and gratitude to royalty; his bow was deeper when the supreme usher led him away from the throne than when he approached it. As he made his way out of the banqueting hall, a score of noblemen, captains of thousands, over-eunuchs, and more trailed at his heels, salaaming, fawning, congratulating, offering all manner of service. Not on the days following his victory at the Isthmia had his head been in such a whirl. He hardly heard the well-meant warning which Artabanus, the shrewd old vizier, gave as he passed the door of the great hall.

"Play the game well, my new Lord Prexaspes. The king can make you satrap or he can crucify you. Play the game well, the stakes are high."

Neither did he hear the conversation betwixt Xerxes and the bow-bearer whilst he was being conducted away.

"Have I done well to honour this man, Mardonius?"

"Your Eternity was never more wise. Bear with his uncourtliness now, for he is truthful, upright, and noble in soul—qualities rare in a Hellene. Give me but time. I will make him a worthy Persian indeed."

"Do not fail therein," ordered the monarch, "for the youth has such beauty, both of body and mind, I am grieved he was born in Athens. Yet there is one short way to wean him from his doomed and miserable country."

"Will Omnipotence but name it?"

"Search out for him a Persian wife, no, three or four wives—although I have heard the custom of these witless Greeks is to be content with only one. There is no surer way to turn his heart than that."

"I thank your Eternity for your commandment. It shall not be forgotten."

Mardonius bowed himself. Xerxes called for more wine. The feast lasted late and ended in an orgy.

CHAPTER XVII
THE CHARMING BY ROXANA

Glaucon's longing for the old life ebbed and flowed. Sometimes the return of memory maddened him. Who had done it?—had forged that damning letter and then hid it with Seuthes? Themistocles? Impossible. Democrates?—"the friend with the understanding heart no less than a brother dear," as Homer said? More impossible. An unknown enemy, then, had stolen the fleet order from Themistocles? But what man had hated Glaucon? One answer remained,—unwittingly the athlete had offended some god, forgotten some vow, or by sheer good fortune had awakened divine jealousy. Poseidon had been implacable toward Odysseus, Athena toward Hector, Artemis toward Niobe,—Glaucon could only pray that his present welcome amongst the Persians might not draw down another outburst of Heaven's anger.

More than all else was the keen longing for Hermione. He saw her in the night. Vainly, amidst the storms of the gathering war, he had sought a messenger to Athens. In this he dared ask no help from Mardonius. Then almost from the blue a bolt fell that made him wish to tear Hermione from his heart.

A Carian slave, a trusted steward at the Athenian silver mines of Laurium, had loved his liberty and escaped to Sardis. The Persians questioned him eagerly, for he knew all the gossip of Athens. Glaucon met the runaway, who did not know then who he was, so many Greek refugees were always fluttering around the king's court. The Carian told of a new honour for Democrates.

"He is elected strategus for next year because of his proud patriotism. There is talk, too, of a more private bit of good fortune."

"What is it?"

"That he has made successful suit to Hermippus of Eleusis for his daughter,—the widow of Glaucon, the dead outlaw. They say the marriage follows at the end of the year of mourning—Sir, you are not well!"

"I was never better." But the other had turned ashen. He quitted the Carian abruptly and shut himself in his chamber. It was good that he wore no sword. He might have slain himself.

Yet, he communed in his heart, was it not best? Was he not dead to Athens? Must Hermione mourn him down to old age? And whom better could she take than Democrates, the man who had sacrificed even friendship for love of country?

Artabanus, the vizier, gave a great feast that night. They drank the pledge, "Victory to the king, destruction to his enemies." The lords all looked on Glaucon to see if he would touch the cup. He drank deeply. They applauded him. He remained long at the wine, the slaves bore him home drunken. In the morning Mardonius said Xerxes ordered him to serve in the cavalry guards, a post full of honour and chance for promotion. Glaucon did not resist. Mardonius sent him a silvered cuirass and a black horse from the steppes of Bactria,—fleet as the north wind. In his new armour he went to the chambers of Artazostra and Roxana. They had never seen him in panoply before. The brilliant mail became him rarely. The ladies were delighted.

"You grow Persian apace, my Lord Prexaspes,"—Roxana always called him by his new name now,—"soon we shall hail you as 'your Magnificence' the satrap of Parthia or Asia or some other kingly province in the East."

"I do well to become Persian," he answered bitterly, unmoved by the admiration, "for yesterday I heard that which makes it more than ever manifest that Glaucon the Athenian is dead. And whether he shall ever rise to live again, Zeus knoweth; but from me it is hid."

Artazostra did not approach, but Roxana came near, as if to draw the buckle of the golden girdle—the gift of Xerxes. He saw the turquoise shining on the tiara that bound her jet-black hair, the fine dark profile of her face, her delicate nostrils, the sweep of drapery that half revealed the form so full of grace. Was there more than passing friendship in the tone with which she spoke to him?

"You have heard from Athens?"

"Yes."

"And the tidings were evil."

"Why call them evil, princess? My friends all believe me dead. Can they mourn for me forever? They can forget me, alas! more easily than I in my lonesomeness can forget them."

"You are very lonely?"—the hand that drew the buckle worked slowly. How soft it was, how delicately the Nile sun had tinted it!

"Do you say you have no friends? None? Not in Sardis? Not among the Persians?"

"I said not that, dear lady,—but when can a man have more than one native country?—and mine is Attica, and Attica is far away."

"And you can never have another? Can new friendships never take the place of those that lie forever dead?"

"I do not know."

"Ah, believe, new home, new friends, new love, are more than possible, will you but open your heart to suffer them."

The voice both thrilled and trembled now, then suddenly ceased. The colour sprang into Roxana's forehead. Glaucon bowed and kissed her hand. It seemed to rise to his lips very willingly.

"I thank you for your fair hopes. Farewell." That was all he said, but as he went forth from Roxana's presence, the pang of the tidings brought by the Carian seemed less keen.

* * * * * * *

The hosts gathered daily. Xerxes spent his time in dicing, hunting, drinking, or amusing himself with his favourite by-play, wood-carving. He held a few solemn state councils, at which he appeared to determine all things and was actually guided by Artabanus and Mardonius. Now, at last, all the colossal machinery which was to crush down Hellas was being set in motion. Glaucon learned how futile was Themistocles's hope of succour to Athens from the Sicilian Greeks, for,—thanks to Mardonius's indefatigable diplomacy,—it was arranged that the Phœnicians of Carthage should launch a powerful armament against the Sicilians, the same moment Xerxes descended on Sparta and Athens. With calm satisfaction Mardonius watched the completion of his efforts. All was ready,—the army of hundreds of thousands, the twelve hundred war-ships, the bridges across the Hellespont, the canal at Mt. Athos. Glaucon's admiration for the son of Gobryas grew apace. Xerxes was the outward head of the attack on Hellas. Mardonius was the soul. He was the idol of the army—its best archer and rider. Unlike his peers, he maintained no huge harem of jealous concubines and conspiring eunuchs. Artazostra he worshipped. Roxana he loved. He had no time for other women. No servant of Xerxes seemed outwardly more obedient than he. Night and day he wrought for the glory of Persia. Therefore, Glaucon looked on him with dread. In him Themistocles and Leonidas would find a worthy foeman.

Daily Glaucon felt the Persian influence stealing upon him. He grew even accustomed to think of himself under his new name. Greeks were about him: Demaratus, the outlawed "half-king" of Sparta, and the sons of Hippias, late tyrant of Athens. He scorned the company of these renegades. Yet sometimes he would ask himself wherein was he better than they,—had Democrates's accusation been true, could he have asked a greater reward from the Barbarian? And what he would do on the day of battle he did not dare to ask of his own soul.

* * * * * * *

Xerxes left Sardis with the host amidst the same splendour with which he had entered. Glaucon rode in the Life Guard, and saw royalty frequently, for the king loved to meet handsome men. Once he held the stirrup as Xerxes dismounted—an honour which provoked much envious grumbling. Artazostra and Roxana travelled in their closed litters with the train of women and eunuchs which followed every Persian army. Thus the myriads rolled onward through Lydia and Mysia, drinking the rivers dry by their numbers; and across the immortal plains of Troy passed that army which was destined to do and suffer greater things than were wrought beside the poet-sung Simois and Scamander, till at last they came to the Hellespont, the green river seven furlongs wide, that sundered conquered Asia from the Europe yet to be conquered.

Here were the two bridges of ships, more than three hundred in each, held by giant cables, and which upbore a firm earthen road, protected by a high bulwark, that the horses and camels might take no fright at the water. Here, also, the fleet met them,—the armaments of the East, Phœnicians, Cilicians, Egyptians, Cyprians,—more triremes and transports than had ever before ridden upon the seas. And as he saw all this power, all directed by one will, Glaucon grew even more despondent. How could puny, faction-rent Hellas bear up against this might? Only when he looked on the myriads passing, and saw how the captains swung long whips and cracked the lash across the backs of their spearmen, as over driven cattle, did a little comfort come. For he knew there was still a fire in Athens and Sparta, a fire not in Susa nor in Babylon, which kindled free souls and free hands to dare and do great things. "Whom will the high Zeus prosper when the *slaves* of Xerxes stand face to face with *men*?"

A proud thought,—but it ceased to comfort him, as all that afternoon he stood near the marble throne of the "Lord of the World," whence Xerxes overlooked his myriads while they filed by, watched the races of swift triremes, and heard the proud assurances of his officers that "no king since the beginning of time, not Thothmes of Egypt, not Sennacherib of Assyria, not Cyrus nor Darius, had arrayed such hosts as his that day."

Then evening came. Glaucon was, after his wont, in the private pavilion of Mardonius,—itself a palace walled with crimson tapestry in lieu of marble. He sat silent and moody for long, the bright fence of the ladies or of the bow-bearer seldom moving him to answer. And at last Artazostra could endure it no more.

"What has tied your tongue, Prexaspes? Surely my brother in one of his pleasantries has not ordered that it be cut out? Your skin is too fair to let you be enrolled amongst his Libyan mutes."

The Hellene answered with a pitiful attempt at laughter.

"Silent, am I? Then silent because I am admiring your noble ladyship's play of wit."

Artazostra shook her head.

"Impossible. Your eyes were glazed like the blue of Egyptian beads. You were not listening to me. You were seeing sights and hearkening to voices far away."

"You press me hard, lady," he confessed; "how can I answer? No man is master of his roving thoughts,—at least, not I."

"You were seeing Athens. Are you so enamoured of your stony country that you believe no other land can be so fair?"

"Stony it is, lady,—you have seen it,—but there is no sun like the sun that gilds the Acropolis; no birds sing like the nightingales from the grove by the Cephissus; no trees speak with the murmur of the olives at Colonus, or on the hill slope at Eleusis-by-the-Sea. I can answer you in the words of Homer, the singer of Hellas, the words he sets on the tongue of a wanderer and outcast, even as I. 'A rugged land, yet nurse of noble men, and for myself I can see naught sweeter than a man's own country.'"

The praise of his native land had brought the colour into the cheeks of the Athenian, his voice rose to enthusiasm. He knew that Roxana was watching him intently.

"Beautiful it must be, dear Hellene," she spoke, as she sat upon the footstool below the couch of her brother, "yet you have not seen all the world. You have not seen the mystic Nile, Memphis, Thebes, and Saïs, our wondrous cities; have not seen how the sun rises over the desert, how it turns the sand hills to red gold, how at sunset the cliffs glow like walls of beryl and sard and golden jasper."

"Tell then of Egypt," said Glaucon, clearly taking pleasure in the music of her voice.

"Not to-night. I have praised it before. Rather I will praise also the rose valleys of Persia and Bactria, whither Mardonius took me after my dear father died."

"Are they very beautiful also?"

"Beautiful as the Egyptian's House of the Blessed, for those who have passed the dread bar of Osiris; beautiful as Airyana-Væya, the home land of the Aryans, whence Ahura-Mazda sent them forth. The winters are short, the summers bright and long. Neither too much rain nor burning heat. The Paradise by Sardis is nothing beside them. One breathes in the roses, and hearkens to the bulbuls—our Aryan nightingales—all day and all night long. The streams bubble with cool water. At Susa the palace is fairer than word may tell. Hither the court comes each summer from the tedious glories of Babylon. The columns of the palace reach up to heaven, but no walls engirdle them, only curtains green, white, and blue,—whilst the warm sweet breeze blows always thither from green prairies."

"You draw a picture fair as the plains of Elysium, dear lady," spoke Glaucon, his own gaze following the light that burned in hers, "and yet I would not seek refuge even in the king's court with all its beauty. There are times when I long to pray the god, 'Give to me wings, eagle wings from Zeus's own bird, and let me go to the ends of the earth, and there in some charmed valley I may find at last the spring of Lethe water, the water of forgetfulness that gives peace.'"

Roxana looked on him; pity was in her eyes, and he knew he was taking pleasure in her pitying.

"The magic water you ask is not to be drunk from goblets," she answered him, "but the charmed valley lies in the vales of Bactria, the 'Roof of the World,' high amid mountains crowned with immortal snows. Every good tree and flower are here, and here winds the mystic Oxus, the great river sweeping northward. And here, if anywhere, on Mazda's wide, green earth, can the trouble-tossed have peace."

"Then it is so beautiful?" said the Athenian.

"Beautiful," answered Mardonius and Artazostra together. And Roxana, with an approving nod from her brother, arose and crossed the tent where hung a simple harp.

"Will my Lord Prexaspes listen," she asked, "if I sing him one of the homely songs of the Aryans in praise of the vales by the Oxus? My skill is small."

"It should suffice to turn the heart of Persephone, even as did Orpheus," answered the Athenian, never taking his gaze from her.

The soft light of the swinging lamps, the heavy fragrance of the frankincense which smouldered on the brazier, the dark lustre of the singer's eyes—all held Glaucon as by a spell. Roxana struck the harp. Her voice was sweet, and more than desire to please throbbed through the strings and song.

"O far away is gliding

The pleasant Oxus's stream,

I see the green glades darkling,

I see the clear pools gleam.

I hear the bulbuls calling

From blooming tree to tree.

Wave, bird, and tree are singing,

'Away! ah, come with me!'

"By Oxus's stream is rising

Great Cyrus's marble halls;

Like rain of purest silver,

His tinkling fountain falls;

To his cool verdant arbours

What joy with thee to flee.

I'll join with bird and river,

'Away! rest there with me!'

"Forget, forget old sorrows,

Forget the dear things lost!

There comes new peace, new brightness,

When darksome waves are crossed;

By Oxus's streams abiding,

From pang and strife set free,

I'll teach thee love and gladness,—

Rest there, for aye, with me!"

The light, the fragrance, the song so pregnant with meaning, all wrought upon Glaucon of Athens. He felt the warm glow in his cheeks; he felt subtle hands outstretching as if drawing forth his spirit. Roxana's eyes were upon him as she ended. Their gaze met. She was very fair, high-born, sensitive. She was inviting him to put away Glaucon the outcast from Hellas, to become body and soul Prexaspes the Persian, "Benefactor of the King," and sharer in all the glories of the conquering race. All the past seemed slipping away from him as unreal. Roxana stood before him in her dark Oriental beauty;

Hermione was in Athens—and they were giving her in marriage to Democrates. What wonder he felt no mastery of himself, though all that day he had kept from wine?

"A simple song," spoke Mardonius, who seemed marvellously pleased at all his sister did, "yet not lacking its sweetness. We Aryans are without the elaborate music the Greeks and Babylonians affect."

"Simplicity is the highest beauty," answered the Greek, as if still in his trance, "and when I hear Euphrosyne, fairest of the Graces, sing with the voice of Erato, the Song-Queen, I grow afraid. For a mortal may not hear things too divine and live."

Roxana replaced the harp and made one of her inimitable Oriental courtesies,—a token at once of gratitude and farewell for the evening. Glaucon never took his gaze from her, until with a rustle and sweep of her blue gauze she had glided out of the tent. He did not see the meaning glances exchanged by Mardonius and Artazostra before the latter left them.

When the two men were alone, the bow-bearer asked a question.

"Dear Prexaspes, do you not think I should bless the twelve archangels I possess so beautiful a sister?"

"She is so fair, I wonder that Zeus does not haste from Olympus to enthrone her in place of Hera."

The bow-bearer laughed.

"No, I crave for her only a mortal husband. Though there are few in Persia, in Media, in the wide East, to whom I dare entrust her. Perhaps,"—his laugh grew lighter,—"I would do well to turn my eyes westward."

Glaucon did not see Roxana again the next day nor for several following, but in those days he thought much less on Hermione and on Athens.

CHAPTER XVIII
DEMOCRATES'S TROUBLES RETURN

All through that year to its close and again to the verge of springtime the sun made violet haze upon the hills and pure fire of the bay at Eleusis-by-the-Sea. Night by night the bird song would be stilled in the old olives along the dark waters. There Hermione would sit looking off into the void, as many another in like plight has sat and wearily waited, asking of the night and the sea the questions that are never answered. As the bay shimmered under the light of morning, she could gaze toward the brown crags of Salamis and the open Ægean beyond. The waves kept their abiding secret. The tall triremes, the red-sailed fishers' boats, came and went from the havens of Athens, but Hermione never saw the ship that had borne away her all.

The roar and scandal following the unmasking of Glaucon had long since abated. Hermippus—himself full five years grayer on account of the calamity—had taken his daughter again to quiet Eleusis, where there was less to remind her of that terrible night at Colonus. She spent the autumn and winter in an unbroken shadow life, with only her mother and old Cleopis for companions. Reasons not yet told to the world gave her a little hope and comfort. But in mere desire to make her dark cloud break, her parents were continually giving Hermione pain. She guessed it long before her father's wishes passed beyond vaguest hints. She heard him praising Democrates, his zeal for Athens and Hellas, his fair worldly prospects, and there needed no diviner to reveal Hermippus's hidden meaning. Once she overheard Cleopis talking with another maid.

"Her Ladyship has taken on terribly, to be sure, but I told her mother 'when a fire blazes too hot, it burns out simply the faster.' Democrates is just the man to console in another year."

"Yes," answered the other wiseacre, "she's far too young and pretty to stay unwedded very long. Aphrodite didn't make her to sit as an old maid carding wool and munching beans. One can see Hermippus's and Lysistra's purpose with half an eye."

"Cleopis, Nania, what is this vile tattling that I hear?"

The young mistress's eyes blazed fury. Nania turned pale. Hermione was quite capable of giving her a sound whipping, but Cleopis mustered a bold front and a ready lie:

"*Ei!* dear little lady, don't flash up so! I was only talking with Nania about how Phryne the scullion maid was making eyes at Scylax the groom."

"I heard you quite otherwise," was the nigh tremulous answer. But Hermione was not anxious to push matters to an issue. From the moment of Glaucon's downfall she had believed—what even her own mother had mildly derided—that Democrates had been the author of her husband's ruin. And now that the intent of her parents ever more clearly dawned on her, she was close upon despair. Hermippus, however,—whatever his purpose,—was considerate, nay kindly. He regarded Hermione's feelings as pardonable, if not laudable. He would wait for time to soothe her. But the consciousness that her father purposed such a fate for her, however far postponed, was enough to double all the unanswered longing, the unstilled pain.

Glaucon was gone. And with him gone, could Hermione's sun ever rise again? Could she hope, across the end of the æons, to clasp hands even in the dim House of Hades with her glorious husband? If there was chance thereof, dark Hades would grow bright as Olympus. How gladly she would fare out to the shade land, when Hermes led down his troops of helpless dead.

"Downward, down the long dark pathway,

Past Oceanus's great streams,

Past the White Rock, past the Sun's gates

Downward to the land of Dreams:

There they reach the wide dim borders

Of the fields of asphodel,

Where the spectres and the spirits

Of wan, outworn mortals dwell."

But was this the home of Glaucon the Fair; should the young, the strong, the pure in heart, share one condemnation with the mean and the guilty? Homer the Wise left all hid. Yet he told of some not doomed to the common lot. Thus ran the promise to Menelaus, espoused to Helen.

"Far away the gods shall bear you:

To the fair Elysian plains,

Where the time fleets gladly, swiftly,

Where bright Rhadamanthus reigns:

Snow is not, nor rain, nor winter,

But clear zephyrs from the west,

Singing round the streams of Ocean

Round the islands of the Blest."

Was the pledge for Menelaus only?

The boats came, the boats went, on the blue bay. But as the spring grew warm, Hermione thought less of them, less almost of the last dread vision of Glaucon.

* * * * * * *

The cloud of the Persian hung ever darkening over Athens. Continual rumours made Xerxes's power terrible even beyond fact. It was hard to go on eating, drinking, frequenting the jury or the gymnasium, when men knew to a certainty the coming summer would bring Athens face to face with slavery or destruction. Wise men grew silent. Fools took to carousing to banish care. But one word not the frailest uttered—"submission." Worldly prudence forbade that. The women would have stabbed the craven to death with their bodkins. For the women were braver than the men. They knew the fate of conquered Ionia: for the men only merciful death, for the women the living death of the Persian harems and indignities words may not utter. Whether Hellas forsook her or aided, Athens had chosen her fate. Xerxes might annihilate her. Conquer her he could not.

Yet the early spring came back sweetly as ever. The warm breeze blew from Egypt. Philomela sang in the olive groves. The snows on Pentelicus faded. Around the city ran bands of children singing the "swallow's song," and beseeching the spring donation of honey cakes:—

"She is here, she is here, the swallow;

Fair seasons bringing,—fair seasons to follow."

And many a housewife, as she rewarded the singers, dropped a silent tear, wondering whether another spring would see the innocents anywhere save in a Persian slave-pen, or, better fate, in Orchus.

Yet to one woman that spring there came consolation. On Hermippus's door hung a glad olive wreath. Hermione had borne a son. "The fairest babe she had ever seen," cried the midwife. "Phœnix," the mother called him, "for in him shall Glaucon the Beautiful live again." Democrates sent a runner every day to Eleusis to inquire for Hermione until all danger was passed. On the "name-day," ten days after the birth, he was absent from the gathering of friends and kinsmen, but sent a valuable statuette to Hermione, who left it, however, to her father to thank him.

The day after Phœnix was born old Conon, Glaucon's father, died. The old man had never recovered from the blow given by the dishonourable death of the son with whom he had so lately quarrelled. He left a great landed estate at Marathon to his new-born grandson. The exact value thereof Democrates inquired into sharply, and when a distant cousin talked of contesting the will, the orator announced he would defend the infant's rights. The would-be plaintiff withdrew at once, not anxious to cross swords with this favourite of the juries, and everybody said that Democrates was showing a most scrupulous regard for his unfortunate friend's memory.

Indeed, seemingly, Democrates ought to have been the happiest man in Athens. He had been elected "strategus," to serve on the board of generals along with Themistocles. He had plenty of money, and gave great banquets to this or that group of prominent citizens. During the winter he had asked Hermippus for his daughter in marriage. The Eumolpid told him that since Glaucon's fearful end, he was welcome as a son-in-law. Still he could not conceal that Hermione never spoke of him save in hate, and in view of her then delicate condition it was well not to press the matter. The orator had seemed well content. "Woman's fantasies would wear away in time." But the rumour of this negotiation, outrunning truth, grew into the lying report of an absolute betrothal,—the report which was to drift to Asia and turn Glaucon's heart to stone, gossip having always wrought more harm than malignant lying.

Yet flies were in Democrates's sweet ointment. He knew Themistocles hardly trusted him as frankly as of yore. Little Simonides, a man of wide influence and keen insight, treated him very coldly. Cimon had cooled also. But worse than all was a haunting dread. Democrates knew, if hardly another in Hellas, that the Cyprian—in other words Mardonius—was safe in Asia, and likewise that he had fled on the *Solon*. Mardonius, then, had escaped the storm. What if the same miracle had saved the outlaw? What if the dead should awake? The chimera haunted Democrates night and day.

Still he was beginning to shake off his terrors. He believed he had washed his hands fairly clean of his treason, even if the water had cost his soul. He joined with all his energies in seconding Themistocles. His voice was loudest at the Pnyx, counselling resistance. He went on successful embassies to Sicyon and Ægina to get pledges of alliance. In the summer he did his uttermost to prepare the army which Themistocles and Evænetus the Spartan led to defend the pass of Tempē. The expedition sailed amid high hopes for a noble defence of Hellas. Democrates was proud and sanguine. Then, like a thunderbolt, there came one night a knock at his door. Bias led to his master no less a visitor than the sleek and smiling Phœnician—Hiram.

The orator tried to cover his terrors by windy bluster. He broke in before the Oriental could finish his elaborate salaam.

"Of all the harpies and gorgons you are the least welcome. Were you not warned when you fled Athens for Argos never to show your face in Attica again?"

"Your Excellency said so," was the bland reply.

"Admirably you obey it. It remains for me to reward the obedience. Bias, go to the street; summon two Scythian watchmen."

The Thracian darted out. Hiram simply stood with hands folded.

"It is well, Excellency, the lad is gone. I have many things to say in confidence to your Nobility. At Lacedæmon my Lord Lycon was gracious enough to give certain commands for me to transmit to you."

"Commands? To me? Earth and gods! am I to be commanded by an adder like you? You shall pay for this on the rack."

"Your slave thinks otherwise," observed Hiram, humbly. "If your Lordship will deign to read this letter, it will save your slave many words and your Lordship many cursings."

He knelt again before he offered a papyrus. Democrates would rather have taken fire, but he could not refuse. And thus he read:—

"Lycon of Lacedæmon to Democrates of Athens, greeting:—Can he who Medizes in the summer Hellenize in the spring? I know your zeal for Themistocles. Was it for this we plucked you back from exposure and ruin? Do then as Hiram bids you, or repay the money you clutched so eagerly. Fail not, or rest confident all the documents you betrayed shall go to Hypsichides the First Archon, your enemy. Use then your eloquence on Attic juries! But you will grow wise; what need of me to threaten? You will hearken to Hiram.

"From Sparta, on the festival of Bellerophon, in the ephorship of Theudas.— *Chaire!*"

Democrates folded the papyrus and stood long, biting his whitened lips in silence. Perhaps he had surmised the intent of the letter the instant Hiram extended it.

"What do you desire?" he said thickly, at last.

"Let my Lord then hearken—" began the Phœnician, to be interrupted by the sudden advent of Bias.

"The Scythians are at the door, *kyrie*," he was shouting; "shall I order them in and drag this lizard out by the tail?"

"No, in Zeus's name, no! Bid them keep without. And do you go also. This honest fellow is on private business which only I must hear."

Bias slammed the door. Perhaps he stood listening. Hiram, at least, glided nearer to his victim and spoke in a smooth whisper, taking no chances of an eavesdropper.

"Excellency, the desire of Lycon is this. The army has been sent to Tempē. At Lacedæmon Lycon used all his power to prevent its despatch, but

Leonidas is omnipotent to-day in Sparta, and besides, since Lycon's calamity at the Isthmia, his prestige, and therefore his influence, is not a little abated. Nevertheless, the army must be recalled from Tempē."

"And the means?"

"Yourself, Excellency. It is within your power to find a thousand good reasons why Themistocles and Evænetus should retreat. And you will do so at once, Excellency."

"Do not think you and your accursed masters can drive me from infamy to infamy. I can be terrible if pushed to bay."

"Your Nobility has read Lycon's letter," observed the Phœnician, with folded arms.

There was a sword lying on the tripod by which Democrates stood; he regretted for all the rest of his life that he had not seized it and ended the snakelike Oriental then and there. The impulse came, and went. The opportunity never returned. The orator's head dropped down upon his breast.

"Go back to Sparta, go back instantly," he spoke in a hoarse whisper. "Tell that Polyphemus you call your master there that I will do his will. And tell him, too, that if ever the day comes for vengeance on him, on the Cyprian, on you,—my vengeance will be terrible."

"Your slave's ears hear the first part of your message with joy,"—Hiram's smile never grew broader,—"the second part, which my Lord speaks in anger,—I will forget."

"Go! go!" ordered the orator, furiously. He clapped his hands. Bias reëntered.

"Tell the constables I don't need them. Here is an obol apiece for their trouble. Conduct this man out. If he comes hither again, do you and the other slaves beat him till there is not a whole spot left on his body."

Hiram's genuflexion was worthy of Xerxes's court.

"My Lord, as always," was his parting compliment, "has shown himself exceeding wise."

Thus the Oriental went. In what a mood Democrates passed the remaining day needs only scant wits to guess. Clearer, clearer in his ears was ringing Æschylus's song of the Furies. He could not silence it.

"With scourge and with ban

We prostrate the man

Who with smooth-woven wile

And a fair-facèd smile

Hath planted a snare for his friend!

Though fleet, we shall find him;

Though strong, we shall bind him,

Who planted a snare for his friend!"

He had intended to be loyal to Hellas,—to strive valiantly for her freedom,—and now! Was the Nemesis coming upon him, not in one great clap, but stealthily, finger by finger, cubit by cubit, until his soul's price was to be utterly paid? Was this the beginning of the recompense for the night scene at Colonus?

The next morning he made a formal visit to the shrine of the Furies in the hill of Areopagus. "An old vow, too long deferred in payment, taken when he joined in his first contest on the Bema," he explained to friends, when he visited this uncanny spot.

Few were the Athenians who would pass that cleft in the Areopagus where the "Avengers" had their grim sanctuary without a quick motion of the hands to avert the evil eye. Thieves and others of evil conscience would make a wide circuit rather than pass this abode of Alecto, Megæra, and Tisiphone, pitiless pursuers of the guilty. The terrible sisters hounded a man through life, and after death to the judgment bar of Minos. With reason, therefore, the guilty dreaded them.

Democrates had brought the proper sacrifices—two black rams, which were duly slaughtered upon the little altar before the shrine and sprinkled with sweetened water. The priestess, a gray hag herself, asked her visitor if he would enter the cavern and proffer his petition to the mighty goddesses. Leaving his friends outside, the orator passed through the door which the priestess seemed to open in the side of the cave. He saw only a jagged, unhewn cranny, barely tall enough for a man to stand upright and reaching far into the sculptured rock. No image: only a few rough votive tablets set up by a grateful suppliant for some mercy from the awful goddesses.

"If you would pray here, *kyrie*," said the hag, "it is needful that I go forth and close the door. The holy Furies love the dark, for is not their home in Tartarus?"

She went forth. As the light vanished, Democrates seemed buried in the rock. Out of the blackness spectres were springing against him. From a cleft he heard a flapping, a bat, an imprisoned bird, or Alecto's direful wings. He held his hands downward, for he had to address infernal goddesses, and prayed in haste.

"O ye sisters, terrible yet gracious, give ear. If by my offerings I have found favour, lift from my heart this crushing load. Deliver me from the fear of the blood guilty. Are ye not divine? Do not the immortals know all things? Ye know, then, how I was tempted, how sore was the compulsion, and how life and love were sweet. Then spare me. Give me back unhaunted slumber. Deliver me from Lycon. Give my soul peace,—and in reward, I swear it by the Styx, by Zeus's own oath, I will build in your honour a temple by your sacred field at Colonus, where men shall gather to reverence you forever."

But here he ceased. In the darkness moved something white. Again a flapping. He was sure the white thing was Glaucon's face. Glaucon had perished at sea. He had never been buried, so his ghost was wandering over the world, seeking vainly for rest. It all came to Democrates in an instant. His knees smote together; his teeth chattered. He sprang back upon the door and forced it open, but never saw the dove that fluttered forth with him.

"A hideous place!" he cried to his waiting friends. "A man must have a stronger heart than mine to love to tarry after his prayer is finished."

Only a few days later Hellas was startled to hear that Tempē had been evacuated without a blow, and the pass left open to Xerxes. It was said Democrates, in his ever commendable activity, had discovered at the last moment the mountain wall was not as defensible as hoped, and any resistance would have been disastrous. Therefore, whilst the retreat was bewailed, everybody praised the foresight of the orator. Everybody—one should say, except two, Bias and Phormio. They had many conferences together, especially after the coming and going of Hiram.

"There is a larger tunny in the sea than yet has entered the meshes," confessed the fishmonger, sorely puzzled, after much vain talk.

But Hermione was caring for none of these things. Her hands were busy with the swaddling clothes. Her thoughts only for that wicker cradle which swung betwixt the pillars, where Hermippus's house looked toward Salamis.

CHAPTER XIX

THE COMMANDMENT OF XERXES

It is easy to praise the blessings of peace. Still easier to paint the horrors of war,—and yet war will remain for all time the greatest game at which human wits can play. For in it every form of courage, physical and moral, and every talent are called into being. If war at once develops the bestial, it also develops as promptly the heroic. Alone of human activities it demands a brute's strength, an iron will, a serpent's intellect, a lion's courage—all in one. And of him who has these things in justest measure, history writes, "He conquered." It was because Mardonius seemed to possess all these, to foresee everything, to surmount everything, that Glaucon despaired for the fate of Hellas, even more than when he beheld the crushing armaments of the Persian.

Yet for long it seemed as if the host would march even to Athens without battle, without invoking Mardonius's skill. The king crossed Thrace and Macedonia, meeting only trembling hospitality from the cities along his route. At Doriscus he had held a review of his army, and smiled when the fawning scribes told how one million seven hundred thousand foot and eighty thousand horse followed his banners.[8] Every fugitive and spy from southern Hellas told how the hearts of the stanchest patriots were sinking, how everywhere save in Athens and Sparta loud voices urged the sending of "earth and water,"—tokens of submission to the irresistible king. At the pass of Tempē covering Thessaly, Glaucon, who knew the hopes of Themistocles, had been certain the Hellenes would make a stand. Rumour had it that ten thousand Greek infantry were indeed there, and ready for battle. But the outlaw's expectations were utterly shattered. To the disgust of the Persian lords, who dearly loved brisk fighting, it was soon told how the cowardly Hellenes had fled by ship, leaving the rich plains of Thessaly bare to the invader.

Thus was blasted Glaucon's last hope. Hellas was doomed. He almost looked to see Themistocles coming as ambassador to bring the homage of Athens. Since his old life seemed closed to the outlaw, he allowed Mardonius to have his will with him,—to teach him to act, speak, think, as an Oriental. He even bowed himself low before the king, an act rewarded by being commanded one evening to play at dice with majesty itself. Xerxes was actually gracious enough to let his new subject win from him three handsome Syrian slave-boys.

"You Hellenes are becoming wise," announced the monarch one day, when the Locrian envoys came with their earth and water. "If you can learn to speak the truth, you will equal even the virtues of the Aryans."

"Your Majesty has not found me a liar," rejoined the Athenian, warmly.

"You gather our virtues apace. I must consider how I can reward you by promotion."

"The king is overwhelmingly generous. Already I fear many of his servants mutter that I am promoted beyond all desert."

"Mutter? mutter against you?" The king's eyes flashed ominously. "By Mazda, it is against me, then, who advanced you! Hearken, Otanes,"—he addressed the general of the Persian footmen, who stood near by,—"who are the disobedient slaves who question my advancement of Prexaspes?"

The general—he had been the loudest grumbler—bowed and kissed the carpet.

"None, your Eternity; on the contrary, there is not one Aryan in the host who does not rejoice the king has found so noble an object for his godlike bounty."

"You hear, Prexaspes," said Xerxes, mollified. "I am glad, for the man who questions my wisdom touching your advancement must be impaled. To-morrow is my birthday, you will not fail to sit with the other great lords at the banquet."

"The king overpowers me with his goodness."

"Do not fail to deserve it. Mardonius is always praising you. Consider also how much better it is to depend on a gracious king than on the clamour of the fickle mob that rules in your helpless cities!"

* * * * * *

The next morning was the royal birthday. The army, pitched in the fertile plain by Thessalian Larissa, feasted on the abundance at hand. The king distributed huge largesses of money. All day long he sat in his palace-like tent, receiving congratulations from even the lowest of his followers, and bound in turn not to reject any reasonable petition. The Magi sacrificed blooded stallions and rare spices to Mithra the "Lord of Wide Pastures," to Vohu-Manu the "Holy Councillor," and all their other angels, desiring them to bless the arms of the king.

The "Perfect Banquet" of the birthday came in the evening. It hardly differed from the feast at Sardis. The royal pavilion had its poles plated with silver, the tapestries were green and purple, the couches were spread with gorgeous coverlets. Only the drinking was more moderate, the ceremonial less rigid. The fortunate guests devoured dainties reserved for the special use of royalty:

the flour of the bread was from Assos, the wine from Helbon, the water to dilute the wine had come in silver flasks from the Choaspes by Susa. The king even distributed the special unguent of lion's fat and palm wine which no subject, unpermitted, could use and shun the death penalty.

Then at the end certain of the fairest of the women came and danced unveiled before the king—this one night when they might show forth their beauty. And last of all danced Roxana. She danced alone; a diaphanous drapery of pink Egyptian cotton blew around her as an evening cloud. From her black hair shone the diamond coronet. To the sensuous swing of the music she wound in and out before the king and his admiring lords, advancing, retreating, rising, swaying, a paragon of agility and grace, feet, body, hands, weaving their charm together. When at the end she fell on her knees before the king, demanding whether she had done well, the applause shook the pavilion. The king looked down on her, smiling.

"Rise, sister of Mardonius. All Eran rejoices in you to-night. And on this evening whose request can I fail to grant? Whose can I grant more gladly than yours? Speak; you shall have it, though it be for half my kingdoms."

The dancer arose, but hung down her flashing coronal. Her blush was enchanting. She stood silent, while the good-humoured king smiled down on her, till Artazostra came from her seat by Mardonius and whispered in her ear. Every neck in the crowded pavilion was craned as Artazostra spoke to Xerxes.

"May it please my royal brother, this is the word of Roxana. 'I love my brother Mardonius; nevertheless, contrary to the Persian custom, he keeps me now to my nineteenth year unwedded. If now I have found favour in the sight of the king, let him command Mardonius to give me to some noble youth who shall do me honour by the valiant deeds and the true service he shall render unto my Lord.'"

"A fair petition! Let the king grant it!" shouted twenty; while others more wise whispered, "This was not done without foreknowledge by Mardonius."

Xerxes smiled benignantly and rubbed his nose with the lion's fat while deliberating.

"An evil precedent, lady, an evil precedent when women demand husbands and do not wait for their fathers' or brothers' good pleasure. But I have promised. The word of the king is not to be broken. Daughter of Gobryas, your petition is granted. Come hither, Mardonius,"—the bow-bearer approached the throne,—"you have heard the bold desire of your sister, and my answer. I must command you to bestow on her a husband."

The bow-bearer bowed obediently.

"I hear the word of the king, and all his mandates are good. This is no meet time for marriage festivities, when the Lord of the World and all the Aryan power goes forth to war. Yet as soon as the impious rebels amongst the Hellenes shall be subdued, I will rejoice to bestow my sister upon whatsoever fortunate servant the king may deign to honour."

"You hear him, lady,"—the royal features assumed a grin, which was reflected throughout the pavilion. "A husband you shall have, but Mardonius shall be revenged. Your fate is in my hands. And shall not I,—guardian of the households of my empire,—give a warning to all bold maidens against lifting their wills too proudly, or presuming upon an overindulgent king? What then shall be just punishment?" The king bent his head, still rubbing his nose, and trying to persuade all about that he was meditating.

"Bardas, satrap of Sogandia, is old; he has but one eye; they say he beats his eleven wives daily with a whip of rhinoceros hide. It would be just if I gave him this woman also in marriage. What think you, Hydarnes?"

"If your Eternity bestows this woman on Bardas, every husband and father in all your kingdoms will applaud your act," smiled the commander.

The threatened lady fell again on her knees, outstretching her hands and beseeching mercy,—never a more charming picture of misery and contrition.

"You tremble, lady," went on the sovran, "and justly. It were better for my empire if my heart were less hard. After all, you danced so elegantly that I must be mollified. There is the young Prince Zophyrus, son of Datis the general,—he has only five wives already. True, he is usually the worse for wine, is not handsome, and killed one of his women not long since because she did not sing to please him. Yes—you shall have Zophyrus—he will surely rule you—"

"Mercy, not Zophyrus, gracious Lord," pleaded the abject Egyptian.

The king looked down on her, with a broader grin than ever.

"You are very hard to please. I ought to punish your wilfulness by some dreadful doom. Do not cry out again. I will not hear you. My decision is fixed. Mardonius shall bestow you in marriage to a man who is not even a Persian by birth, who one year since was a disobedient rebel against my power, who even now contemns and despises many of the good customs of the Aryans. Hark, then, to his name. When Hellas is conquered, I command that Mardonius wed you to the Lord Prexaspes."

The king broke into an uproarious laugh, a signal for the thousand loyal subjects within the great pavilion to roar with laughter also. In the confusion following Artazostra and Roxana disappeared. Fifty hands dragged the appointed bridegroom to the king, showering on him all manner of congratulations. Xerxes's act was a plain proof that he was adopting the beautiful Hellene as one of his personal favourites,—a post of influence and honour not to be despised by a vizier. What "Prexaspes" said when he thanked the king was drowned in the tumult of laughing and cheering. The monarch, delighted to play the gracious god, roared his injunctions to the Athenian so loud that above the din they heard him.

"You will bridle her well, Prexaspes. I know them—those Egyptian fillies! They need a hard curb and the lash at times. Beware the tyranny of your own harem. I would not have the satrapies know how certain bright eyes in the seraglio can make the son of Darius play the fool. There is nothing more dangerous than women. It will take all your courage to master them. A hard task lies before you. I have given you one wife, but you know our good Persian custom—five, ten, or twenty. Take the score, I order you. Then in twelve years you'll be receiving the prize a Persian king bestows every summer on the father of the most children!"

And following this broad hint, the king held his sides with laughter again, a mirth which it is needless to say was echoed and reëchoed till it seemed it could not cease. Only a few ventured to mutter under breath: "The Hellene will have a subsatrapy in the East before the season is over and a treasure of five thousand talents! Mithra wither the upstart!"

* * * * * *

The summer was waning when the host moved southward from Larissa, for mere numbers had made progress slow, and despite Mardonius's providence the question of commissariat sometimes became difficult. Now at last, leaving behind Thrace and Macedonia, the army began to enter Greece itself. As it fared across the teeming plains of Thessaly, it met only welcome from the inhabitants and submissions from fresh embassies. Report came from the fleet—keeping pace with the land army along the coasts—that nowhere had the weak squadrons of the Greeks adventured a stand. Daily the smile of the Lord of the World grew more complacent, as his "table-companions" told him: "The rumour of your Eternity's advent stupefies the miserable Hellenes. Like Atar, the Angel of Fire, your splendour glitters afar. You will enter Athens and Sparta, and no sword leave its sheath, no bow its wrapper."

Every day Mardonius asked of Glaucon, "Will your Hellenes fight?" and the answer was ever more doubting, "I do not know."

Long since Glaucon had given up hope of the defeat of the Persian. Now he prayed devoutly there might be no useless shedding of blood. If only he could turn back and not behold the humiliation of Athens! Of the fate of the old-time friends—Democrates, Cimon, Hermione—he tried not to think. No doubt Hermione was the wife of Democrates. More than a year had sped since the flight from Colonus. Hermione had put off her mourning for the yellow veil of a bride. Glaucon prayed the war might bring her no new sorrow, though Democrates, of course, would resist Persia to the end. As for himself he would never darken their eyes again. He was betrothed to Roxana. With her he would seek one of those valleys in Bactria which she had praised, the remoter the better, and there perhaps was peace.

Thus the host wound through Thessaly, till before them rose, peak on peak, the jagged mountain wall of Othrys and Œta, fading away in violet distance, the bulwark of central Hellas. Then the king's smile became a frown, for the Hellenes, undismayed despite his might, were assembling their fleet at northern Eubœa, and at the same time a tempest had shattered a large part of the royal navy. The Magi offered sacrifice to appease Tishtrya, the Prince of the Wind-ruling Stars, but the king's frown grew blacker at each message. Glaucon was near him when at last the monarch's thunders broke forth.

A hot, sultry day. The king's chariot had just crossed the mountain stream of the Sphercus, when a captain of a hundred came galloping, dismounted, and prostrated himself in the dust.

"Your tidings?" demanded Xerxes, sharply.

"Be gracious, Fountain of Mercy,"—the captain evidently disliked his mission,—"I am sent from the van. We came to a place where the mountains thrust down upon the sea and leave but a narrow road by the ocean. Your slaves found certain Hellenes, rebels against your benignant government, holding a wall and barring all passage to your army."

"And did you not forthwith seize these impudent wretches and drag them hither to be judged by me?"

"Compassion, Omnipotence,"—the messenger trembled,—"they seemed sturdy, well-armed rogues, and the way was narrow and steep where a score can face a thousand. Therefore, your slave came straight with his tidings to the ever gracious king."

"Dog! Coward!" Xerxes plucked the whip from the charioteer's hand and lashed it over the wretch's shoulders. "By the *fravashi*, the soul of Darius my father, no man shall bring so foul a word to me and live!"

"Compassion, Omnipotence, compassion!" groaned the man, writhing like a worm. Already the master-of-punishments was approaching to cover his face with a towel, preparatory to the bow-string, but the royal anger spent itself just enough to avert a tragedy.

"Your life is forfeit, but I am all too merciful! Take then three hundred stripes on the soles of your feet and live to be braver in the future."

"A thousand blessings on your benignity," cried the captain, as they led him away, "I congratulate myself that insignificant as I am the king yet deigns to notice my existence even to recompense my shortcomings."

"Off," ordered the bristling monarch, "or you die the death yet. And do you, Mardonius, take Prexaspes, who somewhat knows this country, spur forward, and discover who are the madmen thus earning their destruction."

The command was obeyed. Glaucon galloped beside the Prince, overtaking the marching army, until as they cantered into the little mud-walled city of Heraclea a second messenger from the van met them with further details.

"The pass is held by seven thousand Grecian men-at-arms. There are no Athenians. There are three hundred come from Sparta."

"And their chief?" asked Glaucon, leaning eagerly.

"Is Leonidas of Lacedæmon."

"Then, O Mardonius," spoke the Athenian, with a throb in his voice not there an hour ago. "There will be battle."

So, whether wise men or mad, the Hellenes were not to lay down their arms without one struggle, and Glaucon knew not whether to be sorry or to be proud.

CHAPTER XX
THERMOPYLÆ

A rugged mountain, an inaccessible morass, and beyond that morass the sea: the mountain thrusting so close upon the morass as barely to leave space for a narrow wagon road. This was the western gate of Thermopylæ. Behind the narrow defile the mountain and swamp-land drew asunder; in the still scanty opening hot springs gushed forth, sacred to Heracles, then again on the eastern side Mt. Œta and the impenetrable swamp drew together, forming the second of the "Hot Gates,"—the gates which Xerxes must unlock if he would continue his march to Athens.

The Great King's couriers reported that the stubborn Hellenes had cast a wall across the entrance, and that so far from showing terror at the advent of majesty, were carelessly diverting themselves by athletic games, and by combing and adorning their hair, a fact which the "Lord Prexaspes" at least comprehended to mean that Leonidas and his Spartans were preparing for desperate battle. Nevertheless, it was hard to persuade the king that at last he confronted men who would resist him to his face. Glaucon said it. Demaratus, the outlawed Spartan, said it. Xerxes, however, remained angry and incredulous. Four long days he and his army sat before the pass, "because," announced his couriers, "he wishes in his benignity to give these madmen a chance to flee away and shun destruction;" "because," spoke those nearest to Mardonius, the brain of the army, "there is hot fighting ahead, and the general is resolved to bring up the picked troops in the rear before risking a battle."

Then on the fifth day either Xerxes's patience was exhausted or Mardonius felt ready. Strong regiments of Median infantry were ordered to charge Leonidas's position, Xerxes not failing to command that they slay as few of the wretches as possible, but drag them prisoners before his outraged presence.

A noble charge. A terrible repulse. For the first time those Asiatics who had forgotten Marathon discovered the overwhelming superiority that the sheathing of heavy armour gave the Greek hoplites over the lighter armed Median spearmen. The short lances and wooden targets of the attackers were pitifully futile against the long spears and brazen shields of the Hellenes. In the narrow pass the vast numbers of Barbarians went for nothing. They could not use their archers, they could not charge with their magnificent cavalry. The dead lay in heaps. The Medes attacked again and again. At last an end came to their courage. The captains laid the lash over their mutinous troops. The men bore the whips in sullen silence. They would not charge again upon those devouring spears.

White with anger, Xerxes turned to Hydarnes and his "Immortals," the infantry of the Life Guard. The general needed no second bidding. The charge was driven home with magnificent spirit. But what the vassal Medes could not accomplish, neither could the lordly Persians. The repulse was bloody. If once Leonidas's line broke and the Persians rushed on with howls of triumph, it was only to see the Hellenes' files close in a twinkling and return to the onset with their foes in confusion. Hydarnes led back his men at last. The king sat on the ivory throne just out of arrow shot, watching the ebb and flow of the battle. Hydarnes approached and prostrated himself.

"Omnipotence, I the least of your slaves put my life at your bidding. Command that I forfeit my head, but my men can do no more. I have lost hundreds. The pass is not to be stormed."

Only the murmur of assent from all the well-tried generals about the throne saved Hydarnes from paying the last penalty. The king's rage was fearful; men trembled to look on him. His words came so thick, the rest could never follow all his curses and commands. Only Mardonius was bold enough to stand up before his face.

"Your Eternity, this is an unlucky day. Is it not sacred to Angra-Mainyu the Evil? The arch-Magian says the holy fire gives forth sparks of ill-omen. Wait, then, till to-morrow. Verethraghna, the Angel of Victory, will then return to your servants."

The bow-bearer led his trembling master to the royal tent, and naught more of Xerxes was seen till the morning. All that night Mardonius never slept, but went unceasingly the round of the host preparing for battle. Glaucon saw little of him. The Athenian himself had been posted among the guard of nobles directly about the person of the king, and he was glad he was set nowhere else, otherwise he might have been ordered to join in the attack. Like every other in the host, he slept under arms, and never returned to Mardonius's pavilion. His heart had been in his eyes all that day. He had believed Leonidas would be swept from the pass at the first onset. Even he had underrated the Spartan prowess. The repulse of the Medes had astonished him. When Hydarnes reeled back, he could hardly conceal his joy. The Hellenes were fighting! The Hellenes were conquering! He forgot he stood almost at Xerxes's side when the last charge failed; and barely in time did he save himself from joining in the shout of triumph raised by the defenders when the decimated Immortals slunk away. He had grown intensely proud of his countrymen, and when he heard the startled Persian lords muttering dark forbodings of the morrow, he all but laughed his gladness in their faces.

So the night passed for him: the hard earth for a bed, a water cruse wrapped in a cloak for a pillow. And just as the first red blush stole over the green

Malian bay and the mist-hung hills of Eubœa beyond, he woke with all the army. Mardonius had used the night well. Chosen contingents from every corps were ready. Cavalrymen had been dismounted. Heavy masses of Assyrian archers and Arabian slingers were advanced to prepare for the attack by overwhelming volleys. The Persian noblemen, stung to madness by their king's reproaches and their own sense of shame, bound themselves by fearful oaths never to draw from the onset until victorious or dead. The attack itself was led by princes of the blood, royal half-brothers of the king. Xerxes sat again on the ivory throne, assured by every obsequious tongue that the sacred fire gave fair omens, that to-day was the day of victory.

The attack was magnificent. For an instant its fury seemed to carry the Hellenes back. Where a Persian fell two stepped over him. The defenders were swept against their wall. The Barbarians appeared to be storming it. Then like the tide the battle turned. The hoplites, locking shields, presented an impenetrable spear hedge. The charge spent itself in empty promise. Mardonius, who had been in the thickest, nevertheless drew off his men skilfully and prepared to renew the combat.

In the interval Glaucon, standing by the king, could see a short, firm figure in black armour going in and out among the Hellenes, ordering their array— Leonidas—he needed no bird to tell him. And as the Athenian stood and watched, saw the Persians mass their files for another battering charge, saw the Great King twist his beard whilst his gleaming eyes followed the fate of his army, an impulse nigh irresistible came over him to run one short bow-shot to that opposite array, and cry in his own Greek tongue:—

"I am a Hellene, too! Look on me come to join you, to live and die with you, with my face against the Barbarian!"

Cruel the fate that set him here, impotent, when on that band of countrymen Queen Nikē was shedding bright glory!

But he was "Glaucon the Traitor" still, to be awarded the traitor's doom by Leonidas. Therefore the "Lord Prexaspes" must stand at his post, guarding the king of the Aryans.

The second charge was as the first, the third was as the second. Mardonius was full of recourses. By repeated attacks he strove to wear the stubborn Hellenes down. The Persians proved their courage seven times. Ten of them died gladly, if their deaths bought that of a single foe. But few as were Leonidas's numbers, they were not so few as to fail to relieve one another at the front of the press,—which front was fearfully narrow. And three times, as his men drifted back in defeat, Xerxes the king "leaped from the throne whereon he sat, in anguish for his army."

At noon new contingents from the rear took the place of the exhausted attackers. The sun beat down with unpitying heat. The wounded lay sweltering in their agony whilst the battle roared over them. Mardonius never stopped to count his dead. Then at last came nightfall. Man could do no more. As the shadows from Œta grew long over the close scene of combat, even the proudest Persians turned away. They had lost thousands. Their defeat was absolute. Before them and to westward and far away ranged the jagged mountains, report had it, unthreaded by a single pass. To the eastward was only the sea,—the sea closed to them by the Greek fleet at the unseen haven of Artemisium. Was the triumph march of the Lord of the World to end in this?

Xerxes spoke no word when they took him to his tent that night, a sign of indescribable anger. Fear, humiliation, rage—all these seemed driving him mad. His chamberlains and eunuchs feared to approach to take off his golden armour. Mardonius came to the royal tent; the king, with curses he had never hurled against the bow-bearer before, refused to see him. The battle was ended. No one was hardy enough to talk of a fresh attack on the morrow. Every captain had to report the loss of scores of his best. As Glaucon rode back to Mardonius's tents, he overheard two infantry officers:—

"A fearful day—the bow-bearer is likely to pay for it. I hope his Majesty confines his anger only to him."

"Yes—Mardonius will walk the Chinvat bridge to-morrow. The king is turning against him. Megabyzus is the bow-bearer's enemy, and already is gone to his Majesty to say that it is Mardonius's blunders that have brought the army to such a plight. The king will catch at that readily."

At the tents Glaucon found Artazostra and Roxana. They were both pale. The news of the great defeat had been brought by a dozen messengers. Mardonius had not arrived. He was not slain, that was certain, but Artazostra feared the worst. The proud daughter of Darius found it hard to bear up.

"My husband has many enemies. Hitherto the king's favour has allowed him to mock them. But if my brother deserts him, his ruin is speedy. Ah! Ahura-Mazda, why hast Thou suffered us to see this day?"

Glaucon said what he could of comfort, which was little. Roxana wept piteously; he was fain to soothe her by his caress,—something he had never ventured before. Artazostra was on the point of calling her eunuchs and setting forth for Xerxes's tent to plead for the life of her husband, when suddenly Pharnuches, Mardonius's body-servant, came with news that dispelled at least the fears of the women.

"I am bidden to tell your Ladyships that my master has silenced the tongues of his enemies and is restored to the king's good favor. And I am bidden also to command the Lord Prexaspes to come to the royal tent. His Majesty has need of him."

Glaucon went, questioning much as to the service to be required. He did not soon forget the scene that followed. The great pavilion was lit by a score of resinous flambeaux. The red light shook over the green and purple hangings, the silver plating of the tent-poles. At one end rose the golden throne of the king; before it in a semicircle the stools of a dozen or more princes and commanders. In the centre stood Mardonius questioning a coarse-featured, ill-favoured fellow, who by his sheepskin dress and leggings Glaucon instantly recognized as a peasant of this Malian country. The king beckoned the Athenian into the midst and was clearly too eager to stand on ceremony.

"Your Greek is better than Mardonius's, good Prexaspes. In a matter like this we dare not trust too many interpreters. This man speaks the rough dialect of his country, and few can understand him. Can you interpret?"

"I am passing familiar with the Locrian and Malian dialect, your Majesty."

"Question this man further as to what he will do for us. We have understood him but lamely."

Glaucon proceeded to comply. The man, who was exceeding awkward and ill at ease in such august company, spoke an outrageous shepherd's jargon which even the Athenian understood with effort. But his business came out speedily. He was Ephialtes, the son of one Eurydemus, a Malian, a dull-witted grazier of the country, brought to Mardonius by hope of reward. The general, partly understanding his purpose, had brought him to the king. In brief, he was prepared, for due compensation, to lead the Persians by an almost unknown mountain path over the ridge of Œta and to the rear of Leonidas's position at Thermopylæ, where the Hellenes, assailed front and rear, would inevitably be destroyed.

As Glaucon interpreted, the shout of relieved gladness from the Persian grandees made the tent-cloths shake. Xerxes's eyes kindled. He clapped his hands.

"Reward? He shall have ten talents! But where? How?"

The man asserted that the path was easy and practicable for a large body of troops. He had often been over it with his sheep and goats. If the Persians would start a force at once—it was already quite dark—they could fall upon Leonidas at dawn. The Spartan would be completely trapped, or forced to open the defile without another spear thrust.

"A care, fellow," warned Mardonius, regarding the man sharply; "you speak glibly, but if this is a trick to lead a band of the king's servants to destruction, understand you play with deadly dice. If the troops march, you shall have your hands knotted together and a soldier walking behind to cut your throat at the first sign of treachery."

Glaucon interpreted the threat. The man did not wince.

"There is no trap. I will guide you."

That was all they could get him to say.

"And do not the Hellenes know of this mountain path and guard it?" persisted the bow-bearer.

Ephialtes thought not; at least if they had, they had not told off any efficient detachment to guard it. Hydarnes cut the matter short by rising from his stool and casting himself before the king.

"A boon, your Eternity, a boon!"

"What is it?" asked the monarch.

"The Immortals have been disgraced. Twice they have been repulsed with ignominy. The shame burns hot in their breasts. Suffer them to redeem their honour. Suffer me to take this man and all the infantry of the Life Guard, and at dawn the Lord of the World shall see his desire over his miserable enemies."

"The words of Hydarnes are good," added Mardonius, incisively, and Xerxes beamed and nodded assent.

"Go, scale the mountain with the Immortals and tell this Ephialtes there await him ten talents and a girdle of honour if the thing goes well; if ill, let him be flayed alive and his skin be made the head of a kettledrum."

The stolid peasant did not blench even at this. Glaucon remained in the tent, translating and hearing all the details: how Hydarnes was to press the attack from the rear at early dawn, how Mardonius was to conduct another onset from the front. At last the general of the guard knelt before the king for the last time.

"Thus I go forth, Omnipotence, and to-morrow, behold your will upon your enemies, or behold me never more."

"I have faithful slaves," said Xerxes, rising and smiling benignantly upon the general and the bow-bearer. "Let us disperse, but first let command be given the Magians to cry all night to Mithra and Tishtrya, and to sacrifice to them a white horse."

"Your Majesty always enlists the blessings of heaven for your servants," bowed Mardonius, as the company broke up and the king went away to his inner tent and his concubines. Glaucon lingered until most of the grandees had gone forth, then the bow-bearer went to him.

"Go back to my tents," ordered Mardonius; "tell Artazostra and Roxana that all is well, that Ahura has delivered me from a great strait and restored me to the king's favour, and that to-morrow the gate of Hellas will be opened."

"You are still bloody and dusty. You have watched all last night and been in the thick all day," expostulated the Athenian; "come to the tents with me and rest."

The bow-bearer shook his head.

"No rest until to-morrow, and then the rest of victory or a longer one. Now go; the women are consuming with their care."

Glaucon wandered back through the long avenues of pavilions. The lights of innumerable camp-fires, the hum of thousands of voices, the snorting of horses, the grumbling of camels, the groans of men wounded—all these and all other sights and sounds from the countless host were lost to him. He walked on by a kind of animal instinct that took him to Mardonius's encampment through the mazes of the canvas city. It was dawning on him with a terrible clearness that he was become a traitor to Hellas in very deed. It was one thing to be a passive onlooker of a battle, another to be a participant in a plot for the ruin of Leonidas. Unless warned betimes the Spartan king and all who followed him infallibly would be captured or slaughtered to a man. And he had heard all—the traitor, the discussion, the design—had even, if without his choice, been partner and helper in the same. The blood of Leonidas and his men would be on his head. Every curse the Athenians had heaped on him once unjustly, he would deserve. Now truly he would be, even in his own mind's eyes, "Glaucon the Traitor, partner to the betrayal of Thermopylæ." The doltish peasant, lured by the great reward, he might forgive,—himself, the high-born Alcmæonid, never.

From this revery he was shaken by finding himself at the entrance to the tents of Mardonius. Artazostra and Roxana came to meet him. When he told of the deliverance of the bow-bearer, he had joy by the light in their eyes. Roxana had never shone in greater beauty. He spoke of the heat of the sun, of his throbbing head. The women bathed his forehead with lavender-water, touching him with their own soft hands. Roxana sang again to him, a low, crooning song of the fragrant Nile, the lotus bells, the nodding palms, the perfumed breeze from the desert. Whilst he watched her through half-closed eyes, the visions of that day of battles left him. He sat wrapped in a dream world, far from stern realities of men and arms. So for a while, as he lounged on the divans, following the play of the torch-light on the face of Roxana as her long fingers plied the strings. What was it to him if Leonidas fought a losing battle? Was not his happiness secure—be it in Hellas, or Egypt, or Bactria? He tried to persuade himself thus. At the end, when he and Roxana stood face to face for the parting, he violated all Oriental custom, yet he knew her brother would not be angry. He took her in his arms and gave her kiss for kiss.

Then he went to his own tent to seek rest. But Hypnos did not come for a long time with his poppies. Once out of the Egyptian's presence the haunting terror had returned, "Glaucon the Traitor!" Those three words were always uppermost. At last, indeed, sleep came and as he slept he dreamed.

CHAPTER XXI
THE THREE HUNDRED—AND ONE

As Glaucon slept he found himself again in Athens. He was on the familiar way from the cool wrestling ground of the Academy and walking toward the city through the suburb of Ceramicus. Just as he came to the three tall pine trees before the gate, after he had passed the tomb of Solon, behold! a fair woman stood in the path and looked on him. She was beyond mortal height and of divine beauty, yet a beauty grave and stern. Her gray eyes cut to his heart like swords. On her right hand hovered a winged Victory, on her shoulder rested an owl, at her feet twined a wise serpent, in her left hand she bore the ægis, the shaggy goat-skin engirt with snakes—emblem of Zeus's lightnings. Glaucon knew that she was Athena Polias, the Warder of Athens, and lifted his hands to adore her. But she only looked on him in silent anger. Fire seemed leaping from her eyes. The more Glaucon besought, the more she turned away. Fear possessed him. "Woe is me," he trembled, "I have enraged a terrible immortal." Then suddenly the woman's countenance was changed. The ægis, the serpent, the Victory, all vanished; he saw Hermione before him, beautiful as on the day she ran to greet him at Eleusis, yet sad as was his last sight of her the moment he fled from Colonus. Seized with infinite longing, he sprang to her. But lo! she drifted back as into the air. It was even as when Odysseus followed the shade of his mother in the shadowy Land of the Dead.

"Yearned he sorely then to clasp her,

Thrice his arms were opened wide:

From his hands so strong, so loving,

Like a dream she seemed to glide,

And away, away she flitted,

Whilst he grasped the empty space,

And a pain shot through him, maddening,

As he strove for her embrace."

He pursued, she drifted farther, farther. Her face was inexpressibly sorrowful. And Glaucon knew that she spoke to him.

"I have believed you innocent, though all Athens calls you 'traitor.' I have been true to you, though all men rise up against me. In what manner have you kept your innocence? Have you had love for another, caresses for another, kisses for another? How will you prove your loyalty to Athens and return?"

"Hermione!" Glaucon cried, not in his dream, but quite aloud. He awoke with a start. Outside the tent sentry was calling to sentry, changing the watch just before the dawning. It was perfectly plain to him what he must do. His dream had only given shape to the ferment in his brain, a ferment never ceasing while his body slept. He must go instantly to the Greek camp and warn Leonidas. If the Spartan did not trust him, no matter, he had done his duty. If Leonidas slew him on the spot, again no matter, life with an eternally gnawing conscience could be bought on too hard terms. He knew, as though Zeus's messenger Iris had spoken it, that Hermione had never believed him guilty, that she had been in all things true to him. He could never betray her trust.

His head now was clear and calm. He arose, threw on his cloak, and buckled about his waist a short sword. The Nubian boy that Mardonius had given him for a body-servant awoke on his mat, and asked wonderingly "whither his Lordship was going?" Glaucon informed him he must be at the front before daybreak, and bade him remain behind and disturb no one. But the Athenian was not to execute his design unhindered. As he passed out of the tent and into the night, where the morning stars were burning, and where the first red was creeping upward from the sea, two figures glided forth from the next pavilion. He knew them and shrank from them. They were Artazostra and Roxana.

"You go forth early, dearest Prexaspes," spoke the Egyptian, throwing back her veil, and even in the starlight he saw the anxious flash of her eyes, "does the battle join so soon that you take so little sleep?"

"It joins early, lady," spoke Glaucon, his wits wandering. In the intensity of his purpose he had not thought of the partings with the people he must henceforth reckon foes. He was sorely beset, when Roxana drew near and laid her hand upon his shoulder.

"Your Greeks will resist terribly," she spoke. "We women dread the battle more than you. Yours is the fierce gladness of the combat, ours only the waiting, the heavy tidings, the sorrow. Therefore Artazostra and I could not sleep, but have been watching together. You will of course be near Mardonius my brother. You will guard him from all danger. Leonidas will resist fearfully when at bay. Ah! what is this?"

In pressing closer she had discovered the Athenian wore no cuirass.

"You will not risk the battle without armour?" was her cry.

"I shall not need it, lady," answered he, and only half conscious what he did, stretched forth as if to put her away. Roxana shrank back, grieved and wondering, but Artazostra seized his arm quickly.

"What is this, Prexaspes? All is not well. Your manner is strange!"

He shook her off, almost savagely.

"Call me not Prexaspes," he cried, not in Persian, but in Greek. "I am Glaucon of Athens; as Glaucon I must live, as Glaucon die. No man—not though he desire it—can disown the land that bore him. And if I dreamed I was a Persian, I wake to find myself a Greek. Therefore forget me forever. I go to my own!"

"Prexaspes, my lover,"—Roxana, strong in fear and passion, clung about his girdle, while again Artazostra seized him,—"last night I was in your arms. Last night you kissed me. Are we not to be happy together? What is this you say?"

He stood one instant silent, then shook himself and put them both aside with a marvellous ease.

"Forget my name," he commanded. "If I have given you sorrow, I repent it. I go to my own. Go you to yours. My place is with Leonidas—to save him, or more like to die with him! Farewell!"

He sprang away from them. He saw Roxana sink upon the ground. He heard Artazostra calling to the horse-boys and the eunuchs,—perhaps she bade them to pursue. Once he looked back, but never twice. He knew the watchwords, and all the sentries let him pass by freely. With a feverish stride he traced the avenues of sleeping tents. Soon he was at the outposts, where strong divisions of Cissian and Babylonian infantrymen were slumbering under arms, ready for the attack the instant the uproar from the rear of the pass told how Hydarnes had completed his circuit. Eos—"Rosy-Fingered Dawn"—was just shimmering above the mist-hung peak of Mt. Telethrius in Eubœa across the bay when Glaucon came to the last Persian outpost.

The pickets saluted with their lances, as he went by them, taking him for a high officer on a reconnoissance before the onset. Next he was on the scene of the former battles. He stumbled over riven shields, shattered spear butts, and many times over ghastlier objects—objects yielding and still warm— dead men, awaiting the crows of the morrow. He walked straight on, while the dawn strengthened and the narrow pass sprang into view, betwixt mountain and morass. Then at last a challenge, not in Persian, but in round clear Doric.

"Halt! Who passes?"

Glaucon held up his right hand, and advanced cautiously. Two men in heavy armour approached, and threatened his breast with their lance points.

"Who are you?"

"A friend, a Hellene—my speech tells that. Take me to Leonidas. I've a story worth telling."

"*Euge!* Master 'Friend,' our general can't be waked for every deserter. We'll call our decarch."

A shout brought the subaltern commanding the Greek outposts. He was a Spartan of less sluggish wits than many of his breed, and presently believed Glaucon when he declared he had reason in asking for Leonidas.

"But your accent is Athenian?" asked the decarch, with wonderment.

"Ay, Athenian," assented Glaucon.

"Curses on you! I thought no Athenian ever Medized. What business had *you* in the Persian camp? Who of your countrymen are there save the sons of Hippias?"

"Not many," rejoined the fugitive, not anxious to have the questions pushed home.

"Well, to Leonidas you shall go, sir Athenian, and state your business. But you are like to get a bearish welcome. Since your pretty Glaucon's treason, our king has not wasted much love even on repentant traitors."

With a soldier on either side, the deserter was marched within the barrier wall. Another encampment, vastly smaller and less luxurious than the Persian, but of martial orderliness, spread out along the pass. The Hellenes were just waking. Some were breakfasting from helmets full of cold boiled peas, others buckled on the well-dinted bronze cuirasses and greaves. Men stared at Glaucon as he was led by them.

"A deserter they take to the chief," ran the whisper, and a little knot of idle Spartans trailed behind, when at last Glaucon's guides halted him before a brown tent barely larger than the others.

A man sat on a camp chest by the entrance, and was busy with an iron spoon eating "black broth"[2] from a huge kettle. In the dim light Glaucon could just see that he wore a purple cloak flung over his black armour, and that the helmet resting beside him was girt by a wreath of gold foil.

The two guards dropped their spears in salute. The man looked upward.

"A deserter," reported one of Glaucon's mentors; "he says he has important news."

"Wait!" ordered the general, making the iron spoon clack steadily.

"The weal of Hellas rests thereon. Listen!" pleaded the nervous Athenian.

"Wait!" was the unruffled answer, and still the iron spoon went on plying. The Spartan lifted a huge morsel from the pot, chewed it deliberately, then put the vessel by. Next he inspected the newcomer from head to toe, then at last gave his permission.

"Well?"

Glaucon's words were like a bursting torrent.

"Fly, your Excellency! I'm from Xerxes's camp. I was at the Persian council. The mountain path is betrayed. Hydarnes and the guard are almost over it. They will fall upon your rear. Fly, or you and all your men are trapped!"

"Well," observed the Spartan, slowly, motioning for the deserter to cease, but Glaucon's fears made that impossible.

"I say I was in Xerxes's own tent. I was interpreter betwixt the king and the traitor. I know all whereof I say. If you do not flee instantly, the blood of these men is on your head."

Leonidas again scanned the deserter with piercing scrutiny, then flung a question.

"Who are you?"

The blood leaped into the Athenian's cheeks. The tongue that had wagged so nimbly clove in his mouth. He grew silent.

"Who are you?"

As the question was repeated, the scrutiny grew yet closer. The soldiers were pressing around, one comrade leaning over another's shoulder. Twenty saw the fugitive's form straighten as he stood in the morning twilight.

"I am Glaucon of Athens, Isthmionices!"

"Ah!" Leonidas's jaw dropped for an instant. He showed no other astonishment, but the listening Spartans raised a yell.

"Death! Stone the traitor!"

Leonidas, without a word, smote the man nearest to him with a spear butt. The soldiers were silent instantly. Then the chief turned back to the deserter.

"Why here?"

Glaucon had never prayed for the gifts of Peitho, "Our Lady Persuasion," more than at that crucial moment. Arguments, supplications, protestations of innocence, curses upon his unknown enemies, rushed to his lips together. He hardly realized what he himself said. Only he knew that at the end the soldiers did not tug at their hilts as before and scowl so threateningly, and Leonidas at last lifted his hand as if to bid him cease.

"*Euge!*" grunted the chief. "So you wish me to believe you a victim of fate, and trust your story? The pass is turned, you say? Masistes the seer said the libation sputtered on the flame with ill-omen when he sacrificed this morning. Then you come. The thing shall be looked into. Call the captains."

* * * * * *

The locharchs and taxiarchs of the Greeks assembled. It was a brief and gloomy council of war. While Euboulus, commanding the Corinthian contingent, was still questioning whether the deserter was worthy of credence, a scout came running down Mt. Œta confirming the worst. The cowardly Phocians watching the mountain trail had fled at the first arrows of Hydarnes. It was merely a question of time before the Immortals would be at Alpeni, the village in Leonidas's rear. There was only one thing to say, and the Spartan chief said it.

"You must retreat."

The taxiarchs of the allied Hellenes under him were already rushing forth to their men to bid them fly for dear life. Only one or two stayed by the tent, marvelling much to observe that Leonidas gave no orders to his

Lacedæmonians to join in the flight. On the contrary, Glaucon, as he stood near, saw the general lift the discarded pot of broth and explore it again with the iron spoon.

"O Father Zeus," cried the incredulous Corinthian leader. "Are you turned mad, Leonidas?"

"Time enough for all things," returned the unmoved Spartan, continuing his breakfast.

"Time!" shouted Euboulus. "Have we not to flee on wings, or be cut off?"

"Fly, then."

"But you and your Spartans?"

"We will stay."

"Stay? A handful against a million? Do I hear aright? What can you do?"

"Die."

"The gods forbid! Suicide is a fearful end. No man should rush on destruction. What requires you to perish?"

"Honour."

"Honour! Have you not won glory enough by holding Xerxes's whole power at bay two days? Is not your life precious to Hellas? What is the gain?"

"Glory to Sparta."

Then in the red morning half-light, folding his big hands across his mailed chest, Leonidas looked from one to another of the little circle. His voice was still in unemotional gutturals when he delivered the longest speech of his life.

"We of Sparta were ordered to defend this pass. The order shall be obeyed. The rest of you must go away—all save the Thebans, whose loyalty I distrust. Tell Leotychides, my colleague at Sparta, to care for Gorgo my wife and Pleistarchus my young son, and to remember that Themistocles the Athenian loves Hellas and gives sage counsel. Pay Strophius of Epidaurus the three hundred drachmæ I owe him for my horse. Likewise—"

A second breathless scout interrupted with the tidings that Hydarnes was on the last stretches of his road. The chief arose, drew the helmet down across his face, and motioned with his spear.

"Go!" he ordered.

The Corinthian would have seized his hand. He shook him off. At Leonidas's elbow was standing the trumpeter for his three hundred from Lacedæmon.

"Blow!" commanded the chief.

The keen blast cut the air. The chief deliberately wrapped the purple mantle around himself and adjusted the gold circlet over his helmet, for on the day of battle a Lacedæmonian was wont to wear his best. And even as he waited there came to him out of the midst of the panic-stricken, dissolving camp, one by one, tall men in armour, who took station beside him—the men of Sparta who had abided steadfast while all others prepared to flee, waiting for the word of the chief.

Presently they stood, a long black line, motionless, silent, whilst the other divisions filed in swift fear past. Only the Thespians—let their names not be forgotten—chose to share the Laconians' glory and their doom and took their stand behind the line of Leonidas. With them stood also the Thebans, but compulsion held them, and they tarried merely to desert and pawn their honour for their lives.

More couriers. Hydarnes's van was in sight of Alpeni now. The retreat of the Corinthians, Tegeans, and other Hellenes became a run; only once Euboulus and his fellow-captains turned to the silent warrior that stood leaning on his spear.

"Are you resolved on madness, Leonidas?"

"*Chaire!* Farewell!" was the only answer he gave them. Euboulus sought no more, but faced another figure, hitherto almost forgotten in the confusion of the retreat.

"Haste, Master Deserter, the Barbarians will give you an overwarm welcome, and you are no Spartan; save yourself!"

Glaucon did not stir.

"Do you not see that it is impossible?" he answered, then strode across to Leonidas. "I must stay."

"Are you also mad? You are young—" The good-hearted Corinthian strove to drag him into the retreating mob.

Glaucon sprang away from him and addressed the silent general.

"Shall not Athens remain by Sparta, if Sparta will accept?"

He could see Leonidas's cold eyes gleam out through the slits in his helmet. The general reached forth his hand.

"Sparta accepts," called he; "they have lied concerning your Medizing! And you, Euboulus, do not filch from him his glory."

"Zeus pity you!" cried Euboulus, running at last. One of the Spartans brought to Glaucon the heavy hoplite's armour and the ponderous spear and shield. He took his place in the line with the others. Leonidas stalked to the right wing of his scant array, the post of honour and of danger. The Thespians closed up behind. Shield was set to shield. Helmets were drawn low. The lance points projected in a bristling hedge in front. All was ready.

The general made no speech to fire his men. There was no wailing, no crying to the gods, no curses upon the tardy ephors at Lacedæmon who had deferred sending their whole strong levy instead of the pitiful three hundred. Sparta had sent this band to hold the pass. They had gone, knowing she might require the supreme sacrifice. Leonidas had spoken for all his men. "Sparta demanded it." What more was to be said?

As for Glaucon he could think of nothing save—in the language of his people—"this was a beautiful manner and place in which to die." "Count no man happy until he meets a happy end," so had said Solon, and of all ends what could be more fortunate than this? Euboulus would tell in Athens, in all Hellas, how he had remained with Leonidas and maintained Athenian honour when Corinthian and Tegean turned away. From "Glaucon the Traitor" he would be raised to "Glaucon the Hero." Hermione, Democrates, and all others he loved would flush with pride and no more with shame when men spoke of him. Could a life of a hundred years add to his glory more than he could win this day?

"Blow!" commanded Leonidas again, and again pealed the trumpet. The line moved beyond the wall toward Xerxes's camp in the open beside the Asopus. Why wait for Hydarnes's coming? They would meet the king of the Aryans face to face and show him the terrible manner in which the men of Lacedæmon knew how to die.

As they passed from the shadow of the mountain, the sun sprang over the hills of Eubœa, making fire of the bay and bathing earth and heavens with glory. In their rear was already shouting. Hydarnes had reached his goal at Alpeni. All retreat was ended. The thin line swept onward. Before them spread the whole host of the Barbarian as far as the eye could reach,—a tossing sea of golden shields, scarlet surcoats, silver lance-heads,—awaiting with its human billows to engulf them. The Laconians halted just beyond bow shot. The line locked tighter. Instinctively every man pressed closer to his comrade. Then before the eyes of Xerxes's host, which kept silence, marvelling, the handful broke forth with their pæan. They threw their well-loved charging song of Tyrtæus in the very face of the king.

"Press the charge, O sons of Sparta!

Ye are sons of men born free:

Press the charge; 'tis where the shields lock,

That your sires would have you be!

Honour's cheaply sold for life,

Press the charge, and join the strife:

Let the coward cling to breath,

Let the base shrink back from death,

Press the charge, let cravens flee!"

Leonidas's spear pointed to the ivory throne, around which and him that sat thereon in blue and scarlet glittered the Persian grandees.

"Onward!"

Immortal ichor seemed in the veins of every Greek. They burst into one shout.

"The king! The king!"

A roar from countless drums, horns, and atabals answered from the Barbarians, as across the narrow plain-land charged the three hundred—and one.

CHAPTER XXII
MARDONIUS GIVES A PROMISE

"Ugh—the dogs died hard, but they are dead," grunted Xerxes, still shivering on the ivory throne. The battle had raged disagreeably close to him.

"They are dead; even so perish all of your Eternity's enemies," rejoined Mardonius, close by. The bow-bearer himself was covered with blood and dust. A Spartan sword had grazed his forehead. He had exposed himself recklessly, as well he might, for it had taken all the efforts of the Persian captains, as well as the ruthless laying of whips over the backs of their men, to make the king's battalions face the frenzied Hellenes, until the closing in of Hydarnes from the rear gave the battle its inevitable ending.

Xerxes was victorious. The gate of Hellas was unlocked. The mountain wall of Œta would hinder him no more. But the triumph had been bought with a price which made Mardonius and every other general in the king's host shake his head.

"Lord," reported Hystaspes, commander of the Scythians, "one man in every seven of my band is slain, and those the bravest."

"Lord," spoke Artabazus, who led the Parthians, "my men swear the Hellenes were possessed by *dævas*. They dare not approach even their dead bodies."

"Lord," asked Hydarnes, "will it please your Eternity to appoint five other officers in the Life Guard, for of my ten lieutenants over the Immortals five are slain?"

But the heaviest news no man save Mardonius dared to bring to the king.

"May it please your Omnipotence," spoke the bow-bearer, "to order the funeral pyres of cedar and precious oils to be prepared for your brothers Abrocomes and Hyperanthes, and command the Magians to offer prayers for the repose of their *fravashis* in Garonmana the Blessed, for it pleased Mazda the Great they should fall before the Hellenes."

Xerxes waved his hand in assent. It was hard to be the "Lord of the World," and be troubled by such little things as the deaths of a few thousand servants, or even of two of his numerous half-brethren, hard at least on a day like this when he had seen his desire over his enemies.

"They shall be well avenged," he announced with kingly dignity, then smiled with satisfaction when they brought him the shield and helmet of Leonidas, the madman, who had dared to contemn his power. But all the generals who stood by were grim and sad. One more such victory would bring the army close to destruction.

Xerxes's happiness, however, was not to be clouded. From childish fears he had passed to childish exultation.

"Have you found the body also of this crazed Spartan?" he inquired of the cavalry officer who had brought the trophies.

"As you say, Omnipotence," rejoined the captain, bowing in the saddle.

"Good, then. Let the head be struck off and the trunk fastened on a cross that all may see it. And you, Mardonius," addressing the bow-bearer, "ride back to the hillock where these madmen made their last stand. If you discover among the corpses any who yet breathe, bring them hither to me, that they may learn the futility of resisting my might."

The bow-bearer shrugged his shoulders. He loved a fair battle and fair treatment of valiant foes. The dishonouring of the corpse of Leonidas was displeasing to more than one high-minded Aryan nobleman. But the king had spoken, and was to be obeyed. Mardonius rode back to the hillock at the mouth of the pass, where the Hellenes had retired—after their spears were broken and they could resist only with swords, stones, or naked hands—for the final death grip.

The slain Barbarians lay in heaps. The Greeks had been crushed at the end, not in close strife, but by showers of arrows. Mardonius dismounted and went with a few followers among the dead. Plunderers were already at their harpy work of stripping the slain. The bow-bearer chased them angrily away. He oversaw the task which his attendants performed as quickly as possible. Their toil was not quite fruitless. Three or four Thespians were still breathing, a few more of the helots who had attended Leonidas's Spartans, but not one of the three hundred but seemed dead, and that too with many wounds.

Snofru, Mardonius's Egyptian body-servant, rose from the ghastly work and grinned with his ivories at his master.

"All the rest are slain, Excellency."

"You have not searched that pile yonder."

Snofru and his helpers resumed their toil. Presently the Egyptian dragged from a bloody heap a body, and raised a yell. "Another one—he breathes!"

"There's life in him. He shall not be left to the crows. Take him forth and lay him with the others that are living."

It was not easy to roll the three corpses from their feebly stirring comrade. When this was done, the stricken man was still encased in his cuirass and helmet. They saw only that his hands were slim and white.

"With care," ordered the humane bow-bearer, "he is a young man. I heard Leonidas took only older men on his desperate venture. Here, rascals, do you not see he is smothered in that helmet? Lift him up, unbuckle the cuirass. By Mithra, he has a strong and noble form! Now the helmet—uncover the face."

But as the Egyptian did so, his master uttered a shout of mingled wonderment and terror.

"Glaucon—Prexaspes, and in Spartan armour!"

What had befallen Glaucon was in no wise miraculous. He had borne his part in the battle until the Hellenes fell back to the fatal hillock. Then in one of the fierce onsets which the Barbarians attempted before they had recourse to the simpler and less glorious method of crushing their foes by arrow fire, a Babylonian's war club had dashed upon his helmet. The stout bronze had saved him from wound, but under the stroke strength and consciousness had left him in a flash. The moment after he fell, the soldier beside him had perished by a javelin, and falling above the Athenian made his body a ghastly shield against the surge and trampling of the battle. Glaucon lay scathless but senseless through the final catastrophe. Now consciousness was returning, but he would have died of suffocation save for Snofru's timely aid.

It was well for the Athenian that Mardonius was a man of ready devices. He had not seen Glaucon at his familiar post beside the king, but had presumed the Hellene had remained at the tents with the women, unwilling to watch the destruction of his people. In the rush and roar of the battle the messenger Artazostra had sent her husband telling of "Prexaspes's" flight had never reached him. But Mardonius could divine what had happened. The swallow must fly south in the autumn. The Athenian had returned to his own. The bow-bearer's wrath at his protégé's desertion was overmastered by the consuming fear that tidings of Prexaspes's disloyalty would get to the king. Xerxes's wrath would be boundless. Had he not proffered his new subject all the good things of his empire? And to be rewarded thus! Glaucon's recompense would be to be sawn asunder or flung into a serpent's cage.

Fortunately Mardonius had only his own personal followers around him. He could count on their discreet loyalty. Vouchsafing no explanations, but bidding them say not a word of their discovery on their heads, he ordered Snofru and his companions to make a litter of cloaks and lances, to throw away Glaucon's tell-tale Spartan armour, and bear him speedily to Artazostra's tents. The stricken man was groaning feebly, moving his limbs, muttering incoherently. The sight of Xerxes driving in person to inspect the battle-field made Mardonius hasten the litter away, while he remained to parley with the king.

"So only a few are alive?" asked Xerxes, leaning over the silver rail of the chariot, and peering on the upturned faces of the dead which were nearly trampled by his horses. "Are any sound enough to set before me?"

"None, your Eternity; even the handful that live are desperately wounded. We have laid them yonder."

"Let them wait, then; all around here seem dead. Ugly hounds!" muttered the monarch, still peering down; "even in death they seem to grit their teeth and defy me. Faugh! The stench is already terrible. It is just as well they are dead. Angra-Mainyu surely possessed them to fight so! It cannot be there are many more who can fight like this left in Hellas, though Demaratus, the Spartan outlaw, says there are. Drive away, Pitiramphes—and you, Mardonius, ride beside me. I cannot abide those corpses. Where is my handkerchief? The one with the Sabæan nard on it. I will hold it to my nose. Most refreshing! And I had a question to ask—I have forgotten what."

"Whether news has come from the fleets before Artemisium?" spoke Mardonius, galloping close to the wheel.

"Not that. Ah! I remember. Where was Prexaspes? I did not see him near me. Did he stay in the tents while these mad men were destroyed? It was not loyal, yet I forgive him. After all, he was once a Hellene."

"May it please your Eternity,"—Mardonius chose his words carefully,—a Persian always loved the truth, and lies to the king were doubly impious,— "Prexaspes was not in the tents but in the thick of the battle."

"Ah!" Xerxes smiled pleasantly, "it was right loyal of him to show his devotion to me thus. And he acquitted himself valiantly?"

"Most valiantly, Omnipotence."

"Doubly good. Yet he ought to have stayed near me. If he had been a true Persian, he would not have withdrawn from the person of the king, even to display his prowess in combat. Still he did well. Where is he?"

"I regret to tell your Eternity he was desperately wounded, though your servant hopes not unto death. He is even now being taken to my tents."

"Where that pretty dancer, your sister, will play the surgeon—ha!" cried the king. "Well, tell him his Lord is grateful. He shall not be forgotten. If his wounds do not mend, call in my body-physicians. And I will send him something in gratitude—a golden cimeter, perhaps, or it may be another cream Nisæan charger."

A general rode up to the chariot with his report, and Mardonius was suffered to gallop to his own tents, blessing Mazda; he had saved the Athenian, yet had not told a lie.

* * * * * *

The ever ready eunuchs of Artazostra ran to tell Mardonius of the Hellene's strange desertion, even before their lord dismounted. Mardonius was not astonished now, however much the tidings pained him. The Greek had escaped more than trifling wounds; ten days would see him sound and hale, but the stunning blow had left his wits still wandering. He had believed himself dead at first, and demanded why Charon took so long with his ferry-boat. He had not recognized Roxana, but spoke one name many times—"Hermione!" And the Egyptian, understanding too well, went to her own tent weeping bitterly.

"He has forsaken us," spoke Artazostra, harshly, to her husband. "He has paid kindness with disloyalty. He has chosen the lot of his desperate race rather than princely state amongst the Aryans. Your sister is in agony."

"And I with her," returned the bow-bearer, gravely, "but let us not forget one thing—this man has saved our lives. And all else weighs small in the balance."

When Mardonius went to him, Glaucon was again himself. He lay on bright pillows, his forehead swathed in linen. His eyes were unnaturally bright.

"You know what has befallen?" asked Mardonius.

"They have told me. I almost alone of all the Hellenes have not been called to the heroes' Elysium, to the glory of Theseus and Achilles, the glory that shall not die. Yet I am content. For plainly the Olympians have destined that I should see and do great things in Hellas, otherwise they would not have kept me back from Leonidas's glory."

The Athenian's voice rang confidently. None of the halting weakness remained that had made it falter once when Mardonius asked him, "Will your Hellenes fight?" He spoke as might one returned crowned with the victor's laurel.

"And wherefore are you grown so bold?" The bow-bearer was troubled as he looked on him. "Nobly you and your handful fought. We Persians honour the brave, and full honour we give to you. But was it not graven upon the stars what should befall? Were not Leonidas, his men, and you all mad—"

"Ah, yes! divinely mad." Brighter still grew the Athenian's eyes. "For that moment of exultation when we charged to meet the king I would again pay a lifetime."

"Yet the gateway of Hellas is unlocked. Your bravest are fallen. Your land is defenceless. What else can be written hereafter save, 'The Hellenes strove with fierce courage to fling back Xerxes. Their valour was foolishness. The god turned against them. The king prevailed.'"

But Glaucon met the Persian's glance with one more bold.

"No, Mardonius, good friend, for do not think that we must be foes one to another because our people are at war,—I can answer you with ease. Leonidas you have slain, and his handful, and you have pierced the mountain wall of Œta, and no doubt your king's host will march even to Athens. But do not dream Hellas is conquered by striding over her land. Before you shall possess the land you must first possess the men. And I say to you, Athens is still left, and Sparta left, free and strong, with men whose hearts and hands can never fail. I doubted once. But now I doubt no more. And our gods will fight for us. Your Ahura-Mazda has still to prevail over Zeus the Thunderer and Athena of the Pure Heart."

"And you?" asked the Persian.

"And as for me, I know I have cast away by my own act all the good things you and your king would fain bestow upon me. Perhaps I deserve death at your hands. I will never plead for respite, but this I know, whether I live or die, it shall be as Glaucon of Athens who owns no king but Zeus, no loyalty save to the land that bore him."

There was stillness in the tent. The wounded man sank back on the pillows, breathing deep, closing his eyes, expectant almost of a burst of wrath from the Persian. But Mardonius answered without trace of anger.

"Friend, your words cut keenly, and your boasts are high. Only the Most High knoweth whether you boast aright. Yet this I say, that much as I desire your friendship, would see you my brother, even,—you know that,—I dare not tell you you do wholly wrong. A man is given one country and one manner of faith in God. He does not choose them. I was born to serve the lord of the Aryans, and to spread the triumphs of Mithra the Glorious, and you were born in Athens. I would it were otherwise. Artazostra and I would fain have made you Persian like ourselves. My sister loves you. Yet we cannot strive against fate. Will you go back to your own people and share their lot, however direful?"

"Since life is given me, I will."

Mardonius stepped to the bedside and gave the Athenian his right hand.

"At the island you saved my life and that of my best beloved. Let it never be said that Mardonius, son of Gobryas, is ungrateful. To-day, in some measure, I have repaid the debt I owe. If you will have it so, as speedily as your strength returns and opportunity offers I will return you to your people. And amongst them may your own gods show you favour, for you will have none from ours!"

Glaucon took the proffered hand in silent gratitude. He was still very weak and rested on the pillows, breathing hard. The bow-bearer went out to his wife and his sister and told his promise. There was little to be said. The Athenian must go his path, and they go theirs, unless he were to be handed over to Xerxes to die a death of torments. And not even Roxana, keenly as pierced her sorrow, would think of that.

CHAPTER XXIII
THE DARKEST HOUR

A city of two hundred thousand awaiting a common sentence of death,— such seemed the doom of Athens.

Every morning the golden majesty of the sun rose above the wall of Hymettus, but few could lift their hands to Lord Helios and give praise for another day of light. "Each sunrise brings Xerxes nearer." The bravest forgot not that.

Yet Athens was never more truly the "Violet-Crowned City" than on these last days before the fearful advent. The sun at morn on Hymettus, the sun at night on Daphni, the nightingales and cicadas in the olives by Cephissus, the hum of bees on the sweet thyme of the mountain, the purple of the hills, the blue and the fire of the bay, the merry tinkle of the goat bells upon the rocks, the laugh of little children in the streets—all these made Athens fair, but could not take the cloud from the hearts of the people.

Trade was at standstill in the Agora. The most careless frequented the temples. Old foes composed their cases before the arbitrator. The courts were closed, but there was meeting after meeting in the Pnyx, with incessant speeches on one theme—how Athens must resist to the bitter end.

And why should not the end be bitter? Argos and Crete had Medized. Corcyra promised and did nothing. Thebes was weakening. Thessaly had sent earth and water. Corinth, Ægina, and a few lesser states were moderately loyal, but great Sparta only procrastinated and despatched no help to her Athenian ally. So every day the Persian thunder-cloud was darkening.

But one man never faltered, nor suffered others about him to falter,— Themistocles. The people heard him gladly—he would never talk of defeat. He had a thousand reasons why the invader should be baffled, from a convenient hexameter in old Bacis's oracle book, up to the fact that the Greeks used the longest spears. If he found it weary work looking the crowding peril in the face and smiling still, he never confessed it. His friends would marvel at his serenity. Only when they saw him sit silent, saw his brows knit, his hand comb at his beard, they knew his inexhaustible brain was weaving the web which should ensnare the lord of the Aryans.

Thus day after day—while men thought dark things in their hearts.

* * * * * *

Hermippus had come down to his city house from Eleusis, and with him his wife and daughter. The Eleusinian was very busy. He was a member of the Areopagus, the old council of ex-archons, an experienced body that found much to do. Hermippus had strained his own resources to provide shields for the hoplites. He was constantly with Themistocles, which implied being much with Democrates. The more he saw of the young orator, the better the Eleusinian liked him. True, not every story ran to Democrates's credit, but Hermippus knew the world, and could forgive a young man if he had occasionally spent a jolly night. Democrates seemed to have forsworn Ionian harp-girls now. His patriotism was self-evident. The Eleusinian saw in him a most desirable protector in the perils of war for Hermione and her child. Hermione's dislike for her husband's destroyer was natural,—nay, in bounds, laudable,—but one must not give way too much to women's phantasies. The lady was making a Cyclops of Democrates by sheer imagination; an interview would dispel her prejudices. Therefore Hermippus planned, and his plan was not hard to execute.

On the day the fleet sailed to Artemisium, Hermione went with her mother to the havens, as all the city went, to wish godspeed to the "wooden wall" of Hellas.

One hundred and twenty-seven triremes were to go forth, and three and fifty to follow, bearing the best and bravest of Athens with them. Themistocles was in absolute command, and perhaps in his heart of hearts Democrates was not mournful if it lay out of his power to do a second ill-turn to his country.

It was again summer, and again such a day as when Glaucon with glad friends had rowed toward Salamis. The Saronian bay flashed fairest azure. The scattered isles and the headlands of Argolis rose in clear beauty. The city had emptied itself. Mothers hung on the necks of sons as the latter strode toward Peiræus; friends clasped hands for the last time as he who remained promised him who went that the wife and little ones should never be forgotten. Only Hermione, as she stood on the hill of Munychia above the triple havens, shed no tear. The ship bearing her all was gone long since. Themistocles would never lead it back. Hermippus was at the quay in Peiræus, taking leave of the admiral. Old Cleopis held the babe as Hermione stood by her mother. The younger woman had suffered her gaze to wander to far Ægina, where a featherlike cloud hung above the topmost summit of the isle, when her mother's voice called her back.

"They go."

A line of streamers blew from the foremast of the *Nausicaä* as the piper on the flag-ship gave the time to the oars. The triple line of blades, pumiced white, splashed with a steady rhythm. The long black hull glided away. The trailing line of consorts swiftly followed. From the hill and the quays a shout uprose from the thousands, to be answered by the fleet,—a cheer or a prayer to sea-ruling Poseidon those who gave it hardly knew. The people stood silent till the last dark hull crept around the southern headland; then, still in silence, the multitudes dissolved. The young and the strong had gone from them. For Athens this was the beginning of the war.

Hermione and Lysistra awaited Hermippus before setting homeward, but the Eleusinian was delayed. The fleet had vanished. The havens were empty. In Cleopis's arms little Phœnix wept. His mother was anxious to be gone, when she was surprised to see a figure climbing the almost deserted slope. A moment more and she was face to face with Democrates, who advanced outstretching his hand and smiling.

The orator wore the dress of his new office of strategus. The purple-edged cloak, the light helmet wreathed with myrtle, the short sword at his side, all became him well. If there were deeper lines about his face than on the day Hermione last saw him, even an enemy would confess a leader of the Athenians had cause to be thoughtful. He was cordially greeted by Lysistra and seemed not at all abashed that Hermione gave only a sullen nod. From the ladies he turned with laughter to Cleopis and her burden.

"A new Athenian!" spoke he, lightly, "and I fear Xerxes will have been chased away before he has a chance to prove his valour. But fear not, there will be more brave days in store."

Hermione shook her head, ill-pleased.

"Blessed be Hera, my babe is too young to know aught of wars. And if we survive this one, will not just Zeus spare us from further bloodshed?"

Democrates, without answering, approached the nurse, and Phœnix—for reasons best known to himself—ceased lamenting and smiled up in the orator's face.

"His mother's features and eyes," cried Democrates. "I swear it—ay, by all Athena's owls—that young Hermes when he lay in Maia's cave on Mt. Cylene was not finer or lustier than he. His mother's face and eyes, I say."

"His father's," corrected Hermione. "Is not his name Phœnix? In him will not Glaucon the Beautiful live again? Will he not grow to man's estate to avenge his murdered father?" The lady spoke without passion, but with a cold bitterness that made Democrates cease from smiling. He turned away from the babe.

"Forgive me, dear lady," he answered her, "I am wiser at ruling the Athenians than at ruling children, but I see nothing of Glaucon about the babe, though much of his beautiful mother."

"You had once a better memory, Democrates," said Hermione, reproachfully.

"I do not understand your Ladyship."

"I mean that Glaucon has been dead one brief year. Can you forget *his* face in so short a while?"

But here Lysistra interposed with all good intent.

"You are fond and foolish, Hermione, and like all young mothers are enraged if all the world does not see his father's image in their first-born."

"Democrates knows what I would say," said the younger woman, soberly.

"Since your Ladyship is pleased to speak in riddles and I am no seer nor oracle-monger, I must confess I cannot follow. But we will contend no more concerning little Phœnix. Enough that he will grow up fair as the Delian Apollo and an unspeakable joy to his mother."

"Her only joy," was Hermione's icy answer. "Wrap up the child, Cleopis. My father is coming. It is a long walk home to the city."

With a rustle of white Hermione went down the slope in advance of her mother. Hermippus and Lysistra were not pleased. Plainly their daughter kept all her prejudice against Democrates. Her cold contempt was more disappointing even than open fury.

Once at home Hermione held little Phœnix long to her heart and wept over him. For the sake of her dead husband's child, if for naught else, how could she suffer them to give her to Democrates? That the orator had destroyed Glaucon in black malice had become a corner-stone in her belief. She could at first give for it only a woman's reason—blind intuition. She could not discuss her conviction with her mother or with any save a strange confidant—Phormio.

She had met the fishmonger in the Agora once when she went with the slaves to buy a mackerel. The auctioneer had astonished everybody by knocking down to her a noble fish an obol under price, then under pretext of showing her a rare Bœotian eel got her aside into his booth and whispered a few words that made the red and white come and go from her cheeks, after which the lady's hand went quickly to her purse, and she spoke quick words about "the evening" and "the garden gate."

Phormio refused the drachma brusquely, but kept the tryst. Cleopis had the key to the garden, and would contrive anything for her mistress—especially as all Athens knew Phormio was harmless save with his tongue. That evening for the first time Hermione heard the true story of Glaucon's escape by the *Solon*, but when the fishmonger paused she hung down her head closer.

"You saved him, then? I bless you. But was the sea more merciful than the executioner?"

The fishmonger let his voice fall lower.

"Democrates is unhappy. Something weighs on his mind. He is afraid."

"Of what?"

"Bias his slave came to see me again last night. Many of his master's doings have been strange to him. Many are riddles still, but one thing at last is plain. Hiram has been to see Democrates once more, despite the previous threats. Bias listened. He could not understand everything, but he heard Lycon's name passed many times, then one thing he caught clearly. '*The Babylonish carpet-seller was the Prince Mardonius.*' 'The Babylonian fled on the *Solon.*' 'The Prince is safe in Sardis.' If Mardonius could escape the storm and wreck, why not Glaucon, a king among swimmers?"

Hermione clapped her hands to her head.

"Don't torture me. I've long since trodden out hope. Why has he sent me no word in all these months of pain?"

"It is not the easiest thing to get a letter across the Ægean in these days of roaring war."

"I dare not believe it. What else did Bias hear?"

"Very little. Hiram was urging something. Democrates always said, 'Impossible.' Hiram went away with a very sour grin. However, Democrates caught Bias lurking."

"And flogged him?"

"No, Bias ran into the street and cried out he would flee to the Temple of Theseus, the slave's sanctuary, and demand that the archon sell him to a kinder master. Then suddenly Democrates forgave him and gave him five drachmæ to say no more about it."

"And so Bias at once told you?" Hermione could not forbear a smile, but her gesture was of desperation. "O Father Zeus—only the testimony of a slave to lean on, I a weak woman and Democrates one of the chief men in Athens! O for strength to wring out all the bitter truth!"

"Peace, *kyria*," said Phormio, not ungently, "Aletheia, Mistress Truth, is a patient dame, but she says her word at last. And you see that hope is not quite dead."

"I dare not cherish it. If I were but a man!" repeated Hermione. But she thanked Phormio many times, would not let him refuse her money, and bade him come often again and bring her all the Agora gossip about the war. "For we are friends," she concluded; "you and I are the only persons who hold Glaucon innocent in all the world. And is that not tie enough?"

So Phormio came frequently, glad perhaps to escape the discipline of his spouse. Now he brought a rumour of Xerxes's progress, now a bit of Bias's tattling about his master. The talebearing counted for little, but went to make Hermione's conviction like adamant. Every night she would speak over Phœnix as she held him whilst he slept.

"Grow fast, *makaire*, grow strong, for there is work for you to do! Your father cries, 'Avenge me well,' even from Hades."

* * * * * * *

After the departure of the fleet Athens seemed silent as the grave. On the streets one met only slaves and graybeards. In the Agora the hucksters' booths were silent, but little groups of white-headed men sat in the shaded porticos and watched eagerly for the appearing of the archon before the government house to read the last despatch of the progress of Xerxes. The Pnyx was deserted. The gymnasia were closed. The more superstitious scanned the heavens for a lucky or unlucky flight of hawks. The priestesses sang litanies all day and all night on the Acropolis where the great altar to Athena smoked with victims continually. At last, after the days of uncertainty and wavering rumour, came surer tidings of battles.

"Leonidas is fighting at Thermopylæ. The fleets are fighting at Artemisium, off Eubœa. The first onsets of the Barbarians have failed, but nothing is decided."

This was the substance, and tantalizingly meagre. And the strong army of Sparta and her allies still tarried at the Isthmus instead of hasting to aid the pitiful handful at Thermopylæ. Therefore the old men wagged their heads, the altars were loaded with victims, and the women wept over their children.

So ended the first day after news came of the fighting. The second was like it—only more tense. Hermione never knew that snail called time to creep more slowly. Never had she chafed more against the iron custom which commanded Athenian gentlewomen to keep, tortoise-like, at home in days of distress and tumult. On the evening of the second day came once more the dusty courier. Leonidas was holding the gate of Hellas. The Barbarians had perished by thousands. At Artemisium, Themistocles and the allied

Greek admirals were making head against the Persian armadas. But still nothing was decided. Still the Spartan host lingered at the Isthmus, and Leonidas must fight his battle alone. The sun sank that night with tens of thousands wishing his car might stand fast. At gray dawn Athens was awake and watching. Men forgot to eat, forgot to drink. One food would have contented—news!

* * * * * *

It was about noon—"the end of market time," had there been any market then at Athens—when Hermione knew by instinct that news had come from the battle and that it was evil. She and her mother had sat since dawn by the upper window, craning forth their heads up the street toward the Agora, where they knew all couriers must hasten. Along the street in all the houses other women were peering forth also. When little Phœnix cried in his cradle, his mother for the first time in his life almost angrily bade him be silent. Cleopis, the only one of the fluttering servants who went placidly about the wonted tasks, vainly coaxed her young mistress with figs and a little wine. Hermippus was at the council. The street, save for the leaning heads of the women, was deserted. Then suddenly came a change.

First a man ran toward the Agora, panting,—his himation blew from his shoulders, he never stopped to recover it. Next shouts, scattered in the beginning, then louder, and coming not as a roar but as a wailing, rising, falling like the billows of the howling sea,—as if the thousands in the market-place groaned in sore agony. Shrill and hideous they rose, and a hand of ice fell on the hearts of the listening women. Then more runners, until the street seemed alive by magic, slaves and old men all crowding to the Agora. And still the shout and ever more dreadful. The women leaned from the windows and cried vainly to the trampling crowd below.

"Tell us! In the name of Athena, tell us!" No answer for long, till at last a runner came not toward the Agora but from it. They had hardly need to hear what he was calling.

"Leonidas is slain. Thermopylæ is turned! Xerxes is advancing!"

Hermione staggered back from the lattice. In the cradle Phœnix awoke; seeing his mother bending over him, he crowed cheerily and flung his chubby fists in her face. She caught him up and again could not fight the tears away.

"Glaucon! Glaucon!" she prayed,—for her husband was all but a deity in her sight,—"hear us wherever you are, even if in the blessed land of Rhadamanthus. Take us thither, your child and me, for there is no peace or shelter left on earth!"

Then, seeing her panic-stricken women flying hither and thither like witless birds, her patrician blood asserted itself. She dashed the drops from her eyes and joined her mother in quieting the maids. Whatever there was to hope or fear, their fate would not be lightened by wild moaning. Soon the direful wailing from the Agora ceased. A blue flag waved over the Council House, a sign that the "Five Hundred" had been called in hurried session. Simultaneously a dense column of smoke leaped up from the market-place. The archons had ordered the hucksters' booths to be burned, as a signal to all Attica that the worst had befallen.

After inexpressibly long waiting Phormio came, then Hermippus, to tell all they knew. Leonidas had perished gloriously. His name was with the immortals, but the mountain wall of Hellas had been unlocked. No Spartan army was in Bœotia. The bravest of Athens were in the fleet. The easy Attic passes of Phyle and Decelea could never be defended. Nothing could save Athens from Xerxes. The calamity had been foreseen, but to foresee is not to realize. That night in Athens no man slept.

CHAPTER XXIV
THE EVACUATION OF ATHENS

It had come at last,—the hour wise men had dreaded, fools had scoffed at, cowards had dared not face. The Barbarian was within five days' march of Attica. The Athenians must bow the knee to the world monarch or go forth exiles from their country.

In the morning after the night of terror came another courier, not this time from Thermopylæ. He bore a letter from Themistocles, who was returning from Eubœa with the whole allied Grecian fleet. The reading of the letter in the Agora was the first rift in the cloud above the city.

"Be strong, prove yourselves sons of Athens. Do what a year ago you so boldly voted. Prepare to evacuate Attica. All is not lost. In three days I will be with you."

There was no time for an assembly at the Pnyx, but the Five Hundred and the Areopagus council acted for the people. It was ordered to remove the entire population of Attica, with all their movable goods, across the bay to Salamis or to the friendly Peloponnesus, and that same noon the heralds went over the land to bear the direful summons.

To Hermione, who in the calm after-years looked back on all this year of agony and stress as on an unreal thing, one time always was stamped on memory as no dream, but vivid, unforgetable,—these days of the great evacuation. Up and down the pleasant plain country of the Mesogia to southward, to the rolling highlands beyond Pentelicus and Parnes, to the slumbering villages by Marathon, to the fertile farm-land by Eleusis, went the proclaimers of ill-tidings.

"Quit your homes, hasten to Athens, take with you what you can, but hasten, or stay as Xerxes's slaves."

For the next two days a piteous multitude was passing through the city. A country of four hundred thousand inhabitants was to be swept clean and left naked and profitless to the invader. Under Hermione's window, as she gazed up and down the street, jostled the army of fugitives, women old and young, shrinking from the bustle and uproar, grandsires on their staves, boys driving the bleating goats or the patient donkeys piled high with pots and panniers, little girls tearfully hugging a pet puppy or hen. But few strong men were seen, for the fleet had not yet rounded Sunium to bear the people away.

The well-loved villas and farmsteads were tenantless. They left the standing grain, the ripening orchards, the groves of the sacred olives. Men rushed for the last time to the shrines where their fathers had prayed,—the temples of

Theseus, Olympian Zeus, Dionysus, Aphrodite. The tombs of the worthies of old, stretching out along the Sacred Way to Eleusis, where Solon, Clisthenes, Miltiades, and many another bulwark of Athens slept, had the last votive wreath hung lovingly upon them. And especially men sought the great temple of the "Rock," to lift their hands to Athena Polias, and vow awful vows of how harm to the Virgin Goddess should be wiped away in blood.

So the throng passed through the city and toward the shore, awaiting the fleet.

It came after eager watching. The whole fighting force of Athens and her Corinthian, Æginetan, and other allies. Before the rest raced a stately ship, the *Nausicaä*, her triple-oar bank flying faster than the spray. The people crowded to the water's edge when the great trireme cast off her pinnace and a well-known figure stepped therein.

"Themistocles is with us!"

He landed at Phaleron, the thousands greeted him as if he were a god. He seemed their only hope—the Atlas upbearing all the fates of Athens. With the glance of his eye, with a few quick words, he chased the terrors from the strategi and archons that crowded up around him.

"Why distressed? Have we not held the Barbarians back nobly at Artemisium? Will we not soon sweep his power from the seas in fair battle?"

With almost a conqueror's train he swept up to the city. A last assembly filled the Pnyx. Themistocles had never been more hopeful, more eloquent. With one voice men voted never to bend the knee to the king. If the gods forbade them to win back their own dear country, they would go together to Italy, to found a new and better Athens far from the Persian's power. And at Themistocles's motion they voted to recall all the political exiles, especially Themistocles's own great enemy Aristeides the Just, banished by the son of Neocles only a few years before. The assembly dispersed—not weeping but with cheers. Already it was time to be quitting the city. Couriers told how the Tartar horsemen were burning the villages beyond Parnes. The magistrates and admirals went to the house of Athena. The last incense smoked before the image. The bucklers hanging on the temple wall were taken down by Cimon and the other young patricians. The statue was reverently lifted, wound in fine linen, and borne swiftly to the fleet.

"Come, *makaira*!" called Hermippus, entering his house to summon his daughter. Hermione sent a last glance around the disordered aula; her mother called to the bevy of pallid, whimpering maids. Cleopis was bearing Phœnix, but Hermione took him from her. Only his own mother should bear him now. They went through the thinning Agora and took one hard look at each familiar building and temple. When they should return to them, the inscrutable god kept hid. So to Peiræus,—and to the rapid pinnaces which bore them across the narrow sea to Salamis, where for the moment at least was peace.

All that day the boats were bearing the people, and late into the night, until the task was accomplished, the like whereof is not found in history. No Athenian who willed was left to the power of Xerxes. One brain and voice planned and directed all. Leonidas, Ajax of the Hellenes, had been taken. Themistocles, their Odysseus, valiant as Ajax and gifted with the craft of the immortals, remained. Could that craft and that valour turn back the might of even the god-king of the Aryans?

CHAPTER XXV
THE ACROPOLIS FLAMES

A few days only Xerxes and his host rested after the dear-bought triumph at Thermopylæ. An expedition sent to plunder Delphi returned discomfited—thanks, said common report, to Apollo himself, who broke off two mountain crags to crush the impious invaders. But no such miracle halted the march on Athens. Bœotia and her cities welcomed the king; Thespiæ and Platæa, which had stood fast for Hellas, were burned. The Peloponnesian army lingered at Corinth, busy with a wall across the Isthmus, instead of risking valorous battle.

"By the soul of my father," the king had sworn, "I believe that after the lesson at Thermopylæ these madmen will not fight again!"

"By land they will not," said Mardonius, always at his lord's elbow, "by sea—it remains for your Eternity to discover."

"Will they really dare to fight by sea?" asked Xerxes, hardly pleased at the suggestion.

"Omnipotence, you have slain Leonidas, but a second great enemy remains. While Themistocles lives, it is likely your slaves will have another opportunity to prove to you their devotion."

"Ah, yes! A stubborn rogue, I hear. Well—if we must fight by sea, it shall be under my own eyes. My loyal Phœnician and Egyptian mariners did not do themselves full justice at Artemisium; they lacked the valour which comes from being in the presence of their king."

"Which makes a dutiful subject fight as ten," quickly added Pharnaspes the fan-bearer.

"Of course," smiled the monarch, "and now I must ask again, Mardonius, how fares it with my handsome Prexaspes?"

"Only indifferently, your Majesty, since you graciously deign to inquire."

"Such a sad wound? That is heavy news. He takes long in recovering. I trust he wants for nothing."

"Nothing, Omnipotence. He has the best surgeons in the camp."

"To-day I will send him Helbon wine from my own table. I miss his comely face about me. I want him here to play at dice. Tell him to recover because his king desires it. If he has become right Persian, that will be better than any physic."

"I have no doubt he will be deeply moved to learn of your Eternity's kindness," rejoined the bow-bearer, who was not sorry that further discussion of this delicate subject was averted by the arch-usher introducing certain cavalry officers with their report on the most practicable line of march through Bœotia.

Glaucon, in fact, was long since out of danger, thanks to the sturdy bronze of his Laconian helmet. He was able to walk, and, if need be, ride, but Mardonius would not suffer him to go outside his own tents. The Athenian would be certain to be recognized, and at once Xerxes would send for him, and how Glaucon, in his new frame of mind, would deport himself before majesty, whether he would not taunt the irascible monarch to his face, the bow-bearer did not know. Therefore the Athenian endured a manner of captivity in the tents with the eunuchs, pages, and women. Artazostra was often with him, and less frequently Roxana. But the Egyptian had lost all power over him now. He treated her with a cold courtesy more painful than contempt. Once or twice Artazostra had tried to turn him back from his purpose, but her words always broke themselves over one barrier.

"I am born a Hellene, lady. My gods are not yours. I must live and die after the manner of my people. And that our gods are strong and will give victory, after that morning with Leonidas I dare not doubt."

When the host advanced south and eastward from Thermopylæ, Glaucon went with it, riding in a closed travelling carriage guarded by Mardonius's eunuchs. All who saw it said that here went one of the bow-bearer's harem women, and as for the king, every day he asked for his favourite, and every day Mardonius told him, "He is even as before," an answer which the bow-bearer prayed to truth-loving Mithra might not be accounted a lie.

It was while the army lay at Platæa that news came which might have shaken Glaucon's purpose, had that purpose been shakable. Euboulus the Corinthian had been slain in a skirmish shortly after the forcing of Thermopylæ. The tidings meant that no one lived who could tell in Athens that on the day of testing the outlaw had cast in his lot with Hellas. Leonidas was dead. The Spartan soldiers who had heard Glaucon avow his identity were dead. In the hurried conference of captains preceding the retreat, Leonidas had told his informant's precise name only to Euboulus. And now Euboulus was slain, doubtless before any word from him of Glaucon's deed could spread abroad. To Athenians Glaucon was still the "Traitor," doubly execrated in this hour of trial. If he returned to his people, would he not be torn in pieces by the mob? But the young Alcmæonid was resolved. Since he had not died at Thermopylæ, no life in the camp of the Barbarian was tolerable. He would trust sovran Athena who had plucked him out of one death to deliver from a second. Therefore he nursed his strength—a caged lion waiting for freedom,—and almost wished the Persian host would advance more swiftly that he might haste onward to his own.

* * * * * *

Glaucon had cherished a hope to see the whole power of the Peloponnesus in array in Bœotia, but that hope proved quickly vain. The oracle was truly to be fulfilled,—the whole of "the land of Cecrops" was to be possessed by the Barbarian. The mountain passes were open. No arrows greeted the Persian vanguard as it cantered down the defiles, and once more the king's courtiers told their smiling master that not another hand would be raised against him.

The fourth month after quitting the Hellespont Xerxes entered Athens. The gates stood ajar. The invaders walked in silent streets as of a city of the dead. A few runaway slaves alone greeted them. Only in the Acropolis a handful of superstitious old men and temple warders had barricaded themselves, trusting that Athena would still defend her holy mountain. For a few days they defended the steep, rolling down huge boulders, but the end was inevitable. The Persians discovered a secret path upward. The defenders were surprised and dashed themselves from the crags or were massacred. A Median spear-man flung a fire-brand. The house of the guardian goddess went up in flame. The red column leaping to heaven was a beacon for leagues around that Xerxes held the length and breadth of Attica.

Glaucon watched the burning temple with grinding teeth. Mardonius's tents were pitched in the eastern city by the fountain of Callirhoë,—a spot of fond memories for the Alcmæonid. Here first he had met Hermione, come with her maids to draw water, and had gone away dreaming of Aphrodite arising from the sea. Often here he had sat with Democrates by the little pool, whilst the cypresses above talked their sweet, monotonous music. Before him rose the Rock of Athena,—the same, yet not the same. The temple of his fathers was vanishing in smoke and ashes. What wonder that he turned to Artazostra at his side with a bitter smile.

"Lady, your people have their will. But do not think Athena Nikephorus, the Lady of Triumphs, will forget this day when we stand against you in battle."

She did not answer him. He knew that many noblemen had advised Xerxes against driving the Greeks to desperation by this sacrilege, but this fact hardly made him the happier.

At dusk the next evening Mardonius suffered him to go with two faithful eunuchs and rove through the deserted city. The Persians were mostly encamped without the walls, and plundering was forbidden. Only Hydarnes with the Immortals pitched on Areopagus, and the king had taken his abode by the Agora. It was like walking through the country of the dead. Everything familiar, everything changed. The eunuchs carried torches. They wandered down one street after another, where the house doors stood open, where the aulas were strewn with the débris of household stuff which the fleeing citizens had abandoned. A deserter had already told Glaucon of his father's death; he was not amazed therefore to find the house of his birth empty and desolate. But everywhere else, also, it was to call back memories of glad days never to return. Here was the school where crusty Pollicharmes had driven the "reading, writing, and music" into Democrates and himself between the blows. Here was the corner Hermes, before which he had sacrificed the day he won his first wreath in the public games. Here was the house of Cimon, in whose dining room he had enjoyed many a bright symposium. He trod the Agora and walked under the porticos where he had lounged in the golden evenings after the brisk stroll from the wrestling ground at Cynosarges, and had chatted and chaffered with light-hearted friends about "the war" and "the king," in the days when the Persian seemed very far away. Last of all an instinct—he could not call it desire—drove him to seek the house of Hermippus.

They had to force the door open with a stone. The first red torch-light that glimmered around the aula told that the Eumolpid had awaited the enemy in Athens, not in Eleusis. The court was littered with all manner of stuff,— crockery, blankets, tables, stools,—which the late inhabitants had been forced to forsake. A tame quail hopped from the tripod by the now cold hearth. Glaucon held out his hand, the bird came quickly, expecting the bit of grain. Had not Hermione possessed such a quail? The outlaw's blood ran quicker. He felt the heat glowing in his forehead.

A chest of clothes stood open by the entrance. He dragged forth the contents—women's dresses and uppermost a white airy gauze of Amorgos that clung to his hands as if he were lifting clouds. Out of its folds fell a pair of white shoes with clasps of gold. Then he recognized this dress Hermione had worn in the Panathenæa and on the night of his ruin. He threw it down, next stood staring over it like a man possessed. The friendly eunuchs watched his strange movements. He could not endure to have them follow him.

"Give me a torch. I return in a moment."

He went up the stair alone to the upper story, to the chambers of the women. Confusion here also,—the more valuable possessions gone, but much remaining. In one corner stood the loom and stretched upon it the half-made web of a shawl. He could trace the pattern clearly wrought in bright wools,— Ariadne sitting desolate awaiting the returning of Theseus. Would the wife or the betrothed of Democrates busy herself with *that*, whatever the griefs in her heart? Glaucon's temples now were throbbing as if to burst.

A second room, and more littered confusion, but in one corner stood a bronze statue,—Apollo bending his bow against the Achæans,—which Glaucon had given to Hermione. At the foot of the statue hung a wreath of purple asters, dead and dry, but he plucked it asunder and set many blossoms in his breast.

A third room, and almost empty. He was moving back in disappointment, when the torch-light shook over something that swung betwixt two beams,—a wicker cradle. The woollen swaddling bands were still in it. One could see the spot on the little pillow with the impress of the tiny head. Glaucon almost dropped the torch. He pressed his hand to his brow.

"Zeus pity me!" he groaned, "preserve my reason. How can I serve Hellas and those I love if thou strikest me mad?"

With feverish anxiety he sent his eyes around that chamber. His search was not in vain. He almost trampled upon the thing that lay at his feet,—a wooden rattle, the toy older than the Egyptian pyramids. He seized it, shook it as a warrior his sword. He scanned it eagerly. Upon the handle were letters carved, but there was a mist before his eyes which took long to pass away. Then he read the rude inscription: "ΦΟΙΝΙΞ : ΥΙΟΣ : ΓΛΑΥΚΟΝΤΟΣ." "Phœnix the son of Glaucon." *His* child. He was the father of a fair son. His wife, he was sure thereof, had not yet been given to Democrates.

Overcome by a thousand emotions, he flung himself upon a chest and pressed the homely toy many times to his lips.

* * * * * *

After a long interval he recovered himself enough to go down to the eunuchs, who were misdoubting his long absence.

"Persian," he said to Mardonius, when he was again at the bow-bearer's tents, "either suffer me to go back to my people right soon or put me to death. My wife has borne me a son. My place is where I can defend him."

Mardonius frowned, but nodded his head.

"You know I desire it otherwise. But my word is given. And the word of a prince of the Aryans is not to be recalled. You know what to expect among your people—perhaps a foul death for a deed of another."

"I know it. I also know that Hellas needs me."

"To fight against us?" asked the bow-bearer, with a sigh. "Yet you shall go. Eran is not so weak that adding one more to her enemies will halt her triumph. To-morrow night a boat shall be ready on the strand. Take it. And after that may your gods guard you, for I can do no more."

All the next day Glaucon sat in the tents and watched the smoke cloud above the Acropolis and the soldiers in the plain hewing down the sacred olives, Athena's trees, which no Athenian might injure and thereafter live. But Glaucon was past cursing now,—endure a little longer and after that, what vengeance!

The gossiping eunuchs told readily what the king had determined. Xerxes was at Phaleron reviewing his fleet. The Hellenes' ships confronted him at Salamis. The Persians had met in council, deliberating one night over their wine, reconsidering the next morning when sober. Their wisdom each time had been to force a battle. Let the king destroy the enemy at Salamis, and he could land troops at ease at the very doors of Sparta, defying the vain wall across the Isthmus. Was not victory certain? Had he not two ships to the Hellenes' one? So the Phœnician vassal kings and all his admirals assured him. Only Artemisia, the martial queen of Halicarnassus, spoke otherwise, but none would hear her.

"To-morrow the war is ended," a cup-bearer had told a butler in Glaucon's hearing, and never noticed how the Athenian took a horseshoe in his slim fingers and straightened it, whilst looking on the scorched columns of the Acropolis.

At length the sun spread his last gold of the evening. The eunuchs called Glaucon to the pavilion of Artazostra, who came forth with Roxana for their farewell. They were in royal purple. The amethysts in their hair were worth a month's revenues of Corinth. Roxana had never been lovelier. Glaucon was again in the simple Greek dress, but he knelt and kissed the robes of both the women. Then rising he spoke to them.

"To you, O princess, my benefactress, I wish all manner of blessing. May you be crowned with happy age, may your fame surpass Semiramis, the conqueror queen of the fables, let the gods refuse only one prayer—the conquest of Hellas. The rest of the world is yours, leave then to us our own."

"And you, sister of Mardonius," he turned to Roxana now, "do not think I despise your love or your beauty. That I have given you pain, is double pain to me. But I loved you only in a dream. My life is not for the rose valleys of Bactria, but for the stony hills by Athens. May Aphrodite give you another love, a brighter fortune than might ever come by linking your fate to mine."

They held out their hands. He kissed them. He saw tears on the long lashes of Roxana.

"Farewell," spoke the women, simply.

"Farewell," he answered. He turned from them. He knew they were re-entering the tent. He never saw the women again.

Mardonius accompanied him all the long way from the fount of Callirhoë to the sea-shore. Glaucon protested, but the bow-bearer would not hearken.

"You have saved my life, Athenian," was his answer, "when you leave me now, it is forever."

The moon was lifting above the gloomy mass of Hymettus and scattering all the Attic plain with her pale gold. The Acropolis Rock loomed high above them. Glaucon, looking upward, saw the moonlight flash on the spear point and shield of a soldier,—a Barbarian standing sentry on the ruined shrine of the Virgin Goddess. Once more the Alcmæonid was leaving Athens, but with very different thoughts than on that other night when he had fled at Phormio's side. They quitted the desolate city and the sleeping camp. The last bars of day had long since dimmed in the west when before them loomed the hill of Munychia clustered also with tents, and beyond it the violet-black vista of the sea. A forest of masts crowded the havens, the fleet of the "Lord of the World" that was to complete his mastery with the returning sun. Mardonius did not lead Glaucon to the ports, but southward, where beyond the little point of Colias spread an open sandy beach. The night waves lapped softly. The wind had sunk to warm puffs from the southward. They heard the rattle of anchor-chains and tackle-blocks, but from far away. Beyond the vague promontory of Peiræus rose dark mountains and headlands, at their foot lay a sprinkling of lights.

"Salamis!" cried Glaucon, pointing. "Yonder are the ships of Hellas."

Mardonius walked with him upon the shelving shore. A skiff, small but stanch, was ready with oars.

"What else will you?" asked the bow-bearer. "Gold?"

"Nothing. Yet take this." Glaucon unclasped from his waist the golden belt Xerxes had bestowed at Sardis. "A Hellene I went forth, a Hellene I return."

He made to kiss the Persian's dress, but Mardonius would not suffer it.

"Did I not desire you for my brother?" he said, and they embraced. As their arms parted, the bow-bearer spoke three words in earnest whisper:—

"Beware of Democrates."

"What do you mean?"

"I can say no more. Yet be wise. Beware of Democrates."

The attendants, faithful body-servants of Mardonius, and mute witnesses of all that passed, were thrusting the skiff into the water. There were no long farewells. Both knew that the parting was absolute, that Glaucon might be dead on the morrow. A last clasping of the hands and quickly the boat was drifting out upon the heaving waters. Glaucon stood one moment watching the figures on the beach and pondering on Mardonius's strange warning. Then he set himself to the oars, rowing westward, skirting the Barbarian fleet as it rode at anchor, observing its numbers and array and how it was aligned for battle. After that, with more rapid stroke, he sent the skiff across the dark ribbon toward Salamis.

CHAPTER XXVI
THEMISTOCLES IS THINKING

Leonidas was taken. Themistocles was left,—left to bear as crushing a load as ever weighed on man,—to fight two battles, one with the Persian, one with his own unheroic allies, and the last was the harder. Three hundred and seventy Greek triremes rode off Salamis, half from Athens, but the commander-in-chief was Eurybiades of Sparta, the sluggard state that sent only sixteen ships, yet the only state the bickering Peloponnesians would obey. Hence Themistocles's sore problems.

Different from the man of unruffled brow who ruled from the bema was he who paced the state cabin of the *Nausicaä* a few nights after the evacuation. For *he* at least knew the morn would bring Hellas her doom. There had been a gloomy council that afternoon. They had seen the Acropolis flame two days before. The great fleet of Xerxes rode off the Attic havens. At the gathering of the Greek chiefs in Eurybiades's cabin Themistocles had spoken one word many times,—"Fight!"

To which Adeimantus, the craven admiral of Corinth, and many another had answered:—

"Delay! Back to the Isthmus! Risk nothing!"

Then at last the son of Neocles silenced them, not with arguments but threats. "Either here in the narrow straits we can fight the king or not at all. In the open seas his numbers can crush us. Either vote to fight here or we Athenians sail for Italy and leave you to stem Xerxes as you can."

There had been sullen silence after that, the admirals misliking the furrow drawn above Themistocles's eyes. Then Eurybiades had haltingly given orders for battle.

That had been the command, but as the Athenian left the Spartan flag-ship in his pinnace he heard Globryas, the admiral of Sicyon, muttering, "Headstrong fool—he shall not destroy us!" and saw Adeimantus turn back for a word in Eurybiades's ear. The Spartan had shaken his head, but Themistocles did not deceive himself. In the battle at morn half of the Hellenes would go to battle asking more "how escape?" than "how conquer?" and that was no question to ask before a victory.

The cabin was empty now save for the admiral. On the deck above the hearty shouts of Ameinias the trierarch, and chanting of the seamen told that on the *Nausicaä* at least there would be no slackness in the fight. The ship was being stripped for action, needless spars and sails sent ashore, extra oars made ready, and grappling-irons placed. "Battle" was what every Athenian prayed for, but amongst the allies Themistocles knew it was otherwise. The crucial hour of his life found him nervous, moody, silent. He repelled the zealous subalterns who came for orders.

"My directions have been given. Execute them. Has Aristeides come yet?" The last question was to Simonides, who had been half-companion, half-counsellor, in all these days of storm.

"He is not yet come from Ægina."

"Leave me, then."

Themistocles's frown deepened. The others went out.

The state cabin was elegant, considering its place. Themistocles had furnished it according to his luxurious taste,—stanchions cased in bronze hammered work, heavy rugs from Carthage, lamps swinging from chains of precious Corinthian brass. Behind a tripod stood an image of Aphrodite of Fair Counsel, the admiral's favourite deity. By force of habit now he crossed the cabin, took the golden box, and shook a few grains of frankincense upon the tripod.

"Attend, O queen," he said mechanically, "and be thou propitious to all my prayers."

He knew the words meant nothing. The puff of night air from the port-hole carried the fragrance from the room. The image wore its unchanging, meaningless smile, and Themistocles smiled too, albeit bitterly.

"So this is the end. A losing fight, cowardice, slavery—no, I shall not live to see that last."

He looked from the port-hole. He could see the lights of the Barbarian fleet clearly. He took long breaths of the clear brine.

"So the tragedy ends—worse than Phrynicus's poorest, when they pelted his chorus from the orchestra with date-stones. And yet—and yet—"

He never formulated what came next even in his own mind.

"*Eu!*" he cried, springing back with part of his old lightness, "I have borne a brave front before it all. I have looked the Cyclops in the face, even when he glowered the fiercest. But it all will pass. I presume Thersytes the caitiff and Agamemnon the king have the same sleep and the same dreams in Orchus. And a few years more or a few less in a man's life make little matter. But it would be sweeter to go out thinking 'I have triumphed' than 'I have failed, and all the things I loved fail with me.' And Athens—"

Again he stopped. When he resumed his monologue, it was in a different key.

"There are many things I cannot understand. They cannot unlock the riddles at Delphi, no seer can read them in the omens of birds. Why was Glaucon blasted? Was he a traitor? What was the truth concerning his treason? Since his going I have lost half my faith in mortal men."

Once more his thoughts wandered.

"How they trust me, my followers of Athens! Is it not better to be a leader of one city of freemen than a Xerxes, master of a hundred million slaves? How they greeted me, as if I were Apollo the Saviour, when I returned to Peiræus! And must it be written by the chroniclers thereafter, 'About this time Themistocles, son of Neocles, aroused the Athenians to hopeless resistance and drew on them utter destruction'? O Father Zeus, must men say *that*? Am I a fool or crazed for wishing to save my land from the fate of Media, Lydia, Babylonia, Egypt, Ionia? Has dark Atropos decreed that the Persians should conquer forever? Then, O Zeus, or whatever be thy name, O Power of Powers, look to thine empire! Xerxes is not a king, but a god; he will besiege Olympus, even thy throne."

He crossed the cabin with hard strides.

"How can I?" he cried half-aloud, beating his forehead. "How can I make these Hellenes fight?"

His hand tightened over his sword-hilt.

"This is the only place where we can fight to advantage. Here in the strait betwixt Salamis and Attica we have space to deploy all our ships, while the Barbarians will be crowded by numbers. And if we once retreat?—Let Adeimantus and the rest prate about—'The wall, the wall across the Isthmus! The king can never storm it.' Nor will he try to, unless his councillors are turned stark mad. Will he not have command of the sea? can he not land his army behind the wall, wherever he wills? Have I not dinned that argument in those doltish Peloponnesians' ears until I have grown hoarse? Earth and gods! suffer me rather to convince a stone statue than a Dorian. The task is less hard. Yet they call themselves reasoning beings."

A knock upon the cabin door. Simonides reëntered.

"You do not come on deck, Themistocles? The men ask for you. Ameinias's cook has prepared a noble supper—anchovies and tunny—will you not join the other officers and drink a cup to Tychē, Lady Fortune, that she prosper us in the morning?"

"I am at odds with Tychē, Simonides. I cannot come with you."

"The case is bad, then?"

"Ay, bad. But keep a brave face before the men. There's no call to pawn our last chance."

"Has it come to that?" quoth the little poet, in curiosity and concern.

"Leave me!" ordered Themistocles, with a sweep of the hand, and Simonides was wise enough to obey.

Themistocles took a pen from the table, but instead of writing on the outspread sheet of papyrus, thrust the reed between his teeth and bit it fiercely.

"How can I? How can I make these Hellenes fight? Tell that, King Zeus, tell that!"

Then quickly his eager brain ran from expedient to expedient.

"Another oracle, some lucky prediction that we shall conquer? But I have shaken the oracle books till there is only chaff in them. Or a bribe to Adeimantus and his fellows? But gold can buy only souls, not courage. Or another brave speech and convincing argument? Had I the tongue of Nestor and the wisdom of Thales, would those doltish Dorians listen?"

Again the knock, still again Simonides. The dapper poet's face was a cubit long.

"Oh, grief to report it! Cimon sends a boat from his ship the *Perseus*. He says the *Dikē*, the Sicyonian ship beside him, is not stripping for battle, but rigging sail on her spars as if to flee away."

"Is that all?" asked Themistocles, calmly.

"And there is also a message that Adeimantus and many other admirals who are minded like him have gone again to Eurybiades to urge him not to fight."

"I expected it."

"Will the Spartan yield?" The little poet was whitening.

"Very likely. Eurybiades would be a coward if he were not too much of a fool."

"And you are not going to him instantly, to confound the faint hearts and urge them to quit themselves like Hellenes?"

"Not yet."

"By the dog of Egypt, man," cried Simonides, seizing his friend's arm, "don't you know that if nothing's done, we'll all walk the asphodel to-morrow?"

"Of course. I am doing all I can."

"All? You stand with folded hands!"

"All—for I am thinking."

"Thinking—oh, make actions of your thoughts!"

"I will."

"When?"

"When the god opens the way. Just now the way is fast closed."

"*Ai!* woe—and it is already far into the evening, and Hellas is lost."

Themistocles laughed almost lightly.

"No, my friend. Hellas will not be lost until to-morrow morning, and much can happen in a night. Now go, and let me think yet more."

Simonides lingered. He was not sure Themistocles was master of himself. But the admiral beckoned peremptorily, the poet's hand was on the cabin door, when a loud knock sounded on the other side. The *prōreus*, commander of the fore-deck and Ameinas's chief lieutenant, entered and saluted swiftly.

"Your business?" questioned the admiral, sharply.

"May it please your Excellency, a deserter."

"A deserter, and how and why here?"

"He came to the *Nausicaä* in a skiff. He swears he has just come from the Barbarians at Phaleron. He demands to see the admiral."

"He is a Barbarian?"

"No, a Greek. He affects to speak a kind of Doric dialect."

Themistocles laughed again, and even more lightly.

"A deserter, you say. Then why, by Athena's owls, has he left 'the Land of Roast Hare' among the Persians, whither so many are betaking themselves? We've not so many deserters to our cause that to-night we can ignore one. Fetch him in."

"But the council with Eurybiades?" implored Simonides, almost on his knees.

"To the harpies with it! I asked Zeus for an omen. It comes—a fair one. There is time to hear this deserter, to confound Adeimantus, and to save Hellas too!"

Themistocles tossed his head. The wavering, the doubting frown was gone. He was himself again. What he hoped for, what device lay in that inexhaustible brain of his, Simonides did not know. But the sight itself of this strong, smiling man gave courage. The officer reëntered, with him a young man, his face in part concealed by a thick beard and a peaked cap drawn low upon his forehead. The stranger came boldly across to Themistocles, spoke a few words, whereat the admiral instantly bade the officer to quit the cabin.

CHAPTER XXVII
THE CRAFT OF ODYSSEUS

The stranger drew back the shaggy cap. Simonides and Themistocles saw a young, well-formed man. With his thick beard and the flickering cabin lamps it was impossible to discover more. The newcomer stood silent as if awaiting remark from the others, and they in turn looked on him.

"Well," spoke the admiral, at length, "who are you? Why are you here?"

"You do not know me?"

"Not in the least, and my memory is good. But your speech now is Attic, not Doric as they told me."

"It may well be Attic, I am Athenian born."

"Athenian? And still to me a stranger? Ah! an instant. Your voice is familiar. Where have I heard it before?"

"The last time," rejoined the stranger, his tones rising, "it was a certain night at Colonus. Democrates and Hermippus were with you—likewise—"

Themistocles leaped back three steps.

"The sea gives up its dead. You are Glaucon son of—"

"Conon," completed the fugitive, folding his arms calmly, but the admiral was not so calm.

"Miserable youth! What harpy, what evil god has brought you hither? What prevents that I give you over to the crew to crucify at the foremast?"

"Nothing hinders! nothing"—Glaucon's voice mounted to shrillness—"save that Athens and Hellas need all their sons this night."

"A loyal son you have been!" darted Themistocles, his lips curling. "Where did you escape the sea?"

"I was washed on Astypalæa."

"Where have you been since?"

"In Sardis."

"Who protected you there?"

"Mardonius."

"Did the Persians treat you so shabbily that you were glad to desert them?"

"They loaded me with riches and honour. Xerxes showered me with benefits."

"And you accompanied their army to Hellas? You went with the other Greek renegades—the sons of Hippias and the rest?"

Glaucon's brow grew very red, but he met Themistocles's arrowlike gaze.

"I did—and yet—"

"Ah, yes—the 'yet,'" observed Themistocles, sarcastically. "I had expected it. Well, I can imagine many motives for coming,—to betray our hopes to the Persians, or even because Athena has put some contrite manhood in your heart. You know, of course, that the resolution we passed recalling the exiles did not extend pardon to traitors."

"I know it."

Themistocles flung himself into a chair. The admiral was in a rare condition for him,—truly at a loss to divine the best word and question.

"Sit also, Simonides," his order, "and you, once Alcmæonid and now outlaw, tell why, after these confessions, I should believe any other part of your story?"

"I do not ask you to believe,"—Glaucon stood like a statue,—"I shall not blame you if you do the worst,—yet you shall hear—"

The admiral made an impatient gesture, commanding "Begin," and the fugitive poured out his tale. All the voyage from Phaleron he had been nerving himself for this ordeal; his composure did not desert now. He related lucidly, briefly, how the fates had dealt with him since he fled Colonus. Only when he told of his abiding with Leonidas Themistocles's gaze grew sharper.

"Tell that again. Be careful. I am very good at detecting lies."

Glaucon repeated unfalteringly.

"What proof that you were with Leonidas?"

"None but my word. Euboulus of Corinth and the Spartans alone knew my name. They are dead."

"Humph! And you expect me to accept the boast of a traitor with a price upon his head?"

"You said you were good at detecting lies."

Themistocles's head went down between his hands; at last he lifted it and gazed the deserter in the face.

"Now, son of Conon, do you still persist that you are innocent? Do you repeat those oaths you swore at Colonus?"

"All. I did not write that letter."

"Who did, then?"

"A malignant god, I said. I will say it again."

Themistocles shook his head.

"Gods take human agencies to ruin a man in these days, even Hermes the Trickster. Again I say, who wrote that letter?"

"Athena knows."

"And unfortunately her Ladyship the Goddess will not tell," cried the admiral, blasphemously. "Let us fall back on easier questions. Did I write it?"

"Absurd."

"Did Democrates?"

"Absurd again, still—"

"Do you not see, dearest outlaw," said Themistocles, mildly, "until you can lay that letter on some other man's shoulders, I cannot answer, 'I believe you'?"

"I did not ask that. I have a simpler request. Will you let me serve Hellas?"

"How do I know you are not a spy sent from Mardonius?"

"Because too many deserters and talebearers are flying to Xerxes now to require that I thrust my head in the Hydra's jaws. You know surely that."

Themistocles raised his eyebrows.

"There's truth said there, Simonides. What do you think?" The last question was to the poet.

"That this Glaucon, whatever his guilt a year ago, comes to-night in good faith."

"*Euge!* that's easily said. But what if he betrays us again?"

"If I understand aright," spoke Simonides, shrewdly, "our case is such there's little left worth betraying."

"Not badly put,"—again Themistocles pressed his forehead, while Glaucon stood as passive as hard marble. Then the admiral suddenly began to rain questions like an arrow volley.

"You come from the king's camp?"

"Yes."

"And have heard the plans of battle?"

"I was not at the council, but nothing is concealed. The Persians are too confident."

"Of course. How do their ships lie?"

"Crowded around the havens of Athens. The vassal Ionians have their ships on the left. The Phœnicians, Xerxes's chief hope, lie on the right, but on the extreme right anchor the Egyptians."

"How do you know this?"

"From the camp-followers' talk. Then, too, I rowed by the whole armada while on my way to Salamis. I have eyes. The moon was shining. I was not mistaken."

"Do you know where rides the trireme of Ariabignes, Xerxes's admiral-in-chief?"

"Off the entrance to Peiræus. It is easy to find her. She is covered with lights."

"Ah! and the Egyptian squadron is on the extreme right and closest to Salamis?"

"Very close."

"If they went up the coast as far as the promontory on Mt. Ægaleos, the strait toward Eleusis would be closed?"

"Certainly."

"And on the south the way is already blocked by the Ionians."

"I had trouble in passing even in my skiff."

More questions, Glaucon not knowing whither they all were drifting. Without warning Themistocles uprose and smote his thigh.

"So you are anxious to serve Hellas?"

"Have I not said it?"

"Dare you die for her?"

"I made the choice once with Leonidas."

"Dare you do a thing which, if it slip, may give you into the hands of the Barbarians to be torn by wild horses or of the Greeks to be crucified?"

"But it shall not slip!"

"*Euge!* that is a noble answer. Now let us come."

"Whither?"

"To Eurybiades's flag-ship. Then I can know whether you must risk the deed."

Themistocles touched a bronze gong; a marine adjutant entered.

"My pinnace," ordered the admiral. As the man went out, Themistocles took a long himation from the locker and wrapped it around the newcomer.

"Since even Simonides and I did not recognize you in your long beard, I doubt if you are in danger of detection to-night. But remember your name is Critias. You can dye your hair if you come safe back from this adventure. Have you eaten?"

"Who has hunger now?"

Themistocles laughed.

"So say all of us. But if the gifts of Demeter cannot strengthen, it is not so with those of Dionysus. Drink."

He took from a hook a leathern bottle and poured out a hornful of hot Chian. Glaucon did not refuse. After he had finished the admiral did likewise. Then Glaucon in turn asked questions.

"Where is my wife?"

"In the town of Salamis, with her father; do you know she has borne—"

"A son. Are both well?"

"Well. The child is fair as the son of Leto."

They could see the light flash out of the eyes of the outlaw. He turned toward the statue and stretched out his hand.

"O Aphrodite, I bless thee!" Then again to the admiral, "And Hermione is not yet given to Democrates in marriage?" The words came swiftly.

"Not yet. Hermippus desires it. Hermione resists. She calls Democrates your destroyer."

Glaucon turned away his face that they might not behold it.

"The god has not yet forgotten mercy," Simonides thought he heard him say.

"The pinnace is waiting, *kyrie*," announced the orderly from the companionway.

"Let the deserter's skiff be towed behind," ordered Themistocles, once on deck, "and let Sicinnus also go with me."

The keen-eyed Asiatic took his place with Themistocles and Glaucon in the stern. The sturdy boatmen sent the pinnace dancing. All through the brief voyage the admiral was at whispers with Sicinnus. As they reached the Spartan flag-ship, half a score of pinnaces trailing behind told how the Peloponnesian admirals were already aboard clamouring at Eurybiades for orders to fly. From the ports of the stern-cabin the glare of many lamps spread wavering bars of light across the water. Voices came, upraised in jarring debate. The marine guard saluted with his spear as Themistocles went up the ladder. Leaving his companions on deck, the admiral hastened below. An instant later he was back and beckoned the Asiatic and the outlaw to the ship's rail.

"Take Sicinnus to the Persian high admiral," was his ominous whisper, "and fail not,—fail not, for I say to you except the god prosper you now, not all Olympus can save our Hellas to-morrow."

Not another word as he turned again to the cabin. The pinnace crew had brought the skiff alongside, Sicinnus entered it, Glaucon took the oars, pulled out a little, as if back to the *Nausicaä*, then sent the head of the skiff around, pointing across the strait, toward the havens of Athens. Sicinnus sat in silence, but Glaucon guessed the errand. The wind was rising and bringing clouds. This would hide the moon and lessen the danger. But above all things speed was needful. The athlete put his strength upon the oars till the heavy skiff shot across the black void of the water.

* * * * * *

It was little short of midnight when Glaucon swung the skiff away from the tall trireme of Ariabignes, the Barbarian's admiral. The deed was done. He had sat in the bobbing boat while Sicinnus had been above with the Persian chiefs. Officers who had exchanged the wine-cup with Glaucon in the days when he stood at Xerxes's side passed through the glare of the battle lanterns swaying above the rail. The Athenian had gripped at the dagger in his belt as he watched them. Better in the instant of discovery to slay one's self than die a few hours afterward by slow tortures! But discovery had not come. Sicinnus had come down the ladder, smiling, jesting, a dozen subalterns salaaming as he went, and offering all manner of service, for had he not been a bearer of great good tidings to the king?

"Till to-morrow," an olive-skinned Cilician navarch had spoken.

"Till to-morrow," waved the messenger, lightly. He did all things coolly, as if he had been bearing an invitation to a feast, took his post in the stern of the skiff deliberately, then turned to the silent man with him.

"Pull."

"Whither?" Glaucon was already tugging the oars.

"To Eurybiades's ship. Themistocles is waiting. And again all speed."

The line of twinkling water betwixt the skiff and the Persian widened. For a few moments Glaucon bent himself silently to his task, then for the first time questioned.

"What have you done?"

Even in the darkness he knew Sicinnus grinned and showed his teeth.

"In the name of Themistocles I have told the Barbarian chiefs that the Hellenes are at strife one with another, that they are meditating a hasty flight, that if the king's captains will but move their ships so as to enclose them, it is likely there will be no battle in the morning, but the Hellenes will fall into the hands of Xerxes unresisting."

"And the Persian answered?"

"That I and my master would not fail of reward for this service to the king. That the Egyptian ships would be swung at once across the strait to cut off all flight by the Hellenes."

The outlaw made no answer, but pulled at the oars. The reaction from the day and evening of strain and peril was upon him. He was unutterably weary, though more in mind than in body. The clumsy skiff seemed only to crawl. Trusting the orders of Sicinnus to steer him aright, he closed his eyes. One picture after another of his old life came up before him now he was in the stadium at Corinth and facing the giant Spartan, now he stood by Hermione on the sacred Rock at Athens, now he was at Xerxes's side with the fleets and the myriads passing before them at the Hellespont, he saw his wife, he saw Roxana, and all other things fair and lovely that had crossed his life. Had he made the best choice? Were the desperate fates of Hellas better than the flower-banked streams of Bactria, whose delights he had forever thrust by? Would his Fortune, guider of every human destiny, bring him at last to a calm haven, or would his life go out amid the crashing ships to-morrow? The oars bumped on the thole-pins. He pulled mechanically, the revery ever deepening, then a sharp hail awoke him.

"O-op! What do you here?"

The call was in Phœnician. Glaucon scarce knew the harsh Semitic speech, but the *lembos*, a many-oared patrol cutter, was nearly on them. A moment more, and seizure would be followed by identification. Life, death, Hellas, Hermione, all flashed before his eyes as he sat numbed, but Sicinnus saved them both.

"The password to-night? You know it," he demanded in quick whisper.

" 'Hystaspes,' " muttered Glaucon, still wool-gathering.

"Who are you? Why here?" An officer in the cutter was rising and upholding an unmasked lantern. "We've been ordered to cruise in the channel and snap up deserters, and by Baal, here are twain! The crows will pick at your eyes to-morrow."

Sicinnus stood upright in the skiff.

"Fool," he answered in good Sidonian, "dare you halt the king's privy messenger? It is not *our* heads that the crows will find the soonest."

The cutter was close beside them, but the officer dropped his lantern.

"Good, then. Give the password."

" 'Hystaspes.' "

They could see the Phœnician's hand rise to his head in salute.

"Forgive my rudeness, worthy sir. It's truly needless to seek deserters to-night with the Hellenes' affairs so desperate, yet we must obey his Eternity's orders."

"I pardon you," quoth the emissary, loftily, "I will commend your vigilance to the admiral."

"May Moloch give your Lordship ten thousand children," called back the mollified Semite.

The crew of the cutter dropped their blades into the water. The boats glided apart. Not till there was a safe stretch betwixt them did Glaucon begin to grow hot, then cold, then hot again. Chill Thanatos had passed and missed by a hair's breadth. Again the bumping of the oars and the slow, slow creeping over the water. The night was darkening. The clouds had hid the moon and all her stars. Sicinnus, shrewd and weatherwise, remarked, "There will be a stiff wind in the morning," and lapsed into silence. Glaucon toiled on resolutely. A fixed conviction was taking possession of his mind,—one that had come on the day he had been preserved at Thermopylæ, now deepened by the event just passed,—that he was being reserved by the god for some crowning service to Hellas, after which should come peace, whether the peace of a warrior who dies in the arms of victory, whether the peace of a life spent after a deed well done, he scarcely knew, and in the meantime, if the storms must beat and the waves rise up against him, he would bear them still. Like the hero of his race, he could say, "Already have I suffered much and much have I toiled in perils of waves and war, let this be added to the tale of those."

Bump—bump, the oars played their monotonous music on the thole-pins. Sicinnus stirred on his seat. He was peering northward anxiously, and Glaucon knew what he was seeking. Through the void of the night their straining eyes saw masses gliding across the face of the water. Ariabignes was making his promise good. Yonder the Egyptian fleet were swinging forth to close the last retreat of the Hellenes. Thus on the north, and southward, too, other triremes were thrusting out, bearing—both watchers wisely guessed— a force to disembark on Psyttaleia, the islet betwixt Salamis and the main, a vantage-point in the coming battle.

The coming battle? It was so silent, ghostlike, far away, imagination scarce could picture it. Was this black slumberous water to be the scene at dawn of a combat beside which that of Hector and Achilles under Troy would be only as a tale that is told? And was he, Glaucon, son of Conon the Alcmæonid, sitting there in the skiff alone with Sicinnus, to have a part therein, in a battle the fame whereof should ring through the ages? Bump, bump—still the monologue of the oars. A fish near by leaped from the water, splashing loudly. Then for an instant the clouds broke. Selene uncovered her face. The silvery flash quickly come, more quickly flying, showed him the headlands of that Attica now in Xerxes's hands. He saw Pentelicus and Hymettus, Parnes and Cithæron, the hills he had wandered over in glad boyhood, the hills where rested his ancestors' dust. It was no dream. He felt his warm blood quicken. He felt the round-bowed skiff spring over the waves, as with unwearied hands he tugged at the oar. There are moments when the dullest mind grows prophetic, and the mind of the Athenian was not dull. The moonlight had vanished. In its place through the magic darkness seemed gathering all the heroes of his people beckoning him and his compeers onward. Perseus was there, and Theseus and Erechtheus, Heracles the Mighty, and Odysseus the Patient, whose intellect Themistocles possessed, Solon the Wise, Periander the Crafty, Diomedes the Undaunted, men of reality, men of fable, sages, warriors, demigods, crowding together, speaking one message: "Be strong, for the heritage of what you do this coming day shall be passed beyond children's children, shall be passed down to peoples to whom the tongue, the gods, yea, the name of Hellas, are but as a dream."

Glaucon felt the weariness fly from him. He was refreshed as never by wine. Then through the void in place of the band of heroes slowly outspread the tracery of a vessel at anchor,—the outermost guardship of the fleet of the Hellenes. They were again amongst friends. The watcher on the trireme was keeping himself awake after the manner of sentries by singing. In the night-stillness the catch from Archilochus rang lustily.

"By my spear I have won my bread,

By spear won my clear, red wine,

On my spear I will lean and drink,—

Show me a merrier life than is mine!"

The trolling called Glaucon back to reality. Guided by Sicinnus, who knew the stations of the Greek fleet better than he, a second time they came beside the Spartan admiral. The lamps were still burning in the stern-cabin. Even before they were alongside, they caught the clamours of fierce debate.

"Still arguing?" quoth Sicinnus to the yawning marine officer who advanced to greet them as they reached the top of the ladder.

"Still arguing," grunted the Spartan. "I think your master has dragged forth all his old arguments and invented a thousand new ones. He talks continuously, as if battling for time, though only Castor knows wherefore. There's surely a majority against him."

The emissary descended the companionway, Themistocles leaped up from his seat in the crowded council. A few whispers, the Asiatic returned to Glaucon on the deck. The two gazed down the companionway, observing everything. They had not long to wait.

CHAPTER XXVIII
BEFORE THE DEATH GRAPPLE

For the fourth time the subaltern who stood at Eurybiades's elbow turned the water-glass that marked the passing of the hours. The lamps in the low-ceiled cabin were flickering dimly. Men glared on one another across the narrow table with drawn and heated faces. Adeimantus of Corinth was rising to reply to the last appeal of the Athenian.

"We have had enough, Eurybiades, of Themistocles's wordy folly. Because the Athenian admiral is resolved to lead all Hellas to destruction, is no reason that we should follow. As for his threat that he will desert us with his ships if we refuse to fight, I fling it in his face that he dare not make it good. Why go all over the well-threshed straw again? Is not the fleet of the king overwhelming? Were we not saved by a miracle from overthrow at Artemisium? Do not the scouts tell us the Persians are advancing beyond Eleusis toward Megara and the Isthmus? Is not our best fighting blood here in the fleet? Then if the Isthmus is threatened, our business is to defend it and save the Peloponnesus, the last remnant of Hellas unconquered. Now then, headstrong son of Neocles, answer that!"

The Corinthian, a tall domineering man, threw back his shoulders like a boxer awaiting battle. Themistocles did not answer, but only smiled up at him from his seat opposite.

"I have silenced you, grinning babbler, at last," thundered Adeimantus, "and I demand of you, O Eurybiades, that we end this tedious debate. If we are to retreat, let us retreat. A vote, I say, a vote!"

Eurybiades rose at the head of the table. He was a heavy, florid individual with more than the average Spartan's slowness of tongue and intellect. Physically he was no coward, but he dreaded responsibility.

"Much has been said," he announced ponderously, "many opinions offered. It would seem the majority of the council favour the decision to retire forthwith. Has Themistocles anything more to say why the vote should not be taken?"

"Nothing," rejoined the Athenian, with an equanimity that made Adeimantus snap his teeth.

"We will therefore take the vote city by city," went on Eurybiades. "Do you, Phlegon of Seriphos, give your vote."

Seriphos—wretched islet—sent only one ship, but thanks to the Greek mania for "equality" Phlegon's vote had equal weight with that of Themistocles.

"Salamis is not defensible," announced the Seriphian, shortly. "Retreat."

"And you, Charmides of Melos?"

"Retreat."

"And you, Phoibodas of Trœzene?"

"Retreat, by all the gods."

"And you, Hippocrates of Ægina?"

"Stay and fight. If you go back to the Isthmus, Ægina must be abandoned to the Barbarians. I am with Themistocles."

"Record his vote," shouted Adeimantus, ill-naturedly, "he is but one against twenty. But I warn you, Eurybiades, do not call for Themistocles's vote, or the rest of us will be angry. The man whose city is under the power of the Barbarian has no vote in this council, however much we condescend to listen to his chatterings."

The Athenian sprang from his seat, his aspect as threatening as Apollo descending Olympus in wrath.

"Where is my country, Adeimantus? Yonder!" he pointed out the open port-hole, "there rides the array of our Athenian ships. What other state in Hellas sends so many and sets better men within them? Athens still lives, though her Acropolis be wrapped in flames. 'Strong-hearted men and naught else are warp and woof of a city.' Do you forget Alcæus's word so soon, O Boaster from Corinth? Yes, by Athena Promachos, Mistress of Battles, while those nine score ships ride on the deep, I have a city fairer, braver, than yours. And will you still deny me equal voice and vote with this noble trierarch from Siphinos with his one, or with his comrade from Melos with his twain?"

Themistocles's voice rang like a trumpet. Adeimantus winced. Eurybiades broke in with soothing tones.

"No one intends to deny your right to vote, Themistocles. The excellent Corinthian did but jest."

"A fitting hour for jesting!" muttered the Athenian, sinking back into his seat.

"The vote, the vote!" urged the Sicyonian chief, from Adeimantus's elbow, and the voting went on. Of more than twenty voices only three—Themistocles's and those of the Æginetan and Megarian admirals—were in favour of abiding the onset. Yet even when Eurybiades arose to announce the decision, the son of Neocles sat with his hands sprawling on the table, his face set in an inscrutable smile as he looked on Adeimantus.

"It is the plain opinion,"—Eurybiades hemmed and hawed with his words,—"the plain opinion, I say, of this council that the allied fleet retire at once to the Isthmus. Therefore, I, as admiral-in-chief, do order each commander to proceed to his own flag-ship and prepare his triremes to retire at dawn."

"Well said," shouted Adeimantus, already on his feet; "now to obey."

But with him rose Themistocles. He stood tall and calm, his thumbs thrust in his girdle. His smile was a little broader, his head held a little higher, than of wont.

"Good Eurybiades, I grieve to blast the wisdom of all these valiant gentlemen, but they cannot retire if they wish."

"Explain!" a dozen shouted.

"Very simply. I have had good reason to know that the king has moved forward the western horn of his fleet, so as to enclose our anchorage at Salamis. It is impossible to retire save through the Persian line of battle."

Perseus upholding the Gorgon's head before Polydectes's guests and turning them to stone wrought hardly more of a miracle than this calm announcement of Themistocles. Men stared at him vacantly, stunned by the tidings, then Adeimantus's frightened wrath broke loose.

"Fox![10] Was this your doing?"

"I did not ask you to thank me, *philotate*," was the easy answer. "It is, however, urgent to consider whether you wish to be taken unresisting in the morning."

The Corinthian shook his fist across the table.

"Liar, as a last device to ruin us, you invent this folly."

"It is easy to see if I lie," rejoined Themistocles; "send out a pinnace and note where the Persians anchor. It will not take long."

For an instant swords seemed about to leap from their scabbards, and the enraged Peloponnesians to sheathe them in the Athenian's breast. He stood unflinching, smiling, while a volley of curses flew over him. Then an orderly summoned him on deck, while Adeimantus and his fellows foamed and contended below. Under the battle lantern Themistocles saw a man who was his elder in years, rugged in feature, with massive forehead and wise gray eyes. This was Aristeides the Just, the admiral's enemy, but their feud had died when Xerxes drew near to Athens.

Hands clasped heartily as the twain stood face to face.

"Our rivalry forever more shall be a rivalry which of us can do most to profit Athens," spoke the returning exile; then Aristeides told how he had even now come from Ægina, how he had heard of the clamours to retreat, how retreat was impossible, for the Persians were pressing in. A laugh from Themistocles interrupted.

"My handiwork! Come to the council. They will not believe me, no, not my oath."

Aristeides told his story, and how his vessel to Salamis had scarce escaped the Egyptian triremes, and how by this time all entrance and exit was surely closed. But even now many an angry captain called him "liar." The strife of words was at white heat when Eurybiades himself silenced the fiercest doubter.

"Captains of Hellas, a trireme of Teos has deserted from the Barbarian to us. Her navarch sends word that all is even as Themistocles and Aristeides tell. The Egyptians hold the passage to Eleusis. Infantry are disembarked on Psyttaleia. The Phœnicians and Ionians enclose us on the eastern strait. We are hemmed in."

* * * * * *

Once more the orderly turned the water-clock. It was past midnight. The clouds had blown apart before the rising wind. The debate must end. Eurybiades stood again to take the votes of the wearied, tense-strung men.

"In view of the report of the Teans, what is your voice and vote?"

Before all the rest up leaped Adeimantus. He was no craven at heart, though an evil genius had possessed him.

"You have your will, Themistocles," he made the concession sullenly yet firmly, "you have your will. May Poseidon prove you in the right. If it is battle or slavery at dawn, the choice is quick. Battle!"

"Battle!" shouted the twenty, arising together, and Eurybiades had no need to declare the vote. The commanders scattered to their flag-ships, to give orders to be ready to fight at dawn. Themistocles went to his pinnace last. He walked proudly. He knew that whatever glory he might gain on the morrow, he could never win a fairer victory than he had won that night. When his barge came alongside, his boat crew knew that his eyes were dancing, that his whole mien was of a man in love with his fortune. Many times, as Glaucon sat beside him, he heard the son of Neocles repeating as in ecstasy:—

"They must fight. They must fight."

* * * * * * *

Glaucon sat mutely in the pinnace which had headed not for the *Nausicaä*, but toward the shore, where a few faint beacons were burning.

"I must confer with the strategi as to the morning," Themistocles declared after a long interval, at which Sicinnus broke in anxiously:—

"You will not sleep, *kyrie?*"

"Sleep?" laughed the admiral, as at an excellent jest, "I have forgotten there was such a god as Hypnos." Then, ignoring Sicinnus, he addressed the outlaw.

"I am grateful to you, my friend," he did not call Glaucon by name before the others, "you have saved me, and I have saved Hellas. You brought me a new plan when I seemed at the last resource. How can the son of Neocles reward you?"

"Give me a part to play to-morrow."

"Thermopylæ was not brisk enough fighting, ha? Can you still fling a javelin?"

"I can try."

"*Euge!* Try you shall." He let his voice drop. "Do not forget your name henceforth is Critias. The *Nausicaä's* crew are mostly from Sunium and the Mesogia. They'd hardly recognize you under that beard; still Sicinnus must alter you."

"Command me, *kyrie*," said the Asiatic.

"A strange time and place, but you must do it. Find some dark dye for this man's hair to-night, and at dawn have him aboard the flag-ship."

"The thing can be done, *kyrie.*"

"After that, lie down and sleep. Because Themistocles is awake, is no cause for others' star-gazing. Sleep sound. Pray Apollo and Hephæstus to make your eye sure, your hand strong. Then awake to see the glory of Hellas."

Confidence, yes, power came through the tones of the admiral's voice. Themistocles went away to the belated council. Sicinnus led his charge through the crooked streets of the town of Salamis. Sailors were sleeping in the open night, and they stumbled over them. At last they found a small tavern where a dozen shipmen sprawled on the earthen floor, and a gaping host was just quenching his last lamp. Sicinnus, however, seemed to know him. There was much protesting and headshaking, at last ended by the glint of a daric. The man grumbled, departed, returned after a tedious interval with a pot of ointment, found Hermes knew where. By a rush-candle's flicker Sicinnus applied the dark dye with a practised hand.

"You know the art well," observed the outlaw.

"Assuredly; the agent of Themistocles must be a Proteus with his disguises."

Sicinnus laid down his pot and brushes. They had no mirror, but Glaucon knew that he was transformed. The host got his daric. Again they went out into the night and forsaking the crowded town sought the seaside. The strand was broad, the sand soft and cool, the circling stars gave three hours yet of night, and they lay down to rest. The sea and the shore stretched away, a magic vista with a thousand mystic shapes springing out of the charmed darkness, made and unmade as overwrought fancy summoned them. As from an unreal world Glaucon—whilst he lay—saw the lights of the scattered ships, heard the clank of chains, the rattling of tacklings. Nature slept. Only man was waking.

"The mountain brows, the rocks, the peaks are sleeping,

Uplands and gorges hush!

The thousand moorland things are silence keeping,

The beasts under each bush

Crouch, and the hived bees

Rest in their honeyed ease;

In the purple sea fish lie as they were dead,

And each bird folds his wing over his head."

The school-learned lines of Alcman, with a thousand other trivial things, swarmed back through the head of Glaucon the Alcmæonid. How much he had lived through that night, how much he would live through,—if indeed he was to live,—upon the morrow! The thought was benumbing in its greatness. His head swam with confused memories. Then at last all things dimmed. Once more he dreamed. He was with Hermione gathering red poppies on the hill above Eleusis. She had filled her basket full. He called to her to wait for him. She ran away. He chased, she fled with laughter and sparkling eyes. He could hear the wavings of her dress, the little cries she flung back over her shoulder. Then by the sacred well near the temple he caught her. He felt her struggling gayly. He felt her warm breath upon his face, her hair was touching his forehead. Rejoicing in his strength, he was bending her head toward his—but here he wakened. Sicinnus had disappeared. A bar of gray gold hung over the water in the east.

"This was the day. *This was the day!*"

Some moments he lay trying to realize the fact in its full moment. A thin mist rested on the black water waiting to be dispelled by the sun. From afar came sounds not of seamen's trumpets, but horns, harps, kettledrums, from the hidden mainland across the strait, as of a host advancing along the shore. "Xerxes goes down to the marge with his myriads," Glaucon told himself. "Have not all his captains bowed and smiled, 'Your Eternity's victory is certain. Come and behold.' " But here the Athenian shut his teeth.

People at length were passing up and down the strand. The coast was waking. The gray bar was becoming silver. Friends passed, deep in talk,—perchance for the last time. Glaucon lay still a moment longer, and as he rested caught a voice so familiar he felt all the blood surge to his forehead,—Democrates's voice.

"I tell you, Hiram,—I told you before,—I have no part in the ordering of the fleet. Were I to interfere with ever so good a heart, it would only breed trouble for us all."

So close were the twain, the orator's trailing chiton almost fell on Glaucon's face. The latter marvelled that his own heart did not spring from its prison in his breast, so fierce were its beatings.

"If my Lord would go to Adeimantus and suggest,"—the other's Greek came with a marked Oriental accent.

"Harpy! Adeimantus is no Medizer. He is pushed to bay now, and is sure to fight. Have you Barbarians no confidence? Has not the king two triremes to our one? Only fools can demand more. Tell Lycon, your master, I have long since done my uttermost to serve him."

"Yet remember, Excellency."

"Begone, scoundrel. Don't threaten again. If I know your power over me, I can also promise you not to go down to Orchus alone, but take excellent pains to have fair company."

"I am sorry to bear such tidings to Lycon, Excellency."

"Away with you!"

"Do not raise your voice, *kyrie*," spoke Hiram, never more blandly, "here is a man asleep."

The hint sent Democrates from the spot almost on a run. Hiram disappeared in the opposite direction. Glaucon rose, shook the sand from his cloak, and stood an instant with his head whirling. The voice of his boyhood friend, of the man who had ruined him because of a suspicion of treason—and now deep in compromising talk with the agent of the chief of the peace party at Sparta! And wherefore had Mardonius spoken those mysterious words at their parting, "Beware of Democrates"? For an instant the problems evoked made him forget even the coming battle.

A clear trumpet-blast down the strand gave a truce to questioning. Sicinnus reappeared, and led Glaucon to one of the great fires roaring on the beach, where the provident Greek sailors were breakfasting on barley porridge and meat broth before dining on spears and arrow-heads. A silent company, no laughter, no jesting. All knew another sun for them might never rise. Glaucon ate not because he hungered, but because duty ordered it. As the light strengthened, the strand grew alive with thousands of men at toil. The triremes drawn on shore went down into the sea on their rollers. More trumpet-blasts sent the rowers aboard their ships. But last of all, before thrusting out to do or die, the Greeks must feast their ears as well as their stomachs. On the sloping beach gathered the officers and the armoured marines,—eighteen from each trireme,—and heard one stirring harangue after another. The old feuds were forgotten. Adeimantus and Eurybiades both spoke bravely. The seers announced that every bird and cloud gave good omen. Prayer was offered to Ajax of Salamis that the hero should fight for his people. Last of all Themistocles spoke, and never to fairer purpose. No boasts, no lip courage, a painting of the noble and the base, the glory of dying as freemen, the infamy of existing as slaves. He told of Marathon, of Thermopylæ, and asked if Leonidas had died as died a fool. He drew tears. He drew vows of vengeance. He never drew applause. Men were too strained for that. At last he sent the thousands forth.

"Go, then. Quit yourselves as Hellenes. That is all the task. And I say to you, in the after days this shall be your joy, to hear the greatest declare of you, 'Reverence this man, for he saved us all at Salamis.'"

The company dispersed, each man to his ship. Themistocles went to his pinnace, and a cheer uprose from sea and land as the boat shot out to the *Nausicaä*. Eurybiades might be chief in name; who did not know that Themistocles was the surest bulwark of Hellas?

The son of Neocles, standing in the boat, uplifted his face to the now golden east.

"Be witness, Helios," he cried aloud, "be witness when thou comest, I have done all things possible. And do thou and thy fellow-gods on bright Olympus rule our battle now; the lot is in your hands!"

CHAPTER XXIX
SALAMIS

Sunrise. The *Nausicaä* was ready. Ameinias the navarch walked the deck above the stern-cabin with nervous strides. All that human forethought could do to prepare the ship had long been done. The slim hull one hundred and fifty feet long had been stripped of every superfluous rope and spar. The masts had been lowered. On the cat-heads hung the anchors weighted with stone to fend off an enemy, astern towed the pinnace ready to drag alongside and break the force of the hostile ram. The heavy-armed marines stood with their long boarding spears, to lead an attack or cast off grappling-irons. But the true weapon of the *Nausicaä* was herself. To send the three-toothed beak through a foeman's side was the end of her being. To meet the shock of collision two heavy cables had been bound horizontally around the hull from stem to stern. The oarsmen,—the *thranites* of the upper tier, the *zygites* of the middle, the *thalamites* of the lower,—one hundred and seventy swart, nervous-eyed men, sat on their benches, and let their hands close tight upon those oars which trailed now in the drifting water, but which soon and eagerly should spring to life. At the belt of every oarsman dangled a sword, for boarders' work was more than likely. Thirty spare rowers rested impatiently on the centre deck, ready to leap wherever needed. On the forecastle commanded the *prōreus*, Ameinias's lieutenant, and with him the *keleustes*, the oar master who must give time on his sounding-board for the rowing, and never fail,—not though the ships around reeled down to watery grave. And finally on the poop by the captain stood the "governor,"—knotted, grizzled, and keen,—the man whose touch upon the heavy steering oars might give the *Nausicaä* life or destruction when the ships charged beak to beak.

"The trireme is ready, admiral," reported Ameinias, as Themistocles came up leisurely from the stern-cabin.

The son of Neocles threw back his helmet, that all might see his calm, untroubled face. He wore a cuirass of silvered scale-armour over his purple chiton. At his side walked a young man, whom the ship's people imagined the deserter of the preceding night, but he had drawn his helmet close.

"This is Critias," said Themistocles, briefly, to the navarch; "he is a good caster. See that he has plenty of darts."

"One of Themistocles's secret agents," muttered the captain to the governor, "we should have guessed it." And they all had other things to think of than the whence and wherefore of this stranger.

It was a weary, nervous interval. Men had said everything, done everything, hoped and feared everything. They were in no mood even to invoke the gods.

In desperation some jested riotously as they gripped the oars on the benches,—demonstrations which the *prōreus* quelled with a loud "Silence in the ship." The morning mist was breaking. A brisk wind was coming with the sun. Clear and strong sang the Notus, the breeze of the kindly south. It covered the blue bay with crisping whitecaps, it sent the surf foaming up along the Attic shore across the strait. Themistocles watched it all with silent eyes, but eyes that spoke of gladness. He knew the waves would beat with full force on the Persian prows, and make their swift movement difficult while the Greeks, taking the galloping surf astern, would suffer little.

"Æolus fights for us. The first omen and a fair one." The word ran in whispers down the benches, and every soul on the trireme rejoiced.

How long did they sit thus? An æon? Would Eurybiades never draw out his line of battle? Would Adeimantus prove craven at the end? Would treachery undo Hellas to-day, as once before at Lade when the Ionian Greeks had faced the Persian fleet in vain? Now as the vapour broke, men began to be able to look about them, and be delivered from their own thoughts. The shores of Salamis were alive,—old men, women, little children,—the fugitives from Attica were crowding to the marge in thousands to watch the deed that should decide their all. And many a bronze-cheeked oarsman arose from his bench to wave farewell to the wife or father or mother, and sank back again,—a clutching in his throat, a mist before his eyes, while his grip upon the oar grew like to steel.

As the *Nausicaä* rode at her place in the long line of ships spread up and down the shore of Salamis, it was easy to detect forms if not faces on the strand. And Glaucon, peering out from his helmet bars, saw Democrates himself standing on the sands and beckoning to Themistocles. Then other figures became clear to him out of the many, this one or that whom he had loved and clasped hands with in the sunlit days gone by. And last of all he saw those his gaze hungered for the most, Hermippus, Lysistra, and another standing at their side all in white, and in her arms she bore something he knew must be her child,—Hermione's son, his son, born to the lot of a free man of Athens or a slave of Xerxes according as his elders played their part this day. Only a glimpse,—the throng of strangers opened to disclose them closed again; Glaucon leaned on a capstan. All the strength for the moment was gone out of him.

"You rowed and wrought too much last night, Critias," spoke Themistocles, who had eyes for everything. "To the cabin, Sicinnus, bring a cup of Chian."

"No wine, for Athena's sake!" cried the outlaw, drawing himself together, "it is passed. I am strong again."

A great shout from the shores and the waiting fleet made him forget even the sight of Hermione.

"They come! The Persians! The Persians!"

The fleet of the Barbarians was advancing from the havens of Athens.

* * * * * * *

The sun rose higher. He was far above Hymettus now, and shooting his bright javelins over mainland, islands, and waters. With his rising the southern breeze sang ever clearer, making the narrow channel betwixt Salamis and Attica white, and tossing each trireme merrily. Not a cloud hung upon Pentelicus, Hymettus, or the purple northern range of Parnes. Over the desolate Acropolis hovered a thin mist,—smoke from the smouldering temple, the sight of which made every Attic sailor blink hard and think of the vengeance.

Yonder on the shore of the mainland the host of the Persian was moving: horsemen in gilded panoply, Hydarnes's spearmen in armour like suns. They stood by myriads in glittering masses about a little spur of Mt. Ægaleos, where a holy close of Heracles looked out upon the sea. To them were coming more horsemen, chariots, litters, and across the strait drifted the thunderous acclamation, "Victory to the king!" For here on the ivory throne, with his mighty men, his captains, his harem, about him, the "Lord of the World" would look down on the battle and see how his slaves could fight.

Now the Barbarians began to move forth by sea. From the havens of Peiræus and their anchorages along the shore swept their galleys,—Phœnician, Cilician, Egyptian, and, sorrow of sorrows, Ionian—Greek arrayed against Greek! Six hundred triremes and more they were, taller in poop and prow than the Hellenes, and braver to look upon.

Each vied with each in the splendour of the scarlet, purple, and gold upon stern and foreship. Their thousands of white oars moved like the onward march of an army as they trampled down the foam. From the masts of their many admirals flew innumerable gay signal-flags. The commands shouted through trumpets in a dozen strange tongues—the shrill pipings of the oar masters, the hoarse shouts of the rowers—went up to heaven in a clamorous babel. "Swallows' chatter," cried the deriding Hellenes, but hearts were beating quicker, breath was coming faster in many a breast by Salamis then,—and no shame. For now was the hour of trial, the wrestle of Olympian Zeus with Ahura-Mazda. Now would a mighty one speak from the heavens to Hellas, and say to her "Die!" or "Be!"

The Barbarians' armadas were forming. Their black beaks, all pointing toward Salamis, stretched in two bristling lines from the islet of Psyttaleia—whence the shields of the landing force glittered—to that brighter glitter on the promontory by Ægaleos where sat the king. To charge their array seemed charging a moving hedge of spears, impenetrable in defence, invincible in attack. Slowly, rocked by the sea and rowing in steady order, the armament approached Salamis. And still the Greek ships lay spread out along the shore, each trireme swinging at the end of the cable which moored her to the land, each mariner listening to the beatings of his own heart and straining his eyes on one ship now—Eurybiades's—which rode at the centre of their line and far ahead.

All could read the order of battle at last as squadron lay against squadron. On the west, under Xerxes's own eye, the Athenians must charge the serried Phœnicians, at the centre the Æginetans must face the Cilicians, on the east Adeimantus and his fellows from Peloponnese must make good against the vassal Ionians. But would the signal to row and strike never come? Had some god numbed Eurybiades's will? Was treachery doing its darkest work? With men so highly wrought moments were precious. The bow strung too long will lose power. And wherefore did Eurybiades tarry?

Every soul in the *Nausicaä* kept his curses soft, and waited—waited till that trailing monster, the Persian fleet, had crept halfway from Psyttaleia toward them, then up the shrouds of the Spartan admiral leaped a flag. Eager hands drew it, yet it seemed mounting as a snail, till at the masthead the clear wind blew it wide,—a plain red banner, but as it spread hundreds of axes were hewing the cables that bound the triremes to the shore, every Greek oar was biting the sea, the ships were leaping away from Salamis. From the strand a shout went up, a prayer more than a cheer, mothers, wives, little ones, calling it together:—

"Zeus prosper you!"

A roar from the fleet, the tearing of countless blades on the thole-pins answered them. Eurybiades had spoken. There was no treason. All now was in the hand of the god.

* * * * * *

Across the strait they went, and the Barbarians seemed springing to meet them. From the mainland a tumult of voices was rising, the myriads around Xerxes encouraging their comrades by sea to play the man. No indecisive, half-hearted battle should this be, as at Artemisium. Persian and Hellene knew that. The keen Phœnicians, who had chafed at being kept from action so long, sent their line of ships sweeping over the waves with furious strokes. The grudges, the commercial rivalries between Greek and Sidonian, were old. No Persian was hotter for Xerxes's cause than his Phœnician vassals that day.

And as they charged, the foemen's lines seemed so dense, their ships so tall, their power so vast, that involuntarily hesitancy came over the Greeks. Their strokes slowed. The whole line lagged. Here an Æginetan galley dropped behind, yonder a Corinthian navarch suffered his men to back water. Even the *keleustes* of the *Nausicaä* slackened his beating on the sounding-board. Eurybiades's ship had drifted behind to the line of her sisters, as in defiance a towering Sidonian sprang ahead of the Barbarian line of battle, twenty trumpets from her poop and foreship asking, "Dare you meet me?" The Greek line became almost stationary. Some ships were backing water. It was a moment which, suffered to slip unchecked, leads to irreparable disaster. Then like a god sprang Themistocles upon the capstan on his poop. He had torn off his helmet. The crews of scores of triremes saw him. His voice was like Stentor's, the herald whose call was strong as fifty common men.

In a lull amidst the howls of the Barbarians his call rang up and down the flagging ships:—

"*O Sons of Hellas! save your land,*

Your children save, your altars and your wives!

Now dare and do, for ye have staked your all!"

"Now dare and do, for ye have staked your all!"

Navarch shouted it to navarch. The cry went up and down the line of the Hellenes, "loud as when billows lash the beetling crags." The trailing oars beat again into the water, and even as the ships once more gained way, Themistocles nodded to Ameinias, and he to the *keleustes*. The master oarsman leaped from his seat and crashed his gavel down upon the sounding-board.

"*Aru! Aru! Aru!* Put it on, my men!"

The *Nausicaä* answered with a leap. Men wrought at the oar butts, tugging like mad, their backs toward the foe, conscious only that duty bade them send the trireme across the waves as a stone whirls from the sling. Thus the men, but Themistocles, on the poop, standing at the captain's and governor's side, never took his gaze from the great Barbarian that leaped defiantly to meet them.

"Can we risk the trick?" his swift question to Ameinias.

The captain nodded. "With this crew—yes."

Two stadia, one stadium, half a stadium, a ship's length, the triremes were charging prow to prow, rushing on a common death, when Ameinias clapped a whistle to his lips and blew shrilly. As one man every rower on the port-side leaped to his feet and dragged his oar inward through its row-hole. The deed was barely done ere the Sidonian was on them. They heard the roaring water round her prow, the cracking of the whips as the petty officers ran up and down the gangways urging on the panting cattle at the oars. Then almost at the shock the governor touched his steering oar. The *Nausicaä* swerved. The prow of the Sidonian rushed past them. A shower of darts pattered down on the deck of the Hellene, but a twinkling later from the Barbarians arose a frightful cry. Right across her triple oar bank, still in full speed, ploughed the Athenian. The Sidonian's oars were snapping like faggots. The luckless rowers were flung from their benches in heaps. In less time than the telling every oar on the Barbarian's port-side had been put out of play. The *diekplous*, favourite trick of the Grecian seamen, had never been done more fairly.

Now was Themistocles's chance. He used it. There was no need for him to give orders to the oar master. Automatically every rower on the port-tiers of the *Nausicaä* had run out his blade again. The governor sent the head of the trireme around with a grim smile locked about his grizzled lips. It was no woman's task which lay before them. Exposing her whole broadside lay the long Sidonian; she was helpless, striving vainly to crawl away with her remaining oar banks. Her people were running to and fro, howling to Baal, Astarte, Moloch, and all their other foul gods, and stretching their hands for help to consorts too far away.

"*Aru! Aru! Aru!*" was the shout of the oar master; again the *Nausicaä* answered with her leap. Straight across the narrow water she shot, the firm hand of the governor never veering now. The stroke grew faster, faster. Then with one instinct men dropped the oars, to trail in the rushing water, and seized stanchions, beams, anything to brace themselves for the shock. The crash which followed was heard on the mainland and on Salamis. The side of the Phœnician was beaten in like an egg-shell. From the *Nausicaä's* poop they saw her open hull reel over, saw the hundreds of upturned, frantic faces, heard the howls of agony, saw the waves leap into the gaping void.—

"Back water," thundered Ameinias, "clear the vortex, she is going down!"

The *Nausicaä's* people staggered to the oars. So busy were they in righting their own ship few saw the crowning horror. A moment more and a few drifting spars, a few bobbing heads, were all that was left of the Phœnician. The Ægean had swallowed her.

A shout was pealing from the ships of the Hellenes. "Zeus is with us! Athena is with us!"

At the outset of the battle, when advantage tells the most, advantage had been won. Themistocles's deed had fused all the Greeks with hopeful courage. Eurybiades was charging. Adeimantus was charging. Their ships and all the rest went racing to meet the foe.

* * * * * *

But the *Nausicaä* had paid for her victory. In the shock of ramming the triple-toothed beak on her prow had been wrenched away. In the *mêlée* of ships which had just begun, she must play her part robbed of her keenest weapon. The sinking of the Barbarian had been met with cheers by the Hellenes, by howls of revengeful rage by the host against them. Not lightly were the Asiatics who fought beneath the eyes of the king to be daunted. They came crowding up the strait in such masses that sheer numbers hindered them, leaving no space for the play of the oars, much less for fine manœuvre. Yet for an instant it seemed as if mere weight would sweep the Hellenes back to Salamis. Then the lines of battle dissolved into confused fragments. Captains singled out an opponent and charged home desperately, unmindful how it fared elsewhere in the battle. Here an Egyptian ran down a Eubœan, there a Sicyonian grappled a Cilician and flung her boarders on to the foeman's decks. To the onlookers the scene could have meant naught save confusion. A hundred duels, a hundred varying victories, but to which side the final glory would fall, who knew?—perchance not even Zeus.

In the roaring *mêlée* the *Nausicaä* had for some moments moved almost aimlessly, her men gathering breath and letting their unscathed comrades pass. Then gradually the battle drifted round them also. A Cyprian, noting they had lost their ram, strove to charge them bow to bow. The skill of the governor avoided that disaster. They ran under the stem of a Tyrian, and Glaucon proved he had not forgotten his skill when he sent his javelins among the officers upon the poop. A second Sidonian swept down on them, but grown wise by her consort's destruction turned aside to lock with an Æginetan galley. How the fight at large was going, who was winning, who losing, Glaucon saw no more than any one else. An arrow grazed his arm. He first learned it when he found his armour bloody. A sling-stone smote the marine next to him on the forehead. The man dropped without a groan. Glaucon flung the body overboard, almost by instinct. Themistocles was everywhere, on the poop, on the foreship, among the rowers' benches, shouting, laughing, cheering, ordering, standing up boldly where the arrows flew thickest, yet never hit. So for a while, till out of the confusion of ships and wrecks came darting a trireme, loftier than her peers. The railing on poop and prow was silver. The shields of the javelin-men that crowded her high fighting decks were gilded. Ten pennons whipped from her masts, and the cry of horns, tambours, and kettledrums blended with the shoutings of her crew. A partially disabled Hellene drifted across her path. She ran the luckless ship down in a twinkling. Then her bow swung. She headed toward the *Nausicaä*.

"Do you know this ship?" asked Themistocles, at Glaucon's side on the poop.

"A Tyrian, the newest in their fleet, but her captain is the admiral Ariamenes, Xerxes's brother."

"She is attacking us, Excellency," called Ameinias, in his chief's ear. The din which covered the sea was beyond telling.

Themistocles measured the water with his eye.

"She will be alongside then in a moment," was his answer, "and the beak is gone?"

"Gone, and ten of our best rowers are dead."

Themistocles drew down the helmet, covering his face.

"*Euge!* Since the choice is to grapple or fly, we had better grapple."

The governor shifted again the steering paddles. The head of the *Nausicaä* fell away toward her attacker, but no signal was given to quicken the oars. The Barbarian, noting what her opponent did, but justly fearing the handiness of the Greeks, slackened also. The two ships drifted slowly together. Long before they closed in unfriendly contact the arrows of the Phœnician pelted over the *Nausicaä* like hail. Rowers fell as they sat on the upper benches; on the poop the *prōreus* lay with half his men. Glaucon never counted how many missiles dinted his helmet and buckler. The next instant the two ships were drifting without steerage-way. The grappling-irons dashed down upon the Athenian, and simultaneously the brown Phœnician boarders were scrambling like cats upon her decks.

"Swords, men!" called Themistocles, never less daunted than at the pinch, "up and feed them with iron!"

Three times the Phœnicians poured as a flood over the *Nausicaä*. Three times they were flung back with loss, but only to rage, call on their gods, and return with tenfold fury. Glaucon had hurled one sheaf of javelins, and tore loose another, eye and arm aiming, casting mechanically. In the lulls he saw how wind and sea were sweeping the two ships landward, until almost in arrow-shot of the rocky point where sat Xerxes and his lords. He saw the king upon his ivory throne and all his mighty men around him. He saw the scribes standing near with parchment and papyrus, inscribing the names of this or that ship which did well or ill in behalf of the lord of the Aryans. He saw the gaudy dresses of the eunuchs, the litters, and from them peering forth the veiled women. Did Artazostra think *now* the Hellenes were mad fools to look her brother's power in the face? From the shores of Attica and of Salamis, where the myriads rejoiced or wept as the scattered battle changed, the cries were rising, falling, like the throb of a tragic chorus,—a chorus of Titans, with the actors gods.

"Another charge!" shouted Ameinias, through the din, "meet them briskly, lads!"

Once more the hoarse Semitic war-shout, the dark-faced Asiatics dropping upon the decks, the whir of javelins, the scream of dying men, the clash of steel on steel. A frantic charge, but stoutly met. Themistocles was in the thickest *mêlée*. With his own spear he dashed two Tyrians overboard, as they sprang upon the poop. The band that had leaped down among the oar benches were hewn in pieces by the seamen. The remnant of the attackers recoiled in howls of despair. On the Phœnician's decks the Greeks saw the officers laying the lash mercilessly across their men, but the disheartened creatures did not stir. Now could be seen Ariamenes, the high admiral himself, a giant warrior in his purple and gilded armour, going up and down the poop, cursing, praying, threatening,—all in vain. The *Nausicaä's* people rose and cheered madly.

"Enough! They have enough! Glory to Athens!"

But here Ameinias gripped Themistocles's arm. The chief turned, and all the Hellenes with him. The cheer died on their lips. A tall trireme was bearing down on them in full charge even while the *Nausicaä* drifted. They were as helpless as the Sidonian they had sent to death. One groan broke from the Athenians.

"Save, Athena! Save! It is Artemisia! The queen of Halicarnassus!"

The heavy trireme of the amazon princess was a magnificent sight as they looked on her. Her oars flew in a flashing rhythm. The foam leaped in a cataract over her ram. The sun made fire of the tossing weapons on her prow. A yell of triumph rose from the Phœnicians. On the *Nausicaä* men dropped sword and spear, moaned, raved, and gazed wildly on Themistocles as if he were a god possessing power to dash the death aside.

"To your places, men!" rang his shout, as he faced the foe unmoved, "and die as Athenians!"

Then even while men glanced up at the sun to greet Helios for the last time, there was a marvel. The threatening beak shot around. The trireme flew past them, her oars leaping madly, her people too intent on escape even to give a flight of javelins. And again the Athenians cheered.

"The *Perseus*! Cimon has saved us."

Not three ships' lengths behind the Halicarnassian raced the ship of the son of Miltiades. They knew now why Artemisia had veered. Well she might; had she struck the *Nausicaä* down, her own broadside would have swung defenceless to the fleet pursuer. The *Perseus* sped past her consort at full speed, Athenian cheering Athenian as she went.

"Need you help?" called Cimon, from his poop, as Themistocles waved his sword.

"None, press on, smite the Barbarian! Athena is with us!"

"Athena is with us! Zeus is with us!"

The *Nausicaä's* crew were lifted from panic to mad enthusiasm. Still above them towered the tall Phœnician, but they could have scaled Mt. Caucasus at that instant.

"Onward! Up and after them," rang Ameinias's blast, "she is our own, we will take her under the king's own eye."

The javelins and arrows were pelting from the Barbarian. The Athenians mocked the shower as they leaped the void from bulwark to bulwark. Vainly the Phœnicians strove to clear the grapples. Too firm! Their foes came on to their decks with long leaps, or here and there ran deftly on projecting spars, for what athlete of Hellas could not run the tight rope? In an instant the long rowers' deck of the Tyrian was won, and the attackers cheered and blessed Athena. But this was only storming the first outpost. Like castles forward and aft reared the prow and poop, whither the sullen defenders retreated. Turning at bay, the Phœnicians swarmed back into the waist, waiting no scourging from their officers. Now their proud admiral himself plunged into the *mêlée*, laying about with a mighty sword worthy of Ajax at Troy, showing he was a prince of the Aryans indeed. It took all the steadiness of Ameinias and his stoutest men to stop the rush, and save the Athenians in turn from being driven overboard. The rush was halted finally, though this was mere respite before a fiercer breaking of the storm. The two ships were drifting yet closer to the strand. Only the fear of striking their own men kept the Persians around the king from clouding the air with arrows. Glaucon saw the grandees near Xerxes's throne brandishing their swords. In imagination he saw the monarch leaping from his throne in agony as at Thermopylæ.

"Back to the charge," pealed Ariamenes's summons to the Tyrians; "will you be cowards and dogs beneath the very eyes of the king?"

The defenders answered with a second rush. Others again hurled darts from the stern and foreship. Then out of the mælstrom of men and weapons came a truce. Athenian and Tyrian drew back, whilst Themistocles and Ariamenes were fighting blade to blade. Twice the giant Persian almost dashed the Hellene down. Twice Themistocles recovered poise, and paid back stroke for stroke. He had smitten the helmet from Ariamenes's head and was swinging for a master-blow when his foot slipped on the bloody plank. He staggered. Before he could recover, the Persian had brought his own weapon up, and flung his might into the downward stroke.

"The admiral—lost!" Athenians shuddered together, but with the groan shot a javelin. Clear through the scales of the cuirass it tore, and into the Persian's shoulder,—Glaucon's cast, never at the Isthmus truer with hand or eye. The ponderous blade turned, grazed the Athenian's corselet, clattered on the deck. The Persian sprang back disarmed and powerless. At sight thereof the Phœnicians flung down their swords. True Orientals, in the fate of their chief they saw decreeing Destiny,—what use to resist it?

"Yield, my Lord, yield," called Glaucon, in Persian, "the battle is against you, and no fault of yours. Save the lives of your men."

Ariamenes gave a toss of his princely head, and with his left hand plucked the javelin from his shoulder.

"A prince of the Aryans knows how to die, but not how to yield," he cast back, and before the Athenians guessed his intent he sprang upon the bulwark. There in the sight of his king he stood and bowed his head and with his left arm made the sign of adoration.

"Seize him!" shouted Ameinias, divining his intent, but too late. The Persian leaped into the water. In his heavy mail he sank like lead. The wave closed over him, as he passed forever from the sight of man.

There was stillness on the Tyrian for a moment. A groan of helpless horror was rising from the Barbarians on the shore. Then the Phœnicians fell upon their knees, crying in their harsh tongue, "Quarter! Quarter!" and embracing and kissing the feet of the victors. Thanks to the moment of quietness given them, the Athenians' blood had cooled a little; they gathered up the weapons cast upon the deck; there was no massacre.

Themistocles mounted the poop of the captured flag-ship, and Glaucon with him. The wind was wafting them again into the centre of the channel. For the first time for many moments they were able to look about them, to ask, "How goes the battle?" Not the petty duel they had fought, but the great battle of battles which was the life-struggle of Hellas. And behold, as they gazed they pressed their hands upon their eyes and looked and looked again, for the thing they saw seemed overgood for truth. Where the great Barbarian line had been pushing up the strait, were only bands of scattered ships, and most of these turning their beaks from Salamis. The waves were strewn with wrecks, and nigh every one a Persian. And right, left, and centre the triumphant Hellenes were pressing home, ramming, grappling, capturing. Even whilst the fight raged, pinnaces were thrusting out from Salamis— Aristeides's deed, they later heard—crowded with martial graybeards who could not look idly on while their sons fought on the ships, and who speedily landed on Psyttaleia to massacre the luckless Persians there stationed. The cheers of the Barbarians were ended now; from the shores came only a beastlike howling which drowned the pæans of the victors. As the *Nausicaä's* people looked, they could see the once haughty Phœnicians and Cilicians thrusting back against the land, and the thousands of footmen running down upon the shore to drag the shattered triremes up and away from the triumphant Hellenes.

The *Nausicaä's* people in wondering gaze stood there for a long time as if transfixed, forgetful how their ship and its prize drifted, forgetful of weariness, forgetful of wounds. Then as one man they turned to the poop of the captured Tyrian, and to Themistocles. *He* had done it—their admiral. He had saved Hellas under the eyes of the vaunting demigod who thought to be her destroyer. They called to Themistocles, they worshipped as if he were the Olympian himself.

CHAPTER XXX
THEMISTOCLES GIVES A PROMISE

After the *Nausicaä* had returned that night to Salamis, after the old men and the women had laughed and wept over the living,—they were too proud to weep over the dead,—after the prudent admirals had set the fleet again in order, for Xerxes might tempt fate again in the morning with his remaining ships, Themistocles found himself once more in his cabin. With him was only Glaucon the Alcmæonid. The admiral's words were few and pointed.

"Son of Conon, last night you gave me the thought whereby I could save Hellas. To-day your javelin saved me from death. I owe you much. I will repay in true coin. To-morrow I can give you back to your wife and all your friends if you will but suffer me."

The younger man flushed a little, but his eyes did not brighten. He felt Themistocles's reservation.

"On what terms?"

"You shall be presented to the Athenians as one who, yielding for a moment to overmastering temptation, has atoned for one error by rendering infinite service."

"Then I am to be 'Glaucon the Traitor' still, even if 'Glaucon the Repentant Traitor'?"

"Your words are hard, son of Conon; what may I say? Have you any new explanation for the letter to Argos?"

"The old one—I did not write it."

"Let us not bandy useless arguments. Do you not see I shall be doing all that is possible?"

"Let me think a little."

The younger Athenian held down his head, and Themistocles saw his brows knitting.

"Son of Neocles," said Glaucon, at length, "I thank you. You are a just man. Whatever of sorrow has or will be mine, you have no part therein, but I cannot return—not to Hermione and my child—on any terms you name."

"Your purpose, then?"

"To-day the gods show mercy to Hellas, later they may show justice to me. The war is far from ended. Can you not let me serve on some ship of the allies where none can recognize me? Thus let me wait a year, and trust that in that year the sphinx will find her riddle answered."

"To wait thus long is hard," spoke the other, kindly.

"I have done many hard things, Themistocles."

"And your wife?"

"Hera pity her! She bade me return when Athens knew me innocent. Better that she wait a little longer, though in sorrow, when I can return to her even as she bade me. Nevertheless, promise one thing."

"Name it."

"That if her parents are about to give her to Democrates or any other, you will prevent."

Themistocles's face lightened. He laid a friendly hand on the young man's shoulder.

"I do not know how to answer your cry of innocency, *philotate*, but this I know, in all Hellas I think none is fairer in body or soul than you. Have no fear for Hermione, and in the year to come may Revealer Apollo make all of your dark things bright."

Glaucon bowed his head. Themistocles had given everything the outlaw could ask, and the latter went out of the cabin.

BOOK III
THE PASSING OF THE PERSIAN

CHAPTER XXXI
DEMOCRATES SURRENDERS

Hellas was saved. But whether forever or only for a year the gods kept hid. Panic-stricken, the "Lord of the World" had fled to Asia after the great disaster. The eunuchs, the harem women, the soft-handed pages, had escaped with their master to luxurious Sardis, the remnant of the fleet fled back across the Ægean. But the brain and right arm of the Persians, Mardonius the Valiant, remained in Hellas. With him were still the Median infantry, the Tartar horse-archers, the matchless Persian lancers,—the backbone of the undefeated army. Hellas was not yet safe.

Democrates had prospered. He had been reëlected strategus. If Themistocles no longer trusted him quite so freely as once, Aristeides, restored now to much of his former power, gave him full confidence. Democrates found constant and honourable employment through the winter in the endless negotiations at Sparta, at Corinth, and elsewhere, while the jealous Greek states wrangled and intrigued, more to humiliate some rival than to advance the safety of Hellas. But amongst all the patriot chiefs none seemed more devoted to the common weal of Hellas than the Athenian orator.

Hermippus at least was convinced of this. The Eleusinian had settled at Trœzene on the Argive coast, a hospitable city that received many an outcast Athenian. He found his daughter's resistance to another marriage increasingly unreasonable. Was not Glaucon dead for more than a year? Ought not any woman to bless Hera who gave her so noble, so eloquent, a husband as Democrates—pious, rich, trusted by the greatest, and with the best of worldly prospects?

"If you truly desire any other worthy man, *makaira*," said Hermippus, once, "you shall not find me obstinate. Can a loving father say more? But if you are simply resolved never to marry, I will give you to him despite your will. A senseless whim must not blast your highest happiness."

"He ruined Glaucon," said Hermione, tearfully.

"At least," returned Lysistra, who like many good women could say exceeding cruel things, "*he* has never been a traitor to his country."

Hermione's answer was to fly to her chamber, and to weep—as many a time before—over Phœnix in the cradle. Here old Cleopis found her, took her in her arms, and sang her the old song about Alphæus chasing Arethusa—a song more fit for Phœnix than his mother, but most comforting. So the contest for the moment passed, but after a conference with Hermippus, Democrates went away on public business to Corinth unusually well pleased with the world and himself.

It was a tedious, jangling conference held at the Isthmus city. Mardonius had tempted the Athenians sorely. In the spring had come his envoys proffering reparation for all injuries in the wars, enlarged territory, and not slavery, but free alliance with the Great King, if they would but join against their fellow-Hellenes. The Athenians had met the tempter as became Athenians. Aristeides had given the envoys the answer of the whole people.

"We know your power. Yet tell it to Mardonius, that so long as Helios moves in the heavens we will not make alliance with Xerxes, but rather trust to the gods whose temples he has burned."

Bravely said, but when the Athenians looked to Sparta for the great army to hasten north and give Mardonius his death-stroke, it was the old wearisome tale of excuses and delay. At the conference in Corinth Aristeides and Democrates had passed from arguments to all but threats, even such as Themistocles had used at Salamis. It was after one of these fruitless debates that Democrates passed out of the gathering at the Corinthian prytaneum, with his colleagues all breathing forth their wrath against Dorian stupidity and evasiveness.

Democrates himself crossed the city Agora, seeking the house of the friendly merchant where he was to sup. He walked briskly, his thoughts more perhaps on the waiting betrothal feast at Trœzene, than on the discussion behind him. The Agora scene had little to interest, the same buyers, booths, and babel as in Athens, only the citadel above was the mount of Acro-Corinthus, not the tawny rock of Athena. And in late months he had begun to find his old fears and terrors flee away. Every day he was growing more certain that his former "missteps"—that was his own name for certain occurrences—could have no malign influence. "After all," he was reflecting, "Nemesis is a very capricious goddess. Often she forgets for a lifetime, and after death—who knows what is beyond the Styx?"

He was on such noble terms with all about him that he could even give ear to the whine of a beggar. The man was sitting on the steps between the pillars of a colonnade, with a tame crow perched upon his fist, and as Democrates passed he began his doggerel prayer:—

"Good master, a handful of barley bestow

On the child of Apollo, the sage, sable crow."

The Athenian began to fumble in his belt for an obol, when he was rudely distracted by a twitch upon his chiton. Turning, he was little pleased to come face to face with no less a giant than Lycon.

"There was an hour, *philotate*," spoke the Spartan, with ill-concealed sneer, "when you did not have so much silver to scatter out to beggars."

Time had not mended Lycon's aspect, nor taken from his eye that sinister twinkle which was so marked a foil to his brutishness.

"I did not invite you, dear fellow," rejoined the Athenian, "to remind me of the fact."

"Yet you should have gratitude, and you have lacked that virtue of late. It was a sorry plight Mardonius's money saved you from two years since, and nobly have you remembered his good service."

"Worthy Lacedæmonian," said Democrates, with what patience he could command, "if you desire to go over all that little business which concerned us then, at least I would suggest not in the open Agora." He started to walk swiftly away. The Spartan's ponderous strides easily kept beside him. Democrates looked vainly for an associate whom he could approach and on some pretext could accompany. None in sight. Lycon kept fast hold of his cloak. For practical purposes Democrates was prisoner.

"Why in Corinth?" he threw out sullenly.

"For three reasons, *philotate*," Lycon grinned over his shoulder, "first, the women at the Grove of Aphrodite here are handsome; second, I am weary of Sparta and its black broth and iron money; third, and here is the rose for my garland, I had need to confer with your noble self."

"Would not Hiram be your dutiful messenger again?" queried the other, vainly watching for escape.

"Hiram is worth twenty talents as a helper;"—Lycon gave a hound-like chuckle,—"still he is not Apollo, and there are too many strings on this lyre for him to play them all. Besides, he failed at Salamis."

"He did! Zeus blast his importunity and yours likewise. Where are you taking me? I warn you in advance, you are 'shearing an ass,'—attempting the impossible,—if you deceive yourself as to my power. I can do nothing more to prevent the war from being pressed against Mardonius. It is only your Laconian ephors that are hindering."

"We shall see, *philotate*, we shall see," grunted the Spartan, exasperatingly cool. "Here is Poseidon's Temple. Let us sit in the shaded portico."

Democrates resigned himself to be led to a stone seat against the wall. The gray old "dog-watcher" by the gate glanced up to see that no dogs were straying into the holy house, noted only two gentlemen come for a chat, and resumed his siesta. Lycon took a long time in opening his business.

"The world has used you well of late, dear fellow."

"Passing well, by Athena's favour."

"You should say by Hermes's favour, but I would trust you Athenians to grow fat on successful villany and then bless the righteous gods."

"I hope you haven't left Sparta just to revile me!" cried Democrates, leaping up, to be thrust back by Lycon's giant paw.

"*Ai!* mix a little honey with your speech, it costs nothing. Well, the length and breadth of my errand is this, Mardonius must fight soon, and must be victorious."

"That is for your brave ephors to say," darted Democrates. "According to their valiant proposals they desire this war to imitate that with Troy,—to last ten years."

"Indeed—but I always held my people surpassed in procrastination, as yours in deceiving. However, their minds will change."

"Aristeides and Themistocles will bless you for that."

Lycon shrugged his great shoulders.

"Then I'll surpass the gods, who can seldom please all men. Still it is quite true."

"I'm glad to hear it."

"Dear Democrates, you know what's befallen in Sparta. Since Leonidas died, his rivals from my own side of the royal house have gathered a great deal more of power. My uncle Nicander is at present head of the board of ephors, and gladly takes my advice."

"Ha!" Democrates began to divine the drift.

"It seemed best to me after the affair at Salamis to give the lie to my calumniators, who hinted that I desired to 'Medize,' and that it was by my intriguing that the late king took so small a force to Thermopylæ."

"All Hellas knows *your* patriotism!" cried Democrates, satirically.

"Even so. I have silenced my fiercest abusers. If I have not yet urged in our assembly that we should fight Mardonius, it is merely because—it is not yet prudent."

"Excellent scoundrel," declared the other, writhing on his seat, "you are no Spartan, but long-winded as a Sicilian."

"Patience, *philotate*, a Spartan must either speak in apothegms or take all day. I have not advised a battle yet because I was not certain of your aid."

"Ay, by Zeus," broke out Democrates, "that ointment I sniffed a long way off. I can give you quick answer. Fly back to Sparta, swift as Boreas; plot, conspire, earn Tartarus, to your heart's content—you'll get no more help from me."

"I expected that speech." Lycon's coolness drove his victim almost frantic.

"In the affair of Tempē I bent to you for the last time," Democrates charged desperately. "I have counted the cost. Perhaps you can use against me certain documents, but I am on a surer footing than once. In the last year I have done such service to Hellas I can even hope to be forgiven, should these old mistakes be proved. And if you drive me to bay, be sure of this, I will see to it that all the dealings betwixt the Barbarian and your noble self are expounded to your admiring countrymen."

"You show truly excellent courage, dear Democrates," cried Lycon, in pseudo-admiration. "That speech was quite worthy of a tragic actor."

"If we're in the theatre, let the chorus sing its last strophe and have done. You disgust me."

"Peace, peace," ordered Lycon, his hand still on the Athenian's shoulder, "I will make all the haste I can, but obstinacy is disagreeable. I repeat, you are needed, sorely needed, by Mardonius to enable him to complete the conquest of Hellas. You shall not call the Persians ungrateful—the tyranny of Athens under the easy suzerainty of the king, is that no dish to whet your appetite?"

"I knew of the offer before."

"A great pity you are not more eager. Hermes seldom sends such chances twice. I hoped to have you for 'my royal brother' when they gave me the like lordship of Lacedæmon. However, the matter does not end with your refusal."

"I have said, 'Do your worst.'"

"And my worst is—Agis."

For an instant Lycon was dismayed. He thought he had slain his victim with one word. Democrates dropped from his clutch and upon the pavement as though stricken through the heart by an arrow. He was pallid as a corpse, at first he only groaned.

"*Eu! eu!* good comrade," cried the Spartan, dragging him up, half triumphant, half sympathetic, "I did not know I was throwing Zeus's thunderbolts."

The Athenian sat with his head on his hands. In all his dealings with the Spartan he had believed he had covered the details of the fate of Glaucon. Lycon could surmise what he liked, but the proof to make the damning charges good Democrates believed he had safe in his own keeping. Only one man could have unlocked the casket of infamy—Agis—and the mention of his name was as a bolt from the blue.

"Where is he? I heard he was killed at Artemisium." Lycon hardly understood his victim's thick whispers.

"Wounded indeed, *philotate*, taken prisoner, and sent to Thebes. There friends of mine found he had a story to tell—greatly to my advantage. It is only a little time since he came to Sparta."

"What lies has he told?"

"Several, dear fellow, although if they are lies, then Aletheia, Lady Truth, must almost own them for her children. At least they are interesting lies; as, for example, how you advised the Cyprian to escape from Athens, how you gave Agis a letter to hide in the boots of Glaucon's messenger, of your interviews with Lampaxo and Archias, of the charming art you possess of imitating handwritings and seals."

"Base-born swine! who will believe him?"

"Base born, Democrates, but hardly swinish. He can tell a very clear story. Likewise, Lampaxo and Archias must testify at the trial, also your slave Bias can tell many interesting things."

"Only if I consent to produce him."

"When did a master ever refuse to let his slave testify, if demanded, unless he wished to blast his own cause with the jury? No, *makaire*, you will not enjoy the day when Themistocles arrays the testimony against you."

Democrates shivered. The late spring sun was warm. He felt no heat. A mere charge of treason he was almost prepared now to endure. If Mistress Fortune helped him, he might refute it, but to be branded before Hellas as the destroyer of his bosom friend, and that by guile the like whereof Tantalus, Sisyphus, and Ixion conjoined had never wrought—what wonder his knees smote together? Why had he not foreseen that Agis would fall into Lycon's hands? Why had he trusted that lying tale from Artemisium? And worst of all, worse than the howls of the people who would tear his body asunder like dogs, not waiting the work of the hemlock, was the thought of Hermione. She hated him now. How she would love him, though he sat on Xerxes's throne, if once her suspicion rose to certainty! He saw himself ruined in life and in love, and blazoned as infamous forever.

Lycon was wise enough to sit some moments, letting his utterance do its work. He was confident, and rightly. Democrates looked on him at last. The workings of the Athenian's face were terrible.

"I am your slave, Spartan. Had you bought me for ten minæ and held the bill of sale, I were not yours more utterly. Your wish?"

Lycon chose his words and answered slowly.

"You must serve Persia. Not for a moment, but for all time. You must place that dreadful gift of yours at our disposal. And in return take what is promised,—the lordship of Athens."

"No word of that," groaned the wretched man, "what will you do?"

"Aristeides is soon going to Sparta to press home his demands that the Lacedæmonians march in full force against Mardonius. I can see to it that his mission succeeds. A great battle will be fought in Bœotia. *We* can see to it that Mardonius is so victorious that all further resistance becomes a dream."

"And my part in this monster's work?"

The demands and propositions with which Lycon answered this despairing question will unfold themselves in due place and time. Suffice it here, that when he let the Athenian go his way Lycon was convinced that Democrates had bound himself heart and soul to forward his enterprise. The orator was no merry guest for his Corinthian hosts that night. He returned to his old manner of drinking unmixed wine. "Thirsty as a Macedonian!" cried his companions, in vain endeavour to drive him into a laugh. They did not know that once more the chorus of the Furies was singing about his ears, and he could not still it by the deepest wine-cup. They did not know that every time he closed his eyes he was seeing the face of Glaucon. That morning he had mocked at Nemesis. That night he heard the beating of her brazen wings.

CHAPTER XXXII
THE STRANGER IN TRŒZENE

Despite exile, life had moved pleasantly for Hermippus's household that spring. The Trœzenians had surpassed all duties to Zeus Xenios—the stranger's god—in entertaining the outcast Athenians. The fugitives had received two obols per day to keep them in figs and porridge. Their children had been suffered to roam and plunder the orchards. But Hermippus had not needed such generosity. He had placed several talents at interest in Corinth; likewise bonds of "guest-friendship" with prominent Trœzenians made his residence very agreeable. He had hired a comfortable house, and could enjoy even luxury with his wife, daughter, young sons, and score of slaves.

Little Phœnix grew marvellously day by day, as if obeying his mother's command to wax strong and avenge his father. Old Cleopis vowed he was the healthiest, least tearful babe, as well as the handsomest, she had ever known,—and she spoke from wide experience. When he was one year old, he was so active they had to tie him in the cradle. When the golden spring days came, he would ride forth upon his nurse's back, surveying the Hellas he was born to inherit, and seeming to find it exceeding good.

But as spring verged on summer, Hermione demanded so much of Cleopis's care that even Phœnix ceased to be the focus of attention. The lordly Alcmæonid fell into the custody of one Niobe, a dark-haired lass of the islands, who treated him well, but cared too much for certain young "serving-gentlemen" to waste on her charge any unreciprocated adoration. So on one day, just as the dying grass told the full reign of the Sun King, she went forth with her precious bundle wriggling in her arms, but her thoughts hardly on Master Phœnix. Procles the steward had been cold of late, he had even cast sly glances at Jocasta, Lysistra's tiring-woman. Mistress Niobe was ready—since fair means of recalling the fickle Apollo failed—to resort to foul. Instead, therefore, of going to the promenade over the sea, she went—burden and all—to the Agora, where she was sure old Dion, who kept a soothsayer's shop, would give due assistance in return for half a drachma.

The market was just thinning. Niobe picked her way amongst the vegetable women, fought off a boy who thrust on her a pair of geese, and found in a quiet corner by a temple porch the booth of Dion, who grinned with his toothless gums in way of greeting. He listened with paternal interest to her story, soothed her when she sniffled at Procles's name, and made her show her silver, then began pulling over his bags and vials of strange powders and liquids.

"Ah, kind Master Dion," began Niobe, for the sixth time, "if only some philtre could make Procles loath that abominable Jocasta!"

"*Eu! eu!*" muttered the old sinner, "it's hard to say what's best,—powder of toad's bone or the mixture of wormwood and adder's fat. The safest thing is to consult the god—"

"What do you mean?"

"Why, my holy cock here, hatched at Delphi with Apollo's blessings on him." Dion pointed with his thumb to the small coop at his feet. "The oracle is simple. You cast before him two piles of corn; if he picks at the one to right we take toad's bone, to left the adder's fat. Heaven will speak to us."

"Excellent," cried Niobe, brightening.

"But, of course, we must use only consecrated corn, that's two obols more."

Niobe's face fell. "I've only this half-drachma."

"Then, *philotata*," said Dion, kindly but firmly, "we had better wait a little longer."

Niobe wept. "*Ai!* woe. 'A little longer' and Jocasta has Procles. I can't ask Hermione again for money. *Ai! ai!*"

Two round tears did not move Dion in the slightest. Niobe was sobbing, at her small wits' end, when a voice sounded behind her.

"What's there wrong, lass? By Zeus, but you carry a handsome child!"

Niobe glanced, and instantly stopped weeping. A young man dressed roughly as a sailor, and with long black hair and beard, had approached her, but despite dress and beard she was quite aware he was far handsomer than even Procles.

"I beg pardon, *kyrie*,"—she said "*kyrie*" by instinct,—"I'm only an honest maid. Dion is terribly extortionate." She cast down her eyes, expecting instant succour from the susceptible seaman, but to her disgust she saw he was admiring only the babe, not herself.

"Ah! Gods and goddesses, what a beautiful child! A girl?"

"A boy," answered Niobe, almost sullenly.

"Blessed the house in Trœzene then that can boast of such a son."

"Oh, he's not Trœzenian, but one of the exiles from Athens," volunteered Dion, who kept all the tittle-tattle of the little city in stock along with his philtres.

"An Athenian! Praised be Athena Polias, then. I am from Athens myself. And his father?"

"The brat will never boast of his father," quoth Dion, rolling his eyes. "He left the world in a way, I wager five minæ, the mother hopes she can hide from her darling, but the babe's of right good stock, an Alcmæonid, and the grandfather is that Hermippus—"

"Hermippus?" The stranger seemed to catch the word out of Dion's mouth. A donkey had broken loose at the upper end of the Agora; he turned and stared at it and its pursuers intently.

"If you're Athenian," went on the soothsayer, "the story's an old one—of Glaucon the Traitor."

The stranger turned back again. For a moment Dion saw he was blinking, but no doubt it was dust. Then he suddenly began to fumble in his girdle.

"What do you want, girl?" he demanded of Niobe, nigh fiercely.

"Two obols."

"Take two drachmæ. I was once a friend to that Glaucon, and traitor though he has been blazed, his child is yet dear to me. Let me take him."

Without waiting her answer he thrust the coin into her hands, and caught the child out of them. Phœnix looked up into the strange, bearded face, and deliberated an instant whether to crow or to weep. Then some friendly god decided him. He laughed as sweetly, as musically, as ever one can at his most august age. With both chubby hands he plucked at the black beard and held tight. The strange sailor answered laugh with laugh, and released himself right gayly. Then whilst Niobe and Dion watched and wondered they saw the sailor kiss the child full fifty times, all the time whispering soft words in his ear, at which Phœnix crowed and laughed yet more.

"An old family servant," threw out Dion, in a whisper.

"Sheep!" retorted the nurse, "do you call yourself wise? Do you think a man with that face and those long hands ever felt the stocks or the whip? He's gentleman born, by Demeter!"

"War makes many changes," rejoined Dion. "*Ai!* is he beside himself or a kidnapper? He is walking off with the babe."

The stranger indeed had seemed to forget them all and was going with swift strides up the Agora, but just before Niobe could begin her outcry he wheeled, and brought his merry burden back to the nurse's arms.

"You ought to be exceeding proud, my girl," he remarked almost severely, "to have such a precious babe in charge. I trust you are dutiful."

"So I strive, *kyrie*, but he grows very strong. One cannot keep the swaddling clothes on him now. They say he will be a mighty athlete like his father."

"Ah, yes—his father—" The sailor looked down.

"You knew Master Glaucon well?" pressed Dion, itching for a new bit of gossip.

"Well," answered the sailor, standing gazing on the child as though something held him fascinated, then shot another question. "And does the babe's lady-mother prosper?"

"She is passing well in body, *kyrie*, but grievously ill in mind. Hera give her a release from all her sorrow!"

"Sorrow?" The man's eyes were opening wider, wider. "What mean you?"

"Why, all Trœzene knows it, I'm sure."

"I'm not from Trœzene. My ship made port from Naxos this morning. Speak, girl!"

He seized Niobe's wrist in a grip which she thought would crush the bone.

"*Ai!* Let go, sir, you hurt. Don't stare so. I'm frightened. I'll tell as fast as I can. Master Democrates has come back from Corinth. Hermippus is resolved to make the *kyria* wed him, however bitterly she resists. It's taken a long time for her father to determine to break her will, but now his mind's made up. The betrothal is in three days, the wedding ten days thereafter."

The sailor had dropped her hand. She shrank at the pallor of his face. He seemed struggling for words; when they came she made nothing of them.

"Themistocles, Themistocles—your promise!"

Then by some giant exercise of will he steadied. His speech grew more coherent.

"Give me the child," he commanded, and Niobe mutely obeyed. He kissed Phœnix on both cheeks, mouth, forehead. They saw that tears were running down his bronzed face. He handed back the babe and again held out money,—a coin for both the slave girl and the soothsayer,—gold half-darics, that they gaped at wonderingly.

"Say nothing!" ordered the sailor, "nothing of what I have said or done, or as Helios shines this noon, I will kill you both."

Not waiting reply, he went down the Agora at a run, and never looked back. It took some moments for Dion and Niobe to recover their equanimity; they would have believed it all a dream, but lo! in their hands gleamed the money.

"There are times," remarked the soothsayer, dubiously at last, "when I begin to think the gods again walk the earth and work wonders. This is a very high matter. Even I with my art dare not meddle with it. It is best to heed the injunction to silence. Wagging tongues always have troubles as their children. Now let us proceed with my sacred cock and his divination."

Niobe got her philtre,—though whether it reconquered Procles is not contained in this history. Likewise, she heeded Dion's injunction. There was something uncanny about the strange sailor; she hid away the half-daric, and related nothing of her adventure even to her confidant Cleopis.

* * * * * * *

Three days later Democrates was not drinking wine at his betrothal feast, but sending this cipher letter by a swift and trusty "distance-runner" to Sparta.

"Democrates to Lycon, greeting:—At Corinth I cursed you. Rejoice therefore; you are my only hope. I am with you whether your path leads to Olympus or to Hades. Tartarus is opened at my feet. You must save me. My words are confused, do you think? Then hear this, and ask if I have not cause for turning mad.

"Yesterday, even as Hermippus hung garlands on his house, and summoned the guests to witness the betrothal contract, Themistocles returned suddenly from Eubœa. He called Hermippus and myself aside. '*Glaucon lives*,' he said, 'and with the god's help we'll prove his innocence.' Hermippus at once broke off the betrothal. No one else knows aught thereof, not even Hermione. Themistocles refuses all further details. 'Glaucon lives,'—I can think of nothing else. Where is he? What does he? How soon will the awful truth go flying through Hellas? I trembled when I heard he was dead. But name my terrors now I know he is alive! Send Hiram. He, if any snake living, can find me my enemy before it is too late. And speed the victory of Mardonius! *Chaire*."

"Glaucon lives." Democrates had only written one least part of his terrors. Two words—but enough to make the orator the most miserable man in Hellas, the most supple of Xerxes's hundred million slaves.

CHAPTER XXXIII
WHAT BEFELL ON THE HILLSIDE

Once more the Persians pressed into Attica, once more the Athenians,—or such few of them as had ventured home in the winter,—fled with their movables to Salamis or Peloponnesus, and an embassy, headed by Aristeides, hastened to Sparta to demand for the last time that the tardy ephors make good their promise in sending forth their infantry to hurl back the invader. If not, Aristeides spoke plainly, his people must perforce close alliance with Mardonius.

Almost to the amazement of the Athenian chiefs, so accustomed were they to Dorian doltishness and immobility, after a ten days' delay and excuses that "they must celebrate their festival the Hyacinthia," the ephors called forth their whole levy. Ten thousand heavy infantrymen with a host of lightly armed "helots"[11] were started northward under the able lead of Pausanias, the regent for Leonidas's young son. Likewise all the allies of Lacedæmon—Corinthians, Sicyonians, Elians, Arcadians—began to hurry toward the Isthmus. Therefore men who had loved Hellas and had almost despaired for her took courage. "At last we will have a great land battle, and an end to the Barbarian."

All was excitement in the Athenian colony at Trœzene. The board of strategi met and voted that now was the time for a crowning effort. Five thousand men-at-arms should march under Aristeides to join against Mardonius in Bœotia. By sea Themistocles should go with every available ship to Delos, meet the allied squadrons there, and use his infallible art in persuading the sluggish Spartan high admiral to conduct a raid across the Ægean at Xerxes's own doors. Of the ten strategi Democrates had called loudest for instant action, so loudly indeed that Themistocles had cautioned him against rashness. Hermippus was old, but experienced men trusted him, therefore he was appointed to command the contingent of his tribe. Democrates was to accompany Aristeides as general adjutant; his diplomatic training would be invaluable in ending the frictions sure to arise amongst the allies. Cimon would go with Themistocles, and so every other man was sent to his place. In the general preparation private problems seemed forgotten. Hermippus and Democrates both announced that the betrothal of Hermione had been postponed, pending the public crisis. The old Eleusinian had not told his daughter, or even his wife, why he had seemed to relax his announced purpose of forcing Hermione to an unwelcome marriage. The young widow knew she had respite—for how long nothing told her, but for every day her agony was postponed she blessed kind Hera. Then came the morning when her father must go forth with his men. She still loved him, despite the grief he was giving her. She did him justice to believe he acted in affection. The gay ribbons that laced his cuirass, the red and blue embroidery that edged his "taxiarch's" cloak, were from the needle of his daughter. Hermione kissed him as she stood with her mother in the aula. He coughed gruffly when he answered their "farewell." The house door closed behind him, and Hermione and Lysistra ran into one another's arms. They had given to Hellas their best, and now must look to Athena.

Hermippus and Aristeides were gone, Democrates remained in Trœzene. His business, he said, was more diplomatic than military, and he was expecting advices from the islands which he must take to Pausanias in person. He had a number of interviews with Themistocles, when it was observed that every time he came away with clouded brow and gruff answers to all who accosted. It began to be hinted that all was not as well as formerly between the admiral and the orator, that Democrates had chosen to tie too closely to Aristeides for the son of Neocles's liking, and that as soon as the campaign was decided, a bitter feud would break out betwixt them. But this was merest gossip. Outwardly Democrates and Themistocles continued friends, dined together, exchanged civilities. On the day when Themistocles was to sail for Delos he walked arm in arm with Democrates to the quay. The hundreds of onlookers saw him embrace the young strategus in a manner belying any rumour of estrangement, whilst Democrates stood on the sand waving his good wishes until the admiral climbed the ladder of the *Nausicaä*.

It was another day and landscape which the stranger in Hellas would have remembered long. The haven of Trœzene, noblest in Peloponnesus, girt by its two mountain promontories, Methana and the holy hill Calauria, opened its bright blue into the deeper blue of the Saronic bay. Under the eye of the beholder Ægina and the coasts of Attica stood forth, a fit frame to the far horizon. Sun, sea, hills, and shore wrought together to make one glorious harmony, endless variety, yet ordered and fashioned into a divine whole. "Euopis," "The Fair-Faced," the beauty-loving dwellers of the country called it, and they named aright.

Something of the beauty touched even Hermione as she stood on the hill slope, gazing across the sea. Only Cleopis was with her. The young widow had less trembling when she looked on the *Nausicaä* than when one year before the stately trireme had sailed for Artemisium. If ill news must come, it would be from the plains of Bœotia. Most of Themistocles's fleet was already at Delos. He led only a dozen sail. When his squadron glided on into the blue deep, the haven seemed deserted save for the Carthaginian trader that swung at her cables close upon the land. As Hermione looked and saw the climbing sun change the tintings of the waters, here spreading a line of green gold amidst the blue, here flashing the waves with dark violet, something of the peace and majesty of the scene entered into her own breast. The waves at the foot of the slope beat in monotonous music. She did not wonder that Thetis, Galatea, and all the hundred Nereids loved their home. Somewhere, far off on that shimmering plain, Glaucon the Beautiful had fallen asleep; whether he waked in the land of Rhadamanthus, whether he had been stolen away by Leucothea and the other nymphs to be their playfellow, she did not know. She was not sad, even to think of him crowned with green seaweed, and sitting under the sea-floor with fish-tailed Tritons at their tables of pearl, while the finny shoals like birds flitted above their heads. Thales the Sage made all life proceed out of the sea. Perchance all life should return to it. Then she would find her husband again, not beyond, but within the realms of great Oceanus. With such beauty spreading out before her eyes the phantasy was almost welcome.

The people had wandered homeward. Cleopis set the parasol on the dry grass where it would shade her mistress and betook herself to the shelter of a rock. If Hermione was pleased to meditate so long, she would not deny her slave a siesta. So the Athenian sat and mused, now sadly, now with a gleam of brightness, for she was too young to have her sun clouded always.

A speaker near by her called her out of her reverie.

"You sit long, *kyria*, and gaze forth as if you were Zeus in Olympus and could look on all the world."

Hermione had not exchanged a word with Democrates since that day she cast scorn on him on that other hill slope at Munychia, but this did not make his intrusion more welcome. With mortification she realized that she had forgotten herself. That she lay on the sunny bank with her feet outstretched and her hair shaken loose on her shoulders. Her feet she instantly covered with her long himation. Her hands flew instantly to her hair. Then she uprose, flushing haughtily.

"It has pleased my father, sir," she spoke with frigid dignity, "to tell me that you are some day perchance to be my husband. The fulfilment lies with the gods. But to-day the strategus Democrates knows our customs too well to thrust himself upon an Attic gentlewoman who finds herself alone save for one servant."

"Ah, *kyria*; pardon the word, it's overcold; *makaira*, I'd say more gladly," Democrates was marvellously at his ease despite her frowns, "your noble father will take nothing amiss if I ask you to sit again that we may talk together."

"I do not think so." Hermione drew herself up at full height. But Democrates deliberately placed himself in the path up the hillside. To have run toward the water seemed folly. She could expect no help from Cleopis, who would hardly oppose a man soon probably to be her master. As the less of evils, Hermione did not indeed sit as desired, but stood facing her unloved lover and hearkening.

"How long I've desired this instant!" Democrates looked as if he might seize her hands to kiss them, but she thrust them behind her. "I know you hate me bitterly because, touching your late husband, I did my duty."

"Your duty?" Nestor's eloquence was in her incredulous echo.

"If I have pained you beyond telling, do you think my act was a pleasant one for me? A bosom friend to ruin, the most sacred bonds to sever, last and not least, to give infinite sorrow to her I love?"

"I hardly understand."

Democrates drew a step nearer.

"Ah! Hera, Artemis, Aphrodite the Golden—by what name shall I call my goddess?" Hermione drew back a step. There was danger in his eyes. "I have loved you, loved you long. Before Glaucon took you in marriage I loved you. But Eros and Hymen hearkened to his prayers, not mine. You became his bride. I wore a bright face at your wedding. You remember I was Glaucon's groomsman, and rode beside you in the bridal car. You loved him, he seemed worthy of you. Therefore I trod my own grief down into my heart, and rejoiced with my friends. But to cease loving you I could not. Truly they say Eros is the strongest god, and pitiless—do not the poets say bloody Ares begat him—"

"Spare me mythologies," interposed Hermione, with another step back.

"As you will, but you shall hearken. I have desired this moment for two years. Not as the weak girl given by her father, but as the fair goddess who comes to me gladly, I do desire you. And I know you will smile on me when you have heard me through."

"Keep back your eloquence. You have destroyed Glaucon. That is enough."

"Hear me." Democrates cried desperately now. Hermione feared even to retreat farther, lest he pass to violence. She summoned courage and looked him in the eye.

"Say on, then. But remember I am a woman and alone save for Cleopis. If you profess to love me, you will not forget that."

But Democrates was passing almost beyond the limits of coherent speech.

"Oh, when you come to me, you will not know what a price I have paid for you. In Homer's day men wooed their wives with costly gifts, but I—have I not paid for you with my soul? My soul, I say—honour, friendship, country, what has weighed against Himeros, 'Master Desire,'—the desire ever for you!"

She hardly understood him, his speech flowed so thick. She knew he was on the edge of reason, and feared to answer lest she drive beyond it.

"Do you hear the price I have paid? Do you still look on in cold hate, lady? Ah, by Zeus, even in your coldest, most forbidding mood you are fair as the Paphian when she sprang above the sea! And I will win you, lady, I will win your heart, for they shall do you homage, even all Athens, and I will make you a queen. Yes! the house of Athena on the Acropolis shall be your palace if you will, and they will cry in the Agora, 'Way, way for Hermione, glorious consort of Democrates our king!'"

"Sir," spoke Hermione, while her hands grew chill, for now she was sure he raved, "I have not the joy to comprehend. There is no king in Athens, please Athena, there never will be. Treason and blasphemy you speak all in one." She sought vainly with her eyes for refuge. None in sight. The hill slope seemed empty save for the scattered brown boulders. Far away a goat was wandering. She motioned to Cleopis. The old woman was staring now, and doubtless thought Democrates was carrying his familiarities too far, but she was a weak creature, and at best could only scream.

"Treason and blasphemy," cried Democrates, dropping on his knees, his frame shaking with dishonest passion, "yes! call them so now. They will be blessed truth for me in a month, for me, for you. Hermes the Trickster is a mighty god. He has befriended Eros. I shall possess Athens and possess you. I shall be the most fortunate mortal upon earth as now I am most miserable. Ah! but I have waited so long." He sprang to his feet. "Tarry, *makaira*, tarry! A kiss!"

Hermione screamed at last shrilly and turned to fly. Instantly Democrates was upon her. In that fluttering white dress escape was hopeless.

"Apollo pursuing Daphne!"—his crazed shout as his arms closed around her,—"but Daphne becomes no laurel this time. Her race is lost. She shall pay the forfeit."

She felt him seize her girdle. He swung her face to face. She saw his wide eyes, his mad smile. His hot breath smote her cheek. Cleopis at last was screaming.

"Mine," he triumphed, while he forced her resisting head to his own, "there is none to hinder!"

But even while the woman's flesh crept back at his impure kiss, a giant power came rending the twain apart. A man had sundered them, sprung from the ground or from heaven belike, or from behind a boulder? He tore

Democrates's hands away as a lion tears a lamb. He dashed the mad orator prone upon the sod, and kicked him twice, as of mingled hatred and contempt. All this Hermione only knew in half, while her senses swam. Then she came to herself enough to see that the stranger was a young man in a sailor's loose dress, his features almost hidden under the dishevelled hair and beard. All this time he uttered no word, but having smitten Democrates down, leaped back, rubbing his hands upon his thigh, as if despising to touch so foul an object. The orator groaned, staggered upward. He wore a sword. It flew from its scabbard as he leaped on the sailor. The stranger put forth his hand, snatched his opponent's wrist, and with lightning dexterity sent the blade spinning back upon the grass. Then he threw Democrates a second time, and the latter did not rise again hastily, but lay cursing. The fall had not been gentle.

But all this while Cleopis was screaming. People were hastening up the hill,—fishermen from a skiff upon the beach, slaves who had been carrying bales to the haven. In a moment they would be surrounded by a dozen. The strange sailor turned as if to fly. He had not spoken one word. Hermione herself at last called to him.

"My preserver! Your name! Blessed be you forever!"

The fisherfolk were very close. Cleopis was still screaming. The sailor looked once into the lady's eyes.

"I am nameless! You owe me nothing!" And with that he was gone up the hill slopes, springing with long bounds that would have mocked pursuing, had any attempted. But Cleopis quenched her outcry instantly; her screams had been drowned by a louder scream from Hermione, who fell upon the greensward, no marble whiter than her face. The nurse ran to her mistress. Democrates staggered to his feet. Whatever else the chastisement had given him, it had restored his balance of mind. He told the fisherfolk a glib story that a sailor wandering along the strand had accosted Hermione, that he himself had chased the villain off, but had tripped whilst trying to follow. If the tale was not of perfect workmanship at all points, there was no one with interest to gainsay it. A few ran up the hill slope, but the sailor was nowhere in sight. Hermione was still speechless. They made a litter of oars and sail-cloth and carried her to her mother. Democrates oiled Cleopis's palm well, that she should tell nothing amiss to Lysistra. It was a long time before Hermione opened her eyes in her chamber. Her first words were:—

"Glaucon! I have seen Glaucon!"

"You have had a strange dream, *philotata*," soothed Lysistra, shifting the pillows, "lie still and rest."

But Hermione shook her shining brown head and repeated, many times:—

"No dream! No dream! I have seen Glaucon face to face. In that instant he spoke and looked on me I knew him. He lives. He saved me. Ah! why does he stay away?"

Lysistra, whose husband had not deemed it prudent to inform her of Themistocles's revelations, was infinitely distressed. She sent for the best physicians of the city, and despatched a slave to the temple of Asclepius at Epidaurus—not distant—to sacrifice two cocks for her daughter's recovery. The doctors looked wise and recommended heavy doses of spiced wine, and if those did not suffice, said that the patient might spend a night in the temple of the Healer, who would no doubt explain the true remedy in a dream. A "wise woman" who had great following among the slaves advised that a young puppy be tied upon Hermione's temples to absorb the disaffection of her brain. Lysistra was barely persuaded not to follow her admonitions. After a few days the patient grew better, recovered strength, took an interest in her child. Yet ever and anon she would repeat over Phœnix's cradle:—

"Your father lives! I have seen him! I have seen him!"

What, however, puzzled Lysistra most, was the fact that Cleopis did not contradict her young mistress in the least, but maintained a mysterious silence about the whole adventure.

CHAPTER XXXIV
THE LOYALTY OF LAMPAXO

The night after his adventure on the hill slope Democrates received in his chambers no less an individual than Hiram. That industrious Phœnician had been several days in Trœzene, occupied in a manner he and his superior discreetly kept to themselves. The orator had a bandage above one eye, where a heavy sandal had kicked him. He was exceedingly pale, and sat in the armchair propped with pillows. That he had awaited Hiram eagerly, betrayed itself by the promptness with which he cut short the inevitable salaam.

"Well, my dear rascal, have you found him?"

"May it please your Excellency to hearken to even the least of your slaves?"

"Do you hear, fox?—have you found him?"

"My Lord shall judge for himself."

"Cerberus eat you, fellow,—though you'd be a poisonous mouthful,—tell your story in as few words as possible. I *know* that he is lurking about Trœzene."

"Compassion, your Lordship, compassion,"—Hiram seemed washing his hands in oil, they waved so soothingly—"if your Benignity will grant it, I have a very worthy woman here who, I think, can tell a story that will be interesting."

"In with her, then."

The person Hiram escorted into the room proved to be no more nor less than Lampaxo. Two years had not removed the wrinkles from her cheek, the sharpness from her nose, the rasping from her tongue. At sight of her Democrates half rose from his seat and held out his hand affably, the demagogue's instinct uppermost.

"Ah! my good dame, whom do I recognize? Are you not the wife of our excellent fishmonger, Phormio? A truly sterling man, and how, pray, is your good husband?"

"Poorly, poorly, *kyrie*." Lampaxo looked down and fumbled her dirty chiton. Such condescension on the part of a magnate barely less than Themistocles or Aristeides was overpowering.

"Poorly? I grieve to learn it. I was informed that he was comfortably settled here until it was safe to return to Attica, and had even opened a prosperous stall in the market-place."

"Of course, *kyrie*; and the trade, considering the times, is not so bad—Athena be praised—and he's not sick in body. It's worse, far worse. I was even on the point of going to your Lordship to state my misgivings, when your good friend, the Phœnician, fell into my company, and I found he was searching for the very thing I wanted to reveal."

"Ah!" Democrates leaned forward and battled against his impatience,—"and what is the matter wherein I can be of service to so deserving a citizen as your husband?"

"I fear me,"—Lampaxo put her apron dutifully to her face and began to sniff,—"your Excellency won't call him 'deserving' any more. Hellas knows your Excellency is patriotism itself. The fact is Phormio has 'Medized.' "

"Medized!" The orator started as became an actor. "Gods and goddesses! what trust is in men if Phormio the Athenian has Medized?"

"Hear my story, *mu! mu!*" groaned Lampaxo. "It's a terrible thing to accuse one's own husband, but duty to Hellas is duty. Your Excellency is a merciful man, if he could only warn Phormio in private."

"Woman,"—Democrates pulled his most consequential frown,—"Medizing is treason. On your duty as a daughter of Athens I charge you tell everything, then rely on my wisdom."

"Certainly, *kyrie*, certainly," gasped Lampaxo, and so she began a recital mingled with many moans and protestations, which Democrates dared not bid her hasten.

The good woman commenced by reminding the strategus how he had visited her and her brother Polus to question them as to the doings of the Babylonish carpet merchant, and how it had seemed plain to them that Glaucon was nothing less than a traitor. Next she proceeded to relate how her husband had enabled the criminal to fly by sea, and her own part therein—for she loudly accused herself of treason in possessing a guilty knowledge of the outlaw's manner of escape. As for Bias, he had just now gone on a message to Megara, but Democrates would surely castigate his own slave. "Still," wound up Lampaxo, "the traitor seemed drowned, and his treason locked up in Phorcys's strong box, and so I said nothing about him. More's the pity."

"The more reason for concealing nothing now."

"Zeus strike me if I keep back anything. It's now about ten days since *he* returned."

" 'He?' Whom do you mean?"

"It's not overeasy to tell, *kyrie*. He calls himself Critias, and wears a long black beard and tangled hair. Phormio brought him home one evening—said he was the *prōreus* of a Melian trireme caulking at Epidaurus, but was once in the fish trade at Peiræus and an old friend. I told Phormio we had enough these days to fill our own bellies, but my husband would be hospitable. I had to bring out my best honey cakes. Your Lordship knows I take just pride in my honey cakes."

"Beyond doubt,"—Democrates's hand twitched with impatience,—"but tell of the stranger."

"At once, *kyrie*; well, we all sat down to sup. Phormio kept pressing wine on the fellow as if we had not only one little jar of yellow Rhodian in the cellar. All the time the sailor barely spoke a few words of island Doric, but my heart misgave. He seemed so refined, so handsome. And near the roots of his hair it was not so dark—as if dyed and needing renewal. Trust a woman's eyes for that. When supper was over Phormio orders me, 'Up the ladder and to bed. I'll come shortly, but leave a blanket and pillow for our friend who sleeps on the hearth.' Your Excellency knows we hired a little house on the 'Carpenter's Street,' very reasonably you will grant—only half a minæ for the winter. I gave the stranger a fine pillow and a blanket embroidered by Stephanium, she was my great-aunt, and left it to me by will, and the beautiful red wool was from Byzantium—"

"But you spoke of Critias?" Democrates could scarce keep upon his seat.

"Yes, *kyrie*. Well, I warned Phormio not to give him any more wine. Then I went up the ladder. O Mother Demeter, how sharply I listened, but the rascals spoke too low together for me to catch anything, save that Critias had dropped his Doric and spoke good Attic now. At last Phormio came up to me, and I pretended to snore. In the morning, lo! the scoundrelly stranger had slipped away. In the evening he returns late. Phormio harbours him again. So for several nights, coming late, going early. Then to-night he comes a bit before his wont. He and Phormio drank more than common. After Phormio sent me away, they talked a long time and in louder voice."

"You overheard?" Democrates gripped his arm-chair.

"Yes, *kyrie*, blessed be Athena! The stranger spoke pure Attic such as your Excellency might use. Many times I heard Hermione named, and yourself once—"

"And how?"

"The stranger said: 'So she will not wed Democrates. She loathes him. Aphrodite shed joy on her forever.' Then Phormio answered him, 'Therefore, dear Glaucon, you should trust the gods a little longer.' "

" 'Glaucon,' said he?" Democrates leaped from the chair.

" 'Glaucon,' on my oath by the Styx. Then I covered my head and wept. I knew my husband harboured the arch-traitor. Heaven can tell how he escaped the sea. As soon as Phormio was sleeping snug beside me, I went down the ladder, intending to call the watch. In the street I met a man, this good Phœnician here,—he explained he was suspecting this 'Critias' himself, and lurked about in hopes of tracing him in the morning. I told my story. He said it was best to come straight to you. And now I have accused my own husband, Excellency. *Ai!* was wife ever harder beset? Phormio is a kindly and commonly obedient man, even if he doesn't know the value of an obol. You will be merciful—"

"Peace," commanded Democrates, with portentous gravity, "justice first, mercy later. Do you solemnly swear you heard Phormio call this stranger 'Glaucon'?"

"Yes, *kyrie*. Woe! woe!"

"And you say he is now asleep in your house?"

"Yes, the wine has made them both very heavy."

"You have done well." Democrates extended his hand again. "You are a worthy daughter of Athens. In years to come they will name you with King Codrus who sacrificed his life for the freedom of Attica, for have you not sacrificed what should be dearer than life,—the fair name of your husband? But courage. Your patriotism may extenuate his crime. Only the traitor must be taken."

"Yes, he was breathing hard when I went out. Ah! seize him quickly."

"Retire," commanded Democrates, with a flourish; "leave me to concert with this excellent Hiram the means of thwarting I know not what gross villany."

The door had hardly closed behind Lampaxo, when Democrates fell as a heap into the cushions. He was ashen and palsied.

"Courage, master,"—Hiram was drawing a suggestive finger across his throat,—"the woman's tale is true metal. Critias shall sleep snug and sweetly to-night, if perchance too soundly."

"What will you do?" shrieked the wretched man.

"The thing is marvellously simple, master. The night is not yet old. Hasdrubal and his crew of Carthaginians are here and by the grace of Baal can serve you. This cackling hen will guide us to the house. Heaven has put your enemy off his guard. He and Phormio will never wake to feel their throats cut. Then a good stone on each foot takes the corpses down in the harbour."

But Democrates dashed his hand in negation.

"No, by the infernal gods, not so! No murder. I cannot bear the curse of the Furies. Seize him, carry him to the ends of the earth, to hardest slavery. Let him never cross my path again. But no bloodshed—"

Hiram almost lost his never failing smile, so much he marvelled.

"But, your Lordship, the man is a giant, mighty as Melkarth.[12] Seizing will be hard. Sheol is the safest prison."

"No." Democrates was still shaking. "His ghost came to me a thousand times, though yet he lived. It would hound me mad if I murdered him."

"*You* would not murder him. Your slave is not afflicted by dreams." Hiram's smile was extremely insinuating.

"Don't quibble with words. It would be I who slew him, though I never struck the blow. You can seize him. Is he not asleep? Call Hasdrubal—bind Glaucon, gag him, drag him to the ship. But he must not die."

"Very good, Excellency." Hiram seldom quarrelled to no purpose with his betters. "Let your Lordship deign to leave this small matter to his slave. By Baal's favour Hasdrubal and six of his crew sleep on shore to-night. Let us pray they be not deep in wine. Wait for me one hour, perhaps two, and your heart and liver shall be comforted."

"Go, go! I will wait and pray to Hermes Dolios."

Hiram even now did not forget his punctilious salaam before departing. Never had he seemed more the beautiful serpent with the shining scales than the instant he bent gracefully at Democrates's feet, the red light falling on his gleaming ear and nose rings, his smooth brown skin and beady eyes. The door turned on its pivots—closed. Democrates heard the retiring footsteps. No doubt the Phœnician was taking Lampaxo with him. The Athenian staggered across the room to his bed and flung himself on it, laughing hysterically. How absolutely his enemy was delivered into his hands! How the Moræ in sending that Carthaginian ship, to do Lycon's business and his, had provided the means of ridding him of the haunting terror! How everything conspired to aid him! He need not even kill Glaucon. He would have no blood guiltiness, he need not dread Alecto and her sister Furies. He could trust Hiram and Hasdrubal to see to it that Glaucon never returned to plague him. And Hermione? Democrates laughed again. He was almost frightened at his own glee.

"A month, my nymph, a month, and you and your dear father, yes, Themistocles himself, will be in no state to answer me 'nay,'—though Glaucon come to claim you."

Thus he lay a long time, while the drip, drip from the water-clock in the corner told how the night was passing. The lamp flickered and burned lower. He never knew the hours to creep so slowly.

* * * * * *

At last, a knock; Scodrus, the yawning valet, ushering in a black and bearded sailor, who crouched eastern fashion at the feet of the strategus.

"You have seized him?"

"Blessed be Moloch, Baal, and Melkarth! They have poured sleep upon my Lord's enemy." The sailor's Greek was harsh and execrable. "Your servants did even as commanded. The woman let us in. The young man my Lord hates was bound and gagged almost ere he could waken, likewise the fishmonger was seized."

"Bravely done. I never forget good service. And the woman?"

"She is retained likewise. I have hastened hither to learn the further will of my Lord."

Democrates arose hastily.

"My himation, staff, and shoes, boy!" he ordered. "I will go forth myself. The prisoners are still at the fishmonger's house?"

"Even so, Excellency."

"I go back with you. I must see this stranger with my own eyes. There must be no mistake."

Scodrus stared widely when he saw his master go out into the dark, for his only escort a black Carthaginian sailor with a dirk a cubit long. Democrates did not even ask for a lantern. None of the servants could fathom their master's doings of late. He gave strappings when they asked questions, and Bias was away.

The streets of Trœzene were utterly deserted when Democrates threaded them. There was no moon, neither he nor his companion were overcertain of the way. Once they missed the right turn, wandered down a blind alley, and plunged into a pile of offal awaiting the scavenger dogs. But finally the seaman stopped at a low door in a narrow street, and a triple rap made it open. The scene was squalid. A rush-candle was burning on a table. Around it squatted seven men who rose and bowed as the strategus entered. In the dim flicker he could just recognize the burly shipmaster Hasdrubal and gigantic Hib, the Libyan "governor," whose ebon face betrayed itself even there.

"We have expected you, *kyrie*," said Hiram, who was one of the group.

"Thanks be to Hermes and to you all. I have told my guide already I will be grateful. Where is he?"

"In the kitchen behind, your Lordship. We were singularly favoured. Hib had the cord around his arms before he wakened. He could scarcely struggle despite his power. The fishmonger awoke before Hasdrubal could nip him. For a moment we feared his outcries would rouse the street. But again the gods blessed us. No one stirred, and we soon throttled him."

"Take the light," ordered Democrates. "Come."

Accompanied by Hiram, the orator entered the kitchen, a small square room. The white-washed ceiling was blacked around the smoke-hole, a few pots and pans lay in the corners, a few dying embers gleamed on the hearth. But Democrates had eyes only for two objects,—human figures tightly bound lying rigid as faggots in the further corner.

"Which is he?" asked Democrates again, stepping softly as though going to danger.

"The further one is Phormio, the nearer is my Lord's enemy. Your Excellency need not fear to draw close. He is quite secure."

"Give me the candle."

Democrates held the light high and trod gently over to the prostrate men. Hiram spoke rightly that his victim was secure. They had lashed him hand and foot, using small chains in lieu of cords. A bit of wood had been thrust into his mouth and tied with twine under the ears. Democrates stood an instant looking down, then very deliberately knelt beside the prisoner and moved the candle closer. He could see now the face hidden half by the tangled black hair and beard and the gag—but who could doubt it?—the deep blue eye, the chiselled profile, the small, fine lips, yes, and the godlike form visible in its comeliness despite the bands. He was gazing upon the man who two years ago had called him "bosom-friend."

The prisoner looked straight upward. The only thing he could move was his eyes, and these followed Democrates's least motion. The orator pressed the candle closer yet. He even put out his hand, and touched the face to brush away the hair. A long look—and he was satisfied. No mistake was possible. Democrates arose and stood over the prisoner, then spoke aloud.

"Glaucon, I have played at dice with Fortune. I have conquered. I did not ruin you willingly. There was no other way. A man must first be a friend to himself, and then friendly to others. I have cast in my lot with the Persians. It was I who wrote that letter which blasted you at Colonus. Very soon there will be a great battle fought in Bœotia. Lycon and I will make it certain that Mardonius conquers. I am to be tyrant of Athens. Hermione shall be my wife." The workings of the prisoner's face made Democrates wince; from Glaucon's throat came rattlings, his eyes were terrible. But the other drove recklessly forward. "As for you, you pass this night out of my life. How you escaped the sea I know not and care less. Hasdrubal will take you to Carthage, and sell you into the interior of Libya. I wish you no misery, only you go where you shall never see Hellas again. I am merciful. Your life is in my hands. But I restore it. I am without blood guiltiness. What I have done you would have done, had you loved as I—had you been under necessity as I. Eros is a great god, but Anangkë, Dame Necessity, is yet mightier. So to-night we part—farewell."

A strong spasm passed through the prisoner's frame. For a moment Democrates thought the bonds would snap. Too strong. The orator swung on his heel and returned to the outer room.

"The night wanes, *kyrie*," remarked Hasdrubal; "if these good people are to be taken to the ship, it must be soon."

"As you will. I do nothing more concerning them."

"Fetch down the woman," ordered Hasdrubal; in the mongrel Greek current amongst Mediterranean sea-folk. Two of his seamen ascended the ladder and returned with Lampaxo, who smirked and simpered at sight of Democrates and bobbed him a courtesy.

"The traitor is seized, your Excellency. I hope your Excellency will see that he drinks hemlock. You will be merciful to my poor husband, even if he must be arrested for the night. Gods and goddesses! what are these men doing to me?"

A stalwart Carthaginian was in the act of knotting a cord around the good woman's arms preparatory to pinioning them.

"*Kyrie! kyrie!*" she screamed, "they are binding me, too! Me—the most loyal woman in Attica."

Democrates scowled and turned his back on her.

"Your Lordship surely intended this woman to be taken also," suggested Hiram, sweetly. "It cannot be he will leave such a dangerous witness at large."

"Of course not. Off with her!"

"*Kyrie! kyrie!*" was her shriek, but quickly ended, for Hasdrubal knitted his fingers around her throat.

"A gag," he ordered, and with a few more struggles Lampaxo stood helpless and silent.

A little later the band was threading its stealthy way down the black streets. Four of the Carthaginians carried Glaucon, slung hands and feet over a pole. They dared not trust him on his feet. Phormio and Lampaxo walked, closely pinioned and pricked on by the captain's dagger. They were soon at the deserted strand, and their ship's pinnace lay upon the beach. Democrates accompanied them as far as the dark marge, and watched while the boat glided out into the gloom of the haven. The orator paced homeward alone. Everything had favoured him. He had even cleared himself of the curse of the Furies and the pursuit of Nemesis. He had, he congratulated himself, shown marvellous qualities of mercy. Glaucon lived? Yes—but the parching sand-plains of Libya would be as fast a prison as the grave, and the life of a slave in Africa was a short one. Glaucon had passed from his horizon forever.

CHAPTER XXXV
MOLOCH BETRAYS THE PHŒNICIAN

Even whilst the boat pulled out to the trader, Hiram suggested that since his superior's "unfortunate scruples" forbade them to shed blood, at least they could disable the most dangerous captive by putting out his eyes. But Hasdrubal, thrifty Semite, would not hearken.

"Is not the fellow worth five hundred shekels in the Carthage market?—but who will give two for a blind dog?"

And once at the ship the prisoners were stowed in the hold so securely that even Hiram ceased to concern himself. In the morning some of the neighbours indeed wondered at Phormio's closed door and the silence of the jangling voice of Lampaxo; but the fishmonger was after all an exile, and might have returned suddenly to Attica, now the Persians had retreated again to Bœotia, and before these surmises could change to misdoubting, the *Bozra* was bearing forth into the Ægean.

The business of Hasdrubal with the *Bozra* at Trœzene appeared simple. The war had disturbed the Greek harvests. He had come accordingly with a cargo of African corn, and was taking a light return lading of olive oil and salt fish. But those who walked along the harbour front remarked that the *Bozra* was hardly a common merchantman. She was a "sea-mouse," long, shallow, and very fast under sail; she also carried again an unwontedly heavy crew. When Hasdrubal's cargo seemed completed, he lingered a couple of days, alleging he was repairing a cable; then the third morning after his nocturnal adventure a cipher letter to Democrates sent the Carthaginian to sea. The letter went thus:—

"Lycon, in the camp of the Greeks in Bœotia, to Democrates in Trœzene, greeting:—The armies have now faced many days. The soothsayers declare that the aggressor is sure to be defeated, still there has been some skirmishing in which your Athenians slew Masistes, Mardonius's chief of cavalry. This, however, is no great loss to us. Your presence with Aristeides is now urgently needed. Send Hasdrubal and Hiram at once to Asia with the papers we arranged in Corinth. Come yourself with speed to the army. Ten days and this merry dice-throwing is ended. *Chaire!*"

Democrates immediately after this gave Hiram a small packet of papyrus sheets rolled very tight, with the ominous injunction to "conceal carefully, weight it with lead, and fling it overboard if there is danger of capture." At which Hiram bowed more elegantly than usual and answered, "Fear not; it shall be guarded as the priests guard the ark of Moloch, and when next your slave comes, it is to salute my Lord as the sovran of Athens."

Hiram smiled fulsomely and departed. An hour later the *Bozra* ran out on the light wind around the point of Calauria and into the sparkling sea to eastward. Democrates stood gazing after her until she was a dark speck on the horizon.

The speck at last vanished. The strategus walked homeward. Glaucon was gone. The fateful packet binding Democrates irrevocably to the Persian cause was gone. He could not turn back. At the gray of morning with a few servants he quitted Trœzene, and hastened to join Aristeides and Pausanias in Bœotia.

* * * * * * *

In the hold of the *Bozra*, where Hasdrubal had stowed his unwilling passengers, there crept just enough sunlight to make darkness visible. The gags had been removed from the prisoners, suffering them to eat, whereupon Lampaxo had raised a truly prodigious outcry which must needs be silenced by a vigorous anointing with Hasdrubal's whip of bullock's hide. Her husband and Glaucon disdained to join a clamour which could never escape the dreary cavern of the hold, and which only drew the hoots of their unmagnanimous guardians. The Carthaginians had not misinterpreted Glaucon's silence, however. They knew well they had a Titan in custody, and did not even unlash his hands. His feet and Phormio's were tied between two beams in lieu of stocks. The giant Hib took it upon himself to feed them bean porridge with a wooden spoon, making the dainty sweeter with tales of the parching heats of Africa and the life of a slave under Libyan task-masters.

So one day, another, and another, while the *Bozra* rocked at anchor, and the prisoners knew that liberty lay two short cable lengths away, yet might have been in Atlantis for all it profited them. Phormio never reviled his wife as the author of their calamity, and Lampaxo, with nigh childish earnestness, would protest that surely Democrates knew not what the sailors did when they bound her.

"So noble a patriot! An evil god bewitched him into letting these harpies take us. Woe! woe! What misfortune!"

To which plaint the others only smiled horribly and ground their teeth.

Phormio as well as Glaucon had heard the avowal of Democrates on the night of the seizure. There was no longer any doubt of the answer to the great riddle. But disheartening, benumbing beyond all personal anguish was the dread for Hellas. The sacrifice at Thermopylæ vain. The glory of Salamis vain. Hellas and Athens enslaved. The will of Xerxes and Mardonius accomplished not because of their valour, but because of their enemies' infamy.

"O gods, if indeed there be gods!" Glaucon was greatly doubting that at last; "if ye have any power, if justice, truth, and honour weigh against iniquity, put that power forth, or never claim the prayers and sacrifice of men again."

Glaucon was past dreading for himself. He prayed that Hermione might be spared a long life of tears, and that Artemis might slay her quickly by her silent arrows. To follow his thoughts in all their dark mazes were profitless. Suffice it that the night which had brooded over his soul from the hour he fled from Colonus was never so dark as now. He was too despairing even to curse.

The last hope fled when they heard the rattling of the cables weighing anchor. Soon the soft slap of the water around the bow and the regular heaving motion told that the *Bozra* was under way. The sea-mouse creaked and groaned through all her timbers and her lading. The foul bilge-water made the hold stifling as a charnel-house. Lampaxo, Hib being absent, began to howl and moan.

"O Queen Hera! O Queen Hera, I die for a breath of air—I, the most patriotic woman in Athens!"

"Silence, goodwife," muttered Phormio, twisting desperately on the filthy straw under him. "Have I not enough to fret about without the addition of your pipings?" And he muttered underbreath the old saw of Hesiod:—

"He who doth a woman trust,

Doth trust a den of thieves."

"Silence below there, you squealing sow," ordered Hib, from the hatchway. "Must I tan your hide again?"

Lampaxo subsided. Phormio tugged vainly at his feet in the stocks. Glaucon said nothing. A terrible hope had come to him. If he could not speedily die, at least he would soon go mad, and that would rescue him from his most terrible enemy—himself.

* * * * * *

The *Bozra*, it has been said, headed not south but eastward. Hasdrubal's commission was to fetch Samos, where the still formidable fleet of the

Barbarian lay, and to put the precious packet from Democrates in the hands of Tigranes, Xerxes's commander-in-chief on the coast of Asia Minor. But although speed had been enjoined, the voyage did not go prosperously. Off Belbina the wind deserted them altogether, and Hasdrubal had been compelled to force his craft along by sweeps,—ponderous oars, worked by three men,—but his progress at best was slow. Off Cythnos the breeze had again arisen, but it was the Eurus from the southeast, worse than useless; the *Bozra* had been obliged to ride at anchor off the island for two days. Then another calm; and at last, "because," said Hasdrubal piously, "he had vowed two black lambs to the Wind God," the breeze came clear and cool from the north, which, if not wholly favourable, enabled the merchantman to plough onward. It was the fifth day, finally, after quitting Trœzene, that the headlands of Naxos came in sight at dawn, and the master began to take comfort. The fleet of the Greeks—a fisherboat had told him—was swinging inactive at Delos well to the north and westward, and he could fairly consider himself in waters dominated by the king.

"A fortunate voyage," the master was boasting to Hiram, as he sat at breakfast in the stern-cabin above a platter of boiled dolphin; "two talents from the Persians for acting as their messenger; a thousand drachmæ profit on the corn; a hundred from Master Democrates in return for our little service, not to mention the profit on the return cargo, and last but not least the three slaves."

"Yes, the three slaves. I had almost forgotten about them."

"You see, my dear Hiram," quoth the master, betwixt two unwontedly huge mouthfuls, "you see what folly it was of you to suggest putting out that handsome fellow's eyes. I am strongly thinking of selling him not to Carthage, but to Babylon. I know a trader at Ephesus who makes a specialty of handsome youths. The satrap Artabozares has commissioned him to find as many good-looking out-runners as possible. Also for his harem—if this Glaucon were only a eunuch—"

Hiram, breaking a large disk of bread, was smiling very suggestively before making reply, when a sailor shouted at the hatch:—

"Ships, master! Ships with oars!"

"In what quarter?" Hasdrubal sprang up, letting the dishes clatter.

"From Myconus. They come up fast. Hib at the masthead counts eleven triremes."

"Baal preserve us!" The master at once clambered on deck. "The Greek fleet may be quitting Delos. We must pray for wind."

It was a gray, hazy day after a dozen bright ones. The northerly breeze seemed falling. The water spread out a sombre lead colour. The heights of Naxos were in sight to starboard, but none too clearly. Much more interesting to Hasdrubal was the line of dots spreading on the horizon to northwest. Despite the distance his keen eyes could catch the rise and fall of the oar banks—war-ships, not traders. Hib was right, and Hasdrubal's face grew longer. No triremes save the Greeks could be bearing thither, and a merchantman, even from nominally neutral Carthage, caught headed for the king's coasts in those days of blazing war was nothing if not fair prize. The master's decision was prompt.

"They are far off. Put the ship before the wind."

The sea-mouse was fleet indeed for a trader, but unlike a trireme must count on her canvas for her speed. With a piping breeze she could mock pursuit. In a calm she was fearfully handicapped. However, for a moment Hasdrubal congratulated himself he could slip away unnoticed. The distance was very great. Then his dark lips cursed.

"Moloch consume me! If I see aright, we are chased."

Two vessels, in fact, seemed turning away from the rest. They were heading straight after the *Bozra*. A long race it would be, but with the gale so light the chances were against the sea-mouse. Hasdrubal had no need to urge his crew to rig out the oars and tug furiously, if they wished to escape a Greek prison and a slave market.

The whole crew, forty black-visaged, black-eyed creatures, were soon busy over the dozen great sweeps in a frantic attempt to force the *Bozra* beyond danger. Panting, yelling, blaspheming, for a while they seemed holding their own, but the master watched with sinking heart the waning breeze. At the end of an hour their pursuers could be distinguished,—a tall trireme behind, but closer, pulling more rapidly, a penteconter, a slim scouting galley working fifty oars in a single bank.

Hasdrubal began to shout desperately: "Wind, Baal, wind! Fill the sails, and seven he-goats await thy altar in Carthage!"

Either the god found the bribe too small or lacked the power to accept it. The breeze did not stiffen. The sailors strove like demons at the sweeps, but almost imperceptibly the gap betwixt them and the war-ships was narrowing.

Hiram, who had been rowing, now left his post to approach the master.

"What of the captives? Crucifixion waits us all if they are found on the ship and tell their story. Kill them at once and fling the bodies overboard."

Hasdrubal shook his head.

"Not yet. Still a good chance. I'll not cast five hundred bright shekels to the fish till harder pressed. The breeze may strengthen." Then he redoubled his shout. "Wind, Baal, wind!"

But a little later the gap betwixt the sea-mouse and the penteconter had so dwindled that even the master's inborn thrift began to yield to prudence.

"Hark you, Hib," he cried from the helm. "Take Adherbal and Lars the Etruscan. It's a good ten furlongs to that cursed galley still, but we must have those prisoners ready on deck. Over they go if the chase gets a bit closer."

The giant Libyan hastened to comply, while all the crew joined in the captain's howl, "Wind, Baal, wind!" and cried reckless vows, while they scanned the fateful stretch of gray-green water behind the stern, whereon liberty if not life depended.

The trireme, pulling only one of her banks, was dropping behind, her navarch leaving the tiring chase to the penteconter, but the latter hung on doggedly.

"Curse those war-ships with their long oars and heavy crews," growled Hib, reappearing above the hatch with the prisoners. "The penteconter's only nine furlongs off."

He had been obliged to release the captives from the stocks, but Hib had taken the precaution to place on the formidable athlete a pair of leg irons joined by a shackle. Not merely were Glaucon's arms pinioned by a stout cord, but the great Libyan was gripping them tightly. Lars and Adherbal conducted the other prisoners, whose feet, however, were not bound. For a moment the three captives stood blinking at the unfamiliar light, unconscious of the situation and their extremity, whilst Hasdrubal for the fortieth time measured the distance. The wind had strengthened a little. Let it strengthen a trifle more and the *Bozra* would hold her own. Still her people were nearly spent with their toiling, and the keen beak and large complement of the man-of-war made resistance madness if she once came alongside.

"Have ready sand-bags," ordered Hasdrubal, "to tie to these wretches' feet. Set them by the boat mast, so the sail can hide our pretty deed from the penteconter. Have ready an axe. We'll bide a little longer, though, before we say 'farewell' to our passengers. The gods may help yet."

Hib and his fellows were marching the prisoners to the poop, when the sight of the war-ship told Phormio all the story. No gag now hindered his tongue.

"Oh, dragons from Carthage, are you going to murder us?" he began in tones more indignant than terrified.

"No, save as Heaven enjoins it!" quoth the master, clapping his hands to urge on the rowing stroke. "Pray, then, your Æolus, Hellene, to stiffen the breeze."

"Pray, then, to Pluto, whelps," bawled the undaunted fishmonger, "to give you a snug berth in Orcus. Ha! but it's a merry thought of you and all your pretty lads stretched on crosses and waiting for the crows."

But a violent screech came from Lampaxo, who had just comprehended the fate awaiting.

"*Ai! ai!* save me, fellow-Hellenes!" she bawled toward the penteconter, "a citizeness of Athens, the most patriotic woman in the city, slaughtered by Barbarians—"

"Silence the squealing sow!" roared Hasdrubal. "They'll hear her on the war-ship. Aft with her and overboard at once."

But as they dragged Lampaxo on the poop, her outcry rose to a tempest till Lars the Etruscan clapped his hand upon her mouth. Her screaming stilled, but his own outcry more than replaced it. In a twinkling the virago's hard teeth closed over his fingers. Two ran from the oars to him. But the woman, conscious that she fought for life or death, held fast. Curses, blows, even a dagger pried betwixt her lips—all bootless. She seemed as a thing possessed. And all the time the Etruscan howled in mortal agony.

The thin dagger, bent too hard, snapped betwixt her teeth. Lars's clamour could surely be heard on the penteconter. Again the breeze was falling.

They seized the fury's throat, and pressed it till she turned black, but the grip of her jaw only tightened.

"*Attatai! attatai!*" groaned the victim, "forbear. Don't throttle her. Her teeth are iron. They are biting through the bone. If you strangle her, they will never relax. *Attatai! attatai!*"

"Nip him tight, little wife," called Phormio, for once regarding his spouse with supreme satisfaction. "It's a dainty morsel you have in your mouth. Chew it well!"

Lampaxo's attackers paused an instant, uncertain how to release the Etruscan. To their threats of torture the woman was deaf as the mainmast, and still the Etruscan screamed.

Glaucon had stood perfectly passive during all this grim by-play. Once Phormio saw his fellow-captive's face twist into a smile, but in the excitement of the moment the fishmonger as well as the Carthaginians almost forgot the Isthmionices, and Hib relaxed his grip and guard. Lars's finger was streaming red, when Hasdrubal threw away the steering-paddle in a rage.

"Silence her forever! The axe, Hib. Split her skull open!"

The axe lay at the Libyan's feet. One instant, only one, betook his hands from the athlete's wrists to seize the weapon, but in that instant the yell from all the crew drowned even the howls of Lars. Had any watched, they might have seen all the muscles in the Alcmæonid's glorious body contract, might have seen the fire spring from his eyes as he put forth a godlike might. Heracles and Athena Polias had been with him when he threw his strength upon the bands that held his arms. The crushing of Lycon down had been no feat like this. In a twinkling the cords about his wrists were snapped. He swung his free hands in the air.

"Athens!" he shouted, whilst the crew stood spellbound. "Hermione! Glaucon is still Glaucon!"

Hib had grasped the axe, but he never knew what smote him once behind the ear and sent him rolling lifeless against the bulwark. In an instant his bright weapon was swinging high above the athlete's head. Glaucon stood terrible as Achilles before the cowering Trojans.

"Woe! woe! he is Melkarth. We are lost men!" groaned the crew.

"At him, fools!" bawled Hasdrubal, first to recover wits, "his feet are still shackled."

But whilst the master called to them, the axe dashed down upon the fetters, and one great stroke smote the coupling-link in twain. The Athenian stood a moment looking right and left, the axe dancing as a toy in his grasp, and a smile on his face inviting, "Prove me."

A javelin singing from the hand of Adherbal flew at him. An imperceptible bending of the body, a red streak on Glaucon's naked side, and it dug into the deck. Yet whilst it quivered, was out again and hurled through the Carthaginian's breast and shoulders. He fell in a heap beside the Libyan.

Another howl from the sailors.

"Not Melkarth, but Baal the Dragon-Slayer. We are lost. Who can contend with him?"

"Cowards!" thundered Hasdrubal, whipping the sword from his thigh, "do you not know these three sniff our true business? If they live when the penteconter comes, it's not prison but Sheol that's waiting. Their lives or ours. One rush and we have this madman down!"

But their terrible adversary gave the master no time to gather his myrmidons. One stroke of the axe had already released Phormio, who clutched the arms of his wife.

"The cabin!" the ready-witted fishmonger commanded, and Lampaxo, scarce knowing what she did, released her ungentle hold on Lars and suffered her husband to drag her down the ladder. Glaucon went last; no man loving death enough to come within reach of the axe. Hasdrubal saw his victims escaping under his eyes and groaned.

"There is only one hatchway. We must force it. Darts, belaying-pins, ballast stones—fling anything down. It's for life or death!"

"The penteconter is four furlongs away!" shrieked a sailor, growing gray under his dark skin.

"And Democrates's despatches are hid in the cabin," added Hiram, chattering. "If they do not go overboard, our deaths will be terrible."

"Hear, King Moloch!" called Hasdrubal, lifting his swarthy arms to heaven, then striking them with his sword till the blood gushed down, "suffer us to escape this calamity and I vow thee even my daughter Tibaït,—a child in her tenth year,—she shall die in thy holy furnace a sacrifice."

"Hear, Baal! Hear, Moloch!" chorussed the crew; and gathering courage from necessity seized boat-hooks, oars, dirks, and all other handy weapons for their attack.

But below the released prisoners had not been idle. Never—Glaucon knew it—had his brain been clearer, his invention more fertile than now, and Phormio was not too old to cease to be a valiant helper. The cabin was small. A few spears and swords stood in the rack about the mast. The athlete bolted the sliding hatch-cover, and tore down the weapons.

"Release your wife," he ordered Phormio; "yonder sea chest is strong. Drag it over to bar the hatch-ladder. Work as Titans if you hope for another sun."

"*Ai, ai, ai!*" screeched Lampaxo, who had released Lars's fingers only to resume her din, "we all perish. They are hewing the hatch-cover with their axes. Hera preserve us! The wood splinters. We die."

"We have no time to die," called the athlete, "but only to save Hellas."

A dozen blows beat the frail hatch-cover to splinters. A dark face with grinning teeth showed itself. A heavy ballast stone grazed the athlete's shoulder, but the intruder fell back with a gurgling in his throat, his hands clutching the empty air. Glaucon had sent a heavy spear clean through him.

More ballast stones, but the Titanic Alcmæonid had torn a mattress from a bunk, and held it as effective shield. By main force the others dragged the chest across to the hatchway, making the entrance doubly narrow. Vainly Hasdrubal stormed at his men to rush down boldly. They barely dared to fling stones and darts, so fast their adversary sped them back, and to the mark.

"A god! a god! We fight against Heaven!" bleated the seamen.

Their groans were answered by the screechings of Lampaxo through the port-hole and the taunts of Phormio.

"Sing, sing, pretty Pisinoë, sweetest of the sirens," tossed the fishmonger, playing his part at Glaucon's side; "lure that dear penteconter a little nearer. And you, brave, gentle sirs, don't try 'to flay a skinned dog' by thrusting down here. Your hands are just itching for the nails, I warrant!"

Hasdrubal redoubled his vows to Moloch. In place of his daughter he substituted his son, though the lad was fourteen years old and the darling of his parents. But the god was not tempted even now. The attack on the cabin had called the sailors from the oars. The penteconter consequently had gained fast upon them. The trireme behind was manning her other banks and drawing down apace. Hiram cast a hopeless glance toward her.

"I know those 'eyes'—those red hawse-holes—the *Nausicaä*. Come what may, Themistocles must not read the packet in the cabin. There is one chance."

He approached the splintered hatchway and outstretched his hands—weaponless.

"Ah, good and gracious Master Glaucon, and your honest friends, your gods of Hellas are very great and have delivered us, your poor slaves, into your hands. Your friends approach. We will resist no longer. Come on deck; and when the ship is taken, entreat the navarch to be merciful and generous."

"Bah!" spat Phormio, "you write your promises in water, or better in oil, black-scaled viper. We know what time of day it is with us, and what for you."

Hiram saw Glaucon's hand rise with a javelin, and shrank shivering.

"They won't hearken. All's lost," he whimpered, his smile becoming ghastly.

"Another rush, men!" pleaded Hasdrubal.

"Lead the charge yourself, master!" retorted the seamen, sullenly.

The captain, swinging a cutlass, leaped down the bloodstained hatch. One moment the desperate fury of his attack carried Glaucon backward. The two fought—sword against axe—in doubtful combat.

"Follow! follow!" called Hasdrubal, dashing Phormio aside with the flat of his blade. "I have him at last!" But just as Hiram was leading down a dozen more, the athlete's axe swept past the sword, and fell like a millstone on the master's skull. He never screamed as he crashed upon the planks.

This was enough. The seamen were at the end of their valour. If they must die, they must die. What use resisting destiny?

Slowly, slowly the moments crept for the three in the cabin. Even Lampaxo grew still. They heard Hiram pleading frantically, vainly, for another attempt, and raving strange things about Democrates, Lycon, and the Persian. Then behind the *Bozra* sounded the rushing of foam around a ram, the bumping of fifty oars plying on the thole-pins. Into their sight shot the pentecounter, the brass glistening on her prow, the white blades leaping in rhythm. Marines in armour stood on the forecastle. A few arrows pattered on the plankings of the *Bozra*. Her abject crew obeyed the demand to surrender. Their helmsman pushed over the steering-paddle, and flung himself upon the deck. The sea-mouse went up into the wind. The grappling-irons rattled over the bulwark. Glaucon heard the Phœnicians whining, "Mercy! mercy!" as they embraced the boarders' feet, then the *prōreus*, in hearty Attic, calling, "Secure the prisoners and rummage the prize!"

Glaucon had suffered many things of late. He had faced intolerable captivity, immediate death. Now around his eyes swam hot mist. He fell upon a sea chest, and for a little cared not for anything around, whilst down his cheeks would flow the tears.

CHAPTER XXXVI
THE READING OF THE RIDDLE

A hard chase. The rowers of the pentaconter were well winded before they caught the *Bozra*. A merchantman making for Asia was, however, undoubted prize; the luckless crew could be sold in the Agora, the cargo of oil, fish, and pottery was likewise of value. Cimon was standing on his poop, listening to the report of his *prōreus*.

"We're all a mina richer for the race, captain, and they've some jars of their good Numidian wine in the forecastle."

But here a seaman interrupted, staring blankly.

"*Kyrie*, here's a strange prize. Five men lie dead on the deck. The planks are bloody. In the cabin are two men and a woman. All three seem mad. They are Greeks. They keep us out, and bawl, 'The navarch! show us the navarch, or Hellas is lost.' And one of them—as true as that I sucked my mother's milk—is Phormio—"

"Phormio the fishmonger,"—Cimon dropped his steering oar,—"on a Carthaginian ship? You're mad yourself, man."

"See with your own eyes, captain. They'll yield to none save you. The prisoners are howling that one of these men is a giant."

For the active son of Miltiades to leap from bulwark to bulwark took an instant. Only when he showed himself did the three in the cabin scramble up the ladder, covered with blood, the red lines of the fetters marked into wrist and ankle. Lampaxo had thrown her dress over her head and was screaming still, despite assurances. The third Hellene's face was hid under a tangle of hair. But Cimon knew the fishmonger. Many a morning had he haggled with him merrily for a fine mackerel or tunny, and the navarch recoiled in horror at his fellow-citizen's plight.

"Infernal gods! You a prisoner here? Where is this cursed vessel from?"

"From Trœzene," gasped the refugee; "if you love Athens and Hellas—"

He turned just in time to fling an arm about Hiram, who—carelessly guarded—was gliding down the hatchway.

"Seize that viper, bind, torture; he knows all. Make him tell or Hellas is lost!"

"Control yourself, friend," adjured Cimon, sorely perplexed, while Hiram struggled and began tugging out a crooked knife, before two brawny seamen nipped him fast and disarmed.

"Ah! you carrion meat," shouted Phormio, shaking his fists under the helpless creature's nose. "Honest men have their day at last. There's a gay hour coming before Zeus claps the lid over you in Tartarus."

"Peace," commanded the navarch, who betwixt Phormio's shouts, Lampaxo's howls, and Hiram's moans was at his wit's end. "Has no one on this ship kept aboard his senses?"

"If you will be so good, sir captain," the third Hellene at last broke his silence, "you will hearken to me."

"Who are you?"

"The *proreus* of the *Alcyone* of Melos. More of myself hereafter. But if you love the weal of Hellas, demand of this Hiram where he concealed the treasonable despatches he received at Trœzene and now has aboard."

"Hiram? O Lord Apollo, I recognize the snake! The one that was always gliding around Lycon at the Isthmus. If despatches he has, I know the way to get them. Now, black-hearted Cyclops,"—Cimon's tone was not gentle,—"where are your papers?"

Hiram had turned gray as a corpse, but his white teeth came together.

"Phormio is mistaken. Your slave has none."

"Bah!" threw out Cimon, "I can smell your lies like garlic. Silent still? Good, see how I am better than Asclepius. I make the dumb talk by a miracle. A cord and belaying-pin, Naon."

The seaman addressed passed a cord about the Phœnician's forehead with a fearful dexterity, and put the iron pin at the back of the skull.

"Twist!" commanded Cimon. Two mariners gripped the victim's arms. Naon pressed the cord tighter, tighter. A beastlike groan came through the lips of the Phœnician. His beady eyes started from his head, but he did not speak.

"Again," thundered the navarch, and as the cord stretched a howl of mortal agony escaped the prisoner.

"Pity! Mercy! My head bursts. I will tell!"

"Tell quick, or we'll squeeze your brains out. Relax a little, Naon."

"In the boat mast." Hiram spit the words out one by one. "In the cabin. There is a peg. Pull it out. The mast is hollowed. You will find the papers. Woe! woe! cursed the day I was born. Cursed my mother for bearing me."

The miserable creature fell to the deck, pressing his hands to his temples and moaning in agony. No one heeded him now. Cimon himself ran below to the mast, and wrenched the peg from its socket. Papyrus sheets were there, rolled compactly, covered with writing and sealed. The navarch turned over the packet curiously, then to the amazement of the sailors seemed to stagger against the mast. He was as pale as Hiram. He thrust the packet into the hands of his *prōreus*, who stood near.

"What make you of this seal? As you fear Athena, tell the truth."

"You need not adjure me so, captain. The device is simple: Theseus slaying the Minotaur."

"And who, in Zeus's name, do you know in Athens who uses a seal like that?"

Silence for a moment, then the *prōreus* himself was pale.

"Your Excellency does not mean—"

"Democrates!" cried the trembling navarch.

"And why not Democrates?" The words came from the released prisoner, who had been so silent, but who had glided down and stood at Cimon's elbow. He spoke in a changed voice now; again the navarch was startled.

"Is Themistocles on the *Nausicaä*?" asked the stranger, whilst Cimon gazed on him spellbound, asking if he himself were growing mad.

"Yes—but your voice, your face, your manner—my head is dizzy."

The stranger touched him gently on the hand.

"Have I so changed, you quite forget me, Cimon?"

The son of Miltiades was a strong man. He had looked on Hiram's tortures with a laugh. To his own death he would have gone with no eyelash trembling. But now the rest saw him blench; then with a cry, at once of wonder and inexpressible joy, his arms closed round the tattered outlaw's neck. Treason or no treason—what matter! He forgot all save that before him was his long-time comrade.

"My friend! My boyhood's friend!" and so for many times they kissed.

The *Nausicaä* had followed the chase at easy distance, ready with aid in case the *Bozra* resisted. Themistocles was in his cabin with Simonides, when Cimon and Glaucon came to him. The admiral heard his young navarch's report, then took the unopened packet and requested Cimon and the poet to withdraw. As their feet sounded on the ladder in the companionway, Themistocles turned on the outlaw, it seemed, fiercely.

"Tell your story."

Glaucon told it: the encounter on the hillside at Trœzene, the seizure in Phormio's house, the coming of Democrates and his boasts over the captives, the voyage and the pursuing. The son of Neocles never hastened the recital, though once or twice he widened it by an incisive question. At the end he demanded:—

"And does Phormio confirm all this?"

"All. Question him."

"Humph! He's a truthful man in everything save the price of fish. Now let us open the packet."

Themistocles was exceeding deliberate. He drew his dagger and pried the wrapper open without breaking the seals or tearing the papyrus. He turned the strips of paper carefully one by one, opened a casket, and drew thence a written sheet which he compared painfully with those before him.

"The same hand," his remark in undertone.

He was so calm that a stranger would have thought him engaged with routine business. Many of the sheets he simply lifted, glanced at, laid down again. They did not seem to interest. So through half the roll, but the outlaw, watching patiently, at last saw he eyebrows of the son of Neocles pressing ever closer,—sign that the inscrutable brain was at its fateful work.

At last he uttered one word, "Cipher."

A sheet lay before him covered with broken words and phrases—seemingly without meaning—but the admiral knew the secret of the Spartan *scytalē*, the "cipher wood." Forth from his casket came a number of rounded sticks of varying lengths. On one after another he wound the sheet spirally until at the fifth trial the scattered words came together. He read with ease. Then Themistocles's brows grew closer than before. He muttered softly in his beard. But still he said nothing aloud. He read the cipher sheet through once, twice; it seemed thrice. Other sheets he fingered delicately, as though he feared the touch of venom. All without haste, but at the end, when Themistocles arose from his seat, the outlaw trembled. Many things he had seen, but never a face so changed. The admiral was neither flushed nor pale. But ten years seemed added to those lines above his eyes. His cheeks were hollowed. Was it fancy that put the gray into his beard and hair? Slowly he rose; slowly he ordered the marine on guard outside the cabin to summon Simonides, Cimon, and all the officers of the flag-ship. They trooped hither and filled the narrow cabin—fifteen or more hale, handsome Athenians, intent on the orders of the admiral. Were they to dash at once for Samos and surprise the Persian? Or what other adventure waited? The breeze had died. The gray breast of the Ægean rocked the *Nausicaä* softly. The thranites of the upper oar bank were alone on the benches, and stroking the great trireme along to a singsong chant about Amphitrite and the Tritons. On the poop above two sailors were grumbling lest the penteconter's people get all the booty of the *Bozra*. Glaucon heard their grunts and complainings whilst he looked on Themistocles's awful face.

The officers ranged themselves and saluted stiffly. Themistocles stood before them, his hands closed over the packet. The first time he started to speak his lips closed desperately. The silence grew awkward. Then the admiral gave his head a toss, and drew his form together as a runner before a race.

"Democrates is a traitor. Unless Athena shows us mercy, Hellas is lost."

"Democrates is a traitor!"

The cry from the startled men rang through the ship. The rowers ceased their chant and their stroking. Themistocles beckoned angrily for silence.

"I did not call you down to wail and groan." He never raised his voice; his calmness made him terrible. But now the questions broke loose as a flood.

"When? How? Declare."

"Peace, men of Athens; you conquered the Persian at Salamis, conquer now yourselves. Harken to this cipher. Then to our task and prove our comrades did not die in vain."

Yet despite him men wept on one another's shoulders as became true Hellenes, whilst Themistocles, whose inexorable face never relaxed, rewound the papyrus on the cipher stick and read in hard voice the words of doom.

"This is the letter secreted on the Carthaginian. The hand is Democrates's, the seals are his. Give ear.

"Democrates the Athenian to Tigranes, commander of the hosts of Xerxes on the coasts of Asia, greeting:—Understand, dear Persian, that Lycon and I as well as the other friends of the king among the Hellenes are prepared to bring all things to pass in a way right pleasing to your master. Even now I depart from Trœzene to join the army of the allied Hellenes in Bœotia, and, the gods helping, we cannot fail. Lycon and I will contrive to separate the Athenians and Spartans from their other allies, to force them to give battle, and at the crisis cause the divisions under our personal commands to retire, breaking the phalanx and making Mardonius's victory certain.

"For your part, excellent Tigranes, you must avoid the Hellenic ships at Delos and come back to Mardonius with your fleet ready to second him at once after his victory, which will be speedy; then with your aid he can readily turn the wall at the Isthmus. I send also letters written, as it were, in the hand of Themistocles. See that they fall into the hands of the other Greek admirals. They will breed more hurt amongst the Hellenes than you can accomplish with all your ships. I send, likewise, lists of such Athenians and Spartans as are friendly to his Majesty, also memoranda of such secret plans of the Greeks as have come to my knowledge.

"From Trœzene, given into the hands of Hiram on the second of Metageitnion, in the archonship of Xanthippus. *Chaire!*"

Themistocles ceased. No man spoke a word. It was as if a god had flung a bolt from heaven. What use to cry against it? Then, in an ominously low voice, Simonides asked a question.

"What are these letters which purport to come from your pen, Themistocles?"

The admiral unrolled another papyrus, and as he looked thereon his fine face contracted with loathing.

"Let another read. I am made to pour contempt and ridicule upon my fellow-captains. I am made to boast 'when the war ends, I will be tyrant of Athens.' A thousand follies and wickednesses are put in my mouth. Were this letter true, I were the vilest wretch escaping Orcus. Since forged—" his hands clinched—"by that man, that man whom I have trusted, loved, cherished, called 'younger brother,' 'oldest son'—" He spat in rising fury and was still.

" 'Fain would I grip his liver in my teeth,' " cried the little poet, even in storm and stress not forgetting his Homer. And the howl from the man-of-war's men was as the howl of beasts desiring their prey. But the admiral's burst of anger ended. He stood again an image of calm power. The voice that had charmed the thousands rang forth in its strength and sweetness.

"Men of Athens, this is no hour for windy rage. Else I should rage the most, for who is more wronged than I? One whom we loved is fallen—later let us weep for him. One whom we trusted is false—later punish him. But now the work is neither to weep nor to punish, but to save Hellas. A great battle impends in Bœotia. Except the Zeus of our sires and Athena of the Pure Eyes be with us, we are men without home, without fatherland. Pausanias and Aristeides must be warned. The *Nausicaä* is the 'Salaminia,'—the swiftest trireme in the fleet. Ours must be the deed, and ours the glory. Enough of this—the men must hear, and then to the oars."

Themistocles had changed from despair to a triumph note. There was uplift even to look upon him. He strode before all his lieutenants up and out upon the poop. The long tiers of benches and the gangways filled with rowers peered up at him. They had seen their officers gather in the cabin, and Dame Rumour, subtlest of Zeus's messengers, had breathed "ill-tidings." Now the admiral stood forth, and in few words told all the heavy tale. Again a great shout, whilst the bronzed men groaned on the benches.

"Democrates is a traitor!"

A deity had fallen from their Olympus; the darling of the Athenians's democracy was sunk to vilest of the vile. But the admiral knew how to play on their two hundred hearts better than Orpheus upon his lyre. Again the note changed from despair to incitement, and when at last he called, "And can we cross the Ægean as never trireme crossed and pluck back Hellas from her fate?" thalamite, zygite, and thranite rose, tossing their brawny arms into the air.

"*We can!*"

Then Themistocles folded his own arms and smiled. He felt the god was still with him.

* * * * * *

Yet, eager as was the will, they could not race forth instantly. Orders must be written to Xanthippus, the Athenian vice-admiral far away, bidding him at all hazards to keep the Persian fleet near Samos. Cimon was long in privy council with Themistocles in the state cabin. At the same time a prisoner was passed aboard the *Nausicaä*, not gently bound,—Hiram, a precious witness, before the dogs had their final meal on him. But the rest of the *Bozra's* people found a quicker release. The penteconter's people decided their fate with a yell.

"Sell such harpies for slaves? The money would stink through our pouches!"

So two by two, tied neck to neck and heel to heel, the wretches were flung overboard, "because we lack place and wood to crucify you," called the *Nausicaä's* governor, as he pushed the last pair off into the leaden sea,—for the day was distant when the destruction of such Barbarian rogues would weigh even on tender consciences.

So the Carthaginians ceased from troubling, but before the penteconter and the *Bozra* bore away to join the remaining fleet, another deed was done in sight of all three ships. For whilst Themistocles was with Cimon, Simonides and Sicinnus had taken Glaucon to the *Nausicaä's* forecastle. Now as the penteconter was casting off, again he came to view, and the shout that greeted him was not of fear this time, but wonder and delight. The Alcmæonid was clean-shaven, his hair clipped close, the black dye even in a manner washed away. He had flung off the rough seaman's dress, and stood forth in all his godlike beauty.

Before all men Cimon, coming from the cabin, ran and kissed him once more, whilst the rowers clapped their hands.

"Apollo—it is Delian Apollo! Glaucon the Beautiful lives again. *Io! Io! pæan!*"

"Yes," spoke Themistocles, in a burst of gladness. "The gods take one friend, they restore another. Œdipus has read the sphinx's riddle. Honour this man, for he is worthy of honour through Hellas!"

The officers ran to the athlete, after them the sailors. They covered his face and hands with kisses. He seemed escaped the Carthaginian to perish in the embrace of his countrymen. Never was his blush more boyish, more divine. Then a bugle-blast sent every man to his station. Cimon leaped across to his smaller ship. The rowers of the *Nausicaä* ran out their oars, the hundred and seventy blades trailed in the water. Every man took a long breath and fixed his eyes on the admiral standing on the poop. He held a golden goblet set with turquoise, and filled with the blood-red Pramnian wine. Loudly Themistocles prayed.

"Zeus of Olympus and Dodona, Zeus Orchios, rewarder of the oath-breaker, to whom the Hellenes do not vainly pray, and thou Athena of the Pure Eyes, give ear. Make our ship swift, our arms strong, our hearts bold. Hold back the battle that we come not too late. Grant that we confound the guilty, put to flight the Barbarian, recompense the traitor. So to you and all other holy gods whose love is for the righteous we will proffer prayer and sacrifice forever. Amen."

He poured out the crimson liquor; far into the sea he flung the golden cup.

"Heaven speed you!" shouted from the penteconter. Themistocles nodded. The *keleustes* smote his gavel upon the sounding-board. The triple oar bank rose as one and plunged into the foam. A long "h-a!" went up from the benches. The race to save Hellas was begun.

CHAPTER XXXVII
THE RACE TO SAVE HELLAS

The chase had cost the Athenians dear. Before the *Bozra* had submitted to her fate, she had led the *Nausicaä* and her consort well down into the southern Ægean. A little more and they would have lifted the shaggy headlands of Crete. The route before the great trireme was a long one. Two thousand stadia,[13] as the crow flies, sundered them from the Euripus, the nearest point whence they could despatch a runner to Pausanias and Aristeides; and what with the twistings around the scattered Cyclades the route was one-fourth longer. But men had ceased reckoning distance. Their hearts were in the flying oars, and at first the *Nausicaä* ran leaping across the waves as leaps the dolphin,—the long gleaming blades springing like shuttles in the hands of the ready crew. They had taken from the penteconter all her spare rowers, and to make the great ship bound over the steel-gray deep was children's play. "We must save Hellas, and we can!" That was the thought of all from Themistocles to the meanest thranite.

So at the beginning when the task seemed light and hands were strong. The breeze that had betrayed the *Bozra* ever sank lower. Presently it died altogether. The sails they set hung limp on the mast. The navarch had them furled. The sea spread out before them, a glassy, leaden-coloured floor; the waves roaring in their wake faded in a wide ripple far behind. To hearten his men the *keleustes* ceased his beating on the sounding-board, and clapped lips to his pipe. The whole trireme chorussed the familiar song together:—

"Fast and more fast

O'er the foam-spray we're passed.

And our creaking sails swell

To the swift-breathing blast,

For Poseidon's wild steeds

With their manifold feet,

Like a hundred white nymphs

On the blue sea-floor fleet.

And we wake as we go

Gray old Phorcys below,

Whilst on shell-clustered trumpets

    The loud Tritons blow!

    The loud Tritons blow!

"All of Æolus's train

Springing o'er the blue main

To our pæans reply

With their long, long refrain;

And the sea-folk upleap

From their dark weedy caves;

With a clear, briny laugh

They dance over the waves;

Now their mistress below,—

See bright Thetis go,

As she leads the mad revels,

    While loud Tritons blow!

    While loud Tritons blow!

"With the foam gliding white,

Where the light flash is bright.

We feel the live keel

Leaping on with delight;

And in melody wild

Men and Nereids and wind

Sing and laugh all their praise,

To the bluff seagods kind;

Whilst deep down below,

Where no storm blasts may go,

On their care-charming trumpets

The loud Tritons blow,

The loud Tritons blow."

Bravely thus for a while, but at last Themistocles, watching from the poop with eyes that nothing evaded, saw how here and there the dip of the blades was weakening, here and there a breast was heaving rapidly, a mouth was panting for air.

"The relief," he ordered. And the spare rowers ran gladly to the places of those who seemed the weariest. Only a partial respite. Fifty supernumeraries were a poor stop-gap for the one hundred and seventy. Only the weakest could be relieved, and even those wept and pled to continue at the benches a little longer. The thunderous threat of Ameinias, that he who refused a proffered relief must stand all day by the mast with an iron anchor on his shoulder, alone sufficed to make the malcontents give place. Yet after a little while the singing died. Breath was too precious to waste. It was mockery to troll of "Æolus's winds" whilst the sea was one motionless mirror of gray. The monotonous "beat," "beat" of the *keleustes's* hammer, and the creaking of the oars in their leathered holes alone broke the stillness that reigned through the length of the trireme. The penteconter and her prize had long since faded below the horizon. With almost wistful eyes men watched the islets as they glided past one after another, Thera now, then Ios, and presently the greater Paros and Naxos lay before them. They relieved oars whenever possible. The supernumeraries needed no urging after their scanty rest to spring to the place of him who was fainting, but hardly any man spoke a word.

The first time the relief went in Glaucon had stepped forward.

"I am strong. I am able to pull an oar," he had cried almost angrily when Themistocles laid his hand upon him, but the admiral would have none of it.

"You shall not. Sooner will I go on to the bench myself. You have been through the gates of Tartarus these last days, and need all your strength. Are you not the Isthmionices,—the swiftest runner in Hellas?"

Then Glaucon had stepped back and said no more. He knew now for what Themistocles reserved him,—that after the *Nausicaä* made land he must run, as never man ran before across wide Bœotia to bear the tidings to Pausanias.

They were betwixt Paros and Naxos at last. Wine and barley cakes soaked in oil were passed among the men at the oars. They ate without leaving the benches. And still the sea spread out glassy, motionless, and the pennon hung limp on the mainmast. The *keleustes* slowed his beatings, but the men did not obey him. No whipped cattle were they, such as rowed the triremes of Phœnicia, but freemen born, sons of Athens, who called it joy to die for her in time of need. Therefore despite the *keleustes's* beats, despite Themistocles's command, the rowing might not slacken. And the black wave around the *Nausicaä's* bow sang its monotonous music.

But Themistocles ever turned his face eastward, until men thought he was awaiting some foe in chase, and presently—just as a rower among the zygites fell back with the blood gushing from mouth and nostrils—the admiral pointed his finger toward the sky-line of the morning.

"Look! Athena is with us!"

And for the first time in hours those panting, straining men let the hot oar butts slip from their hands, even trail in the darkling water, whilst they rose, looked, and blessed their gods.

It was coming, the strong kind Eurus out of the south and east. They could see the black ripple springing over the glassy sea; they could hear the singing of the cordage; they could catch the sweet sniff of the brine. Admiral and rower lifted their hands together at this manifest favour of heaven.

"Poseidon is with us! Athena is with us! Æolus is with us! We can save Hellas!"

Soon the sun burst forth above the mist. All the wide ocean floor was adance with sparkling wavelets. No need of Ameinias's lusty call to bend again the sails. The smaller canvas on the foremast and great spread on the mainmast were bellying to the piping gale. A fair wind, but no storm. The oars were but helpers now,—men laughed, hugged one another as boys, wept as girls, and let the benignant wind gods labour for them. Delos the Holy they passed, and Tenos, and soon the heights of Andros lifted, as the ship with its lading of fate flew over the island-strewn sea. At last, just as the day was leaving them, they saw Helios going down into the fire-tinged waves in a parting burst of glory. Darkness next, but the kindly wind failed not. Through the night no man on that trireme slumbered. Breeze or calm, he who had an obol's weight of power spent it at the oars.

Long after midnight Themistocles and Glaucon clambered the giddy cordage to the ship's top above the swelling mainsail. On the narrow platform, with the stars above, the dim tracery of the wide sail, the still dimmer tracery of the long ship below, they seemed transported to another world. Far beneath by the glimmer of the lanterns they saw the rowers swaying at their toil. In the wake the phosphorous bubbles ran away, opalescent gleams springing upward, as if torches of Doris and her dancing Nereids. So much had admiral and outlaw lived through this day they had thought little of themselves. Now calmer thought returned. Glaucon could tell of many things he had heard and thought, of the conversation overheard the morning before Salamis, of what Phormio had related during the weary captivity in the hold of the *Bozra*. Themistocles pondered long. Yet for Glaucon when standing even on that calm pinnacle the trireme must creep over the deep too slowly.

"O give me wings, Father Zeus," was his prayer; "yes, the wings of Icarus. Let me fly but once to confound the traitor and deliver thy Hellas,—after that, like Icarus let me fall. I am content to die."

But Themistocles pressed close against his side. "Ask for no wings,"—in the admiral's voice was a tremor not there when he sped confidence through the crew,—"if it be destined we save Hellas, it is destined; if we are to die, we die. 'No man of woman born, coward or brave, can shun the fate assigned.' Hector said that to Andromache, and the Trojan was right. But we shall save Hellas. Zeus and Athena are great gods. They did not give us glory at Salamis to make that glory tenfold vain. We shall save Hellas. Yet I have fear—"

"Of what, then?"

"Fear that Themistocles will be too merciful to be just. Ah! pity me."

"I understand—Democrates."

"I pray he may escape to the Persians, or that Ares may slay him in fair battle. If not—"

"What will you do?"

The admiral's hold upon the younger Athenian's arm tightened.

"I will prove that Aristeides is not the only man in Hellas who deserves the name of 'Just.' When I was young, my tutor would predict great things of me. 'You will be nothing small, Themistocles, but great, whether for good or ill, I know not,—but great you will be.' And I have always struggled upward. I have always prospered. I am the first man in Hellas. I have set my will against all the power of Persia. Zeus willing, I shall conquer. But the Olympians demand their price. For saving Hellas I must pay—Democrates. I loved him."

The two men stood in silence long, whilst below the oars and the rushing water played their music. At last the admiral relaxed his hand on Glaucon.

"*Eu!* They will call me 'Saviour of Hellas' if all goes well. I shall be greater than Solon, or Lycurgus, or Periander, and in return I must do justice to a friend. Fair recompense!"

The laugh of the son of Neocles was harsher than a cry. The other answered nothing. Themistocles set his foot on the ladder.

"I must return to the men. I would go to an oar, only they will not let me."

The admiral left Glaucon for a moment alone. All around him was the night,—the stars, the black æther, the blacker sea,—but he was not lonely. He felt as when in the foot-race he turned for the last burst toward the goal. One more struggle, one supreme summons of strength and will, and after that the triumph and the rest.—Hellas, Athens, Hermione, he was speeding back to all. Once again all the things past floated out of the dream-world and before him,—the wreck, the lotus-eating at Sardis, Thermopylæ, Salamis, the agony on the *Bozra*. Now came the end, the end promised in the moment of vision whilst he pulled the boat at Salamis. What was it? He tried not to ask. Enough it was to be the end. He, like Themistocles, had supreme confidence that the treason would be thwarted. The gods were cruel, but not so cruel that after so many deliverances they would crush him at the last. "The miracles of Zeus are never wrought in vain." Had not Zeus wrought miracles for him once and twice? The proverb was great comfort.

Suddenly whilst he built his palace of phantasy, a cry from the foreship dissolved it.

"Attica, Attica, hail, all hail!"

He saw upon the sky-line the dim tracery of the Athenian headlands "like a shield laid on the misty deep." Again men were springing from the oars, laughing, weeping, embracing, whilst under the clear, unflagging wind the *Nausicaä* sped up the narrowing strait betwixt Eubœa and the mainland. Dawn glowed at last, unveiling the brown Attic shoreline with Pentelicus the marble-fretted and all his darker peers.

Hour by hour they ran onward. They skirted the long low coast of Eubœa to the starboard. They saw Marathon and its plain of fair memories stretching to port, and now the strait grew closer yet, and it needed all the governor's skill at the steering-oars to keep the *Nausicaä* from the threatening rocks. Marathon was behind at last. The trireme rounded the last promontory; the bay grew wider; the prow was set more to westward. Every man—the faintest—struggled back to his oar if he had left it—this was the last hundred stadia to Oropus, and after that the *Nausicaä* might do no more. Once again the *keleustes* piped, and his note was swift and feverish. The blades shot faster, faster, as the trireme raced down the sandy shore of the Attic "Diacria." Once in the strait they saw a brown-sailed fisherboat, and the helm swerved enough to bring her within hail. The fishermen stared at the flying trireme and her straining, wide-eyed men.

"Has there been a battle?" cried Ameinias.

"Not yet. We are from Styra on Eubœa; we expect the news daily. The armies are almost together."

"And where are they?"

"Near to Platæa."

That was all. The war-ship left the fishermen rocking in her wake, but again Themistocles drew his eyebrows close together, while Glaucon tightened the buckle on his belt. Platæa,—the name meant that the courier must traverse the breadth of Bœotia, and with the armies face to face how long would Zeus hold back the battle? How long indeed, with Democrates and Lycon intent on bringing battle to pass? The ship was more than ever silent as she rushed on the last stretch of her course. More men fell at the oars with blood upon their faces. The supernumeraries tossed them aside like logs of wood, and leaped upon their benches. Themistocles had vanished with Simonides in the cabin; all knew their work,—preparing letters to Aristeides and Pausanias to warn of the bitter truth. Then the haven at last: the white-stuccoed houses of Oropus clustering down upon the shore, the little mole, a few doltish peasants by the landing gaping at the great trireme. No others greeted them, for the terror of Mardonius's Tartar raiders had driven all but the poorest to some safe shelter. The oars slipped from numb fingers; the anchor plunged into the green water; the mainsail rattled down the mast. Men sat on the benches motionless, gulping down the clear air. They had done their part. The rest lay in the hands of the gods, and in the speed of him who two days since they had called "Glaucon the Traitor." The messenger came from the cabin, half stripped, on his head a felt skullcap, on his feet high hunter's boots laced up to the knees. He had never shone in more noble beauty. The crew watched Themistocles place a papyrus roll in Glaucon's belt, and press his mouth to the messenger's ear in parting admonition. Glaucon gave his right hand to Themistocles, his left to Simonides. Fifty men were ready to man the pinnace to take him ashore. On the beach the *Nausicaä's* people saw him stand an instant, as he turned his face upward to the "dawn-facing" gods of Hellas, praying for strength and swiftness.

"Apollo speed you!" called two hundred after him. He answered from the beach with a wave of his beautiful arms. A moment later he was hid behind a clump of olives. The *Nausicaä's* people knew the ordeal before him, but many a man said Glaucon had the easier task. He could run till life failed him. They now could only fold their hands and wait.

* * * * * *

It was long past noon when Glaucon left the desolate village of Oropus behind him. The day was hot, but after the manner of Greece not sultry, and the brisk breeze was stirring on the hill slopes. Over the distant mountains hung a tint of deep violet. It was early in Bœdromion.[14] The fields—where indeed the Barbarian cavalry men had not deliberately burned them—were seared brown by the long dry summer. Here and there great black crows were picking, and a red fox would whisk out of a thicket and go with long bounds across the unharvested fields to some safer refuge. Glaucon knew his route. Three hundred and sixty stadia lay before him, and those not over the well-beaten course in the gymnasium, but by rocky goat trails and by-paths that made his task no easier. He started off slowly. He was too good an athlete to waste his speed by one fierce burst at the outset. At first his road was no bad one, for he skirted the willow-hung Asopus, the boundary stream betwixt Attica and Bœotia. But he feared to keep too long upon this highway to Tanagra, and of the dangers of the road he soon met grim warnings.

First, it was a farmstead in black ruin, with the carcass of a horse half burned lying before the gate. Next, it was the body of a woman, three days slain, and in the centre of the road,—no pleasant sight, for the crows had been at their banquet,—and hardened though the Alcmæonid was to war, he stopped long enough to cast the ceremonial handful of dust on the poor remains, as symbolic burial, and sped a wish to King Pluto to give peace to the wanderer's spirit. Next, people met him: an old man, his wife, his young son,—wretched shepherd-folk dressed in sheepskins,—the boy helping his elders as they tottered along on their staves toward the mountain. At sight of Glaucon they feebly made to fly, but he held out his hand, showing he was unarmed, and they halted also.

"Whence and whither, good father?"

Whereat the old man began to shake all over and tell a mumbling story, how they had been set upon by the Scythian troopers in their little farm near Œnophytæ, how he had seen the farmhouse burn, his two daughters swung shrieking upon the steeds of the wild Barbarians, and as for himself and his wife and son, Athena knew what saved them! They had lost all but life, and fearful for that were seeking a cave on Mt. Parnes. Would not the young man come with them, a thousand dangers lurked upon the way? But Glaucon did not wait to hear the story out. On he sped up the rocky road.

"Ah, Mardonius! ah, Artazostra!" he was speaking in his heart, "noble and brave you are to your peers, but this is your rare handiwork,—and though you once called me friend, Zeus and Dikē still rule, there is a price for this and you shall tell it out."

Yet he bethought himself of the old man's warning, and left the beaten way. At the long steady trot learned in the stadium, he went onward under the greenwood behind the gleaming river, where the vines and branches whipped on his face; and now and again he crossed a half-dried brook, where he swept up a little water in his hands, and said a quick prayer to the friendly nymphs of the stream. Once or twice he sped through fig orchards, and snatched at the ripe fruit as he ran, eating without slackening his course. Presently the river began to bend away to westward. He knew if he followed it, he came soon to Tanagra, but whether that town were held by the Persians or burned by them, who could tell? He quitted the Asopus and its friendly foliage. The bare wide plain of Bœotia was opening. Concealment was impossible, unless indeed he turned far eastward toward Attica and took refuge on the foothills of the mountains. But speed was more precious than safety. He passed Scolus, and found the village desolate, burned. No human being greeted him, only one or two starving dogs rushed forth to snap, bristle, and be chased away by a well-sent stone. Here and yonder in the fields were still the clusters of crows picking at carrion,—more tokens that Mardonius's Tartar raiders had done their work too well. Then at last, an hour or more before the sunset, just as the spurs of Cithæron, the long mountain over against Attica, began to thrust their bald summits up before the runner's ken, far ahead upon the way approached a cloud of dust. The Athenian paused in his run, dashed into the barren field, and flung himself flat between the furrows. He heard the hoof-beats of the wiry steppe horses, the clatter of targets and scabbards, the shrill shouts of the raiders. He lifted his head enough to see the red streamers on their lance tips flutter past. He let the noise die away before he dared to take the road once more. The time he lost was redeemed by a burst of speed. His head was growing very hot, but it was not time to think of that.

Already the hills were spreading their shadows, and Platæa was many stadia away. Knowledge of how much remained made him reckless. He ran on without his former caution. The plain was again changing to undulating foothills. He had passed Erythræ now,—another village burned and deserted. He mounted a slope, was descending to mount another, when lo! over the hill before came eight riders at full speed. What must be done, must be done quickly. To plunge into the fallow field again were madness, the horsemen had surely seen him, and their sure-footed beasts could run over the furrows like rabbits. Glaucon stood stock still and stretched forth both hands, to show the horsemen he did not resist them.

"O Athena Polias," uprose the prayer from his heart, "if thou lovest not me, forget not thy love for Hellas, for Athens, for Hermione my wife."

The riders were on him instantly, their crooked swords flew out. They surrounded their captive, uttering outlandish cries and chatterings, ogling, muttering, pointing with their swords and lances as if debating among themselves whether to let the stranger go or hew him in pieces. Glaucon stood motionless, looking from one to another and asking for wisdom in his soul. Seven were Tartars, low-browed, yellow-skinned, flat of nose, with the grins of apes. He might expect the worst from these. But the eighth showed a long blond beard under his leather helm, and Glaucon rejoiced; the chief of the band was a Persian and more amenable.

The Tartars continued gesturing and debating, flourishing their steel points right at the prisoner's breast. He regarded them calmly, so calmly that the Persian gave vent to his admiration.

"Down with your lance-head, Rūkhs. By Mithra, I think this Hellene is brave as he is beautiful! See how he stands. We must have him to the Prince."

"Excellency," spoke Glaucon, in his best court Persian, "I am a courier to the Lord Mardonius. If you are faithful servants of his Eternity the king, where is your camp?"

The chief started.

"On the life of my father, you speak Persian as if you dwelled in Eran at the king's own doors! What do you here alone upon this road in Hellas?"

Glaucon put out his hand before answering, caught the tip of Rūkhs's lance, and snapped it short like a reed. He knew the way to win the admiration of the Barbarians. They yelled with delight, all at least save Rūkhs.

"Strong as he is brave and handsome," cried the Persian. "Again—who are you?"

The Alcmæonid drew himself to full height and gave his head its lordliest poise.

"Understand, Persian, that I have indeed lived long at the king's gates. Yes,— I have learned my Aryan at the Lord Mardonius's own table, for I am the son of Attaginus of Thebes, who is not the least of the friends of his Eternity in Hellas."

The mention of one of the foremost Medizers of Greece made the subaltern bend in his saddle. His tone became even obsequious.

"Ah, I understand. Your Excellency is a courier. You have despatches from the king?"

"Despatches of moment just landed from Asia. Now tell me where the army is encamped."

"By the Asopus, much to northward. The Hellenes lie to south. Here, Rūkhs, take the noble courier behind you on the horse, and conduct him to the general."

"Heaven bless your generosity," cried the runner, with almost precipitate haste, "but I know the country well, and the worthy Rūkhs will not thank me if I deprive him of his share in your booty."

"Ah, yes, we have heard of a farm across the hills at Eleutheræ that's not yet been plundered,—handsome wenches, and we'll make the father dig up his pot of money. Mazda speed you, sir, for we are off."

"Yeh! yeh!" yelled the seven Tartars, none more loudly than Rūkhs, who had no hankering for conducting a courier back into the camp. So the riders came and went, whilst Glaucon drew his girdle one notch tighter and ran onward through the gathering evening.

The adventure had been a warning. Once Athena had saved him, not perchance twice,—again he took to the fields. He did not love the sight of the sun ever lower, on the long brown ridge of Helicon far to west. Until now he scarce thought enough of self to realize the terrible draughts he had made upon his treasure-house of strength. Could it be that he—the Isthmionices, who had crushed down the giant of Sparta before the cheering myriads—could faint like a weary girl, when the weal of Hellas was his to win or lose? Why did his tongue burn in his throat as a coal? Why did those feet—so swift, so ready when he sped from Oropus—lift so heavily?

As a flash it came over him what he had endured,—the slow agony on the *Bozra*, the bursting of the bands, the fight for life, the scene with Themistocles, the sleepless night on the trireme. Now he was running as the wild hare runs before the baying chase. Could it be that all this race was vain?

"For Hellas! For Hermione!"

Whilst he groaned through his gritted teeth, some malignant god made him misstep, stumble. He fell between the hard furrows, bruising his face and hands. After a moment he rose, but rose to sink back again with keen pain shooting through an ankle. He had turned it. For an instant he sat motionless, taking breath, then his teeth came together harder.

"Themistocles trusts me. I carry the fate of Hellas. I can die, but I cannot fail."

It was quite dusk now. The brief southern twilight was ending in pale bars of gold above Helicon. Glaucon rose again; the cold sweat sprang out upon his forehead. Before his eyes rose darkness, but he did not faint. Some kind destiny set a stout pole upright in the field,—perhaps for vines to clamber,— he clutched it, and stood until his sight cleared and the pain a little abated. He tore the pole from the ground, and reached the roadway. He must take his chance of meeting more raiders. He had one vast comfort,—if there had been no battle fought that day, there would be none before dawn. But he had still weary stadia before him, and running was out of the question. Ever and anon he would stop his hobbling, take air, and stare at the vague tracery of the hills,—Cithæron to southward, Helicon to west, and northward the wide dark Theban plain. He gave up counting how many times he halted, how many times he spoke the magic words, "For Hellas! For Hermione!" and forced onward his way. The moon failed, even the stars were clouded. A kind of brute instinct guided him. At last—he guessed it was nearly midnight—he caught once more the flashings of a shallow river and the dim outlines of shrubbery beside the bank—again the Asopus. He must take care or he would wander straight into Mardonius's camp. Therefore he stopped awhile, drank the cool water, and let the stream purl around his burning foot. Then he set his face to the south, for there lay Platæa. There he would find the Hellenes.

He was almost unconscious of everything save the fierce pain and the need to go forward even to the end. At moments he thought he saw the mountains springing out of their gloom,—Helicon and Cithæron beckoning him on, as with living fingers.

"Not too late. Marathon was not vain, nor Thermopylæ, nor Salamis. You can save Hellas."

Who spoke that? He stared into the solitary night. Was he not alone? Then phantasms came as on a flood. He was in a kind of euthanasy. The pain of his foot had ceased. He saw the Paradise by Sardis and its bending feathery palms; he heard the tinkling of the Lydian harps, and Roxana singing of the magic Oxus, and the rose valleys of Eran. Next Roxana became Hermione. He was standing at her side on the knoll of Colonus, and watching the sun sink behind Daphni making the Acropolis glow with red fire and gold. Yet all the time he knew he was going onward. He must not stop.

"For Hellas! For Hermione!"

At last even the vision of the Violet-Crowned City faded to mist. Had he reached the end,—the rest by the fields of Rhadamanthus, away from human strife? The night was ever darkening. He saw nothing, felt nothing, thought nothing save that he was still going onward, onward.

* * * * * *

At some time betwixt midnight and dawning an Athenian outpost was pacing his beat outside the lines of Aristeides. The allied Hellenes were retiring from their position by the Asopus to a more convenient spot by Platæa, less exposed to the dreaded Persian cavalry, but on the night march the contingents had become disordered. The Athenians were halting under arms,—awaiting orders from Pausanias the commander-in-chief. The outpost—Hippon, a worthy charcoal-burner of Archarnæ—was creeping gingerly behind the willow hedges, having a well-grounded fear of Tartar arrows. Presently his fox-keen ears caught footfalls from the road. His shield went up. He couched his spear. His eyes, sharpened by the long darkness, saw a man hardly running, nor walking, yet dragging one foot and leaning on a staff. Here was no Tartar, and Hippon sprang out boldly.

"Halt, stranger, tell your business."

"For Aristeides." The apparition seemed holding out something in his hand.

"That's not the watchword. Give it, or I must arrest you."

"For Aristeides."

"Zeus smite you, fellow, can't you speak Greek? What have you got for our general?"

"For Aristeides."

The stranger was hoarse as a crow. He was pushing aside the spear and forcing a packet into Hippon's hands. The latter, sorely puzzled, whistled through his fingers. A moment more the locharch of the scouting division and three comrades appeared.

"Why the alarm? Where's the enemy?"

"No enemy, but a madman. Find what he wants."

The locharch in earlier days had kept an oil booth in the Athens Agora and knew the local celebrities as well as Phormio.

"Now, friend," he spoke, "your business, and shortly; we've no time for chaffering."

"For Aristeides."

"The fourth time he's said it,—sheep!" cried Hippon, but as he spoke the newcomer fell forward heavily, groaned once, and lay on the roadway silent as the dead. The locharch drew forth the horn lantern he had masked under his chalmys and leaned over the stranger. The light fell on the seal of the packet gripped in the rigid fingers.

"Themistocles's seal," he cried, and hastily turned the fallen man's face upward to the light, when the lantern almost dropped from his own hand.

"Glaucon the Alcmæonid! Glaucon the Traitor who was dead! He or his shade come back from Tartarus."

The four soldiers stood quaking like aspen, but their leader was of stouter stuff. Never had his native Attic shrewdness guided him to more purpose.

"Ghost, traitor, what not, this man has run himself all but to death. Look on his face. And Themistocles does not send a courier for nothing. This packet is for Aristeides, and to Aristeides take it with speed."

Hippon seized the papyrus. He thought it would fade out of his hands like a spectre. It did not. The sentinel dropped his spear and ran breathless toward Platæa, where he knew was his general.

CHAPTER XXXVIII
THE COUNCIL OF MARDONIUS

Never since Salamis had Persian hopes been higher than that night. What if the Spartans were in the field at last, and the incessant skirmishing had been partly to Pausanias's advantage? Secure in his fortified camp by the Asopus, Mardonius could confidently wait the turn of the tide. His light Tartar cavalry had cut to pieces the convoys bringing provisions to the Hellenes. Rumour told that Pausanias's army was ill fed, and his captains were at loggerheads. Time was fighting for Mardonius. A joyful letter he had sent to Sardis the preceding morning: "Let the king have patience. In forty days I shall be banqueting even in Sparta."

In the evening the Prince sat at council with his commanders. Xerxes had left behind his own war pavilion, and here the Persians met. Mardonius sat on the high seat of the dais. Gold, purple, a hundred torches, made the scene worthy of the monarch himself. Beside the general stood a young page,— beautiful as Armaiti, fairest of the archangels. All looked on the page, but discreetly kept their thoughts to whispers, though many had guessed the secret of Mardonius's companion.

The debate was long and vehement. Especially Artabazus, general of the rear-guard, was loud in asserting no battle should be risked. He was a crafty man, who, the Prince suspected, was his personal enemy, but his opinion was worth respecting.

"I repeat what I said before. The Hellenes showed how they could fight at Thermopylæ. Let us retire to Thebes."

"Bravely said, valiant general," sneered Mardonius, none too civilly.

"It is mine to speak, yours to follow my opinion as you list. I say we can conquer these Hellenes with folded hands. Retreat to Thebes; money is plentiful with us; we can melt our gold cups into coin. Sprinkle bribes among the hostile chiefs. We know their weakness. Not steel but gold will unlock the way to Sparta."

The generalissimo stood up proudly.

"Bribes and stealth? Did Cyrus and Darius win us empire with these? No, by the Fiend-Smiter, it was sharp steel and the song of the bow-string that made Eran to prosper, and prosper to this day. But lest Artabazus think that in putting on the lion I have forgotten the fox, let the strangers now come to us stand forth, that he and every other may know how I have done all things for the glory of my master and the Persian name."

He smote with his commander's mace upon the bronze ewer on the table. Instantly there appeared two soldiers, between them two men, one of slight, one of gigantic, stature, but both in Grecian dress. Artabazus sprang to his feet.

"Who are these men—Thebans?"

"From greater cities than Thebes. You see two new servants of the king, therefore friends of us all. Behold Lycon of Sparta and Democrates, friend of Themistocles."

His speech was Persian, but the newcomers both understood when he named them. The tall Laconian straightened his bull neck, as in defiance. The Athenian flushed. His head seemed sinking betwixt his shoulders. Much wormwood had he drunk of late, but none bitterer than this,—to be welcomed at the councils of the Barbarian. Artabazus salaamed to his superior half mockingly.

"Verily, son of Gobryas, I was wrong. You are guileful as a Greek. There can be no higher praise."

The Prince's nostrils twitched. Perhaps he was not saying all he felt.

"Let your praise await the issue," he rejoined coldly. "Suffice it that these friends were long convinced of the wisdom of aiding his Eternity, and to-night come from the camp of the Hellenes to tell all that has passed and why we should make ready for battle at the dawning." He turned to the Greeks, ordering in their own tongue, "Speak forth, I am interpreter for the council."

An awkward instant followed. Lycon looked on Democrates.

"You are an Athenian, your tongue is readiest," he whispered.

"And you the first to Medize. Finish your handiwork," the retort.

"We are waiting," prompted Mardonius, and Lycon held up his great head and began in short sentences which the general deftly turned into Persian.

"Your cavalry has made our position by the Asopus intolerable. All the springs are exposed. We have to fight every time we try to draw water. To-day was a meeting of the commanders, many opinions, much wrangling, but all said we must retire. The town of Platæa is best. It is strong, with plenty of water. You cannot attack it. To-night our camp has been struck. The troops begin to retire, but in disorder. The contingent of each city marches by itself. The Athenians, thanks to Democrates, delay retreating; the Spartans I have delayed also. I have persuaded Amompharetus, my cousin, who leads the Pitanate *mora*,[15] and who was not at the council, that it is cowardly for a Spartan to retreat. He is a sheep-skulled fool and has believed me. Consequently, he and his men are holding back. The other Spartans wait for them. At dawn you will find the Athenians and Spartans alone near their old camping ground, their allies straggling in the rear. Attack boldly. When the onset joins, Democrates and I will order our own divisions to retire. The phalanxes will be broken up. With your cavalry you will have them at mercy, for once the spear-hedge is shattered, they are lost. The battle will not cost you twenty men."

Artabazus rose again and showed his teeth.

"A faithful servant of the king, Mardonius,—and so well is all provided, do we brave Aryans need even to string our bows?"

The Prince winced at the sarcasm.

"I am serving the king, not my own pleasure," he retorted stiffly. "The son of Gobryas is too well known to have slurs cast on his courage. And now what questions would my captains ask these Greeks? Promptly—they must be again in their own lines, or they are missed."

An officer here or there threw an interrogation. Lycon answered briefly. Democrates kept sullen silence. He was clearly present more to prove the good faith of his Medizing than for anything he might say. Mardonius smote the ewer again. The soldiers escorted the two Hellenes forth. As the curtains closed behind them, the curious saw that the features of the beautiful page by the general's side were contracted with disgust. Mardonius himself spat violently.

"Dogs, and sons of dogs, let Angra-Mainyu wither them forever. Bear witness, men of Persia, how, for the sake of our Lord the King, I hold converse even with these vilest of the vile!"

Soon the council was broken up. The final commands were given. Every officer knew his task. The cavalry was to be ready to charge across the Asopus at gray dawn. With Lycon and Democrates playing their part the issue was certain, too certain for many a grizzled captain who loved the ring of steel. In his own tent Mardonius held in his arms the beautiful page— Artazostra! Her wonderful face had never shone up at his more brightly than on that night, as he drew back his lips from a long fond kiss.

"To-morrow—the triumph. You will be conqueror of Hellas. Xerxes will make you satrap. I wish we could conquer in fairer fight, but what wrong to vanquish these Hellenes with their own sly weapons? Do you remember what Glaucon said?"

"What thing?"

"That Zeus and Athena were greater than Mazda the Pure and glorious Mithra? To-morrow will prove him wrong. I wonder whether he yet lives,— whether he will ever confess that Persia is irresistible."

"I do not know. From the evening we parted at Phaleron he has faded from our world."

"He was fair as the Amesha-Spentas, was he not? Poor Roxana—she is again in Sardis now. I hope she has ceased to eat her heart out with vain longing for her lover. He was noble minded and spoke the truth. How rare in a Hellene. But what will you do with these two gold-bought traitors, 'friends of the king' indeed?"

Mardonius's face grew stern.

"I have promised them the lordships of Athens and of Sparta. The pledge shall be fulfilled, but after that,"—Artazostra understood his sinister smile,— "there are many ways of removing an unwelcome vassal prince, if I be the satrap of Hellas."

"And you are that in the morning."

"For your sake," was his cry, as again he kissed her, "I would I were not satrap of Hellas only, but lord of all the world, that I might give it to you, O daughter of Darius and Atossa."

"I am mistress of the world," she answered, "for my world is Mardonius. To-morrow the battle, the glory, and then what next—Sicily, Carthage, Italy? For Mazda will give us all things."

* * * * * *

Otherwise talked Democrates and Lycon as they quitted the Persian pickets and made their way across the black plain, back to the lines of the Hellenes.

"You should be happy to-night," said the Athenian.

"Assuredly. I draw up my net and find it very full of mullets quite to my liking."

"Take care it be not so full that it break."

"Dear Democrates,"—Lycon slapped his paw on the other's shoulder,— "why always imagine evil? Hermes is a very safe guide. I only hope our victory will be so complete Sparta will submit without fighting. It will be awkward to rule a plundered city."

"I shudder at the thought of being amongst even conquered Athenians; I shall see a tyrannicide in every boy in the Agora."

"A stout Persian garrison in your Acropolis is the surest physic against that."

"By the dog, Lycon, you speak like a Scythian. Hellene you surely are not."

"Hellene I am, and show my native wisdom in seeing that Persia must conquer and trimming sail accordingly."

"Persia is not irresistible. With a fair battle—"

"It will not be a fair battle. What can save Pausanias? Nothing—except a miracle sent from Zeus."

"Such as what?"

"As merciful Hiram's relenting and releasing your dear Glaucon." Lycon's chuckle was loud.

"Never, as you hope me to be anything save your mortal enemy, mention that name again."

"As you like it—it's no very pretty tale, I grant, even amongst Medizers. Yet it was most imprudent to let him live."

"You have never heard the Furies, Lycon." Democrates's voice was so grave as to dry up the Spartan's banter. "But I shall never see him again, and I shall possess Hermione."

"A pretty consolation. *Eu!* here are our outposts. We must pass for officers reconnoitring the enemy. You know your part to-morrow. At the first charge bid your division 'wheel to rear.' Three words, and the thing is done."

Lycon gave the watchword promptly to one of Pausanias's outposts. The man saluted his officers, and said that the Greeks of the lesser states had retreated far to the rear, that Amompharetus still refused to move his division, that the Spartans waited for him, and the Athenians for the Spartans.

"Noble tidings," whispered the giant, as the two stood an instant, before each went to his own men. "Behold how Hermes helps us—a great deity."

"Sometimes I think Nemesis is greater," said Democrates, once again refusing Lycon's proffered hand.

"By noon you'll laugh at Nemesis, *philotate*, when we both drink Helbon wine in Xerxes's tent!" and away went Lycon into the dark.

Democrates went his own way also. Soon he was in the fallow-field, where under the warm night the Athenians were stretched, each man in armour, his helmet for a pillow. A few torches were moving. From a distance came the hum from a group of officers in excited conversation. As the orator picked his way among the sleeping men, a locharch with a lantern accosted him suddenly.

"You are Democrates the strategus?"

"Certainly."

"Aristeides summons you at once. Come."

There was no reason for refusing. Democrates followed.

CHAPTER XXXIX
THE AVENGING OF LEONIDAS

Morning at last, ruddy and windy. The Persian host had been long prepared. The Tartar cavalry with their bulls-hide targets and long lances, the heavy Persian cuirassiers, the Median and Assyrian archers with their ponderous wicker-shields, stood in rank waiting only the word that should dash them as sling-stones on Pausanias and his ill-starred following. The Magi had sacrificed a stallion, and reported that the holy fire gave every favouring sign. Mardonius went from his tent, all his eunuchs bowing their foreheads to the earth and chorussing, "Victory to our Lord, to Persia, and to the King."

They brought Mardonius his favourite horse, a white steed of the sacred breed of Nisæa. The Prince had bound around his turban the gemmed tiara Xerxes had given him on his wedding-day. Few could wield the Babylonish cimeter that danced in the chieftain's hand. The captains cheered him loudly, as they might have cheered the king.

"Life to the general! To the satrap of Hellas!"

But beside the Nisæan pranced another, lighter and with a lighter mount. The rider was cased in silvered scale-armour, and bore only a steel-tipped reed.

"The general's page," ran the whisper, and other whispers, far softer, followed. None heard the quick words passed back and forth betwixt the two riders.

"You may be riding to death, Artazostra. What place is a battle for women?"

"What place is the camp for the daughter of Darius, when her husband rides to war? We triumph together; we perish together. It shall be as Mazda decrees."

Mardonius answered nothing. Long since he had learned the folly of setting his will against that of the masterful princess at his side. And was not victory certain? Was not Artazostra doing even as Semiramis of Nineveh had done of old?

"The army is ready, Excellency," declared an adjutant, bowing in his saddle.

"Forward, then, but slowly, to await the reconnoitring parties sent toward the Greeks."

In the gray morning the host wound out of the stockaded camp. The women and grooms called fair wishes after them. The far slopes of Cithæron were reddening. A breeze whistled down the hills. It would disperse the mist. Soon the leader of the scouts came galloping, leaped down and salaamed to the general. "Let my Lord's liver find peace. All is even as our friends declared. The enemy have in part fled far away. The Athenians halt on a foot-hill of the mountain. The Laconians sit in companies on the ground, waiting their division that will not retreat. Let my Lord charge, and glory waits for Eran!"

Mardonius's cimeter swung high.

"Forward, all! Mazda fights for us. Bid our allies the Thebans[16] attack the Athenians. Ours is the nobler prey—even the men of Sparta."

"Victory to the king!" thundered the thousands. Confident of triumph, Mardonius suffered the ranks to be broken, as his myriads rushed onward. Over the Asopus and its shallow fords they swept, and raced across the plain-land. Horse mingled with foot; Persians with Tartars. The howlings in a score of tongues, the bray of cymbals and kettledrums, the clamour of spear-butts beaten on armour—who may tell it? Having unleashed his wild beasts, Mardonius dashed before to guide their ragings as he might. The white Nisæan and its companion led the way across the hard plain. Behind, as when in the springtime flood the watery wall goes crashing down the valley, so spread the thousands. A god looking from heaven would not have forgotten that sight of whirling plumes, plunging steeds, flying steel, in all the æons.

Five stadia, six, seven, eight,—so Mardonius led. Already before him he could see the glistering crests and long files of the Spartans—the prey he would crush with one stroke as a vulture swoops over the sparrow. Then nigh involuntarily his hand drew rein. What came to greet him? A man on foot—no horseman even. A man of huge stature running at headlong speed.

The risen sun was now dazzling. The general clapped his hand above his eyes. Then a tug on the bridle sent the Nisæan on his haunches.

"Lycon, as Mazda made me!"

The Spartan was beside them soon, he had run so swiftly. He was so dazed he barely heeded Mardonius's call to halt and tell his tale. He was almost naked. His face was black with fear, never more brutish or loathsome.

"All is betrayed. Democrates is seized. Pausanias and Aristeides are warned. They will give you fair battle. I barely escaped."

"Who betrayed you?" cried the Prince.

"Glaucon the Alcmæonid, he is risen from the dead. *Ai!* woe! no fault of mine."

Never before had the son of Gobryas smiled so fiercely as when the giant cowered beneath his darting eyes. The general's sword whistled down on the skull of the traitor. The Laconian sprawled in the dust without a groan. Mardonius laughed horribly.

"A fair price then for unlucky villany. Blessed be Mithra, who suffers me to give recompense. Wish me joy,"—as his captains came galloping around him,—"our duty to the king is finished. We shall win Hellas in fair battle."

"Then it were well, Excellency," thrust in Artabazus, "since the plot is foiled, to retire to the camp."

Mardonius's eyes flashed lightnings.

"Woman's counsel that! Are we not here to conquer Hellas? Yes, by Mithra the Glorious, we will fight, though every *dæva* in hell joins against us. Re-form the ranks. Halt the charge. Let the bowmen crush the Spartans with their arrows. Then we will see if these Greeks are stouter than Babylonian, Lydian, and Egyptian who played their game with Persia to sore cost. And you, Artabazus, to your rear-guard, and do your duty well."

The general bowed stiffly. He knew the son of Gobryas, and that disobedience would have brought Mardonius's cimeter upon his own helmet. By a great effort the charge was stayed,—barely in time,—for to have flung that disorganized horde on the waiting Spartan spears would have been worse than madness. A single stadium sundered the two hosts when Mardonius brought his men to a stand, set his strong divisions of bowmen in array behind their wall of shields, and drew up his cavalry on the flanks of the bowmen. Battle he would give, but it must be cautious battle now, and he did not love the silence which reigned among the motionless lines of the Spartans.

It was bright day at last. The two armies—the whole strength of the Barbarian, the Spartans with only their Tegean allies—stood facing, as athletes measuring strength before the grapple. The Spartan line was thinner than Mardonius's: no cavalry, few bowmen, but shield was set beside shield, and everywhere tossed the black and scarlet plumes of the helmets. Men who remembered Thermopylæ gripped their spear-stocks tighter. No long postponing now. On this narrow field, this bit of pebble and greensward, the gods would cast the last dice for the destiny of Hellas. All knew that.

The stolidity of the Spartans was maddening. They stood like bronze statues. In clear view at the front was a tall man in scarlet chlamys, and two more in white,—Pausanias and his seers examining the entrails of doves, seeking a fair omen for the battle. Mardonius drew the turban lower over his eyes.

"An end to this truce. Begin your arrows."

A cloud of bolts answered him. The Persian archers emptied their quivers. They could see men falling among the foe, but still Pausanias stood beside the seers, still he gave no signal to advance. The omens doubtless were unfavourable. His men never shifted a foot as the storm of death flew over them. Their rigidity was more terrifying than any battle-shout. What were these men whose iron discipline bound so fast that they could be pelted to death, and no eyelash seem to quiver? The archers renewed their volley. They shot against a rock. The Barbarians joined in one rending yell,—their answer was silence.

Deliberately, arrows dropping around him as tree-blossoms in the gale, Pausanias raised his hand. The omens were good. The gods permitted battle. Deliberately, while men fell dying, he walked to his post on the right wing. Deliberately, while heaven seemed shaking with the Barbarians' clamour, his hand went up again. Through a lull in the tumult pealed a trumpet. *Then the Spartans marched.*

Slowly their lines of bristling spear-points and nodding crests moved on like the sea-waves. Shrill above the booming Tartar drums, the blaring Persian war-horns pierced the screams of their pipers. And the Barbarians heard that which had never met their ears before,—the chanting of their foes as the long line crept nearer.

"Ah!—la—la—la—la! Ah!—la—la—la—la!" deep, prolonged, bellowed in chorus from every bronze visor which peered above the serried shields.

"Faster," stormed the Persian captains to their slingers and bowmen, "beat these madmen down." The rain of arrows and sling-stones was like hail, like hail it rattled from the shields and helms. Here, there, a form sank, the inexorable phalanx closed and swept onward.

"Ah!—la—la—la! Ah!—la—la—la!"

The chant never ceased. The pipers screamed more shrilly. Eight deep, unhasting, unresting, Pausanias was bringing his heavy infantry across the two hundred paces betwixt himself and Mardonius. His Spartan spearmen might be unlearned, doltish, but they knew how to do one deed and that surpassingly well,—to march in line though lightnings dashed from heaven, and to thrust home with their lances. And not a pitiful three hundred, but ten thousand bold and strong stood against the Barbarian that morning. Mardonius was facing the finest infantry in the world, and the avenging of Leonidas was nigh.

"Ah!—la—la—la! Ah!—la—la—la!"

Flesh and blood in the Persian host could not wait the death grip longer. "Let us charge, or let us flee," many a stout officer cried to his chief, and he sitting stern-eyed on the white horse gave to a Tartar troop its word, "Go!"

Then like a mountain stream the wild Tartars charged. The clods flew high under the hoofs. The yell of the riders, the shock of spears on shields, the cry of dying men and dying beasts, the stamping, the dust-cloud, took but a moment. The chant of the Spartans ceased—an instant. An instant the long phalanx halted, from end to end bent and swayed. Then the dust-cloud passed, the chanting renewed. Half of the Tartars were spurring back, with shivered lances, bleeding steeds. The rest,—but the phalanx shook now here, now there, as the impenetrable infantry strode over red forms that had been men and horses. And still the Spartans marched, still the pipes and the war-chant.

Then for the first time fear entered the heart of Mardonius, son of Gobryas, and he called to the thousand picked horsemen, who rode beside him,—not Tartars these, but Persians and Medes of lordly stock, men who had gone forth conquering and to conquer.

"Now as your fathers followed Cyrus the Invincible and Darius the Dauntless, follow you me. Since for the honour of Eran and the king I ride this day."

"We ride. For Eran and the king!" shouted the thousand. All the host joined. Mardonius led straight against the Spartan right wing where Pausanias's life-guard marched.

* * * * * *

Old soldiers of Lacedæmon fighting their battles in the after days, when a warrior of Platæa was as a god to each youth in Hellas, would tell how the Persian cavalrymen rode their phalanx down.

"And say never," they always added, "the Barbarians know not how to fight and how to die. Fools say it, not we of Platæa. For our first line seemed broken in a twinkling. The Pitanate *mora* was cut to pieces; Athena Promachus and Ares the City-Waster alone turned back that charge when Mardonius led the way."

But turned it was. And the thousand horse, no thousand now, drifted to the cover of their shield wall, raging, undaunted, yet beaten back.

Then at last the phalanx locked with the Persian footmen and their rampart of wicker shields. At short spear length men grinned in each other's faces, while their veins were turned to fire. Many a soldier—Spartan, Aryan—had seen his twenty fights, but never a fight like this. And the Persians—those that knew Greek—heard words flung through their foemen's helmets that made each Hellene fight as ten.

"Remember Leonidas! Remember Thermopylæ!"

Orders there were none; the trumpets were drowned in the tumult. Each man fought as he stood, knowing only he must slay the man before him, while slowly, as though by a cord tighter and ever tighter drawn, the Persian shield wall was bending back before the unrelenting thrusting of the Spartans. Then as a cord snaps so broke the barrier. One instant down and the Hellenes were sweeping the light-armed Asiatic footmen before them, as the scythe sweeps down the standing grain. So with the Persian infantry, for their scanty armour and short spears were at terrible disadvantage, but the strength of the Barbarian was not spent. Many times Mardonius led the cavalry in headlong charge, each repulse the prelude to a fiercer shock.

"For Mazda, for Eran, for the king!"

The call of the Prince was a call that turned his wild horsemen into demons, but demons who strove with gods. The phalanx was shaken, halted even, broken never; and foot by foot, fathom by fathom, it brushed the Barbarian horde back across the blood-bathed plain,—and to Mardonius's shout, a more terrible always answered:—

"Remember Leonidas! Remember Thermopylæ!"

The Prince seemed to bear a charmed life as he fought. He was in the thickest fray. He sent the white Nisæan against the Laconian spears and beat down a dozen lance-points with his sword. If one man's valour could have turned the tide, his would have wrought the miracle. And always behind, almost in reach of the Grecian sling-stones, rode that other,—the page in the silvered mail,—nor did any harm come to this rider. But after the fight had raged so long that men sank unwounded,—gasping, stricken by the heat and press,— the Prince drew back a little from the fray to a rising in the plain, where close by a rural temple of Demeter he could watch the drifting fight, and he saw the Aryans yielding ground finger by finger, yet yielding, and the phalanx impregnable as ever. Then he sent an aide with an urgent message.

"To Artabazus and the reserve. Bid him take from the camp all the guards, every man, every eunuch that can lift a spear, and come with speed, or the day is lost."

The adjutant's spurs grew red as he pricked away, while Mardonius wheeled the Nisæan and plunged back into the thickest fight.

"For Mazda, for Eran, for the king!"

His battle-call pealed even above the hellish din. The Persian nobles who had never ridden to aught save victory turned again. Their last charge was their fiercest. They bent the phalanx back like an inverted bow. Their footmen, reckless of self, plunged on the Greeks and snapped off the spear-points with their naked hands. Mardonius was never prouder of his host than in that hour. Proud—but the charge was vain. As the tide swept back, as the files of the Spartans locked once more, he knew his men had done their uttermost. They had fought since dawn. Their shield wall was broken. Their quivers were empty. Was not Mazda turning against them? Had not enough been dared for that king who lounged at ease in Sardis?

"For Mazda, for Eran, for the king!"

Mardonius's shout had no answer. Here, there, he saw horsemen and footmen, now singly, now in small companies, drifting backward across the plain to the last refuge of the defeated, the stockaded camp by the Asopus. The Prince called on his cavalry, so few about him now.

"Shall we die as scared dogs? Remember the Aryan glory. Another charge!"

His bravest seemed never to hear him. The onward thrust of the phalanx quickened. It was gaining ground swiftly at last. Then the Spartans were dashing forward like men possessed.

"The Athenians have vanquished the Thebans. They come to join us. On, men of Lacedæmon, ours alone must be this victory!"

The shout of Pausanias was echoed by his captains. To the left and not far off charged a second phalanx,—five thousand nodding crests and gleaming points,—Aristeides bringing his whole array to his allies' succour. But his help was not needed. The sight of his coming dashed out the last courage of the Barbarians. Before the redoubled shock of the Spartans the Asiatics crumbled like sand. Even whilst these broke once more, the adjutant drew rein beside Mardonius.

"Lord, Artabazus is coward or traitor. Believing the battle lost, he has fled. There is no help to bring."

The Prince bowed his head an instant, while the flight surged round him. The Nisæan was covered with blood, but his rider spurred him across the path of a squadron of flying Medians.

"Turn! Are you grown women!" Mardonius smote the nearest with his sword. "If we cannot as Aryans conquer, let us at least as Aryans die!"

"*Ai! ai!* Mithra deserts us. Artabazus is fled. Save who can!"

They swept past him. He flung himself before a band of Tartars. He had better pleaded with the north wind to stay its course. Horse, foot, Babylonians, Ethiopians, Persians, Medes, were huddled in fleeing rout. "To the camp," their cry, but Mardonius, looking on the onrushing phalanxes knew there was no refuge there....

And now sing it, O mountains and rivers of Hellas. Sing it, Asopus, to Spartan Eurotas, and you to hill-girt Alphæus. And let the maidens, white-robed and poppy-crowned, sweep in thanksgiving up to the welcoming temples,—honouring Zeus of the Thunders, Poseidon the Earth-Shaker, Athena the Mighty in War. The Barbarian is vanquished. The ordeal is ended. Thermopylæ was not in vain, nor Salamis. Hellas is saved, and with her saved the world.

* * * * * *

Again on the knoll by the temple, apart from the rushing fugitives, Mardonius reined. His companion was once more beside him. He leaned that she might hear him through the tumult.

"The battle is lost. The camp is defenceless. What shall we do?"

Artazostra flung back the gold-laced cap and let the sun play over her face and hair.

"We are Aryans," was all her answer.

He understood, but even whilst he was reaching out to catch her bridle that their horses might run together, he saw her lithe form bend. The arrow from a Laconian helot had smitten through the silvered mail. He saw the red spring out over her breast. With a quick grasp he swung her before him on the white horse. She smiled up in his face, never lovelier.

"Glaucon was right," she said,—their lips were very close,—"Zeus and Athena are greater than Mazda and Mithra. The future belongs to Hellas. But we have naught for shame. We have fought as Aryans, as the children of conquerors and kings. We shall be glad together in Garonmana the Blessed, and what is left to dread?"

A quiver passed through her. The Spartan spear-line was close. Mardonius looked once across the field. His men were fleeing like sheep. And so it passed,—the dream of a satrapy of Hellas, of wider conquests, of an empire of the world. He kissed the face of Artazostra and pressed her still form against his breast.

"For Mazda, for Eran, for the king!" he shouted, and threw away his sword. Then he turned the head of his wounded steed and rode on the Spartan lances.

CHAPTER XL
THE SONG OF THE FURIES

Themistocles had started from Oropus with Simonides, a small guard of mariners, and a fettered prisoner, as soon as the *Nausicaä's* people were a little rested. Half the night they themselves were plodding on wearily. At Tanagra the following afternoon a runner with a palm branch met them.

"Mardonius is slain. Artabazus with the rear-guard has fled northward. The Athenians aided by the Spartans stormed the camp. Glory to Athena, who gives us victory!"

"And the traitors?" Themistocles showed surprisingly little joy.

"Lycon's body was found drifting in the Asopus. Democrates lies fettered by Aristeides's tents."

Then the other Athenians broke forth into pæans, but Themistocles bowed his head and was still, though the messenger told how Pausanias and his allies had taken countless treasure, and now were making ready to attack disloyal Thebes. So the admiral and his escort went at leisure across Bœotia, till they reached the Hellenic host still camped near the battle-field. There Themistocles was long in conference with Aristeides and Pausanias. After midnight he left Aristeides's tent.

"Where is the prisoner?" he asked of the sentinel before the headquarters.

"Your Excellency means the traitor?"

"I do."

"I will guide you." The soldier took a torch and led the way. The two went down dark avenues of tents, and halted at one where five hoplites stood guard with their spears ready, five more slept before the entrance.

"We watch him closely, *kyrie*," explained the decarch, saluting. "Naturally we fear suicide as well as escape. Two more are within the tent."

"Withdraw them. Do you all stand at distance. For what happens I will be responsible."

The two guards inside emerged yawning. Themistocles took the torch and entered the squalid hair-cloth pavilion. The sentries noticed he had a casket under his cloak.

"The prisoner sleeps," said a hoplite, "in spite of his fetters."

Themistocles set down the casket and carefully drew the tent-flap. With silent tread he approached the slumberer. The face was upturned; white it was, but it showed the same winsome features that had won the clappings a hundred times in the Pnyx. The sleep seemed heavy, dreamless.

Themistocles's own lips tightened as he stood in contemplation, then he bent to touch the other's shoulder.

"Democrates,"—no answer. "Democrates,"—still silence. "Democrates,"—a stirring, a clanking of metal. The eyes opened,—for one instant a smile.

"*Ei*, Themistocles, it is you?" to be succeeded by a flash of unspeakable horror. "O Zeus, the gyves! That I should come to this!"

The prisoner rose to a sitting posture upon his truss of straw. His fettered hands seized his head.

"Peace," ordered the admiral, gently. "Do not rave. I have sent the sentries away. No one will hear us."

Democrates grew calmer. "You are merciful. You do not know how I was tempted. You will save me."

"I will do all I can." Themistocles's voice was solemn as an æolian harp, but the prisoner caught at everything eagerly.

"Ah, you can do so much. Pausanias fought the battle, but they call you the true saviour of Hellas. They will do anything you say."

"I am glad." Themistocles's face was impenetrable as the sphinx's. Democrates seized the admiral's red chlamys with his fettered hands.

"You will save me! I will fly to Sicily, Carthage, the Tin Isles, as you wish. Have you forgotten our old-time friendship?"

"I loved you," spoke the admiral, tremulously.

"Ah, recall that love to-night!"

"I do."

"O piteous Zeus, why then is your face so awful? If you will aid me to escape—"

"I will aid you."

"Blessings, blessings, but quick! I fear to be stoned to death by the soldiers in the morning. They threaten to crucify—"

"They shall not."

"Blessings, blessings,—can I escape to-night?"

"Yes," but Themistocles's tone made the prisoner's blood run chill. He cowered helplessly. The admiral stood, his own fine face covered with a mingling of pity, contempt, pain.

"Democrates, hearken,"—his voice was hard as flint. "We have seized your camp chest, found the key to your ciphers, and know all your correspondence with Lycon. We have discovered your fearful power of forgery. Hermes the Trickster gave it you for your own destruction. We have brought Hiram hither from the ship. This night he has ridden the 'Little Horse.'[17] He has howled out everything. We have seized Bias and heard his story. There is nothing to conceal. From the beginning of your peculation of the public money, till the moment when, the prisoners say, you were in Mardonius's camp, all is known to us. You need not confess. There is nothing worth confessing."

"I am glad,"—great beads were on the prisoner's brow,—"but you do not realize the temptation. Have you never yourself been betwixt Scylla and Charybdis? Have I not vowed every false step should be the last? I fought against Lycon. I fought against Mardonius. They were too strong. Athena knoweth I did not crave the tyranny of Athens! It was not that which drove me to betray Hellas."

"I believe you. But why did you not trust me at the first?"

"I hardly understand."

"When first your need of money drove you to crime, why did you not come to me? You knew I loved you. You knew I looked on you as my political son and heir in the great work of making Athens the light of Hellas. I would have given you the gold,—yes, fifty talents."

"*Ai, ai,* if I had only dared! I thought of it. I was afraid."

"Right." Themistocles's lip was curling. "You are more coward than knave or traitor. Phobos, Black Fear, has been your leading god, not Hermes. And now—"

"But you have promised I shall escape."

"You shall."

"To-night? What is that you have?" Themistocles was opening the casket.

"The papers seized in your chest. They implicate many noble Hellenes in Corinth, Sicyon, Sparta. Behold—" Themistocles held one papyrus after another in the torch-flame,—"here is crumbling to ashes the evidence that would destroy them all as Medizers. Mardonius is dead. Let the war die with him. Hellas is safe."

"Blessings, blessings! Help me to escape. You have a sword. Pry off these gyves. How easy for you to let me fly!"

"Wait!" The admiral's peremptory voice silenced the prisoner. Themistocles finished his task. Suddenly, however, Democrates howled with animal fear.

"What are you taking now—a goblet?"

"Wait." Themistocles was indeed holding a silver cup and flask. "Have I not said you should escape this captivity—to-night?"

"Be quick, then, the night wanes fast."

The admiral strode over beside the creature who plucked at his hem.

"Give ear again, Democrates. Your crimes against Athens and Hellas were wrought under sore temptation. The money you stole from the public chest, if not returned already, I will myself make good. So much is forgiven."

"You are a true friend, Themistocles." The prisoner's voice was husky, but the admiral's eyes flashed like flint-stones struck by the steel.

"Friend!" he echoed. "Yes, by Zeus Orcios, guardian of oaths and friendship, you had a friend. Where is he now?"

Democrates lay on the turf floor of the tent, not even groaning.

"You had a friend,"—the admiral's intensity was awful. "You blasted his good name, you sought his life, you sought his wife, you broke every bond, human or divine, to destroy him. At last, to silence conscience' sting, you thought you did a deed of mercy in sending him in captivity to a death in life. Fool! Nemesis is not mocked. Glaucon has lain at death's door. He has saved Hellas, but at a price. The surgeons say he will live, but that his foot is crippled. Glaucon can never run again. You have brought him misery. You have brought anguish to Hermione, the noblest woman in Hellas, whom you—ah! mockery—professed to hold in love! You have done worse than murder. Yet I have promised you shall escape this night. Rise up."

Democrates staggered to his feet clumsily, only half knowing what he did. Themistocles was extending the silver cup. "Escape. Drink!"

"What is this cup?" The prisoner had turned gray.

"Hemlock, coward! Did you not bid Glaucon to take his life that night in Colonus? The death you proffered him in his innocency I proffer you now in your guilt. Drink!"

"You have called me friend. You have said you loved me. I dare not die. A little time! Pity! Mercy! What god can I invoke?"

"None. Cerberus himself would not hearken to such as you. Drink."

"Pity, by our old-time friendship!"

The admiral's tall form straightened.

"Themistocles the Friend is dead; Themistocles the Just is here,—drink."

"But you promised escape?" The prisoner's whisper was just audible.

"Ay, truly, from the court-martial before the roaring camp in the morning, the unmasking of all your accomplices, the deeper shame of every one-time friend, the blazoning of your infamy in public evidence through Hellas, the soldiers howling for your blood, the stoning, perchance the plucking in pieces. By the gods Olympian, by the gods Infernal, do your past lovers one last service—drink!"

That was not all Themistocles said, that was all Democrates heard. In his ears sounded, even once again, the song of the Furies,—never so clearly as now.

"With scourge and with ban

We prostrate the man

Who with smooth-woven wile

And a fair-facèd smile

Hath planted a snare for his friend!

Though fleet, we shall find him,

Though strong, we shall bind him,

Who planted a snare for his friend!"

Nemesis—Nemesis, the implacable goddess, had come for her own at last. Democrates took the cup.

CHAPTER XLI
THE BRIGHTNESS OF HELIOS

The day that disloyal Thebes surrendered came the tidings of the crowning of the Hellenes' victories. At Mycale by Samos the Greek fleets had disembarked their crews and defeated the Persians almost at the doors of the Great King in Sardis. Artabazus had escaped through Thrace to Asia in caitiff flight. The war—at least the perilous part thereof—was at end. There might be more battles with the Barbarian, but no second Salamis or Platæa.

The Spartans had found the body of Mardonius pierced with five lances—all in front. Pausanias had honoured the brave dead,—the Persian had been carried from the battle-ground on a shield, and covered by the red cloak of a Laconian general. But the body mysteriously disappeared. Its fate was never known. Perhaps the curious would have gladly heard what Glaucon on his sick-bed told Themistocles, and what Sicinnus did afterward. Certain it is that the shrewd Asiatic later displayed a costly ring which the satrap Zariaspes, Mardonius's cousin, sent him "for a great service to the house of Gobryas."

* * * * * * *

On the same day that Thebes capitulated the household of Hermippus left Trœzene to return to Athens. When they had told Hermione all that had befallen,—the great good, the little ill,—she had not fainted, though Cleopis had been sure thereof. The colour had risen to her cheeks, the love-light to her eyes. She went to the cradle where Phœnix cooed and tossed his baby feet.

"Little one, little one," she said, while he beamed up at her, "you have not to avenge your father now. You have a better, greater task, to be as fair in body and still more in mind as he."

Then came the rush of tears, the sobbing, the laughter, and Lysistra and Cleopis, who feared the shock of too much joy, were glad.

The *Nausicaä* bore them to Peiræus. The harbour towns were in black ruins, for Mardonius had wasted everything before retiring to Bœotia for his last battle. In Athens, as they entered it, the houses were roofless, the streets scattered with rubbish. But Hermione did not think of these things. The Agora at last,—the porticos were only shattered, fire-scarred pillars,—and everywhere were tents and booths and bustle,—the brisk Athenians wasting no time in lamentation, but busy rebuilding and making good the loss. Above Hermione's head rose a few blackened columns,—all that was left of the holy house of Athena,—but the crystalline air and the red Rock of the Acropolis no Persian had been able to take away.

And even as Hermione crossed the Agora she heard a shouting, a word running from lip to lip as a wave leaps over the sea.

In the centre of the buzzing mart she stopped. All the blood sprang to her face, then left it. She passed her fingers over her hair, and waited with twitching, upturned face. Through the hucksters' booths, amid the clamouring buyers and sellers, went a runner, striking left and right with his staff, for the people were packing close, and he had much ado to clear the way. Horsemen next, prancing chargers, the prizes from the Barbarian, and after them a litter. Noble youths bore it, sons of the Eupatrid houses of Athens. At sight of the litter the buzz of the Agora became a roar.

"The beautiful! The fortunate! The deliverer! *Io! Io, pæan!*"

Hermione stood; only her eyes followed the litter. Its curtains were flung back; she saw some one within, lying on purple cushions. She saw the features, beautiful as Pentelic marble and as pale. She cared not for the people. She cared not that Phœnix, frighted by the shouting, had begun to wail. The statue in the litter moved, rose on one elbow.

"Ah, dearest and best,"—his voice had the old-time ring, his head the old-time poise,—"you need not fear to call me husband now!"

"Glaucon," she cried. "I am not fit to be your wife. I am not fit to kiss your feet."

* * * * * *

They set the litter down. Even little Simonides, though a king among the curious, found the Acropolis peculiarly worthy of his study. Enough that Hermione's hands were pressing her husband, and these two cared not whether a thousand watched or only Helios on high. Penelope was greeting the returning Odysseus:—

"Welcome even as to shipmen

On the swelling, raging sea;

When Poseidon flings the whirlwind,

- 337 -

When a thousand blasts roam free,

Then at last the land appeareth;—

E'en so welcome in her sight

Was her lord, her arms long clasped him,

And her eyes shone pure and bright."

After a long time Glaucon commanded, "Bring me our child," and Cleopis gladly obeyed. Phœnix ceased weeping and thrust his red fists in his father's face.

"*Ei*, pretty snail," said Glaucon, pressing him fast by one hand, whilst he held his mother by the other, "if I say you are a merry wight, the nurse will not marvel any more."

But Hermione had already heard from Niobe of the adventure in the market-place at Trœzene.

The young men were just taking up the litter, when the Agora again broke into cheers. Themistocles, saviour of Hellas, had crossed to Glaucon. The admiral—never more worshipped than now, when every plan he wove seemed perfect as a god's—took Glaucon and Hermione, one by each hand.

"Ah, *philotatoi*," he said, "to all of us is given by the sisters above so much bliss and so much sorrow. Some drink the bitter first, some the sweet. And you have drained the bitter to the lees. Therefore look up at the Sun-King boldly. He will not darken for you again."

"Where now?" asked Hermione, in all things looking to her husband.

"To the Acropolis," ordered Glaucon. "If the temple is desolate, the Rock is still holy. Let us give thanks to Athena."

He even would have left the litter, had not Themistocles firmly forbidden. In time the Alcmæonid's strength would return, though never the speed that had left the stadia behind whilst he raced to save Hellas.

They mounted the Rock. From above, in the old-time brightness, the noonday light, the sunlight of Athens, sprang down to them. Hermione, looking on Glaucon's face, saw him gaze eagerly upon her, his child, the sacred Rock, and the glory from Helios. Then his face wore a strange smile she could not understand. She did not know that he was saying in his heart:—

"And I thought for the rose vales of Bactria to forfeit—this!"

They were on the summit. The litter was set down on the projecting spur by the southwest corner. The area of the Acropolis was desolation, ashes, drums of overturned pillars, a few lone and scarred columns. The works of man were in ruin, but the works of the god, of yesterday, to-day, and forever were yet the same. They turned their backs on the ruin. Westward they looked— across land and sea, beautiful always, most beautiful now, for had they not been redeemed with blood and tears? The Barbarian was vanquished; the impossible accomplished. Hellas and Athens were their own, with none to take away.

They saw the blue bay of Phaleron. They saw the craggy height of Munychia, Salamis with its strait of the victory, farther yet the brown dome of Acro-Corinthus and the wide breast of the clear Saronian sea. To the left was Hymettus the Shaggy, to right the long crest of Daphni, behind them rose Pentelicus, home of the marble that should take the shape of the gods. With one voice they fell to praising Athens and Hellas, wisely or foolishly, according to their wit. Only Hermione and Glaucon kept silence, hand within hand, and speaking fast,—not with their lips,—but with their eyes.

Then at the end Themistocles spoke, and as always spoke the best.

"We have flung back the Barbarian. We have set our might against the God-King and have conquered. Athens lies in ruins. We shall rebuild her. We shall make her more truly than before the 'Beautiful,' the 'Violet-Crowned City,' worthy of the guardian Athena. The conquering of the Persian was hard. The making of Athens immortal by the beauty of our lives, and words, and deeds is harder. Yet in this also we shall conquer. Yea, verily, for the day shall come that wherever the eye is charmed by the beautiful, the heart is thrilled by the noble, or the soul yearns after the perfect,—there in the spirit shall stand Athens."

* * * * * * *

After they had prayed to the goddess, they went down from the Rock and its vision of beauty. Below a mule car met them. They set Glaucon and Hermione with the babe therein, and these three were driven over the Sacred

Way toward the purple-bosomed hills, through the olive groves and the pine trees, across the slope of Daphni, to rest and peace in Eleusis-by-the-Sea.

Milton Keynes UK
Ingram Content Group UK Ltd.
UKHW021916231124
451423UK00006B/765

9 789362 922045